ONE WICKED KISS

Elizabeth held out one hand to ward off Northam's final advance. She had no defense against the decidedly wicked gleam in his eye.

"Never say you mean to do me harm," she said a shade breathlessly.

"You misread me, Lady Elizabeth, and do me a grave injustice." His mare pranced closer to Elizabeth's. Northam lifted Elizabeth from her saddle with very little effort and brought her to sit down in front of him.

"You are not struggling." Her face was close to his. There was a fine pink hue rising like cream to the surface of her skin. "You are either very well mannered or unafraid."

"I am both."

Though no challenge had been issued, that statement, cool in its delivery and confident of its truth, raised a rogue's patient smile. He had only intended to take her hat, perhaps make her beg prettily to have it returned. But her mouth was parted. The full lips were flushed a deep rose. Her skin glowed and her mouth—that mouth again—was faintly damp and trembling.

Northam watched her brush impatiently at the fine curling tendrils clinging to her temples. The arrangement of her gold and ginger hair, pulled back from her face in a French braid, enhanced the finely exotic shape of her eyes. She was regarding him without censure, waiting, it seemed, for him to be done with his game.

Northam knew that no matter what his intentions had been they were of little account now. He bent his head and laid his lips over hers. Her mouth—her splendid mouth—was soft and yielding . . .

Books by Jo Goodman

The Captain's Lady
Crystal Passion
Seaswept Abandon
Velvet Night
Violet Fire
Scarlet Lies
Tempting Torment
Midnight Princess
Passion's Sweet Revenge
Sweet Fire
Wild Sweet Ecstasy
Rogue's Mistress
Forever in My Heart
Always in My Dreams
Only in My Arms
My Steadfast Heart
My Reckless Heart
With All My Heart
More Than You Know
More Than You Wished
Let Me Be the One

Published by Zebra Books

LET ME BE THE ONE

Jo Goodman

ZEBRA BOOKS
KENSINGTON PUBLISHING CORP.
http://www.kensingtonbooks.com

ZEBRA BOOKS are published by

Kensington Publishing Corp.
850 Third Avenue
New York, NY 10022

All Kensington titles, imprints and distributed lines are available at special quantity discounts for bulk purchases for sales promotion, premiums, fund-raising, educational or institutional use.

Special book excerpts or customized printings can also be created to fit specific needs. For details, write or phone the office of the Kensington Special Sales Manager: Kensington Publishing Corp., 850 Third Avenue, New York, NY 10022. Attn. Special Sales Department. Phone: 1-800-221-2647.

Zebra and the Z logo Reg. U.S. Pat. & TM Off.

First Printing: September 2002
10 9 8 7 6 5 4 3 2 1

Printed in the United States of America

For the real Compass Club—
Butz, Buddy, Johnny, and Karl
No, guys, I'm not giving you a cut, but thanks for
letting me glimpse your secret, twisted minds!

North. South. East. West.
Friends for life, we have confessed.
All other truths, we'll deny.
For we are soldier, sailor, tinker, spy.
> —Compass Club Charter
> Hambrick Hall

Prologue

April 1796

"I should very much like to see your quim."

Madame Fortuna, née Bess Bowles, stared over the curved horizon of the crystal ball she held between her hands. Her dark eyes narrowed only fractionally, but it was sufficient to pin her young patron back in his chair. His thin face flushed and Bess felt her own palms grow warm, just as if she held his cheeks in the cup of her hands instead of the cooler crystal. It surprised her, this connection. She practiced her craft as a seer of fortunes and futures with a certain theatrical flair but without any real talent. Her mother and grandmother had had the second sight and she had seen—without benefit of crystals and cards—what heartache it had visited upon them.

Bess Bowles contented herself with being a charlatan, taking the coin of men and women who ought to know better and didn't. She was an amusement, escorted into great country homes and London salons to entertain the guests with her readings. Tea leaves. Tarot. Palms. And, of course, the crystal. She had a repertoire of fortunes and dire warnings she had not begun to exhaust, and she was well into her thirtieth year of exploiting the human desire to know one's fate.

Yet this young ruffian had not asked what his future held. He simply wanted to see her quim.

Bess pushed the crystal ball aside. She noticed the boy's gaze didn't shift to follow the movement. He held her own unwavering stare, though she considered this was done with some difficulty. *Brave little soldier.*

The vision of him as a young man handsomely turned out in regimental dress came to her so clearly that Bess had to cough to cover her choked surprise. Perhaps she deserved the moniker and reputation of Madame Fortuna after all. That unsettled Bess Bowles enough to dissolve the vision in her mind's eye. Better to show the rapscallion her quim.

A small round table separated Bess from her patron. Her hands fell away from the crystal ball. She drew her palms along the scarred surface of the table until they were directly in front of her; then she laced her fingers together. Her knuckles, swollen slightly with rheumatism that was particularly plaguing today, showed whitely.

She looked the boy up and down again. His fair skin flushed under her scrutiny, but he didn't flinch in his seat. He was a towhead. His thatch of white-blond hair covered his scalp in several directions, including straight up. He looked as if he wanted to run a hand through it now. To keep from smiling Bess reminded herself of the bold request he had put to her. She really should box his ears.

In a voice that was a raspy, reedy version of her own husky one, she demanded, "How old are you?"

He blinked, genuinely surprised. "Don't you know?"

She *would* box his ears. "Don't be impudent."

He flushed more deeply. "I most humbly beg your pardon, Madame." He squared his shoulders and drew himself up in the chair so that his height might be seen to its full advantage. The effect was opposite of what he wished, making his shoulders seem thinner against the broad back rails of the chair and actually lifting his feet so they dangled an inch off the floor. Still, he responded with dignity. "On my next birthday I will be—"

"Ten," Bess said, cutting him off.

"I'm ten now."

"That's what I said, isn't it?"

"I will *be* eleven."

"Will you?" she asked darkly. "A lot can happen to a boy before his eleventh birthday." She watched him swallow hard; his small Adam's apple bobbed visibly and his collar looked as if it had tightened uncomfortably. This was better than boxing his ears. "Very well, my young earl."

"Oh, but I'm not—"

You will be. The thought came to her with such clarity that for a moment Bess believed she had spoken aloud. The boy seemed arrested as well. Indeed, he had cut himself off and was now regarding her with a look that could only be described as stricken, yet Bess knew by the press of her lips that she had not parted them to say the words. How did he know? How had *she*?

Bess unfolded her hands and waved one dismissively. "It signifies nothing," she said. "Everyone who sits where you're sitting is 'my lord' this or 'my lady' that. It does even the meanest crofter good to give himself airs from time to time. That's the way of it, is it not? There's no harm in it." As she spoke, Bess studied the face across from her. A small amount of color had returned to his cheeks, but it was a pale imitation of the rosy flush that had pinkened them earlier. He wanted to be satisfied with her explanation, but clearly he was guarded. She understood. For this boy to secure his title, his father and brother would have to die. And they would. She could not measure the time left, only know that for all concerned it would be too soon. Bess felt it with absolute certainty. Now, in some manner that defied a reasonable explanation, the boy understood it as well.

Bess rubbed her hands together. Her palms were not as dry as she might have wished. She had not asked for this second sight. On the contrary, she was quite satisfied with the gift passing her by. She sighed, her attention wandering back to the boy. Her prolonged silence had raised his watchfulness again. She supposed it was time to show him her quim.

"I imagine your friends put you up to this," she said.

The boy hesitated, but then honesty compelled him to admit, "They're not my friends precisely."

"Aaah, yes. Then it was older boys who say you can be their friend if you do this one small thing."

"That's right."

"And those three boys I saw standing with you earlier? They look to be of an age with you."

"Oh, yes. *Those* are my friends, Madame. We came to the fair together."

"I see. Then why aren't they here with you? The same challenge was put to them as well, was it not?"

"The very same," he admitted. "But we're light in the pockets, you see, and so we drew broom straws. I'm to tell them all about your quim."

"Is that so? And who will report to the young villains who sent you here?"

"We all will. It's no good if only one of us can be their friend. We're being particular about that. I shall have to be very precise in my description so they will have no difficulty convincing the Bishops we were here."

"The Bishops," Bess said under her breath. She had been right to call them young villains. Year after year for more than a hundred years, boys passed through the cobbled court-yards of Hambrick Hall on their way to a superlative educa-tion. Among the graduates would be those who would shape the nation with their thinking, their sense of honor, and their acceptance of duty. Many names changed, but many more remained the same. It was the legacy of fathers, grandfathers, and great-grandfathers who had covered the same cobbles before, accepting their achievements and bearing their fail-ures with the sort of stoic reserve other young men might express in the face of searing humiliation. Thanks in no small part to the Society of Bishops, Hambrick Hall had much to offer in the way of humiliation.

As initiations went, Bess thought, this one was fairly harmless. On the other hand, she was fairly certain the Bishops did not expect this boy and his three friends to be successful.

Bess pointed to the door of her traveling wagon. "Ask your friends to come in here." At daybreak she would be leaving for another fairgrounds far north of London. She didn't have to worry that tomorrow would bring a visit from the entire Society of Bishops demanding to see what she showed this quartet. "Go on. I'm not like to make this offer again."

Chapter One

It was their laughter that drew her attention. Elizabeth Penrose leaned to her left until her vision was unobstructed by the easel in front of her. The stool wobbled a bit as she shifted. A paintbrush dangled from her fingers. She failed to notice the fat droplet of blue-black watercolor collecting at the tip, gathering size and weight enough to break free and fall squarely on the one part of her lavender muslin gown that was unprotected by a smock.

It was a pure pleasure to hear their laughter. Unrestrained, it had almost a musical quality. Four voices, all of them with a slightly different pitch, gave it a certain harmony. Elizabeth's eyes darted quickly to some of the other guests, and she saw more heads than hers had turned in the direction of the laughter. She did not think for a moment that the men had meant to call attention to themselves. Not above a half hour ago they had been circulating among the baron's guests, slipping in and out of the small conversational groups that had formed naturally once everyone had taken their fill of the picnic repast.

Blankets covered a good portion of the gently sloping hillside. Like patches of a quilt, they were shaped into a larger whole by the strips of grass and wildflowers between them. In various states of repose the guests enjoyed the late afternoon sunshine, the occasional breeze, and the steady rushing rhythm of the stream running swiftly between its banks.

Elizabeth blinked as the men laughed again, heads thrown back, strong throats exposed. Although the tenor was deep, there was something unmistakably youthful in the sound of it. Mischievous, she thought. She could not help smiling herself, feeling not so much an eavesdropper as a coconspirator, even though she had no idea what had prompted their great good humor.

That they knew one another was not surprising, she supposed. With the exception of Mr. Marchman, they were all members of the peerage and breathed the perfumed air of the *ton*. What was interesting was that they appeared to be fast friends, not rivals, yet until they had slowly gravitated toward the same unoccupied stretch of blanket, Elizabeth could not have said for certain that they shared more than a polite nodding acquaintance.

They dispelled that notion once again as the Earl of Northam plucked three ripened peaches from the basket beside him, drew his legs under himself tailor-fashion, and began to juggle. Fresh gales of laughter, a little ribald this time, practically erupted from the others. For reasons she did not entirely understand, Elizabeth Penrose felt a certain amount of heat in her cheeks. Though confident no one had noticed her, she nonetheless sought protection by ducking behind her easel.

It was only as she began to apply brush to paper that she realized the Earl of Northam had stolen most of the subjects of her still life.

Brendan David Hampton, the juggling, *thieving* sixth Earl of Northam, lost his rhythm when one of his friends pitched him another peach. "Devil a bit, East," he said, grinning, "but I could never get the hang of four." He gathered the peaches before they rolled off the blanket and lightly tossed one to each of the others. The one he kept for himself he held up in the palm of his hand and pretended to study it.

"Tender-skinned. A copse of fine hair covering it. A delicate blush deepening to ruby at the cleft." Northam split the peach. "Succulent when parted. Moist. Scented. And the heart of it is revealed lying nestled at the center of the sweet delicate flesh."

Quietly, so that his lips barely moved, he said, "Gentlemen, I give you Madame Fortuna's quim. God bless her." He paused. "And God bless naive Hambrick boys."

Matthew Forrester, Viscount Southerton, South to his boyhood friends from Hambrick, almost choked on the bite he had taken. He coughed hard, torn between opposing forces of laughter and swallowing. Mr. Marchman leaned toward him helpfully and pounded the viscount on the back. Because he used more force than was strictly necessary, South glared at him meaningfully. The threat of retaliation went unregarded because it was difficult for any one of them to take South seriously when his cheeks were flushed and his eyes were glistening with tears. To avoid another blow between his shoulders, he had to roll off the blanket entirely.

"It's not dignified," he muttered, brushing himself off. "Knew this would happen if we got this close. Someone always brings up Madame Fortuna. It's amusing until someone's choking and someone else is trying to kill him by separating his cranium from his spine."

"I believe you were the one to mention her first," Mr. Marchman pointed out calmly. He bit into his own peach. "And if I wanted to really separate your head from your shoulders, I'd use my knife."

Gabriel Whitney, Marquess of Eastlyn, glanced automatically at Marchman's right boot. "You're carrying your blade, West?"

Marchman's answer held no hint of the humor his friend had inserted into the question, though whether this absence was attributable to the question itself or the nickname attached to it was unclear. "Always," he said. He changed the subject, his gaze turning to Northam. "You don't appear to be enjoying the fruits of your labor."

Indeed, Northam was still holding each half of his peach in his open palms. He was not looking at his comrades but rather beyond them, to where an easel had been set up in a patch of bluebells. The young woman who had been painting there had removed her pad and was packing her supplies. Northam was not naturally given to expressions of remorse, but as he glanced at the split peach in his hands, a shadow of regret briefly darkened his eyes. "I believe, friends, I must make my apologies to the lady. I fear I have confiscated the subjects of her work."

Eastlyn glanced over his shoulder. One of his brows kicked up. "Aaah, yes. Lady Elizabeth Penrose. I escorted her in to dinner last evening. You'd know that, North, if you had arrived on time. The very same goes for the rest of you."

Northam scowled at him, but there was no real heat in it. "A difference of opinion with my mother delayed me until today. She, being of the opinion that it is time for me to take a wife. I, being of the opinion that the time has not yet arrived, nor is it imminently approaching."

Moving back to the blanket, Southerton nodded. "I'm familiar with that argument. Tell me, do you suspect it is a daughter-in-law she wishes or grandchildren?"

Northam did not hesitate. "Grandchildren."

"Just so. It is the same with my mother, though she never speaks of it plainly. Why do you suppose that is?"

Eastlyn casually drew back his arm, then snapped it forward, letting his peach pit fly in a long arc toward the stream, where it landed with a satisfying *plop*. "She doesn't speak plainly for the same reason no mother speaks plainly about such things: She doesn't want to believe her dearest son knows anything about how he might go about conceiving an heir."

Marchman nodded. "East is right, though it pains me to admit it." He rested his watchful glance on each of them in turn. "Does this mean I shall soon be wishing you happy and kissing your brides? It appeals to me, you know. The idea of the three of you leg-shackled and me with an open field.''

The Earl of Northam tossed both peach halves at Marchman, who caught them neatly. ''I don't think there is a field you haven't plowed, West.'' He stood, brushing his hands lightly together. ''I am off to make amends,'' he said. ''Endeavor not to embarrass me while I am in the presence of the lady.''

''Have a care, North,'' Eastlyn said. ''She's Rosemont's daughter and a particular favorite of our host and hostess.''

''I don't intend to compromise her,'' North said dryly. ''Merely want to speak to her.''

Eastlyn, Southerton, and Marchman watched him walk off. Eastlyn leaned back on his elbows and crossed his long legs at the ankles. Sunlight glancing off his chestnut hair gave it a streak of fire. A half-smile played casually across his lips and his dark brown eyes glinted. ''I say he will be married before year's end.''

''To Libby Penrose?'' Southerton asked incredulously. ''You're daft.''

Now Marchman regarded Southerton with interest. ''Libby? That appellation signifies some familiarity. You know her?''

Southerton shrugged. ''Never saw her before today. Arriving late with North has its disadvantages. My sister knows her, though. They made their debut at the same time. She wrote me letters filled with the most excruciatingly painful details of her first Season. Of course it was all a delight to her, but I can tell you I was almost grateful to be in the admiral's service and not in London. Lady Elizabeth figured prominently in those missives. Emma found much that she admired about Libby—as she called her—but I can't say that I remember any of the particulars. I do know that Lady Elizabeth was considered something of a bluestocking, which endeared her to Emma, but made her debut rather less than successful. Now that I think on it, Libby was older than Emma by, oh, two or three years, it seems. Why, that would make her twenty-six now.''

''My God,'' Marchman said, pretending to be much struck by this. ''I do believe she has one foot planted. Yes, that is precisely what I noticed about her on first acquaintance. Her toes are practically curling up in anticipation of her own imminent demise.''

The viscount gave him a sour look. ''Make light of me at your own peril, West. You know perfectly well what I mean. The blush is off the peach, as it were. The Dowager Countess of Northam won't approve of her.''

Eastlyn's deep chuckle drew his friends' attention. ''All the more reason North's interest might be engaged.''

''True,'' Southerton said, more thoughtful now. ''Too true. North's rather predictable in that regard. His mother may regret getting what she's wished for.''

Evan Marchman's head tilted to one side as he regarded his companions consideringly. ''A wager? I believe there is one in the making. I have a sovereign that says North will present the dowager countess with a daughter-in-law by year's end.''

Viscount Southerton laughed. ''A sovereign, eh? Very well, if I'm to wager an entire sovereign, you'll have to be more specific. Is it Libby Penrose he'll take to the altar?''

Marchman glanced back to where Northam was standing beside Lady Elizabeth. Northam's features were politely fixed and serenely impenetrable. He could have been wishing himself anywhere else or finding himself thoroughly entertained. If Elizabeth Penrose was in anyway an accomplished woman, and something of a bluestocking to boot, then Marchman was of a mind to wager that Northam was entertained. ''Agreed,'' he said. ''It's Lady Elizabeth he'll marry. East, will you hold our sovereigns?''

''A pleasure.'' Eastlyn held out his hands and collected one gold piece from each man.

* * *

"What is it?" Elizabeth asked. She was immediately sensitive to the shift in the earl's attention, brief though it was. When he looked back at her his eyes had darkened fractionally, the only indication in an otherwise implacable expression that something was not quite as it should be. When he did not answer immediately Elizabeth glanced in the direction of his former companions. One of the men was putting something in the pocket of his jacket and the other two were shaking hands. They appeared amiable in the extreme. "Do you wish to rejoin them?" She flushed a little at the thought that she had been unable to hold this man's regard even for so short a time. She was credited with being a good conversationalist and an even better listener. At dinner parties she was often placed beside the hostess's most difficult guest. She had a manner of quieting the bombast, enlivening the dullard, flattering the peacock, and delivering the perfect riposte to the boor.

Perhaps her skill had been too much refined upon, Elizabeth thought, for she was possessed of none of it now. She looked up at the earl. His hair was like a helmet of sunshine. A gentle breeze caused a few strands to flutter against his temple. He pushed them back absently. White-gold light surrounded his head; shadow passed across his face.

"Would you walk with me, Lady Elizabeth?" He surprised himself with the invitation. The words had not formed clearly in his head before he heard himself give them voice. It was not strictly a desire for her company that persuaded him to make the offer, but a desire to move her away from the speculations of his friends. He had planned to make her acquaintance later, in a less public manner, but seized a moment that was less forced. He hoped she had not seen the money changing hands; hoped even more that if she had seen it, she would not divine it had anything to do with her. Southerton and Marchman should have had more sense than to make their wager so openly. He did not have to know the particulars to know it had something to do with him, and therefore with Elizabeth Penrose. He had taken part in similar wagers over the years, beginning most spectacularly with Madame Fortuna and the challenge issued by the Bishops at Hambrick. This was very different. Most definitely different. He had asked his hostess for an introduction so he could apologize to Elizabeth Penrose. He was hardly of a mind to seduce the Earl of Rosemont's daughter, no matter what those three court jesters on the blanket thought.

"A walk?" Elizabeth asked. Really, she sounded as hopelessly naive as a girl fresh out of the schoolroom. She had *never* been that.

He smiled, softening the corners of a mouth that could be obdurate when it was set. "Yes, a walk. One foot in front of the other. Side by side, if you like. Well within the view of every one of the baroness's fifty closest friends, confidants, and cousins, and most assuredly within sight of her husband. South warned me at the outset that you are a particular favorite of the baron and his wife."

"South?"

Northam tipped his chin toward the blanket where Southerton was stretching his length along the edge, looking for all the world as if he intended to nap. "Viscount Southerton. We call him South."

At that moment Southerton yawned widely enough for Elizabeth to fancy she saw his tonsils. She made no attempt to school her smile at the sight. Her generous mouth tilted up at the corners and the ridge of her teeth showed whitely.

Northam saw the same thing she did. He grinned. "There's a sight." He shook his head, wondering if he could pretend at this late juncture that he was not at all well connected with South or the others.

"I knew his sister Lady Emma. We made our debut during the same Season."

"And I know Emma as well," he said. "Though I missed her debut. That aside, this association virtually makes us friends of long acquaintance."

"I would not go so far as to say that."

"You do not have to. I have already said it."

Elizabeth laughed. "So you have." She sobered slightly, her beautifully arched brows relaxing their raised curve.

"You would not be embarrassed to walk with me?" She was not looking at the earl, but at the uneven path that followed the stream's meandering route. "I fear I shall give you cause to regret your invitation."

"Embarrass me? I should think not." Whatever was she talking about?

Of course he didn't know, Elizabeth realized. He had arrived late to the picnic, with the viscount following soon afterward. He had missed the dinner party entirely the evening before, and clearly her escort to the table, the Marquess of Eastlyn, had not mentioned her infirmity. Unlike most of the guests who had walked to the picnic area, she had ridden. Her mount was contentedly grazing some fifty yards away at the edge of the wood.

Elizabeth rose to her feet with fluid grace. She set the box of watercolors she had been holding on the stool and slipped out of her smock. She brushed ineffectually at the stain on her gown, sighing when she realized there was nothing to be done about it now. "I should like very much to walk with you," she said, looking up at him, her decision made. "May I take your arm?"

"Of course." He raised his elbow, surprised when she grasped it firmly. Elizabeth Penrose was taller than he had imagined she would be. Sitting on the stool she had appeared to be of no more than average height, perhaps even porcelain petite. That was before he realized she was all leg, and most of it had been tucked under her stool and hidden by the paint-streaked smock. When she unfolded, her chin came to his shoulder and her eyes, wide and almond-shaped, were not far below his own. She was slender but not fragile; graceful but not dainty. The grip on his arm was firm, and there was strength revealed in the raised veins and bloodless knuckles of her hand.

When he took his first step, he understood why. Elizabeth Penrose limped heavily beside him. He sensed her hesitation, as if she were anticipating that he would put a halt to their walk before it had strictly begun. Northam had no intention of doing that. "This way," he said. He escorted her past the long table laden with the picked-over picnic feast. It looked incongruous here in the middle of a field, draped with white linen tablecloths and covered with silver and crystal service. There were platters heaped high with chicken and beef and trout, bowls filled with melons, oranges, and peaches. The towers of breads, cakes, and pies arranged at one end were yet largely untouched.

Elizabeth followed the path of his gaze to the table. "You disapprove," she said.

"It is the indulgence in excess." He grimaced. "Forgive me. That sounded priggish to my own ears." Out of the corner of his eye he saw her slight smile. "Our hosts have presented us with a feast that would have fed Wellington's army for a month."

Her smile widened at this exaggeration. "Then it is a good thing the war is already won. It does not serve the national interest to deny Wellington. As it happens, the baroness will direct the servants to give the remains to the foundling home in Merrimac. It will not go for slops." Elizabeth was aware of the heads turning in their direction. Their halting progress to the footpath was causing comment among the guests. There was no point in ignoring it. "We are the subject of speculation, my lord, and we have yet to reach the stream."

"If they find us a rich topic of conversation, then I am heartily glad to be away from it."

"You seemed to be enjoying yourself a short while ago with your friends."

"Reminiscing. Our school days. We were all at Hambrick Hall together. You can be sure there was nothing the least edifying about our conversation." Depending on one's knowledge and perspective, that was not entirely true. Perhaps Elizabeth Penrose would have found it most educational. He had—when he was ten. "Here we are," he said as they reached the trampled footpath. "Shall we take a moment to appreciate the view?"

"I don't require a rest," she said with some asperity.

Northam glanced at her. His brows were considerably darker than his hair, and one of them had risen to give him a perfectly arch look. "Might I appreciate the view, then? You are at liberty to wander away on your own."

Elizabeth turned her head and faced the stream. It was a pleasant enough vantage point to enjoy the steady rush of the water and the eddying breeze, though she had no doubt he was taking the pause for her. The bank was dotted with patches of daisies and wild geraniums. On the other side grass grew knee high and the blades swayed and twisted, turning the hillside silver green when their undersides were exposed. Grass gave way to a wooded area that was highly regarded by the locals for its abundance of wildlife. The fact that the baron was not zealous in his pursuit of poachers meant that the villagers in Battenburn, and as far away as Merrimac and Stoneshire, were well fed even in lean times.

Behind her Elizabeth heard the hum of conversation. It was not so different than the drone of the bees that were diving into a hole in the bank. They came and went in pairs or threes, sought out a spray of coneflowers, then danced lightly on the large purple petals before returning to their home.

"Shall we continue?" Northam asked.

"If you've taken your fill of the view."

He smiled. "I believe I have." Northam felt her grip tighten on his arm as they turned. The footpath was sufficiently wide for him to remain at her side. He was conscious of the path's gentle dips and rocky inclines in a way he would not have been if his partner had been hale. "Are you staying with our hosts?" he asked.

"Yes. I came ahead two weeks before they did. Louise and Harrison are not fond of rusticating in the country, even in the halcyon days of summer. It was my pleasure to see that all was in order before they arrived."

"I understand you are Rosemont's daughter."

Elizabeth did not mistake this comment as a non sequitur. She followed the line of his reasoning. "You think it is odd that the baron and baroness would engage me in such a manner?"

"I did not assume they hired you for such tasks as readying

their home for their arrival, but yes, you are in the right of it that I find it peculiar you would be traveling with them and not occupied similarly with your own father's estates.''

"My father has my stepmother to offer companionship and counsel. My younger brother is there to get underfoot. Father has never raised any objection to the time I spend away from home.''

North did not miss the coolness in her voice. It was the singular lack of affect that gave her words chilling preciseness. He did not know what it meant and he didn't press. He filed it away for examination in a private moment. "My invitation is for a fortnight,'' he said.

"I know.'' She looked at him askance, the merest smile lifting the corners of her mouth. "I wrote it.''

He laughed. "So you do their correspondence also.''

"The baroness will tell you that she is hopelessly muddle-headed when it comes to organizing her affairs. Battenburn had a Mr. Alexander who managed small concerns for him, but he has since gone on and I have gladly taken on those duties.''

"You are an unpaid companion.''

"More like a daughter,'' Elizabeth corrected him. "I am regarded as family. They have no children.''

Since neither the baron nor baroness had reached their fortieth year, children were not strictly out of the question. Northam supposed that Elizabeth was privy to circumstances of a personal nature explaining why the couple, at least fifteen years into their marriage, remained childless. "I do not know either of them well. The invitation was unexpected.''

"But welcome,'' Elizabeth said.

"How do you arrive at that conclusion?''

"Why, the fact that you responded favorably. Your absence last evening, along with that of your friend Viscount Southerton, caused some consternation and the last-minute rearrangement of the seating, but you are here now, so one might reasonably conclude that you welcomed the invitation.''

"I welcomed the diversion. There is a difference."

She understood that very well. It was the difference between running *to* and running *from*. What she did not understand was why the Earl of Northam was sharing that with her. Judging by his subsequent silence, his lordship was wondering much the same thing.

Elizabeth lifted her face to the sun moments before a stand of trees blocked its heat and light. Her bonnet was lying on the ground not far from her case of watercolors and brushes. She had no illusions that her fair skin was not pinkening, but she was supremely unconcerned by it. More bothersome was the pain in her hip. She paused in her awkward stride and felt Northam stop, immediately solicitous.

"Shall I fetch a chair for you?" he asked. "Your stool?"

She could only imagine how foolish she would look sitting at the stream's edge in a straight-backed chair, once again calling attention to her infirmity. "No, thank you. If you will but give me a moment, I only require—"

Elizabeth halted, her breath seized as Northam bent and lifted her. He held her against his chest, her legs dangling over one forearm while the other cradled her back. She blinked at him owlishly, dark amber eyes startled at first, then faintly accusing.

"It is only a short distance to those rocks," he said calmly. "You could put your arms around my neck."

"I could put my hands around your throat." She noticed he was not at all disturbed by this observation. Reluctantly, she raised her arms and slid them in place. Over his shoulder Elizabeth saw the baroness turn away from her circle of friends, obviously prompted to do so, and wave gaily to her, a happy smile brightening her face. The baron, deep in discussion with a clutch of politics-minded men, also turned and gave her a similarly warm acknowledgment. On the blanket where Northam's three friends still staked their territory, they exchanged friendly chucks to the upper arm in some sort of ritual of manly approbation that Elizabeth only vaguely understood.

"Your friends appear to approve of your behavior," she said. "Else they are preparing to brawl."

He laughed then, unrestrained, rumbling, deep and clear. He had to stop in midstride to steady himself and Elizabeth. She felt the vibration of his chest tickle her fingertips where she clutched him. Northam caught his breath and moved on, shaking his head, still smiling to himself as if he could see precisely the behavior that elicited her comment. "They cannot help themselves," he said. "I do not offer that as an excuse, merely as the truth of the situation."

"I certainly could find no fault with the marquess last evening. He was without exception considerate. I am sure he did not engage a single guest in fisticuffs."

"East was there alone."

East? she wondered. Marquess of Eastlyn, of course. Elizabeth rather liked the notion that these four friends clung to childhood familiarities. "Hardly alone. The baron's table was a squeeze."

Northam set her down on an outcropping of rock. He removed a handkerchief from inside his frock coat and placed it on the stone. "Please," he said. "Allow me to help you sit. The sun has warmed this spot nicely." He aided Elizabeth's balance and eased her onto the square of linen, then dropped easily beside her. Neither the close fit of his frock coat, nor the objections he anticipated from his valet that evening, stopped Northam from removing it. He glanced at Elizabeth as he rolled up the sleeves of his shirt. "You don't mind?"

His lack of regard for convention startled her. In spite of the warmth of the afternoon, no other man had gone so far as to remove his frock coat. Many of them, she suspected, could *not* have removed it without the help of a valet. Instead of looking untidy, Northam managed an air of informal elegance, and Elizabeth suspected that if she were to turn her head and survey the guests, the female half would be looking in his direction with some admiration, while the males in their midst would be straining to relieve themselves of their own outer wear. It came to her then that this man had little regard for convention because he helped set the standard.

"You would put your jacket back on if I minded?" she asked.

"No, not at all," he said. "But I wondered if you did."

She laughed. "You say the most unexpected things."

His own smile was brief. "Do I? I assure you, I am quite serious."

"And I believe you. There can be no good reason for men to swelter in their frock coats while the ladies enjoy a modicum of comfort in muslin and the shade of parasols. I confess, however, I had not given the matter any thought before now. It did not occur to me that you were in any way uncomfortable."

"Deuced uncomfortable. But it is our lot to suffer in silence. I am told it impresses the ladies." He glanced sideways to measure the effect of his words. Elizabeth appeared vastly unimpressed, which Northam approved of immensely.

What Elizabeth found to her liking was his plainspeaking. "I am not wearing a bonnet," she said in the manner of a confession.

"I noticed." His gaze passed briefly over her hair. She was not strictly a brunette. Streaks of gold lent her hair a permanently sun-kissed coloring. It was one of the first things he noticed about her. Those strands of glinting, curling gold were what caught his eye each time she peeked out from behind her easel. "Would you put it on if I said I objected?"

Elizabeth did not answer immediately. She gave the question serious thought. "You know," she said finally, "I do not believe I would."

His eyebrows lifted as he challenged her in dry tones. "Not even if I commented on the spray of freckles appearing on your nose?"

She shook her head. "I don't freckle."

"Then for the simple protection of your fair skin from the sun?"

"No, not even then. Not today. It is a glorious sort of day to be bareheaded, is it not?"

"Indeed."

Elizabeth felt the urge to laugh again. She gave in to it because it seemed so natural and right, as if surrendering were a victory of a kind, not one that came in the aftermath of a battle, but one that arrived in the course of time, like spring treading lightly on the heels of winter. She could not say that, of course. He could not possibly understand what she barely understood herself. Still, he was in some way responsible for this moment, while she could take comfort that she finally had the capacity to enjoy it.

Northam picked up the threads of their earlier conversation regarding his friend Eastlyn. "As to the matter of his lordship, the marquess, what I meant was that without Marchman, South, or me being present at the baron's table . . . well, it is not the same thing at all. There is a tendency—regrettable, some would say—to encourage one another in certain lapses in conduct."

Elizabeth pulled her gaze away from Northam's forearms before he noticed she was staring. They were not nearly so pale as her own and the fine hairs that covered them were like gold dust. She concluded this was not the first time this summer that his lordship had rolled his sleeves to his elbows and enjoyed the out of doors in a more natural state. "Lapses in conduct," she murmured before her thoughts continued down a most wayward path. "I suspect you are putting a good face on it. No doubt you were all terrors in your days at Hambrick Hall."

"Terrors?" He shook his head. "No, not even the worst we could come up with would inspire someone to call us terrors. We were . . ." He paused, searching for the right description. "Cheerfully annoying."

"I see. And now?"

"Now we are simply ill-mannered."

Elizabeth laughed. "I rather doubt anyone thinks so, else you would not be so in demand."

"In demand?"

"Oh, come now. There is no need to be modest. You must know it is quite a coup for the hostess when you accept an invitation."

"Are you speaking of me alone, or of me and my friends?"

"Actually I was referring to you all individually because, in truth, I did not know you were fast friends."

"So the baron and baroness are very well pleased to have all of us here?"

"Well, yes. Can you doubt it? Though I don't understand about Mr. Marchman. I don't remember writing out his invitation, and I cannot say with any certainty when he arrived."

"West came as a favor to me—with our hostess's blessing, of course. It seems she answered this correspondence on her own."

"As she is wont to do from time to time. I do wonder that she never mentioned it to me." The oversight was odd. The baroness usually made a point to apprise her of all changes. "He was not at dinner last night either." And his absence had not caused the same disturbance that Northam's and Southerton's had. Clearly Lady Battenburn hadn't been expecting him until the picnic.

"No, he is only here for the day. When we finish our business he will be leaving."

Though curiosity goaded her, Elizabeth could not inquire about the nature of their business. "Why do you call him West?"

Northam shrugged. "We had to call him something, and the other directions were already taken."

Northam. Southerton. Eastlyn. It was easy for Elizabeth to imagine that as a young boy at Hambrick, Marchman must have despaired of fitting in. "Poor Mr. Marchman."

"I would not refine on West's tender feelings too long. He will grow into his name the same as we all have."

Elizabeth's brow puckered. She turned to look at Northam. "What do you mean?"

"I was not Northam at Hambrick," he said.

She expected more in the way of explanation, but Northam fell silent. He was not looking at her, but staring out across the stream to the bank, the field, and the wood beyond. She followed the direction of his gaze and could see nothing remarkable to capture his attention. Birds fluttered in and out of the boughs, making them dip and sway. A rabbit stilled in the grassy bank, his senses made wary by the slow, halting progress of a snapping turtle up from the water.

In profile Northam appeared unapproachable. The lines of his face were drawn with sharp, bold strokes. There was nothing forgiving about the set of his mouth, no weakness in the hard cast of his jaw. He did not seem to be thinking so much as steeling himself. Even his nose, with that slight bump on the bridge, was thrust forward aggressively. Only his long dark lashes, in perfect contrast to his thatch of sun-colored hair, made him seem in the least vulnerable.

Then he turned on her, and every impression of a granite-like countenance faded from Elizabeth's mind. He smiled easily, a trifle sheepishly, and offered an apology for wool-gathering. Elizabeth accepted him at his word and did not challenge his explanation. She did not believe for a moment that his mind had been anywhere but in the present. He had not been collecting his thoughts. He had been collecting himself. Perhaps it had something to do with his business with Mr. Marchman, but she did not think so.

"Had you many invitations for this time?" she asked. In honor of Wellington's victory at Waterloo three years past, invitations to celebrate barraged the *ton* like cannon shot. This was a battle from which Wellington himself would have run. Every hostess threw herself into the fray. A reputation for sponsoring the premiere event could be set for a lifetime or positively ruined by those who did not arrive at her gala. Thus far, the baroness had done very well for herself. The fortnight affair at her country home gave people time to come and go at their leisure. Over the course of the occupation—this was war, after all—the very best of society would collect at Battenburn.

"Many invitations?" Northam mused. "It was impossible

to remove oneself from the line of fire. But it was not difficult to decide among them. I very much wanted to be here.''

Elizabeth smiled warmly, accepting this on behalf of their hostess. ''The baroness will be so gratified to know. To choose her party among all the others ... well, you can imagine that she would take this as a high compliment indeed. You don't mind if I tell her, do you?''

''Not at all, though perhaps you should not tell her the *reason* I wanted to be here.''

Elizabeth's smile faltered, then faded completely. A small vertical crease appeared between her brows. ''I don't understand.''

''Don't you?''

''I just said so, didn't I?''

One of his brows lifted at the impatience communicated in her tone. ''Then I have overestimated your perceptiveness or been sadly lacking in my attention toward you.''

''I believe I am perceptive, my lord.''

He nodded. ''I believe so, too. That means I have not made my interest clear.''

Elizabeth wished herself anywhere but where she was. The sun no longer seemed so warm, and beneath her fingertips the stone was cool. Her desire to leave was clearly communicated in her face.

''Now I have made you uncomfortable,'' Northam said calmly.

''No, it's just that—''

''Please. Do not prevaricate. I can see plainly that you wish I had not spoken so openly. Perhaps I can ease your mind, since my interest has caused some offense.''

Elizabeth did not know where to look. She was mortified that he had so easily discerned her thoughts. She was not an artless ingenue. At six and twenty years she had learned something about schooling her features and presenting a public face. She had an urge to turn away, much as he had done earlier, until she was all of a piece again. Instead, she regarded him boldly and stayed her ground. She only wished there was something she could do about the color in her cheeks.

"I am not offended by your interest," she said coolly. "Merely made suspicious by it. I am politely referred to as 'firmly on the shelf' since I marked my twenty-sixth year in April. I am regarded as a bluestocking because I continued to read and show an aptitude for studies after I left the schoolroom. While it is well known that a handsome settlement will accompany me into marriage, it is also well known that I have no wish to turn over the handling of my fortune. It has not escaped your notice that I am ungainly—some would say crippled. I am not the sort of companion one chooses for life, but rather for rounding out the numbers at a dinner party. And finally, if all of that were not enough to dissuade would-be suitors, my father is the Earl of Rosemont, a difficult and contentious individual in the best of circumstances. It stretches my imagination to think of the man who would embrace him as a father-in-law."

Northam said nothing for a moment. He regarded her set face, the challenge in the almond-shaped eyes. He noticed that they were almost the same color as her hair, and like her hair, they were flecked with gold. "Indeed," he said dryly. "Then I count myself as much relieved that my interest in you is not in the nature of leg-shackling. I do not believe I would want the most disagreeable Earl of Rosemont as a member of the family."

Some gremlin thought prompted Elizabeth to point out, "He certainly would not want you."

Northam took no offense; rather he was amused. "It is just as well."

"Nor would I," she added firmly.

His amusement deepened, but he was careful not to reveal it. He was also more than a little intrigued. It was clear to him that when Elizabeth Penrose mistook his interest and attention as an overture to pursuit, she was not flattered by it. Panicked was the word that came to mind. "Then we are agreed. We would not suit."

"No, indeed."

"It is good, then, that the colonel had no expectations in that regard. I am not of a mind to disappoint him."

"The colonel?" Elizabeth felt her breath catch. "You know Blackwood?"

"I do. He was my commander in India."

"How is he?" she asked softly.

"Well. He inquires the same about you."

Suddenly Elizabeth understood. "He asked you to look after me."

"Something like that. He has not heard from you for months. It is my understanding this is unusual."

"I have been remiss in my correspondence."

"No doubt you have little time for you own. Attending to the baroness's affairs must occupy your energies."

Elizabeth did not think she mistook the note of censure in his tone. "What is your relationship to Blackwood?"

"As I said, he was my commander in India."

"That is a connection. Not a relationship." There was some relationship, she thought, that would lead Northam to believe he had the privilege of taking her to task.

"You have never served under him. In the military it is possible for one to be very much like the other. When the colonel leads, others are inspired to follow. I was merely one of many. And when he asks a favor of me, even in his retirement, it does not occur to refuse."

Elizabeth nodded. She understood perfectly the loyalty and admiration the colonel inspired. Before the wasting illness that left him without the use of his legs, Blackwood stood firm for a promotion that would have put him squarely in Wellington's boots. It might have been Blackwood in command at Waterloo. When Elizabeth had pointed this out to the colonel, he laughed without any tinge of regret. *"God forbid, m'girl,"* he had said. *"Boney might have got the best of me, and then where would we be? Speaking French, I tell you. That would be the way of it, and not at all to the king's liking. Wellington's brilliant. Always was."*

"Colonel Blackwood is my mother's cousin," said Elizabeth. "After she died he fancied himself my guardian. That did not endear him to my father, who found the colonel's inquiries interfering. It was just as well he was often abroad. Had he served here, I probably would have been forbidden to visit him. As it turned out, I was able to write him steadily over the years. I believe the colonel watched me grow up through my letters.''

"Then you are close.''

"Yes, I like to think we are.'' Elizabeth's fine features did not so much soften as ease. "I will write to him this very evening and allay his concerns. It is something of a surprise that he has not commanded me to appear.''

"He entertained it. He thought you might refuse.''

"And it would never do to mutiny in front of one of his soldiers. That's what you are, is it not? One of his soldiers.''

"I believe I said as much. It makes little difference that I no longer wear a uniform. Neither does he.''

Elizabeth looked down at her hands. They were folded quietly in her lap, yet she knew if she unclasped them the finest of tremors would be running through her fingers. "What precisely is the nature of your assignment?'' she asked calmly. "You've been quite clear that it does not involve leg-shackling.''

Northam listened for any note of disappointment in her tone and heard none. His impression remained that she was relieved. He decided to press her a bit. "I am not considered a bad catch, you know. Mothers parade their daughters in front of me. At Almack's I am often called upon to partner young girls who are taking their first waltz.''

"Now *that* is high praise indeed.''

He went on as if she had not commented. "I am thought to be not without some qualities to recommend me. I have been told I have a modestly handsome face. I have my wits about me. On occasion I have been known to use them.'' Northam saw that while Lady Elizabeth appeared to be studying the pattern of violets in her dress, she was also tamping down a smile. "I am a steady friend. I attend church more Sundays than I fish. I make wagers as the mood strikes me, but I have never gambled what I could not afford to lose. I am passionate about horses and Mrs. Wedge's roast beef. There is little else that raises my blood. I drink in moderation and I speak tolerably well of others.''

"You, sir, are a paragon, and I find myself regretting the colonel did not fancy himself a matchmaker.'' She glanced at him and made no effort to hide the laughter in her eyes. "Does that satisfy your wounded sensibilities?''

"It certainly helps. Thank you.''

"Who is Mrs. Wedge?''

"The cook at Hampton Cross. She's been in residence since there *was* a Hampton Cross.'' He saw Elizabeth's skeptical look. He held up his right hand, palm out. "It is only a slight exaggeration, I swear it. She was easily a hundred years old when I was boy. It is of constant amazement to me that she does not age at all, while I continue to grow older.''

A strand of hair loosed itself from the ribbon wound through Elizabeth's curls. She tucked it behind her ear only to have it fall forward again. It tickled her as the breeze buffeted it against her cheek. "Every home must have one Mrs. Wedge,'' she said. "At Rosemont we have Mrs. Gatchel. I cannot say that her roast beef is in any way remarkable, but I have never tasted a steak-and-kidney pie that compares.''

Northam's eyes were fixed on the hair fluttering at Elizabeth's cheek. "I do not think I can summon any sort of passion for steak-and-kidney pie.''

Elizabeth brushed at the strand again, this time a bit self-consciously. "I see your point.'' From somewhere behind her there was a shriek of laughter. Elizabeth turned to look back on the guests. Lord Allen was gesticulating wildly to a group of avid onlookers. She faintly could hear them calling out to him. "They're playing charades,'' she said. "Perhaps you would care to join them?''

"No,'' Northam said firmly. "I would not.''

"It appears your friends are going to enter the game.''

"That does not entice me in the least.'' He drew in a

breath, bracing himself, and gallantly posed the question. "Would you prefer to play?"

She laughed. He was so obviously hoping for a negative response. "No. I'm not very good at the pantomime."

"Neither am I."

Elizabeth could not resist goading him a bit. "But I rather enjoy watching."

"Very well," he said somewhat stiffly. "I will escort you back."

"Have a care, my lord. If you give into this whim, where will it end? Next you will be putting on your frock coat because I insist." In fact, he was already picking it up. "Please, do not trouble yourself. We can watch from here. It's better, I believe. As long as the players do not completely obscure our view we can make our own guesses and be right every time. Look! Lord Allen is hopping mad."

"A hop toad is more like it."

Whatever the robust Lord Allen was trying to communicate to the other players was finally identified, and the baroness herself commanded center stage. Louise Edmunds, the Honorable Lady Battenburn, favored the group with her wide, engaging smile. She was an attractive woman just shy of her fortieth year. Her figure erred on the the side of plumpness, but somehow she made it seem earthy and voluptuous. She removed her flowered bonnet and handed it to Lord Southerton.

Under his breath Northam said, "She will be fortunate if South doesn't clamp that bouquet on his head and call himself a garden."

"He is being quite considerate of it. Look how gingerly he has it tucked under his arm." Her attention went back to Lady Battenburn. "But what is her ladyship doing?"

The baroness was threading her fingers through her hair and making the russet curls stand out wildly.

"She has certainly entered into the spirit of the game," Northam said.

"She looks positively mad like that." Elizabeth bit her lower lip as Louise flung her arms out to the side and began to spin in a tight circle. Her cambric dress puffed out like a balloon as she continued to twirl. "Why, I believe she is a dervish."

"Or a whirligig," Northam offered dryly.

"Or she has taken complete leave of her senses."

"In which case she may be Mad George himself."

Elizabeth's mouth flattened and she gave him a quelling look. "Her ladyship would not make light of the king's regrettable condition."

"I beg your pardon."

It occurred to Elizabeth that Northam should beg Louise's pardon, but she knew she would not repeat his comment. She considered further defense of their hostess and decided nothing was served by belaboring the point. Elizabeth turned her back on the festivities when Louise gave up her turn to Lord Southerton. He entered into the game wearing her hat, and the wry look that Northam cast in Elizabeth's direction was the perfect I-told-you-so.

"What will you tell the colonel about me?" she asked.

Northam was not caught off guard by the change in subject. He had been expecting it. To his way of thinking, her attention to the guests had been a diversion. She hoped to catch him out at something, as if she expected his purpose to be something other than what he had already related.

"I intend to tell him the truth," he said. "That you are well and appear to be enjoying yourself at Battenburn. I shall inform him that while he would not entirely approve of this company, you are able to hold your own. I doubt that a fortnight spent here at Battenburn will add anything of merit, but I am honor bound to try." He paused a beat. "Oh, and I may mention that in spite of the lessons he paid for, you have no talent for watercolors."

Chapter Two

"He told me I had no talent for watercolors." Elizabeth's feet were propped on an upholstered stool in her hostess's bedchamber. The crewelwork under her heels was a repeating pattern of tiny pink roses and mint green leaves. The wing chair where she sat in front of the empty fireplace almost swallowed her whole. The windows had been thrown open to permit the air to circulate on this warm evening, and the ivory damask bed curtains rippled at the head of the four-poster when caught by the breeze.

The baroness poked her head out from behind a silk dressing screen. "But you *have* no talent for watercolors," she said. "You've said so yourself, and I believe Harrison has remarked upon that very thing a time or two. Harrison, of course, has no artistic sense and you should never give any weight to his opinion in the matters of painting, theater, or poetry." Louise's head and the slope of one white shoulder disappeared behind the screen again. Her maid helped her shimmy into her nightgown. "However did you respond to Northam's observation?"

This was the part that Elizabeth was still mulling over. "I laughed."

When Louise appeared from behind the screen this time she was wearing her full nightdress. Her russet curls were tucked under a white cap and her face had been scrubbed clean. Wearing a voluminous cotton nightgown that enveloped her like a cloud, she looked younger than her years. As she moved, the hem of her gown shifted and revealed a pair of blue kid slippers on dainty feet. Louise dismissed her maid and poured the tea herself. She served Elizabeth, then sat opposite her in a matching wing chair.

"How did you laugh, dear?" she asked with some concern. "I mean, what was the tone? Diverted? Gay? Or were you stunned into that response? Was it an uneasy sort of laughter to conceal your hurt? That is often the way of it when we cannot recover quickly enough to deliver a set down."

Elizabeth shook her head. "Not at all. I took no offense. I know. I can hardly credit it myself, but I was genuinely amused. Perhaps it was the manner in which he said it, so matter-of-fact that it did not occur to me to take umbrage. And then, as you have already pointed out, it is something I know as well, though you must admit it is highly unusual to have it remarked upon so boldly."

"Highly unusual," Lady Battenburn agreed. She sipped her tea. "My, that is too hot." She added more milk to her cup, sipped again, and pronounced herself satisfied. Her keen attention then turned to Elizabeth, and she leveled her with a shrewd glance. "He did seem to regard you with favor this afternoon. Harrison commented the very same to me as we were walking back to the house."

"It signifies nothing." Under Louise's knowing regard Elizabeth felt herself shrink a little. "You and the baron must not make too much of it. Lord Northam was merely making amends. He did, after all, steal my still life."

"A simple apology would have sufficed for that transgression," Louise said. "I thought it most romantic when he carried you to the bank. One might even say that he swept you off your feet."

"Pray, do not tie your hopes to that wagon."

"But he *did* sweep you off your feet."

"Only in the most literal sense. I assure you, Louise, my heart is still my own."

The baroness sighed. "Now, *that* is too bad." Her eyes dropped to where Elizabeth's feet were resting on the stool. "I noticed you were limping heavily this afternoon. Has it been very uncomfortable for you?"

Elizabeth did not answer immediately. She stared at her feet for a moment, then wriggled her toes inside the soft kid slippers. "You know it has. The ache in my back is ..." She stopped herself, for there was nothing to be gained by complaining. Some things could not be changed.

"You will do the recommended exercises for your hip, will you not?"

"Yes." The response was somewhat reluctantly given. "And those for my back, so you needn't trouble yourself to ask."

Louise raised one brow. "You are most definitely not feeling at all the thing. Your tone is a trifle sharp, m'dear, and all I did was inquire about the state of your health."

"Please," Elizabeth said softly, closing her eyes. She rested her head against the back of the wing chair and made an effort to compose herself. It was more difficult than in any time in recent memory. "I cannot do this tonight. Might we speak of something else?"

"Certainly."

Elizabeth opened one eye and regarded the baroness with a measure of skepticism. Louise's short response was calculated, and Elizabeth Penrose was not fooled by it. "Do not feign that I have trampled on your tender feelings. It doesn't suit."

Louise made an elegant shrug and sipped her tea. She said nothing.

Sighing, Elizabeth raised her own cup and drank. "Very well," she said at length. "I apologize for my curtness. It was never my intention to give offense."

"You might say it with more feeling."

"I have none." It was not far from the truth. *Tired* was a paltry word to describe Elizabeth's state of mind. What she wanted was nothing more than to excuse herself and retire to her own bedchamber. It was the baroness's habit, however, to conduct a postmortem following any affair she deemed of a certain social importance. Louise's energy was virtually without limits and she thrived on the intrigues and complications that were an inevitable consequence of gathering members of the *ton* together. With twelve days still to unfold in front of her, Elizabeth had no illusions that she would find much in the way of respite. Indeed, the busy schedule she had drawn for herself in preparing for the Battenburn affair was likely to have been the calm before the storm.

Without tensing a single muscle, Elizabeth steeled herself. "What else would you like to know, Louise?"

Satisfied, the baroness smiled widely. Dimples hollowed out the corners of her mouth and cradled her full lips between them. "Did you enjoy the earl's attentions?"

"The time we spent together was brief, but yes, I rather enjoyed myself."

"Then you were not uncomfortable? I have heard that he makes some young women uncomfortable."

Elizabeth felt compelled to point out the obvious. "But then, I am not a young woman."

"You are hardly an ape-leader, m'dear." Louise held up one hand, halting Elizabeth's reply. "Never fear, I am changing the subject. What do you know about his friend Mr. Marchman?"

"I was intending to ask you much the same thing. I understand you personally approved his attending."

"I did not see that I had much choice. His lordship asked it as a favor. Highly irregular, but there you have it. I could have refused, but what would have been the point? No doubt Northam would have been unable to attend, and that would not have served. Mr. Marchman appeared to be a most unexceptional personage. They are of an age, are they not?"

"I understand they attended Hambrick Hall together."

Louise was thoughtful. She finished her tea and set the cup and saucer on the silver tray at her side. "Schoolmates.

You don't suppose they were . . . you know what tricks young boys get up to . . . you don't think they . . ."

"No!"

"It's just that I've heard . . ."

"No," Elizabeth said, quietly this time.

"There are always rumors, you know. Why, Lord Efton once told me that . . ." Her voice trailed off yet again. "And the Duke of . . ." She waved her hand airily, and her eyes followed the movement of her fluttering fingers. "I suppose it is neither here nor there, that is, unless you were to become involved. You don't want to be one leg of *that* sort of triangle, Libby. It can mean nothing but heartbreak."

"Louise, there is no triangle of *any* sort. Mr. Marchman and the earl are friends, I am certain of it. Lord Northam said he asked Mr. Marchman to meet him here on some matter of business."

"Business? Surely not." The baroness could not keep the horror out of her voice. "Oh, that is really too bad of him. Are you certain it is not political in nature?"

"I am certain of nothing. He merely said it was business. I suppose that it might mean anything. The earl is not a *cit*, Louise. He is not likely to set up shop in your parlor and manufacture goods for your guests."

"You really are too bad this evening, but I forgive you. It's just that I know so little about Mr. Marchman, and it is always unsettling to have a cipher under one's roof."

"I believe he's already left. I did not have the impression he was staying into the evening."

Louise was stunned by this revelation. "But he did not seek me out to make his good-byes."

"Perhaps he thought he would give offense."

"That is unfair."

"I apologize."

"I have never been unkind to a *cit*."

"I regret my wayward tongue, Louise." Elizabeth watched the baroness draw in a deep breath, her bosom visibly swelling with the effort, and waited to see if Louise had been successfully placated.

"I cannot seem to stay angry with you," she said finally.

Elizabeth did not respond to this. Instead, she said, "Perhaps Mr. Marchman spoke to his lordship. You did retire to your room immediately upon returning from the picnic and did not reappear for more than an hour. The baron may have accepted his regrets on leaving."

"Yes, you're right. I am certain that's what happened. I will speak to Harrison when he comes to bed."

Stifling a yawn by sheer force of will, Elizabeth risked a glance at the clock on the mantel. It was just minutes short of midnight. The baron might not remove himself from the card table for several more hours. Elizabeth hoped Louise did not expect her to entertain in the interim.

"What of the others?" asked Louise. She settled comfortably into her chair, drawing her legs up and to one side. In contrast to Elizabeth's heavy-lidded expression, Louise was alert, her features showing none of the strain of playing hostess to her grand gathering. Her dark lashes fluttered as she fanned herself with one hand, feigning a sudden rise in her temperature. "I declare, that Lord Southerton is a most handsome gentleman." She treated Elizabeth to an arch look. "Did you not find the viscount so?"

"I spent so little time in his company, I did not form an opinion."

"It is not a matter of time," said Louise, "but of eyesight. It requires but a glance in his direction." She smiled and added coyly, "Then perhaps your mind was more engaged with the earl than you would have me believe."

"Are you matchmaking or communicating your own designs on the viscount?"

"Bah! I am doing neither and shame on you for suggesting it. You will resist all efforts to the former, and as to the latter, everyone knows I remain besotted with my own dear Harrison."

It occurred to Elizabeth to remind Louise that she was not everyone. She held her tongue, even in her weariness recognizing the comment as unnecessarily waspish and incendiary. "What of Lord Eastlyn? Was the marquess not also to your liking?"

"Heavens, yes. What is there to find the least objectionable?"

"Indeed," Elizabeth said wryly. "Did you know they were all Hambrick boys when you extended the invitation?"

"Do you mean to say that Southerton and Eastlyn also attended? Why, I had no idea. So that is the source of their friendship. I knew they were acquainted, of course, but not that they shared a history at Hambrick. And Mr. Marchman as well. I suppose it is impossible for members of the *ton* not to live in one another's pockets. Where would one go to escape? The colonies?" She shuddered, and her nightgown shivered with her.

"I do not believe they call themselves the colonies any longer."

Louise's response was a dismissive wave. "What of Eastlyn and his fiancée?"

"I did not know he was engaged."

"I understand it is all but a done thing."

Which meant it only existed in the minds and wagging tongues of the gossipmongers. "I wonder if the marquess knows he has a fiancée?"

The manor at Battenburn was an imposing stone structure whose main hall had been built in the time of Henry VIII. The first baron had done the king a significant favor that ultimately led to the annulment of his marriage with Anne of Cleves. As a reward, Henry extended land and a title to an otherwise minor figure in his court. Since then Battenburn had largely prospered, and the manse had grown accordingly.

The inside of the house did not reflect the changing architectural styles as much as the outside. While turrets and crenelated parapets gave Battenburn the cold appearance of a keep, the interior warren of rooms was surprisingly warm and inviting. The labyrinth of passages and staircases would have confounded Theseus's search for the Minotaur, but guests at Battenburn were generally charmed and intrigued by the home's history as sanctuary for the currently out-of-favor. More than once, the king's—or queen's—men had arrived at Battenburn to take some dissenter of royal policy in custody, only to discover they could not be found. The maze of hallways and hidden passages seemed to turn in on itself, offering protection to earls, marquesses, barons, and even a duke over the course of two and one-half centuries.

Northam and Eastlyn turned simultaneously as the door to Northam's bedchamber opened. Pale flickering light from a stubby candle illuminated the crack before a figure stepped into the opening. Southerton's eyes darted about the room, finally settling with some relief on the occupants. "At last," he said under his breath. He shut the door behind him and placed his candlestick on a table beside the door. "I despaired of ever finding you. Don't know that I can find my way back to my own chamber so I may camp here. Whose room is this? Yours, East?"

"Mine," Northam said. He motioned Southerton to come closer and indicated the rocker beside the bed. Eastlyn was lounging comfortably across a padded window seat. "East only just found it himself."

"Left a trail of crumbs to find my way back."

"Used candle wax myself," Southerton said, dropping into the rocker. He stretched out his long, athletic frame with such fluid grace, it was difficult to tell he was sitting in a chair and not a chaise. One hand lifted to his hair and he raked it back while his gray eyes darted from friend to friend. "West's gone?"

"Hours ago," Northam said. "Assignment from the colonel."

Southerton nodded, expecting as much. "I thought that might have something to do with him being here. These affairs have never been to his liking. You delivered Blackwood's message?"

"I did."

Neither Eastlyn nor Southerton asked their friend if he knew the nature of the assignment. It was unlikely that he did, and if he did, he would only tell them what the colonel wanted them to know. It was always that way. Caution was Blackwood's operating principle. Without a word or signal passing between them, they unanimously abandoned the subject of Mr. Marchman's disappearance.

The Marquess of Eastlyn picked up the tumbler of Scotch that he had balanced on the narrow window ledge and raised it just short of his lips. "You are going to tell us about her, aren't you, North? There's a wager, you know."

Northam's mouth pulled to one side, communicating his displeasure. He noted, rightly, that Southerton and Eastlyn were unmoved by what he thought. "I saw money exchanging hands. You might have practiced more discretion. How much is the wager?"

"An entire sovereign," Southerton said. "East's holding the money for Marchman and me."

"So much," Northam said dryly. "Can you trust him?"

The viscount cast a dubious look in the direction of East-lyn, who merely waved him off, not deigning to comment on the slight. "I suppose I shall have to." He looked back at Northam. "Is that why you took her off, because you saw us make the wager?"

"Can you doubt it?" He looked around for his own drink and spied it on the mantel, where he had left it when Eastlyn first joined him. Northam rose from his chair and retrieved it, then remained standing at the fireplace. His shoulder rested against the mantelpiece and he looked remarkably at his ease. "How long will you each be staying?"

Southerton eyed the decanter and remaining glass on the silver tray resting at the foot of the bed but made no move to get it. "Haven't changed my mind," he said. "I'll be here the fortnight unless you want me gone before then." He arched an eyebrow in Northam's direction and received a small, negative shake of the head in reply.

"I am for home on Friday," Eastlyn said. "I will inform Battenburn and his lady tomorrow. It appears I must extricate myself from the most damnable coil."

Northam's mouth twitched at the corners. "Something to do with your fiancée?" he asked innocently.

The marquess could not rouse more indignation than a brief sour look. He sighed and pressed the cool crystal tumbler he was holding against his forehead. The gesture, in anticipation of the headache that was sure to present itself directly, lent him the appearance of being deeply put upon. It was rather too much for the others. They laughed openly.

"It is all very well that you find my predicament amusing," Eastlyn said. "I assure you, it is not. I am not engaged. I have never been engaged. I have no intention of becoming engaged." He said this as if by rote, in the youthful tones he had once used for declining Latin verbs at Hambrick. "I should like to know how this rumor began."

Northam and Southerton said in unison, "Marchman."

"Hah! I don't believe it." He lowered his tumbler. "West might enjoy seeing me in a tangle, but he would not be so cruel as to involve another. This predicament most definitely involves an innocent." He glanced at his friends and saw they were duly sobered by this reminder. "It seems likely that Lady Sophia will hear of our engagement before I can assure her of its falseness. I fear she will be in expectation of a proposal when she sees me. Worse, she may have already found a priest to perform the nuptials. I might be walking into a trap, and while I find her company unexceptional in the extreme, she does not deserve to be treated shabbily."

Southerton nodded. "You're right, of course."

Northam added, "West, in fact, is the one who warned us the story was circulating. He was concerned you would hear of it from someone other than one of us. Apparently you did."

"Lady Caroline took me aside, ostensibly to inquire of the particulars regarding my engagement. I say ostensibly because the Lady Caro seemed more intent on divining the direction of my bedchamber."

"Did you decline or accept the invitation?" Southerton asked.

"Declined." Eastlyn shrugged. "Had to. Didn't know how to get there myself. Seems I'm in the east wing on the north side of the house. Or it may be the reverse. Can't understand how it's possible either way. I simply try to keep the courtyard on my left and hope that I'll spy something familiar." He took another swallow of his drink. "In any event, I am resigned to being celibate until it is perfectly clear to the wags that there is no engagement. Lady Sophia deserves that much at least."

"And how will Mrs. Sawyer feel about that?" Northam asked, referring to Eastlyn's mistress. "She is likely to object, is she not?"

The marquess pressed the tumbler back to his brow. There was most definitely the beginnings of a headache starting behind his eyes, no matter what his friends believed. "Mrs. Sawyer is no longer under my protection, nor has she been these last twenty days." His long fingers tightened briefly on the tumbler before he removed it to knock back the remainder of his drink. "I had not considered it until now, but Mrs. Sawyer may be the source of the rumor."

The same thought had occurred to the others. They withheld comment, trusting Eastlyn to know they would lend themselves in any way that was required. Mrs. Sawyer had never been a favorite.

Eastlyn acknowledged the silence and what it meant with a slight nod. He rose from his comfortable position on the window seat and went to the foot of the bed. He poured himself another drink, then lifted the decanter in question, first at Northam, then Southerton. The viscount accepted the offer while Northam refused.

"You know," Eastlyn said as he handed over a drink, "North's neatly managed to avoid the subject of Lady Elizabeth."

"Practices roundaboutation better than anyone I know," Southerton said. "His mama agrees with me."

"My mother said it first," Northam said quellingly.

Southerton's smile was genial. "Did she? Then I suppose I agree with her."

Northam sighed as Eastlyn encouraged the viscount's foolery by laughing. "Lady Elizabeth is rather more provocative than she first appears and rather less sanguine than she would have others believe."

Eastlyn stretched out at the window again. "Which means precisely what?"

"It means what it means," Northam said. "I do not really wish to discuss her."

Eastlyn and Southerton exchanged glances.

Northam pointed to each of them in turn. "I am serious about this."

They nodded in unison, identically bland smiles creasing their handsome faces.

Rolling his eyes, the earl offered one other observation. "She would not have me as a gift."

The Baron Battenburn slipped through the connecting door to his wife's room. He was still dressed in fine evening wear: a cutaway coat with tight-fitting sleeves, striped vest in two shades of gray, high-collared white shirt with points so sharp they might have drawn blood, black trousers with a strap under each shoe to maintain their line. Only his neckcloth looked worse for wear after a long night at cards. The folds were no longer as crisp as they had been at dinner and there was some indication that he had been moved to tug on them from time to time.

Louise's welcoming smile faded when she saw the state of his stock. "How much did you lose, Battenburn?"

In spite of this less than auspicious greeting, Harrison Edmunds, the Right Honorable Lord Battenburn, crossed the room to his lady's side and dutifully kissed the rounded cheek she presented to him. It was not until he stepped back that he noticed Elizabeth Penrose almost secreted away in her wing chair. Her legs were curled under her, and the stool, which she had most assuredly been using earlier for her comfort, was lying overturned in front of her. Battenburn regarded it pointedly, then turned the same regard on Elizabeth.

"Has it offended you in some way?" he asked. He touched the toe of his shoe to one of the legs and righted it with no effort.

"No, my lord," said Elizabeth. And it was true. Her legs offended her, stretched out as they had been, her hip aching and the small of her back so pinched with pain that it might have been in a vise. She was offended by what she had become. She looked away, afraid to hold the baron's gaze for fear she would lose all composure and humiliate herself in front of him.

"Leave off, Harrison," Louise said. "Libby is overset. It has been a very long day for her. For all of us." She watched her husband go to her bed and sit on the edge. Always fastidious about his appearance, Louise was not surprised when he touched his neckcloth, straightening and creasing the folds between his fingertips. His posture was relaxed but not weary. His shoulders never slumped; he carried himself like an athlete, which he was. An avid horseman and boxer, her husband appreciated the importance of interests outside the political arena. Louise wished that gambling was not one of those interests. He smiled in her direction, a slight and slightly rueful lifting of his full mouth. She withheld her response, her own mouth set in the flattest line her generously curved lips would permit.

"Five hundred pounds," he said. "Almost all of it to Southerton. I thought I might recover my losses when he left the table, but sadly, that was not the way of it."

Elizabeth glimpsed the merest flash of relief in Louise's eyes. No doubt she was thinking it was a sum that could be easily managed and even replaced. Elizabeth's own stomach twisted in response. She hugged herself, pressing her forearms tightly against her midriff in an attempt to quell the roiling.

"So Southerton is a cardsharp," Louise said. Her mouth had loosened its disapproving line. "Does he enjoy himself at the table?"

Battenburn tugged at his jacket sleeves, straightening the line of them. "I would not pronounce him a sharp. He is rather more lucky than skilled. He passed the time at the table, but I suspect he did so from an ulterior motive."

"Really? Pray, what motive?"

"The desire to remove himself from the presence of Lady Powell. She was of a single mind this evening to capture Southerton's complete attentions. I fear she is in her room now plotting tomorrow's activities so she may contrive to have him to herself."

Louise's brow lifted. "So that is the way of it. Lady Powell is a sufficiently attractive and witty companion. She is also a widow with no desire to marry again. I wonder what Southerton finds objectionable?"

"Perhaps the way she fairly launched herself at him," Elizabeth said dryly. "I thought she would topple him when he entered the music room this evening."

Louise looked at her husband for confirmation of this observation. She had been late to the entertainment, delaying the start because of a loose clasp on her diamond necklace. It required ten minutes in her bedchamber for her maid to repair the clasp to her satisfaction. Now she wondered if she had missed something worth seeing by insisting on wearing that particular piece. "I shall look forward to the morrow, then," she said. "It will be quite delicious to see who prevails. I only hope Lady Grace does not make a cake of herself. She cannot hold her seat, and tomorrow is the hunt. I should not like to see her trampled. Perhaps I shall speak to her, confidentially, of course. Subtlety is called for on her part."

"I am not certain she will welcome your insights, dear," Harrison said. "Though your instincts on matters such as these are far superior to mine, I think it would not come amiss if you were to watch first, see how the matter progresses, and offer advice when it will be more agreeable. In the meantime we shall all pray she doesn't draw the hounds down on her."

Louise recognized the truth of this, but she could not completely veil her disappointment. "You know how I love

to bring a couple together. It is above all things satisfying
to know one has had a part in it. In what other way can a
man or woman discover their true nature if it is not through
love?''

"Or lust," Harrison said under his breath.

Elizabeth dropped her eyes to her lap. She knotted her
fingers into a single fist.

"I heard that," Louise said. "And it is very bad of you
to say such things. Observe: Libby is mortified. She heard
also—as you intended we should."

Harrison's clear blue eyes settled on Elizabeth. They were
neither cruel nor kind, but neutral in their regard of her bent
head and huddled figure. "I most humbly apologize, Lady
Elizabeth, for my plainspeaking. My wife's notions are
highly romantic and of dubious validity. We all know what
part lust plays, whether we say it or not. I am for saying
it.''

Louise sighed. "That is no sort of apology at all," she
said, though there was no heat in her words. "I have been
trying to persuade our dear Elizabeth to set her cap for
Northam. I'm afraid you have cooled that argument with
your talk of the baser motivations.''

Elizabeth vaulted from her chair as gracefully as her aches
would permit. "If you will both excuse me, I wish most
sincerely to retire.''

The baron was on his feet immediately. "Of course. Do
you require an escort to your room?''

She shook her head. Her smile was slight. "No, do not
trouble yourself. If you will but recall, I know the way.''
The house had initially presented the same challenges to her
as it did to all the guests, but Elizabeth had been a frequent
visitor to Battenburn, often without the baron and baroness
in residence, and she had grown comfortable enough with
the maze of halls to find her way even without benefit of a
candle. It was a test of sorts, and when she demonstrated
her accomplishment to her hosts, they declared it a rite of
passage—pun intended, they said in unison.

"Let her go," Louise said to her husband. "I told you,

it has been a trying day. Northam's attentions were rather
more than she wanted, I think. He informed her that she had
no talent for watercolors.''

"Indeed," the baron said, his tone as dry as dust.

Elizabeth slipped out of the bedchamber as Battenburn
was inquiring of his wife to provide more of the particulars.

The manor was quiet when Northam left his room. The
servants had not yet been roused from their beds to begin
preparations for another day's entertainment. From his limited observations, Northam believed the baron and baroness
were exacting employers. There seemed to be no guest who
was unattended, no whim that was not satisfied. He had
overheard Lady Armitage complain that the floral arrangement in her chambers was not at all to her liking. Very plain,
she had said. Insipid, really. It was not long afterward that
he spied one of the maids ducking into a backstairs passage
with an armload of roses. Later, when Lady Armitage commented that her room was a veritable garden, Northam felt
certain she had been the recipient of the flowers.

Most assuredly it was not the baron and baroness who
directed these things—more likely it was Lady Elizabeth
Penrose—but she could not be acting outside the expectations of the baron and baroness. He wondered again at the
arrangement that existed between the Earl of Rosemont's
daughter and his hosts. It was something of a curiosity
to Colonel Blackwood as well, which ultimately made it
Northam's concern. It was, perhaps, not the most auspicious
of assignments the colonel had trusted him with, and certainly it was not the most dangerous, but it was proving to
be not without some rewards. Northam could think of many
less pleasant ways to pass his time than living in the pocket
of Lady Elizabeth.

Northam wandered the hallways of Battenburn, familiariz-
ing himself with the twists and turns as he had not been able
to earlier, when the majority of guests were still roaming. He
did not want to be included in the games of hide and seek

that were being played among some of the more adventurous guests. Lady Grace Powell, the lovely widow with a fortune and, by all accounts, no designs on a second marriage, had made her interests in South clear within minutes of their introduction. The viscount, never one to appreciate the strategy of a full frontal assault, had been in retreat most of the evening. Northam suspected his friend was sleeping soundly—and alone—in his own room, providing his candle wax trail had led him back to it.

The same could not be said of some of the other guests. Southerton had also mentioned seeing Lord Allen and Lady Heathering secreted in a room that appeared to be a linen closet. The viscount came upon them by accident and backed away with all alacrity when he realized his error. "One would think they would have the good sense to hold the door shut," he said. "Lord Heathering might have stumbled on them."

Northam suspected the cuckolded Lord Heathering would have to have left the arms of Mrs. Flagg in order to make that discovery. These lapses in discretion were the exception and Northam truly had no way of knowing to what extent the other guests at Battenburn were seizing the opportunities presented by too much fine wine and the great hall's peculiar architecture. He suspected this rout was in no way different from any of the others he might have attended this month. Any exposition of affairs would serve as a nine-days' wonder, nothing more.

Northam eventually found his way to the grand staircase. Potted ferns stood at post on either side of the landing. He was careful not to bump into one of the urns and send it crashing to the parquet floor below. Beneath his feet was a dark wine carpet runner. He held up his candlestick to make sure he found the first step, then started down. Northam had been shown the library earlier in the day when he expressed an interest in the baron's collection. He had no difficulty coming to it again. The handle turned noiselessly for him and he let himself in. The addition of light from an oil lamp made him blink. It took a moment to see beyond the circle of light at the corner of the baron's desk and to the occupant of the baron's chair.

"Lady Elizabeth," he said. Surprise made his manner somewhat stiff. Lulled by the stillness that had settled over the house, he had neglected to look for signs of occupancy before he opened the door. "Forgive me. I did not know this room was in use."

Elizabeth's eyebrows arched fractionally. She had the feeling she was not being apologized to at all, but rather taken to task for interrupting *him*. She placed her quill down slowly and, in the same deliberate motion, lifted her chin. She was wearing a hunter green flannel shawl across her shoulders, and now she adjusted the ends so they covered more of her bosom. Her cotton nightdress was less revealing than the gown she had chosen to wear at the musicale, but since it was clearly intended for the bedroom, she felt more exposed. To his credit, Northam's eyes remained on her face. Far from being insulted, Elizabeth was relieved. "May I assist you in some way?" she asked in polite but reserved accents.

Northam remained where he was. "I thought I might find something to read."

"How fortunate you have come upon the library, then."

"It is not by accident," he assured her, "but by design."

Elizabeth withheld comment, her skepticism communicated by her silence.

Northam lowered his candle and his gaze fell on the quill and foolscap in front of Elizabeth. "Your letter to the colonel?" She nodded. "It is rather late, is it not, to be composing your missive?"

"Months late. As you pointed out this afternoon."

He did not correct the meaning she took from his question, suspecting that the misunderstanding was deliberate. "May I intrude upon you long enough to search for a book?"

She made a graceful sweep with her arm, indicating he could go where he would. Elizabeth made no attempt to return to her writing, but chose to watch Northam instead. "Is there one in particular you have in mind?"

"The one containing Malthus's *Essay on the Principle of Population,*" he said. "I believe I saw it earlier."

"Are you certain hot milk would not be more to your liking?" He laughed out loud at that, and Elizabeth was reminded anew how very enjoyable that sound was. She regretted she was not a more amusing person, for listening to his laughter would surely be a pleasure. "It is to your right. One shelf up."

Northam's index finger swept the gold-embossed bindings, guiding his eyes. He stopped suddenly and raised his candle. The yellow light burnished the dark leather spines, deepening and enriching their color. "Ho," he said, his interest arrested by one particular book. "What's this?" He picked out the book carefully, grinning as he examined the cover. "*Castle Rackrent,*" he read aloud. " 'A Gothic novel.' " He checked the spine for the author's name. "By Maria Edgeworth. A pseudonym, no doubt, for who would willingly give over their name to the penning of a Gothic novel?"

"That is very small of you. It is highly entertaining."

Still grinning, Northam somehow managed to arch one brow. His bright crosshatch of yellow hair gleamed in the candlelight. "Is it?" he asked, his tone signifying great cynicism. "Is it yours?"

"It is her ladyship's," Elizabeth said coolly. "But yes, I have read it. That is how I know it is entertaining. You, on the other hand, have no experience by which to judge its content."

"Well said, my lady." He slipped the book under his arm and continued to search out the Malthus essay. "Aaah. Here it is." Northam put the candle down in order to take the collection of essays from the shelf. He fanned through the pages, making certain it contained what he was looking for, then folded it under his arm with the Edgeworth Gothic tome.

Amused that he intended to take *Castle Rackrent* with him, Elizabeth nevertheless did not comment. He did it for show, no doubt, because she had managed to sting him a bit with her comment. The Earl of Northam probably considered himself to be of a liberal bent. It was the fashion among the younger set. The baroness said he was two and thirty, which clearly placed him on the outer edge of that wave of thinking.

Elizabeth leaned back in her chair, finding her breathing coming easier now that Northam's mission was accomplished. She could not have said that she found his presence uncomfortable when he had first entered the library, but now that he was preparing to leave, she knew for a fact that it was true.

Northam did not set off for the door, however, but approached the dark walnut desk instead. "Will you send my regards to the colonel?" he asked.

"Of course." She made no effort to pick up the quill.

"Shall I wait and escort you back to your room?"

That was the last thing she wanted. Evenly she said, "It is not necessary. I know my way much better than you."

"Then perhaps you would be my escort?"

Elizabeth shook her head, her smile a trifle forced. "That would not be seemly, my lord. Someone might attach the wrong meaning to our association. You are adequately attired." Indeed, he had not changed from his tailored evening jacket and trousers. "While I . . ." Her voice trailed off because modesty forbade her from calling attention to her nightclothes. Unconsciously her hands tightened on the tails of her shawl.

"While you are very much in the common mode for this late hour," he finished for her. "I understand." Still, he hesitated. He studied her raised face, the fine curve of her brow and cheek, the more strongly etched curve of her mouth. Her eyes, almond-shaped and nearly a perfect match for her gold and ginger hair, were her most arresting feature, but only if he did not allow himself to gaze below the prim neckline of her nightshift or refine on what was hidden beneath her flannel shawl. "I wonder if you would ride at my side at the hunt tomorrow?"

She blinked up at him, the invitation outside of anything

she expected to hear. For a moment she could not speak. Finally her voice came coolly. "I am flattered at the honor you—"

"It is an invitation to ride, Lady Elizabeth, not a proposal of marriage."

If Elizabeth had been standing, she would have taken a step backward. As it was, the lightly mocking tone pinned her back into the chair. It was on occasions such as this that Elizabeth had cause to remember she was every inch of her the Earl of Rosemont's daughter. "I should accept your offer," she began, "for the pleasure of making you regret it. I will restrain myself, however, not because you don't deserve it, but because it is not worthy of me. In any event you will find my seat on a horse as singularly lacking as my talent for painting. It is on those grounds that I must decline your invitation, my lord ."

"A fine, cutting riposte," Northam said in the neutral tones of an observer, not the target. He hitched one hip on the corner of the desk and laid down his books. Crossing his arms in front of him, his posture casual yet somehow challenging, he continued. "I assure you, I will be vastly entertained by your attempts to make me regret my request, for I find your company, even at its most provoking, is more to my liking than that of any other number of your sex I could name." He gave her no chance to insert a single word, though he thought she was warming nicely to an entire harangue. "As for it not being worthy of you, I concede your point. Your sensibilities are far more refined than mine, so I understand your reluctance to extend yourself on my account. Your point of refusal, though, is a transparent piece of work. You cannot pretend that you were in the least offended this afternoon when I commented on your lack of talent for watercolors. Not when you so clearly found it amusing—and true. Lastly, as to the matter of your seat, I had reason to observe you riding back to the keep and I could find no cause for any sentiment save admiration. Lady Battenburn also informed me that you are an accomplished horsewoman."

"You spoke of me to her?" she asked incredulously.

Northam remained unperturbed. "I believe her ladyship saw the direction of my interest and was moved to comment."

Elizabeth doubted the baroness had confined herself to a mere comment. She saw now that Northam's invitation had Louise's fingerprints all over it. "Louise is trying her hand at matchmaking," Elizabeth said, going straight to the heart of it.

"I know. Her remarks could not properly be called hints. She commented on your qualities with all the subtlety of a Greek chorus." Northam regarded Elizabeth closely and correctly judged she was unamused. "It could not hurt to permit her to think she has succeeded, could it? I believe she will rest her attentions elsewhere if we appear to fall in with her plans."

Elizabeth's gold-flecked eyes narrowed. "I believe you are as manipulative as Louise," she said after a moment.

Northam's brief smile was unapologetic. "What say you, Lady Elizabeth? Aren't you the least bit intrigued that Lady Battenburn thinks we would suit?"

Intrigued? No, that was not the word. Terrified. That was a far better descriptor. "You would be better served to attach your interests to another of my sex," she said. "For all that you might find them less entertaining, you will also find them less taxing." Elizabeth could see by his patient regard that she had not dissuaded him in the least. "Oh, very well, my lord. I shall accompany you on the hunt. As for the remainder of your stay at Battenburn, we shall see."

Northam scooped up his books and candle. He let the light flicker over the promise of sunlight in Elizabeth's hair. "Good evening," he said, his tone gentle now, respectful.

Elizabeth Penrose made no reply. Her gaze dropped away from his with a certain deliberateness that was not avoidance or surrender, but dismissal. She heard Northam chuckle softly and take his leave. When she looked up from her letter as the door closed, her vision was blurred by tears, and the hand lying over the quill was shaking.

* * *

Brendan David Hampton, Earl of Northam, woke with a start. He had only just fallen asleep, or so it seemed. Souderton was no respecter of anyone's respite but his own. He closed the door loudly behind himself and proceeded into the room without waiting for an invitation.

Northam opened one eye, saw who it was, and rearranged his pillow so it was *over* his head. He did not care in the least if he suffocated, only that he died in his sleep. "Go away," he muttered in the event Southerton could not interpret his mood.

Southerton blithely ignored his friend. "I have confiscated a tea service from one of the maids. Apparently it was intended for Lady Heathering, but I am confident that lady will thank me for my timely interference. She is still ensconced with Lord Allen, though they have moved from the linen closet to his room. I stumbled upon them yet again trying to find my way here."

Since Southerton had been one of the finest navigators in the Royal Navy, it seemed highly unlikely to Northam that his sense of direction had suddenly become impaired. "What are you up to, South?" he asked, lifting the pillow just enough for his voice to carry.

Grinning, Southerton said, "Returning a favor."

Northam realized this was something he did *not* want to know. He pushed one hand out from under the covers and held it up. There was blessed silence. "What are you doing here? Where is Brill?"

"Your valet is deuced unhappy with you. Most everyone else is risen these last two hours and he hasn't been able to turn you out. I am here as the sacrificial lamb. If I do not have my heart cut out, Brill will let himself in directly." Southerton poured a cup of tea, added a single lump of sugar, and carried it to the bed. "Here. Take this. You will feel more the thing after you drink something." His clear gray eyes dropped to the books on top of the bedside table. "Never say you only nodded off."

Northam sat up slowly, raked back his hair in a tired gesture, then took the offered cup and saucer. "I was reading."

Southerton lifted the uppermost book. "*Castle Rackrent*. A Gothic novel." One brow kicked up. "Kept you awake, did it?"

"I confess I was reeled in like a gaping trout."

The viscount laughed. He set the book aside and picked up the essays. "Now this has the sandman's grit all through it. I take it you intended to fall asleep perusing it."

"My thought exactly."

"Perhaps tonight."

"I have to finish *Rackrent*."

Southerton laughed again. He put down the book and crossed the room to the wing chair. He dropped into it, seemed to remember himself, rose, walked to the rocker, and began an obvious investigation of the area.

"What are you looking for?"

"My snuffbox."

"You don't take snuff."

"True, but I have a very nice box. You've seen it. The black enameled one with the gold trim and diamonds set into the lid. I like to carry it when I play cards. Superstitious, I know, but there you have it. With Lady Powell in pursuit of me yesterday, it seemed inordinately good judgment to have a fall-back position. Hence, the card game. I was certain I had the box." His eyes wandered to the edge of the bed. He bent, raised the covers, and looked under the frame. "But as you noted, I do not take snuff, so it is not as if I pulled it out and used it. I will have my valet look again in my room. Perhaps it is only that I am so used to having it with me that I have convinced myself of the fact of it."

Northam stared at his cup of tea. "No doubt that's the explanation."

With some reluctance Southerton gave up the search and returned to his chair. "It's only that it was my grandfather's. A wedding present from my grandmother. The sentiment is worth more than the box."

"The lid was encrusted with diamonds," Northam reminded him. "You place a great deal of value on sentiment."

Southerton grinned. "At least five hundred pounds." He motioned to Northam to drink up. "I think I hear Brill scratching at your door. Finish that so you can take breakfast with me. I dare not announce myself in the dining room with Lady Powell prowling about. You will save me from her, won't you?"

"You but have to give the signal."

There was just the briefest hesitation before Southerton replied, "I will count on that."

Northam eyed his friend over the rim of his teacup. "Apparently you are not as set on avoiding the widow today as you were last night."

"It was a long night."

Northam's lips twisted wryly. "May I suggest *Castle Rackren?*"

Chapter Three

Rain delayed the start of the hunt for several hours. During that time there was much sky-watching among the male guests at Battenburn. Spurious predictions abounded and wagers were made on the strength of them. Louise quietly commiserated with Ladies Powell and Heathering that she shouldn't be surprised if there was not a path worn into the carpets. Even as she spoke, thunder rumbled and her husband and three of his friends dutifully left their seats for the windows to gauge the change in the weather.

For a while there was talk of postponing the hunt until the morrow. No one wanted to see their mounts mired in mud and come up lame. When the sun reappeared in the early afternoon and beat hard on the fields and treetops surrounding Battenburn, it was agreed there should be no waiting beyond a single hour.

The men gathered at the rear of the manor, all fashionably turned out in their pinks, while their horses were brought to them from the stable. In their bright scarlet, double-breasted cutaway coats with the claw-hammer tails, brass buttons flashing in the sun, they could not fail to catch a woman's eye. It might have put a damper on some of the strutting had they known there was general agreement among their admirers that they resembled nothing so much as banty roosters. There was much giggling in the ranks of the female observers, likening their top hats to a cock's comb, and the inevitable acknowledgment that they *were* coxcombs.

Few women joined the foxhunt or wanted to. By and large, the sport was a masculine pursuit. Women, being forced to ride sidesaddle, were necessarily excluded because of the danger. Elizabeth Penrose had participated in several hunts since being taken under the wing of the Battenburns. Their willingness to sanction this activity for her inevitably silenced the whispering about it. She was indifferent about their blessing, imagining that she would have been strong-headed enough to ride to the hounds without it. It was not the chase she enjoyed, or the ultimate surrender of the fox to the hounds. It was the freedom she found intoxicating, the opportunity to go hell-bent for leather across fields and fences, to *fly* over water jumps and drive hard into the woods at a speed that could kill her if she or her horse miscalculated.

She limped rather painfully to where a groom held her mount, aware of the stares she received by virtue of her slow, halting progress. She knew by now how to read the expressions of those who stared in her direction. There would be those who pitied her and those who found something to admire. These reactions she considered to be but two sides of the same coin, for they both focused on the obvious physical infirmity. Among those who knew her well there would be little reaction. Lady Battenburn would not countenance any remarks that brought more attention to her. The baron did not publicly recognize her limitations. Friends took their cue from this acceptance, and gradually what was different about her became unexceptional. By the end of the fortnight at Battenburn she would elicit no more comments for her ungainliness than she did for the shape of her nose.

Elizabeth accepted a leg up from the groom and settled comfortably into her saddle. Her mount, a silver gelding that could cover distances with the speed and smoothness of a bullet, pranced lightly while she fawned over him and patted his neck.

"He's a fine animal," Northam said approvingly, coming

abreast of Elizabeth. He looked her mount over from forelock
to fetlock and could see nothing but prime horseflesh. His
expression was admiring and a shade envious. When he
looked at Elizabeth he saw she was amused. "Have I done
something?"

She shook her head, her eyes bright with silent laughter.

Northam frowned, a small crease appearing between his
brows. "Are you quite—"

Southerton came upon them then, interrupting his friend.
"Aaah, Lady Elizabeth. How fine you are looking this afternoon. The fresh air and anticipation of the hunt agrees most
favorably with you. Indeed, I believe one could pluck the
roses from your cheeks, so pronounced are they."

She blushed a little at what she believed was outrageous
flattery, deepening the very roses upon which Southerton
had settled his gaze. "You are too kind, my lord."

Elizabeth's riding habit was black wool serge, fitting
rather more loosely than the tailored jackets the men wore.
The skirt was cut long to preserve modesty as she rode with
one leg hitched around the pommel, but even so there was
a tantalizing glimpse of slender ankles bound tightly in black
leather riding boots. Elizabeth steadied the gelding, then
adjusted the sheer black scarf that held her top hat securely
to her head. "I fear I am sadly out of place among all this
scarlet."

"Nonsense," Southerton said grandly. "What do you
think the pinks are in aid of, if not to attract the attention
of a lovely little pigeon such as yourself?"

Although she was not at all certain she liked being compared to a pigeon, Elizabeth's laughter was bright, encouraging Lord Southerton to expand his thinking.

"It is the way of every species, is it not?" he asked. "The
males spread their bright feathers or puff their chests to
garner the notice of the females. I think it is precisely this
that the tailors had in mind when they fashioned the scarlet
jackets. I assure you, the fox is not at all interested in our
plumage."

"You have given this matter some thought," Elizabeth

said, her mouth still curved in a tempered smile. Her eyes darted briefly to Northam. There was no reproach in her look, only a deepening amusement.

"Of course." Southerton followed Elizabeth's glance. "Never say North has failed to comment on how splendid you look."

"He has been filled with admiration for my Becket." Recognizing his name, the gelding danced in place again. "His lordship noted quite rightly that this is a prime animal."

Southerton rolled his eyes, neatly avoiding the daggers Northam was shooting in his direction. "I might have known. He owns a pair of perfectly matched grays himself and has been known to haunt Tattersall's the evening before an auction. Still, his passion for horses is no excuse for—"

Northam sighed heavily, bringing Southerton to an abrupt halt. "Perhaps I should excuse myself," he said wryly. "Or is it sufficient for me to own that I have been suitably chastised?'

Elizabeth leaned over and rested her gloved hand on his scarlet forearm. She patted it lightly in much the same manner she had used to soothe Becket. Though scarcely aware of her actions, or the implications, her gesture was not lost on either of the men. Southerton laughed loud and hard while the tips of Northam's ears reddened.

Understanding came slowly to Elizabeth. Her eyes widened and she withdrew her hand quickly. Too embarrassed for words, she surreptitiously tickled Becket with her riding crop and did nothing to hold him back when he surged ahead.

Northam and Southerton watched her head straight for the flock of scarlet coats taking their positions for the start of the hunt. "She has a fine seat," Southerton said conversationally.

Northam's reply was an unintelligible grunt. He pulled his mount around. "Find East, won't you?"

Southerton grinned good-naturedly. "You know, I am of the opinion it is not so terrible a thing to be treated like a horse when the Lady Elizabeth is in the saddle."

''The lady's horse,'' Northam said without inflection, ''is a gelding.''

There was an infinitesimal pause on Southerton's part. ''I think I'll find East.''

''A fine idea.''

Elizabeth was in conversation with Lord Allen and Mr. Rutherford when Northam drew close. He did not interrupt or give any indication he was interested in their discussion, which indeed, he was not. He noticed that Elizabeth said very little but gave the impression of being deeply engaged in the matter at hand. Without making her own opinion known she was able to leave each man thinking she had agreed with him.

''You could be a diplomat,'' Northam said as they found their place. Forty hounds were barking frantically, worked up to an almost rabid frenzy as they caught the scent of a fox in the wind. The horses sensed their excitement and beat at the ground. He noticed that Elizabeth had no difficulty reining Becket in and maintaining her seat. ''That was very skillfully maneuvered.''

Not certain if he was still referring to her diplomacy with Allen and Rutherford or her adroitness with Becket, Elizabeth made a brief nod and gave her attention to the groundskeeper and hounds. ''Will you want to hang back?'' she asked.

''Only if it is your wish.''

''I will flank the other riders. It is safer that way. Do not think you have to accompany me or see to my welfare. There can be no sport for you in that.'' She lifted her chin to indicate the woods. ''Do you see that break in the oaks? That is where I will allow Becket to charge. No fox has ever been run to ground there as the cover is sparse. The creature that has been bedeviling the sheep was last sighted in the thickest part of the wood. It will be a squeeze to rival Almack's during the Season.''

''I believe I shall stay with you.''

She nodded, smiling faintly. ''They are ready to give the call.'' Alert to every shift in the landscape, Elizabeth

straightened suddenly and extended her riding crop toward
the far edge of the field. ''Oh, look! There he is, my lord.
He is a game one! I believe he is teasing the hounds!''

Northam caught only a glimpse of a slim snout, a burnished russet pelt, and a white-tagged tail before it disappeared into the tall green grass. The blades bent and swayed
as if an invisible finger were drawing a path through the
field. The fox leaped once, suddenly, avoiding an obstacle
that was hidden in the grass, then disappeared again, this
time into the wood.

The braying, barking hunting hounds were released. They
nearly overran one another as instinct and training urged
them forward on the scent of the fox. They were halfway
across the field before the hunting horns blared. *Tan-ti-veee.
Tan-ti-veee. Tan-ti-veee.* Shouting, the riders released their
straining mounts and they broke free en masse. Great clumps
of damp earth and grass were thrown up as the hooves
pounded out their own rhythm. Riding whips whistled
through the air as the first wave of scarlet crested a knoll
and claw-hammer tails rippled in the wind.

Northam glanced over at Elizabeth. The fine features of
her face were set without tension or fear. Her concentration
was complete, yet she made it seem effortless. If she had
known how she looked she would not have let him see. Here
was a face naked save for joy, stripped of every defense
and all caution. Release made her appear so vulnerable that
it seemed to him a violation of her secret self to stare so
openly.

''Be careful!'' she shouted.

He saw the worn remains of an old stone fence the same
time his horse did. Here, hidden among the tall shafts of lush
green grass, was the obstacle the fox had jumped. Northam
prepared himself as he would not have done if Elizabeth
had not called to him. He would be forever in her debt for
saving him from an ignominious fall. Before he could call
out his thanks, her mount was sailing across the old fence
and he had to give chase.

Elizabeth's prediction of how the riders would cluster as

they neared the wood was proving true. He held his powerful black mare back just enough for Elizabeth's Becket to maintain the lead, then he followed them as they veered toward the dark opening in the oaks. Another rider had split from the hunting party and taken that direction also. Northam recognized the powerful chest and shoulders of Battenburn's cinnamon-colored mare as she charged in front of them.

The sun seemed to wink out as they drove hard into the wood. Hounds and horses could be heard crashing through the thicket. Of necessity, the speed of the animals slowed. The baron's bright scarlet jacket gave Northam and Elizabeth a figure to follow, and the path unfolded in front of them as if a carpet was being laid.

Cunning, Northam thought, not for the first time. Lady Elizabeth Penrose was clever and cunning. Far from being put off by this observation, Northam numbered it among her most intriguing assets.

Northam became aware that there was another incremental change in the concentration of their light. Overhead the canopy of boughs was becoming less dense and shafts of sunlight speared every opening between the branches like transparent lances. Raindrops that had clung to the bright green surface of the leaves were shaken free and fell on them with surprising force. Thirty yards to their front, Battenburn had cleared the trees and was pounding into another open field bordered by a rock-strewn road. When Elizabeth and Northam also broke through the woods, Northam saw they were now ahead of the other riders. Charging in a pack, the hounds continued their enthusiastic pursuit of the harried red fox.

Elizabeth maneuvered Becket toward the hounds on a diagonal. Confronted by the shallow stream that bisected the pasture, the dogs hesitated only a moment before splashing through and picking up the scent on the other side. Battenburn, Elizabeth, and Northam followed, while the pounding of the animals gaining on them from behind thundered in their ears.

The bucolic landscape was made lively with the successive passage of fox, hounds, horses, and riders. Cows scattered across the gentle hillside. Calves lowed piteously in a frantic search for their mothers. A family of ducks contentedly cleaning themselves at the stream were startled into flight. In a distant field, sheep herded themselves into the beginnings of a wool blanket and starlings and wrens and larks flew out of the treetops and underbrush.

A haywagon stood abandoned at the side of the road. Scattered sheaves littered the ground like gold dust. The wagon's broken axle and missing wheel caused the flat bed to rise at a steep angle, making for an irresistible jump for the most daring riders. Battenburn, Northam, and Elizabeth wisely avoided it and gained more ground on their quarry.

At Battenburn, the guests who had not taken part gathered on the crenelated roof. Here, high above even the treetops, they had a largely unrestricted view of the hunt. From their vantage point the spread of scarlet across pasture and orchard, over footbridges and fences, was not without a certain orchestrated beauty. They applauded the appearance of the lead riders and wagered on the identity of those at the fore. The baroness produced a spyglass that delighted them all, and they took turns describing the progress of the hunt in exceptionally fine narration.

It had to end, of course, and badly, if one's sympathies lay with the fox. The wily predator could neither escape the hounds nor the hooves and was finally run to ground near the edge of the Battenburn estate. The hounds circled the large oak whose roots had been exposed by the fox's earth. They clawed the trunk and climbed over each other in an attempt to bring him out of his hollow.

Elizabeth turned her mount around before the hounds were given their due. Without looking behind she knew Northam was following. Becket's silver-gray coat shone with the proof of his heroic exertions. She patted his neck and praised him but did not let him slow for long. Northam kept pace with her as they left the others and took a circuitous route back to Battenburn.

"Look!" Elizabeth pointed to the parapets, where glimpses

of lavender, cherry, and daffodil gowns could be seen in the low intervals between the stone merlons. Feathers and ribbons adorning hats were lifted gaily in the breeze. She raised her arm and made a graceful arc with it, hailing the observers. "They're watching from there. Wave to them."

Northam tipped his hat instead, a small gesture that could not have been seen properly, or at least he hoped that was so.

Elizabeth laughed. In contrast to Northam's slightly affronted expression, there was high color in her cheeks and her wide smile was radiant. Vitality clung to her like the scent of the sweet lavender salts she bathed in. "I collect it is not so easy for you to make a spectacle of yourself when your friends are absent."

"I said as much yesterday, if you will but recall."

Whether it was high spirits in the aftermath of the hunt or a more elemental desire to drop this unsettling man a peg or two, some gremlin of mischief urged the Lady Elizabeth to raise her riding crop. Before Northam could guess her intention, she caught the brim of his top hat with the tip and sent it toppling over the back of his head. It bounced on the rump of his mare before he could catch it and fell to the ground.

She took no time to enjoy his startled expression and applied her crop to Becket's rump instead. Northam followed, but not before he climbed down from his horse to retrieve his hat, brush it off, straighten the brim, and settle it back—at the proper roguish angle—on his head. It was not out of a slavish adherence to fashion that he did so; indeed, he had already demonstrated to Elizabeth by removing his jacket at the picnic that he was no devotee of Brummell. It was rather that he wanted to give her time and distance, allow her to wonder if he intended retribution, perhaps lower her guard for a moment, then conclude finally, and correctly, that he would accept nothing less than a full accounting for her actions.

Becket wove through the trees with all the confidence and grace of the woman on his back. When she urged him to increase his pace, he obliged. When she sent him toward the fence, he cleared it. He would have burst his great heart for her if she had asked it, but Elizabeth Penrose did not. When she saw that Northam was gaining ground and nothing short of riding astride or testing Becket's limits would save her, Elizabeth eased up and allowed herself to be overtaken.

It was perhaps good that he came upon her out of sight of the parapet for the designs he had on her person did not invite an audience. Still flushed of face and smiling, Elizabeth held out one hand to ward off Northam's final advance. She had no defense against the decidedly wicked gleam in his eye.

"Never say you mean to do me harm," she said a shade breathlessly.

"You misread me, Lady Elizabeth, and do me a grave injustice." At Northam's direction his mare pranced closer to Becket. The animals snorted and tossed their heads, eyeing each other first, then preening.

Elizabeth glanced at Becket, sensing betrayal in his attention to the mare. It was in that moment's distraction that she finally lost her seat.

Northam lifted Elizabeth from her saddle with very little effort and brought her to sit down in front him. There was a tiny rush of air escaping her lips that could have been protest or simply an indication of her discomfort, perched as she was half on and half off his saddle.

"You are not struggling." Her face was close to his. There was a fine pink hue rising like cream to the surface of her skin. "You are either very well mannered or unafraid."

"I am both."

Though no challenge had been issued, that statement, cool in its delivery and confident of its truth, raised a rogue's patient smile. He had only intended to take her hat, perhaps make her beg prettily to have it returned without a crease or a bruise. He might have kept the sheer black scarf as a souvenir no matter how she pleaded for it, just to remind her that he had had the upper hand in the end.

But her mouth was parted. The full lips were flushed a

deep rose. There was a hint of pink tongue as she pressed it briefly against the ridge of her front teeth. Her skin glowed and her mouth—that mouth again—was faintly damp and trembling.

Northam raised his gloved hands and tugged on the transparent scarf secured against her cheek and chin. The bow was easily undone and the hat dropped behind her head and into his hands. He fixed it behind his back with one hand while the other twisted so that the scarf was wrapped around his wrist. The deed was done so quickly that from Elizabeth's perspective it seemed to have been accomplished by sleight of hand.

Northam watched her brush impatiently at the fine curling tendrils clinging to her temples. A few drier strands fluttered against her forehead. The arrangement of her gold and ginger hair, pulled back from her face in a French braid, enhanced the faintly exotic shape of her eyes. She was regarding him without censure, waiting, it seemed, for him to be done with his game and return her hat, unharmed, to her head.

Northam knew that no matter what his intentions had been they were of little account now.

He bent his head and laid his lips over hers. Her mouth—her splendid mouth—was soft and yielding. That dark space between her parted lips opened and invited him in. Warm. Moist. She sucked in her breath and drew in his lower lip. Her teeth touched the sensitive underside and she bit gently, so very gently; then those small perfect teeth moved sideways in a sawing motion, tugging and suckling. Delicate. Precise.

And all the blood in Northam's head surged to his groin.

The last time Elizabeth Penrose had engaged in a kiss, she had been deeply, irrevocably in love. Even in retrospect she could not see it differently. To rename that experience of her heart as an infatuation was to make it so much less than it had been and she would not trivialize it. Certainly there had been moments of exhilaration. That wildly intense and ultimately exhausting joy had made her heart pound and blood roar in her ears. She had known light-headedness on hearing her name said in a particular way; had felt a delicious sort of apprehension when she recognized a distinct step approaching. Those sensations were real and abiding. Time had not diminished them. She had embraced them then and remained unashamed of them now, but she had never once mistaken them for love.

She had experienced love as something more than those feelings. Love made room for conflict. It allowed for the expression of more than one view and invited the paradox that disagreement was vital to harmony. Love required accepting and meant changing oneself rather than demanding change of others. Love was tender and thorny. Cruel and kind. It nurtured trust but forgave betrayal. It was not an accident of attraction; it demanded sentient beings, attention and consciousness.

Elizabeth Penrose had known it once. Not a dalliance. Not a flirtation. Not a yearning. She had loved, and having loved, she also knew there would be no second time for her.

She would not permit it.

This dark, sweet, deep kiss had nothing to do with love. It was the absence of that very emotion that made it tolerable.

They drew back slowly and at the same time. She held his steady, assessing gaze, not turning away disingenuously or affecting an accusation where none was deserved. When his gloved hand cupped the side of her face she did not try to escape it. His thumb brushed her bottom lip, then just touched the damp underside. She could taste leather and salt and sense the vitality of the man.

His eyes were dark mirrors as they searched her features, reflecting what he saw and giving no hint of what he thought. There was no smile, no mockery or judgment. The remnants of passion were fading, replaced by something more measured and pensive. Color had returned to his face. He breathed evenly through slightly flared nostrils. His brow was smooth and the cant of his head was coolly inquiring. There was no hint of tension in the line of his lean jaw, no muscle working in his cheek or cords visible in his strong throat.

Northam's hand fell away from her face slowly. The touch of his thumb on her mouth lingered. She felt the pressure of it there even as he was drawing his hand down the length of her arm and settling it at her waist. From behind his back he brought around her hat and placed it on her head. It was only then that her eyes darted away from his. It was as if the return of the hat erased this short passage of time, that they were both back in the moment before it had been recklessly removed and could choose a different course, one where intentions counted for something.

Northam lifted Elizabeth onto her mount. She took up the reins as Becket shifted under her weight. She stared straight ahead to the opening in the trees some twenty yards in front of them, then drew Becket's attention away from the mare with a snap of the reins. A moment later Northam fell in behind.

When they cleared the woods they could see what looked to be the rest of the hunting party crossing a distant field in pairs and threes. For the first time Elizabeth realized how far she and Northam had separated themselves from the others. She felt the nascent stirrings of panic.

Northam saw the direction of her gaze and was not insensitive to her fears. Drawing closer he bid her stop and listen, indicating the shelter of trees they had just left. "The light brigade," he said dryly.

Frowning, Elizabeth glanced behind her and saw the boughs trembling in the wake of thundering hooves. She had been deaf to the sound until Northam pointed it out. It was only when Southerton and Eastlyn charged into the clearing that she understood his reference to the light brigade. They were his friends. She doubted most sincerely that they had followed to make repairs to *her* reputation. "I believe they mean to rescue you, my lord."

He gave her an odd look. "That would be the last thing they mean to do."

Southerton reached Elizabeth's side first, or at least claimed that he did. "You owe me a shilling," he told Eastlyn.

"Hah! I had to twist my head one hundred eighty degrees to watch you arrive."

"By all means," Southerton said. "Allow me the pleasure of completing that rotation for you."

Eastlyn looked at Elizabeth. "My lady, perhaps you would settle the dispute. What say you? Choose a direction. Is it South or East?"

Elizabeth's attention was caught by a movement in her peripheral vision. Northam had directed his mare to make a small retreat and now, outside of his friends' sight, he was shaking his head at her, warning her not to take sides.

Knowing very well the cause of Elizabeth's hesitation, Eastlyn said, "Pay no attention to North. He is no Solomon and therefore is excused from giving an opinion on the reasonable grounds that he has none. South and I are quite willing to accept your judgment in the matter of my clear victory."

Elizabeth pressed the back of one hand to her lips to quell a bit of hysterical laughter. She wondered at their foolery when she knew they were not fools. Northam did not strike her as a person who would suffer them. Her voice was not quite her own as she asked, "The wager is a shilling, you say?"

"That's right," Southerton said. "You must have seen—"

Elizabeth regarded him quizzically as he stopped midsentence and did not continue. His head was cocked to one side, his manner suddenly alert. She noticed that Eastlyn was watchful as well. Northam's glance had darted toward the perimeter of the wood and she realized they were all in expectation of something appearing . . . or someone. She had only just drawn this conclusion when a small entourage including Battenburn, Lord Allen, and Mr. Rutherford entered the open field.

More to herself than to her companions, Elizabeth said, "It seems odd they would come this way."

"We did, didn't we?" Northam said.

A small crease appeared between Elizabeth's brows. She had the impression that Northam meant his statement as something more than a mere observation, as if the arrival of the others was no mere chance occurrence. When the baron's party had crossed half the distance toward them, Elizabeth steadied Becket. For no reason that she could determine, Battenburn suddenly veered to his right and headed toward the stable. The others in his group responded in kind, taking the sharp turn in direction with rather less skill than the baron had demonstrated on his mount.

"I believe they are playing at following the leader," said Elizabeth.

Northam and the others did not disabuse her of that notion. She was correct, after a fashion. Elizabeth Penrose seemed to have no idea that she had been the leader. "We may as well set our own pace," Northam said, bringing his mare around. "We are sadly out of the chase now."

"There's still the matter of my shilling," Southerton said, pointing at Eastlyn.

Before the marquess could reply, Elizabeth held up her hand. "Oh, I beg you, please allow me to settle the matter as you asked. I declare the race a tie and will give you each a shilling upon our return." She saw immediately that the men were inordinately pleased by her decision, and she could not help but laugh at the sly, mischievous exchange between them. It was not as if Northam had not warned her. "I take it you two have been quite successful in emptying the pockets of women in this manner for some time. It is really too bad of you."

Southerton nodded agreeably. "We are scoundrels, Lady Elizabeth. It is just as well you know the truth at the outset."

"The trick," Northam said, a wry twist to his mouth, "is to pay them no attention."

"And you?" she asked. "Do you count yourself as one of them?"

"Most definitely. But I will not be ignored."

Elizabeth's beautifully arched brows lifted a fraction. It occurred to her to wonder how she had come to this pass. In reluctantly accepting the attentions of one, it seemed she had come under the scrutiny of all. She could only think it

was a fortunate thing that Mr. Marchman's business had
taken him off. She was quite certain she could not have
managed a fourth pair of eyes watching her.

Contrary to Northam's last words, Elizabeth deliberately
turned away from him. She heard him chuckle under his
breath and ignored this also. "I understand, Lord Southerton,
that a snuffbox in your possession has come up missing.
Lady Battenburn is distressed that it might have been
stolen."

Southerton waved that concern aside. "I never suggested
such. Indeed, I had not entertained the notion myself. I hope
you will do whatever you can to influence Lady Battenburn
that this is not the case."

"More likely he misplaced the thing," said Eastlyn. "It
will turn up directly."

"Which is precisely why I mentioned it to the baroness.
In the event that it is discovered following my departure, it
can be returned to me."

"Of course," said Elizabeth. "It is of some sentimental
value, I gather."

Southerton nodded. "It belonged to my grandfather."

"Then, save for finding the box, I don't know what I can
do to ease Louise's distress. You'll let us know, won't you,
if the box is recovered elsewhere?"

"Of course."

Eastlyn removed his hat long enough to rake back his
chestnut hair. "I hadn't considered the possibility of theft
myself," he said, thoughtful now. "Plain to see why it would
occur to Lady Battenburn, though. This rascal, the one they
call the Gentleman Thief in the *Gazette*, could be in our
midst. Stands to reason with the plethora of activity in the
country estates right now, he would move from London to
where the pickings are more to his fancy."

Southerton considered this. "The Gentleman Thief, eh?
It bears some thinking. He is credited with lifting Lady
Carver's diamond brooch at the Winthrop ball last winter.
As I understand it, Lady Carver was wearing the brooch at
the time." In deference to Elizabeth's presence, the viscount

did not laugh and was careful not to catch the eye of either Eastlyn or North. It was known to each of them, as well as the *ton*, that the lady was possessed of such an ample bosom, the thief could have found shelter beneath it for the entire evening without fear of discovery. When Southerton was certain the urge for ribald humor had passed him by, he met Elizabeth's eyes and saw they were troubled. "Do not concern yourself," he said. "The box will reappear. It is highly unlikely the Gentleman Thief is among Battenburn's guests."

"I hope you are right," Elizabeth said softly.

Northam moved abreast of her and explained to the others, "Lady Elizabeth was responsible for writing out the invitations. No doubt she believes it makes her accountable for the thief's behavior, if it should be discovered there really *is* a thief at Battenburn. The idea that it is this particular Gentleman Thief is fanciful, I think. There are more likely suspects."

Elizabeth bristled. "I take it you mean the servants. That is very unfair of you, my lord."

Northam took no offense. "Not unfair; merely a practical observation. I would be surprised if Lady Battenburn has not already called the staff into account and ordered a search of their quarters." One of his dark brows kicked up as he regarded Elizabeth's faint flush. "Aaah, then she *has* done so, and you were the one charged with communicating this unpleasantness to the staff."

"I spoke with Jennings," she said quietly. "As butler, it became his unpleasant task."

Southerton sighed. "I regret I mentioned the matter of the snuffbox at all. It seems to have caused an inordinate amount of trouble."

Eastlyn chuckled, pointing a finger at him. "And you'll look every bit the cake when it turns up in your St. James residence. Don't think we won't have some fun with you then."

Northam saw that Elizabeth did not share their humor. He changed the subject. "Did you notice, South, that we were observed during the hunt from the parapet? I believe Lady Powell was among those watching. She would have had no trouble picking you out on that spawn of Satan.''

Southerton snorted. "I see you are bent on having fun with me now, but please do not disparage this fine animal.'' He patted the neck of the great black beast he was riding. His mount's nature was in every way the opposite of his imposing size and strength. Under Southerton's attention the stallion shook his head and showed off his thick mane. "Griffin has tender feelings and a gentle temperament.'' He looked up at the parapet and saw Lady Powell was leaning forward through a notch in the wall. He recognized the instrument in her hand as a spyglass. "Lord," he said under his breath, "she *is* watching me." Southerton smiled wanly, still not certain he wanted to encourage her interest.

Elizabeth raised her own face to the roof. This time she did not wave. "It must be a splendid view.''

Northam was struck by this. "Do you mean to say you have never been up there?''

"Never.''

"Then we should—''

She stopped him, shaking her head firmly. "If you mean to include me, then I must disabuse you of that notion.''

Eastlyn glanced up and saw Lady Powell's spyglass was still riveted on them. "I shouldn't wonder if she topples head over bucket,'' he observed mildly. "Quite a distance to the ground.'' He looked back at Elizabeth. "Do you have some fear of heights?''

"No,'' she said with a certain ironic nuance in her voice. "A fear of falling.'' Elizabeth did not miss Eastlyn's stricken look or the way his dark eyes darted to her hip. She would not let him be embarrassed for inadvertently calling attention to her infirmity. "It would be so much easier if people would simply ask what happened. One assumes after a while that everyone knows, then someone, like yourself, steps into it and reminds me that my ungainly gait is often a matter of speculation. On no account should you be chagrined. It is a simple enough tale: I fell from the ladder in the library at

Rosemont. It was an accident that did not need to happen, and would not have happened if I had shown any patience. I did not fall far, but I landed hard and awkwardly. It has been five years and the bones have set as they will." She shrugged. "I do not climb ladders or step out onto parapets and I am not in demand as a dance partner, but this, perhaps, is fortunate, since I was ever at cross purposes with my dancing master. It is more important to me that my fears have not prevented me from riding and for that I am grateful."

"As am I," Eastlyn said. It was not gallantry that gave rise to the comment, or the need to make some amends, but the simple expression of sincerity. He offered the ultimate compliment. "You are a bruising rider, Lady Elizabeth."

Though he spoke no more than the truth, Elizabeth could feel herself flushing. "Perhaps you would allow me the opportunity to win back my shilling." With no more warning than that, she and Becket were off like a shot in the direction of the stable.

Lady Battenburn rested her head against the back of the tub. A folded towel supported her nape. Her throat was exposed and droplets of water had pooled in the hollow at its base. Ribbons of steam spiraled from the tub. Her fair skin glowed in the candlelight like the petals of a rose damp with morning dew. Her eyes were closed, the dark lashes making faint shadows on her cheeks.

"I noticed your dance card was filled this evening," she said. "That is certainly a good sign."

Elizabeth sat in the same wing chair she had occupied the previous night. She had removed her slippers and rested her heels on the stool. Her toes twitched inside her stockings. She stretched and curled deliberately, easing the ache in her feet. "It is a sign they feel pity for me," she said. "This afternoon I had cause to tell Eastlyn the story of how I was injured. Lord Northam and Southerton heard it also. I would not put too much stock in their attentions this evening."

Lady Battenburn pooh-poohed this comment with a dilatory wave of her hand. "It was not only those three who attended you. Why, you danced with Rutherford, Lord Heathering, Framingham, and . . ." Her voice trailed off. "I shall have to review your dance card to refresh my memory, the list was so long. I do not believe you completed a single set with Harrison. He sulked in the card room again, I think."

"Hardly sulking. He must have been relieved not to do his duty dance with me." In any event, the baron needed no encouragement to retire to the card room. "As for the others who asked me to dance, they were merely following in Eastlyn's wake. The marquess and his friends set certain expectations without giving voice to a single word. I said as much to Lord Northam tonight, but he was having none of it."

"I am not surprised, since it was very nearly insulting for you to have said so." Louise touched a finger to her mouth and tapped her lips lightly. "It is too bad Eastlyn is leaving on Friday. I must say I was devastated by the news. He will miss the treasure hunt, and I had thought after seeing you with him on the dance floor that I would make you his partner."

Then it was a very good thing the marquess was leaving. "I think if you set your mind to it, you can make a proper match of Lady Powell and Lord Southerton. There is interest there, to be sure."

Louise would not be moved from her course. She flicked water in Elizabeth's direction, not caring that she made the carpet damp. "What about the earl? He rode with you at the hunt." When Elizabeth did not reply the baroness thrust out her lower lip. "You intend to be difficult, don't you? Then I am going to concentrate my efforts on bringing Northam around. You should do the same, Libby. Harrison says the earl would make a most suitable partner for you."

"Are you looking for me to leave?" Elizabeth asked.

Louise's lashes flew open. Her head swiveled in Elizabeth's direction and she took measure of the seriousness of the question. "Leave? I do hope you know by now that it is impossible for you to leave us. Harrison and I could not possibly countenance such a thing. It is only that we are trying to set you up properly. It is fitting that you take a husband, Libby. You can leave our nest, as it were, and still be under our wing."

The stool tipped as Elizabeth stood with a speed and force that spoke to her agitation. She made no effort to right it before she turned her back on Louise and crossed the room to the window. Had she always known this day would come? she wondered. She didn't like to think so. "It is calculating," she said quietly.

"Of course it is," Louise said flatly. "How naive you would be if you believed otherwise. Proposals invariably turn on matters of mutual benefit. Money. Title. Power. Influence. These things are always considered. Love matches, to the extent they exist at all, are formed when the interests of all parties are in equilibrium."

"That is very cynical."

"It is *true*."

Elizabeth pressed her forehead to a windowpane. The glass was cool against her skin. "I do not think I can do it."

"What's that?" Louise sat up in the tub. The towel behind her neck slipped into the water. She retrieved it and slapped it on the carpet with all the flair of laying down a gauntlet.

The sound startled Elizabeth and she spun around.

"Speak up, Elizabeth," Louise said sternly. "You know I cannot abide mulishness."

Elizabeth's nostrils flared slightly as she took a steadying breath. She let it out slowly, calming herself so she could think clearly. "I said, I do not think I can do it."

"Do what?" Louise exclaimed. "Pray, do not be such a child. There is nothing for you to do. Northam will be brought around, just as I said. It shall all be accomplished so skillfully that he will think it was his idea. Men really have no sense of how they are led about and it would only subvert our interests to rub their noses in it. You will leave the particulars up to me. I shall see to everything."

Elizabeth knew Louise thought this settled the matter. She had only one card to play. "My father will—"

"Will be delighted," said Louise. "Oh, that may be putting too pretty a bow on the thing, but you take my meaning. He will not protest, Elizabeth, and indeed, he may be relieved. The opportunity for you to begin a family of your own will offer him some respite, will it not?"

Chilled of a sudden, her face drained of all color, Elizabeth moved away from the window. Even knowing the answer, she forced herself to ask, "You have spoken to him of this?"

"Corresponded only. Not the particulars, naturally, but the *idea* of it all. I have leave to act as I think is best." Louise's voice took on a husky, soothing subtlety. "Poor Libby. Is it really so bad? Or is it just that you had permitted yourself to believe you held the reins of your own fate? One does not, you know. It is the nature of fate that it is done *to* you, not *by* you. Surely you can find some cause to rejoice that it is Northam that has been chosen. Harrison had been considering Mr. Rutherford, but there is only the slightest chance he will inherit someday. His prospects are little better than Mr. Marchman's."

Elizabeth pressed one hand to her temple. Her head felt as if it had been stuffed with cotton batting. Louise's plan surpassed anything she had considered in regard to her future. That her father had been in agreement was not in itself surprising; that he had been apprised of this turn was.

"It is all rather too much, isn't it?" Louise asked. She felt at a loss herself. It was difficult to console Elizabeth from her bath. "Get me my robe, dear. There's a good girl. You must know that I have the very best intentions where you are concerned. Have I not considered your feelings in so many ways over the years? But you are six and twenty, Elizabeth, and while the existence of your limp is unenviable, it is not tragic. It was not meant to protect you from the circumstances of living your life." Louise rose gracefully from the tub and slipped into the robe Elizabeth held out to her. She belted it tightly about her waist and the material clung tenaciously to her damp and voluptuous curves. "Is there someone else,

Libby? Someone else who has struck you as more fitting? I have despaired of seeing you catch anyone's eye. You are so very good at keeping suitors at a distance.''

Elizabeth righted the overturned footstool. ''I don't know what you mean.'' But she did, and she knew Louise knew it. Elizabeth almost wished the baroness would take her to task for her lie. She could accept these small cruelties. It was the little kindnesses she found unbearable. In the face of Louise's tactical silence, Elizabeth said, ''No. There is no one else.''

Louise nodded, pleased with this confirmation. ''I observed you from the parapet this afteroon. It seemed that you engaged in a small flirtation with the earl. Did I mistake that?''

For a moment Elizabeth thought she had been spied in the act of returning Northam's kiss. The memory of his mouth on hers, her tongue against his lips, stirred a response that ran under the surface of her skin from the back of her neck all the way to her toes. Reason asserted itself, and she suppressed the memory and the stirrings. It was not the kiss that had been seen, but her playful, spontaneous act of knocking Northam's hat off his head. He had run her to ground in the woods, and while Louise couldn't know for certain that anything untoward had occurred there, her fanciful, romantic, and ultimately shrewd notions were filling in for the facts she lacked.

Elizabeth wanted to reach back in time and rub out a moment's recklessness. Regret nearly stilled her heart. At her sides her knuckles were white. She came to awareness gradually and realized that Louise was speaking to her again.

''It is too bad that Northam's friends followed you into the woods. Harrison had cause to curse his regrettable luck that he could not have arrived sooner.''

Elizabeth's palms were clammy. She resisted the urge to open her fists and wipe them in the folds of her aqua silk gown. ''Do you mean to say the baron and his friends deliberately followed us?''

Louise thought she would lose all patience with Elizabeth's obtuseness. ''I mean exactly that. If you are to be compromised, then it should be the baron who finds you and demands satisfaction on behalf of your father. It does no good at all for Northam's friends to come upon the scene first and drive you out as if they were beating rabbits from the thicket.''

Elizabeth could have told Louise that Eastlyn and Souther-ton had not come upon her and Lord Northam in a clinch, but she was no longer certain it was true. She had heard nothing of their approach until Northam pointed it out after they had left the woods. Now she had cause to wonder if the earl had not been aware of them earlier. The three friends seemed to share an uncanny sense among them.

"I cannot be easily compromised, Louise. As you have pointed out, I am six and twenty, an age that implies some maturity and the license to give my consent.''

"Fiddlesticks. You are the Earl of Rosemont's daughter and your reputation can be ruined as easily as a gel's in the first flush of maidenhood. It is all in how one manages the aftermath, I assure you.''

Elizabeth had cause to know Louise Edmunds, the Right Honorable Lady Battenburn, was a master of manipulating the aftermath. "It seems it is all arranged, then.''

"More or less.'' She regarded Elizabeth's bleak expression with concern. "You are overset, m'dear. I always forget how easily shocked you are. One would think that by this time . . .'' She lifted her hands helplessly. "But no, you have no head for matters such as these. It is just as well that the baron and I have taken you into our bosom. I shudder when I think of how you would have gotten on without us.''

Elizabeth suppressed her own shudder. She said with credible calm, "Will you excuse me?''

"Of course. I have kept you too long as it is. Harrison, I fear, is still at the card table. I only hope the outcome will be different from last night's debacle.''

Elizabeth did not comment. She let herself out and hurried down the hallway to her own suite in the north wing. Once she was inside she leaned over the washstand in her bathing room and emptied the contents of her stomach into the porcelain basin.

Chapter Four

It was still the middle of the night when Northam roused himself from his bed. He dressed in the dark and took no candlestick with him when he left his room. Four nights had passed since Southerton's snuffbox had gone missing, and the earl thought he might have missed his one and only opportunity to surprise the Gentleman Thief.

He shook his head, his mouth set derisively as he considered that moniker. It showed a lamentable lack of creativity on the part of the *Gazette's* writers, though Northam supposed it was accurate enough. Still, there were more colorful cant expressions that could have been made to serve and given this sneaksman an excess of notoriety that might have made him easier to apprehend.

This particular thief—if the stories could be believed—expressed no interest in celebrity and, when confronted from time to time as he inevitably had been by those whose jewels he was lifting, made an elegant leg and apologized for the necessity of his activity. Southerton, sleeping as he always had in the very deepest embrace of Morpheus, had not been awakened by the Gentleman Thief, and would not have been moved to shoot the fellow if he had. It was much more likely that South would have inquired as to whether a decent living could be made lifting snuffboxes, earbobs, necklaces, and the like, and then questioned the man as to all the particulars of his profession. In short, South would have talked the man to death, or at least engaged him in pointless conversation until help arrived in the form of the marquess. One could at least count on Eastlyn to shoot the intruder first and ask for the particulars later.

Northam yawned so widely that his jaw cracked. In the stillness of the manse it sounded like a shot. He hoped that lapse in good sense was the only one he had.

Tonight, he decided, he would go up to the roof. At first he had concentrated on finding the secret passages that Battenburn was famous for, then reasoned that the thief would not use his precious time in a similar study. Every London town house the thief visited was not riddled with corridors between the walls and panels that opened into parlors and galleries. The Gentleman Thief was known to scale walls and trellises to gain his entry, at least when he was not invited through the front door.

What intrigued the *ton* about this thief was that he appeared to be one of their own. Lady Carver's emerald brooch had indeed been stolen from her person at the Winthrop winter ball. It was impossible for her to say at what point she had lost the brooch. When she discovered it gone it might have been minutes or hours since she had had it last. Neither was she inclined to believe it was stolen. It was the theft of Lord Adamson's watch that same evening that made the squeeze suspect the Gentleman Thief was moving among them. With the finely honed skill of a *boman prig* raised in the criminal dens around Covent Garden or Holborn, this thief was able to *speak to the tattler*, or remove watches, and *chive the froe*, cant for cutting out a woman's pockets. The term *boman prig*, as it was applied occasionally to the Gentleman, was something of an honor and meant to mark him as an adept in his trade.

The question raised by the newspapers who reported the Gentleman's activities, was whether this thief had studied his craft in one of the slum academies, and later learned the manner of a gentlemen, or if he had prepared for *rum-*

hustling while he was still attending public school at Eton, Harrow, or Hambrick. This chicken-or-egg poser presented no dilemma for members of the *ton*. To a person they were convinced this thief was a real gentleman, for they could not conceive that just any man could pass among them, participate in their entertainments, or dance with their daughters during the Season, without the kind of bearing, grace, and good form that was bred in the bone. To suppose otherwise, to think even for a moment that one could be taught to affect a position in society that was not one's birthright, would have turned the social order on its ear. It was far more reasonable, and much less threatening, to hold the opinion that a gentleman had chosen to study and embrace the practices of a thief.

Though he was regularly denounced in the papers, it had escaped no one's notice that he was good at his craft. Pride warred with annoyance that the *beau monde* was being filched by one of their own.

Northam carefully opened the door that led to the roof. It swung soundlessly on well-oiled hinges, leading him to conclude that it was a much-used passage. Stepping outside, he understood why guests at Battenburn would come here. The night sky was limitless, spreading out in all directions without any barriers to mark its beginning and end. He had chosen tonight to explore the parapet for two reasons: The lack of a moon presented what he thought was a good opportunity to the thief; and it was a perfect condition for stargazing. If the Gentleman Thief decided to sleep in his own bed this evening, rather than scale the stone walls at Battenburn, Northam at least could make the best of his watch.

The earl walked the perimeter of the roof, stopping occasionally to lean over the parapet and study the recesses in the wall beneath him. With his eyes already adjusted to the dark, the star-lit sky presented him with sufficient illumination to view the shadows where the windows were set and follow the different routes a thief might take to move from room to room using the outside wall for access.

Northam had never been present at a private entertainment

where the Gentleman Thief had done his work. While Lady Carver was having her brooch removed, Northam had been staying with the Pollards and deftly avoiding an entanglement with their oldest daughter. There had been a rash of thefts that same winter, all of which could not properly be attributed to the Gentleman but which were laid at his door nonetheless.

No less a personage than the Dowager Duchess of Hammersly had had three ropes of perfectly matched pearls removed from her neck. Sapphire earbobs, ebony hair combs set with diamond chips, gold watches and fobs, bracelets, necklaces, and tiaras had all been taken at one time or another during that winter. The Gentleman had never struck so recklessly before or since. In the five years this sneaksman had been robbing the rich and giving . . . well, giving to himself . . . his established pattern was to openly steal at relatively few functions of the *ton*. He seemed to prefer to visit the town homes of the best-kept mistresses, where he could take jewelry that would be replaced by their protectors and not cause a terrible kick up among the society matrons. It did the Gentleman Thief's reputation no harm that on occasion a put-upon mistress would claim a bauble had been stolen when it was in fact pawned by her to repay gaming debts.

Northam had had months to try to sort through the facts and fictions of this case and he was still not certain he knew one from the other. It was absurd to believe that every time a purse was lifted in the crush at Drury Lane, it was the Gentleman Thief practicing his specialty. The intermission at the theater, known as the *breaking-up of the spell* in the cant of the thieves, had been a prime time for picking pockets as long as Drury Lane had existed.

The accounts that involved somewhat reliable reporters among the *ton* had been marginally more helpful. Lord Gaithers had surprised the thief in his study and been able to provide a modest description of the man, though Northam doubted the Gentleman Thief was quite the bruiser Gaithers depicted. More likely his lordship exaggerated some of the particulars to explain how he had had his primed pistol taken from him and been brained with the butt of it.

Similarly, Sir Anthony Palmer and his wife were visited by the thief and relieved of an exquisite emerald and diamond bracelet and two ruby stickpins. They provided what was perhaps a better picture of the thief as long as one accounted for their advanced age and failing eyesight.

The Gentleman Thief was no fool.

Northam, under the direction of Colonel Blackwood—whose authority to act in this matter he did not question—had been gathering such evidence as existed for better than six months. This involved the delicate work of speaking to all the Gentleman's victims among the peerage in a way that did not raise their hackles, or even lead them to suspect they were being interviewed. He compiled information about the guest lists at hundreds of parties over the last five years and painstakingly searched for the commonalities. He forced himself to examine the broader picture, taking into account what was happening beyond the sometimes narrow interests of the *ton*. How might have Napoleon's victories and defeats influenced the timing of the thefts, for instance, or the Treaty of Ghent that ended the war with America? What celebrations brought out the very finest jewelry, and when did society's anxieties keep what was best locked away?

The idea of this larger influence intrigued him. Thinking on it, though, made him very tired. Perhaps if it were only jewelry the Gentleman had his eye on, North's own task would be made easier. Complicating his assignment were the things that had gone missing that few wanted to report or discuss.

After circling the roof's perimeter a second time, Northam found a relatively comfortable place for himself in one of the notches in the wall. Removing his telescope from an inside pocket, he extended its length and raised it to his right eye. The clear night gave him opportunity to study the constellations and visible planets. It had always been a hobby of his, this interest in the stars. Camped out in a remote Indian pass, he had often lain outside his tent and stared at the patterns of light in the blue-black sky. The domed shape of the heavens, an illusion his eyes insisted on seeing, gave him the sensation of being held in the cupped hands of the Creator. It was a peaceful thought that had lulled him to sleep, and one he had carried into the thunder of battle.

He roughly estimated the passage of time by noting the change in the position of Sagittarius relative to the landmarks he had fixed on the horizon. Hours later, when the southern-most star appeared to dip behind a distant stand of trees, Northam admitted to himself it was another night gone begging for sleep. He collapsed his scope for the final time and returned it to his jacket.

Stretching his legs, he eased himself down against the stone until he was sitting on the roof. He should have been more tired than he was, having roused himself from a comfortable bed every night since arriving at Battenburn. A lot of work had gone into determining that this particular fortnight of reveling presented prime pickings for the Gentleman Thief. The theft of Southerton's snuffbox seemed to indicate that he and the colonel had properly narrowed the playing field. It did not mean, however, that the Gentleman would limit himself to Battenburn's guests. Travel to another country manor was not out of the question. It was this line of thinking that led to Marchman being dispatched to Rhylstone, west of London. Eastlyn and Southerton had nothing but their own suspicions regarding his assignment, and history had proven it was better that way. Their association with the colonel had presented them all with danger from time to time, but it was a fact they were in more danger when they were tripping over each other in pursuit of the same end. To the extent it was possible, the colonel kept them on parallel assignments and avoided entanglements that set them at cross-purposes.

North found a natural cradle in the stone for the back of his head and rested it there. He crossed his arms in front of his chest, his legs at the ankles, and closed his eyes. For some men this posture would be a precursor to sleep, but not for Northam. He imagined that it was under an apple tree, in just this position, that Newton had found the intellectual acuity to postulate the existence of gravity. He did not flatter himself that he was in the same cerebral league as Sir Isaac, but he considered this exact arrangement of head, arms, and legs to promote the best cognitive powers.

He therefore applied himself to consideration in the matter of Lady Elizabeth Anne Penrose. She had been avoiding him these last few days. East and South had both been moved to remark on it, and Northam's lack of response had not kept them from making this observation again the following day.

People Northam considered far less astute than either of his friends also felt free to comment. Over whist, Lord Battenburn asked Northam if he had given Lady Elizabeth some offense. The bald question startled Northam enough that he dropped a diamond when he meant to throw a heart and reneged on the hand. Lady Powell, still in pursuit of South, wondered aloud if Elizabeth's strategy of avoidance was not perhaps a tactic she should use herself. Oddly, it was the baroness who was quiet on the matter, making Northam curious whether she was encouraging Elizabeth's retreat or merely shrewd enough not to make her opinion known.

Sighing, Northam wondered what theories Sir Isaac might have advanced about women if he had never been conked on the head with that apple. After all, Elizabeth Penrose exerted a gravitational pull every bit the equal of the one that kept the moon orbiting the earth. At least she did on him. Southerton and Eastlyn found her a pleasant enough companion, more than tolerably attractive, and sufficiently quick-witted to keep them entertained, but neither of them seemed to know the exact moment she entered a room or showed the ability to single out the threads of her conversation in the midst of so many others.

Northam was not a little concerned about his proficiency in doing both these things. He reminded himself that East had his own difficulties with Lady Sophia and a discarded mistress to sort out, and one part of South's clever mind was given over to the problem of Lady Powell's self-serving interests. They were not so free as he to be drawn to the Earl of Rosemont's daughter.

Only part of his interest could be attributed to her connection to the colonel. Certainly it had been at the root of their introduction, but it was not what sustained his attraction to her. The kiss, without a doubt, had something to do with it. If he was any judge—and Northam assured himself he was—Lady Elizabeth was no green girl. When he was being uncharitable, he wondered what looseness of morals allowed her to take so much pleasure in a kiss. When he was in a more reasonable frame of mind, he considered what good fortune it was to find a woman whose passion equaled his own.

He had thought a great deal about the kiss they shared, his mouth lowering on hers, her tongue sweeping the soft, sensitive underside of his lips. He could sometimes still feel the edge of her small white teeth pressing against his skin, the wetness and warmth of her mouth on his. She had sucked in his lower lip as she had drawn a breath, tugging on it with precise, delicate nibbles. Openmouthed. Hot. His own tongue had curled around hers. Deep. And deeper.

A soft, guttural growl rose at the back of Northam's throat. His trousers were becoming uncomfortably tight. He reckoned with the temptation to unbutton his fly and take himself in hand. The tension release and comfort afforded by a little masturbatory gratification hardly seemed worth the effort just now. Because Northam had heretofore been of the opinion that sexual pleasure, even when achieved through self-indulgence, was *always* worth the effort, he took it as a sign he was either falling asleep or falling in love. At six o'clock in the morning he was understandably muzzy on what distinguished one from the other.

It was a scream that woke him. For a moment he imagined himself trapped in the pages of a Gothic novel, where all screams were described as bloodcurdling. Northam promised himself he was done reading the likes of *Castle Rackrent*. The scream rose again, less shrilly than before, but managed to sustain the warbling notes with all the tragic passion of an operatic lament.

Northam rose to his feet and shook out his legs. Leaning over the parapet, he was able to vaguely determine which rooms were the likely origin of the scream. He was not so foolish as to attempt to scale down the wall to the open window. Instead he left the roof and hurried down the steep spiral staircase to the main hallway. If he had not already fixed the source of the caterwauling in his own mind, it would have been easily found by the crush outside Lady Battenburn's bedchamber.

The door to her room was flung wide and guests who had been moved to investigate were pressing themselves into the opening and craning to see what manner of injury had taken place.

The baroness sat at the foot of her bed. Her heels dangled several inches above the floor, making her seem younger and more vulnerable than her earthy appearance would otherwise suggest. She was fanning herself with one hand, which had the effect of changing the pitch of her scream. The other hand was being held by her husband, who soothed and patted it in the hope it offered enough comfort for blessed silence to follow.

"It is Lady Battenburn's diamond necklace," he told the crowd gathered in the doorway. "It has been stolen."

It seemed to Northam that something more than a stolen necklace was causing Louise to scream like a banshee. How had the lady come to miss the piece of jewelry at this hour of the morning? From his position outside the circle of onlookers, Northam reached past Allen and Heathering and politely tapped Eastlyn on the shoulder. That worthy had somehow found himself near the center of the crush.

East managed to swivel his head. He grinned when he saw Northam. "Excuse me," he said to those around him. "Let me out. That's it. Lift your arm. View's better at the front." He extricated himself without too much difficultly, and the guests realigned themselves quickly. "South is sleeping?" he asked Northam.

"I suppose he must be. He's not here." He again surveyed the bodies jammed in the tight circle around the doorway. "No, he's not here."

Eastlyn raked back a fallen lock of chestnut hair. His tone was admiring. "He can damn near sleep through anything."

Northam nodded and pointed to the pistol that Eastlyn was carrying. "You, on the other hand . . ."

Eastlyn tucked the pistol away. "I was already awake. I wanted to make an early start of it to London." He glanced back toward the door when the last notes of Lady Battenburn's scream faded away. The crowd seemed to swell slightly as they heaved a collective sigh of relief. East rolled his eyes. "I had my doubts that would ever stop."

Northam had wondered the same thing. "How soon did you arrive?"

"A minute, no more, after she first cried out. I would have been here sooner, but I got lost again. I should have been at the forefront of the charge, instead I was in the middle."

"Did you see anyone leaving her room?"

"No. Rutherford was already here. Heathering, too. Allen came from the opposite direction and we arrived almost together. Do you think the lady surprised the thief?"

"It occurs to me that was the cause of all her screaming."

Eastlyn gave his friend a considering look. "Where did you come from?"

"The roof."

There was only a fractional widening to East's eyes. "Alone?"

"Very much so."

"Lady Battenburn had one arm extended in the direction of the open window when I arrived. I thought she was merely reaching for her husband, who provided little calming influence, by the way. It suggests to me now that she may have seen the thief leave by that route."

Northam mulled this over. "Can you assist in a search without shooting anyone, most particularly me?"

One corner of Eastlyn's mouth kicked up. "I can certainly try."

"Not precisely the assurance I was looking for."

Eastlyn's grin deepened. "It's all I can promise. Am I searching for the necklace or the thief?"

"Either. Both." Northam drew East farther away from the guests as their circle began to loosen, and they milled about, contemplating their next step. "Be careful. The others are bound to get underfoot."

Elizabeth Penrose stirred sleepily. Her cheek rubbed against the back of her hand in a languorous, feline movement. She murmured something, her lips parting and shaping themselves around words that could not be understood by the man standing over her. Northam knew he should step away from her bed, let himself out of her room as quietly as he had entered, but there was that unmistakable pull she exerted, and he was learning sleep did not diminish its force.

She lay on her side with the sheet and blankets tangled close by but not covering her. Her nightshift was a loose-fitting batiste chemise, devoid of even the simplest ornamentation. The neckline was low and rounded and gaped slightly above the shadowed cleavage of her breasts. The hem had ridden up to her knees, and where one slim leg was extended Northam had a very nice view of a finely rounded calf and trim ankle. Her arms were bare, the chemise having only short sleeves. The fine hairs on her forearms were glazed golden by the early morning light.

When his eyes, dark at the centers now and as reflective as mirrors, reached Elizabeth's face again, he saw it was too late to beat a retreat.

Elizabeth bolted upright. As her mouth opened wider than her eyes, Northam was moved to take action. In the event she had practiced screaming in the same school that had tutored Lady Battenburn, Northam considered it the wisest course to shut her up. Because he doubted she would be receptive to a kiss, he clamped his hand across the lower part of her face and kept it there even when she managed to bite him.

He gritted his own teeth and punctuated his pain with a short grunt. It seemed to satisfy her and she let off.

To get better leverage, Northam sat down on the edge of the bed. The back of Elizabeth's head was pressed against an intricately carved walnut headboard and he suspected it was very nearly painful. Over the edge of his hand her eyes no longer expressed any surprise or fear but had narrowed accusingly and remained unblinking and steady in their regard. He eased his hold a fraction, not removing his hand but giving her space enough to tickle his palm with her breath.

"Can I count on your discretion not to scream?" he asked.

She nodded. The last thing Elizabeth wanted was to call attention to his presence in her room. Her initial reaction had been predicated on primitive instincts of survival. Once she recognized Northam as her intruder, fear of the man was replaced by fear of the situation. Her voice fairly hissed. "What are you doing here? Haven't you the least sense of what is proper? My God, if you are discovered . . ."

"I shall hide behind the truth," he said calmly, "and hope for the best."

Elizabeth's brow puckered. Her eyes were still narrowed, but the expression was less accusing and more suspicious. "What truth is that?"

"Oh, I see," Northam said, pretending only now to comprehend the root of her concern. "You think I could not resist you, is that it? That the interlude we shared in the woods, for all that it was brief, served to whet my appetite for a larger feast?" He shook his head, letting his hand drop away completely now. It hovered a moment just inches above the curve of her breasts before dropping to rest on the bed beside her hip. "The truth, Lady Elizabeth, is that the baroness has been robbed, probably by the Gentleman Thief, and has awakened a goodly portion of her guests with more screaming than occurs in a Gothic novel."

Elizabeth blinked.

Northam took this as a good sign. "East and I are making a search. There will be others in our wake, but we are the first."

"How . . . *heroic*."

He ignored her sarcasm. "Yes, well, there you have it. When I opened the door to this room I had no idea that it was yours."

"Yes, but once you knew, you didn't leave."

Northam glanced around. Her bedchamber was appointed with a chaise longue near the fireplace and a secretary and chair by the window. A vanity and damask-covered stool were situated against one wall. A door he supposed led to her dressing room stood slightly ajar. A round walnut table flanked one side of her bed. It held a single book, a collection of short stories by the American writer Washington Irving, and two candlesticks. "I had to conduct a search," he said, bringing his dark glance to bear on her again.

"And have you?" There was unaccountably a small catch in her voice. "Finished conducting it, I mean?"

His eyes dropped to her mouth. "Presently."

Elizabeth could feel herself being drawn toward him as if his glance were a liquid, swirling vortex. The beautiful cobalt color of his irises was so deep a blue, it was barely differentiated from the black pupils. His nose was strong, and even with the bump on the bridge it was perfect really, as perfect as his mouth, and the brilliant color of . . .

"Lady Elizabeth?"

She blinked again.

"Where did you go?" he asked.

That perfect mouth, set with just a hint of amusement, was an homage to the greatest sculptors of the Renaissance. Elizabeth had to press her nails into her palms to think of something else besides those lips covering hers. "I want you to leave," she said.

He nodded. "In a moment. You know, if you had not been so bent on avoiding me these last days, I would not be reduced to this rather foolhardy tryst."

"This is *not* a tryst."

"A rendezvous, then."

"It is not that either."

The edge of panic in her tone made Northam put a period to his teasing. "But you have been avoiding me," he said, the merest inflection at the end making it a question.

"Yes."

He welcomed her honesty. "Why?"

"Because nothing can come of it." She shook her head and pushed at the strands of hair that fell against her temple. "No, that isn't precisely true. It is because nothing *should* come of it. You would do so much better to leave me in peace, my lord. Your life cannot be your own once it has become part of mine."

Northam frowned. Elizabeth's speech was candid but also enigmatic. He did not believe she had set out to intrigue him further; indeed, her intentions seemed to be quite the opposite, yet Northam knew himself to be responding to that pull again. "I think you are a riddle, Lady Elizabeth."

"No," she said earnestly, "I'm not. I'm exactly what you think I am: a whore."

It was not the word that shocked him, but that it came so fiercely from the lips of Elizabeth Penrose. Northam actually reared back. His spine stiffened, and for a moment he was his grandfather, all stuff and starch, sitting at the head of the dinner table delivering a lecture on what was acceptable behavior in a moral society. Each platitude carried the reso- nance of a commandment from God. *Thou shall not take a harlot to wive.* The old earl had never uttered that exact sentiment, but the spirit of it was with Northam now.

"Elizabeth."

He said her name in the exact tone one used when trying to encourage an unreasonable child to see reason. Elizabeth had no patience for it. His next line of attack would be to tell her that she was speaking nonsense, and Elizabeth knew she might very well hit him if provoked in that fashion. To save them both from that end, she lifted her chin and fired the first volley. "You know nothing about me save what the colonel told you and what you've gleaned on our short acquaintance. It is not enough for you to make accurate judgments. Whatever you have observed in me that speaks of good character is false. I cannot say it more plainly than that.''

Northam was frowning deeply now. He absently raked his fingers through his hair, trying to make sense of what she was telling him. ''Why are you set on presenting yourself in such a manner?''

''Do not mistake my sincerity and believe I mean to intrigue you with this confession. I find it to be perfectly odious that I must say these things at all. There is no pleasure in it and I accept that you may well come to despise me.''

''Indeed,'' he said dryly. ''That seems to be your intent.''

Elizabeth shook her head. ''No. You are wrong. I intend only to give you a choice. It is better that you hear the truth from me than discover I have misled you.''

''And what truth is that? Do you mean to name yourself a whore again?''

''It is no more than you have thought yourself.'' She did not avert her eyes but watched him openly, daring him to deny it. ''I do not blame you. Indeed, had you not at least considered the possibility, you could not be counted as very perceptive. Admit it, my lord, my response to your kiss surprised you.''

Northam said quietly, ''It rocked me back on my heels.'' He noticed that, if anything, she paled a bit more. She demanded answers but was not completely braced to hear them. ''It does not mean I thought you a whore.''

Elizabeth collected herself again. She was having none of it. ''But you wondered at my experience.''

''You are six and twenty. Was I wrong to assume you had been kissed before?''

''Why will you not say it?'' she asked. ''That you are in my room now speaks to your thinking. You are not sitting with Miss Caruthers, pretending your presence has something to do with a thief. This is not Lady Martha's room. Or Miss Stevens's.''

Northam held up one hand, stopping her before she named

every young unmarried woman invited to Battenburn. He could have reminded her that all of these women were chaperoned by mothers or great-aunts or companions, and attending to them in their rooms would have been impossible, but this was also the argument that Elizabeth was bent on making. "I take your point."

"Then say it. Say why you have really come here."

Northam had no liking for being cornered and he had no intention of putting into words what he did not fully understand himself. She was correct that he would not have stepped beyond the doorway of Lady Martha's room, or that of the misses Caruthers and Stevens. He would not have even opened their doors without an invitation to do so, yet when his knock was unanswered outside this bedchamber, he let himself in. He could admit to himself, if not to her, that he suspected she was the room's occupant. Rather than making him take a step backward, it had had the opposite effect. He had stood over her sleeping figure, watching her, some part of him hoping that she would wake and . . .

"Coward," she said softly.

Northam's head shot up. He did not want to believe he had heard her correctly, but then he remembered she had called herself a whore. What inhibition would she have, then, from naming him a coward? "If your purpose is to provoke me, my lady, then consider that you have been successful."

Elizabeth took no satisfaction in it. She pressed on as Northam came to his feet, his back partially turned to her. "Would you rather I allowed you to seduce me? Should I have played the innocent for you, then accepted your contempt as my due? What words would you have flung at my head? Tart? Harlot? Or perhaps you would have said nothing, and gone off to lick your wounded pride in silence, salving your conscience for taking me with the knowledge that there was at least one other before you. I am no innocent, Northam, and I will not permit you to pretend to my face that I am."

He took a step away from the bed, almost certain he meant to slap her if he did not.

Elizabeth kicked away the tangle of blankets and rose from the bed. She stood behind Northam, just inches to one side. Her hand lifted to touch his shoulder, and then she thought better of it and let it fall again. "I am not the sort of woman one marries."

Thou shalt not take a harlot to wive.

"Not if one has the ability to exercise choice. You must not be alone with me again, Northam. In any circumstances. It will go badly for you if you're discovered. I would rather you did not come to despise me for what is out of my hands."

He made no reply, and after a moment Elizabeth realized he would not. She stepped past him, the ache in the small of her back serving as a reminder of what she must do. She limped to her dressing room and returned wearing a fine wool shawl over her shoulders.

On the threshold, she stopped. She had expected him to use her brief absence as a way to excuse himself. Retrieving the shawl had been nothing more than a pretext to permit him a graceful exit.

"Can I do nothing to convince you to leave?" she asked.

Northam saw her glance toward the door as if she expected discovery was imminent. Perhaps it was, he thought, but he realized he did not care a great deal one way or the other. What he did care about was that she would not think him a coward, and taking the opportunity she presented to flee seemed a most cowardly act.

Elizabeth released the breath she had been holding as Northam walked to the door. She waited, drawing the shawl more closely about her shoulders, not because she was cold but because her tight grip on the fringed ends stilled the tremor in her fingertips. Her eyes dropped to his hand as he placed it on the brass knob, then lowered when his fingers drifted over it and fell to the key. Elizabeth's stomach twisted in the same motion as his wrist. Her breath was caught on the turn of the key.

Northam dropped the key on top of Elizabeth's vanity. From inside his jacket he removed the small telescope and stood it on end beside the key. He stared at them both a moment, studying their placement as if it held some significance, knowing it was not so at all but that what he required was time. He felt her eyes on him, regarding him with a measure of uncertainty now. She could not know what he intended, not when he remained undecided himself.

Turning, Northam saw he had been right about what he would see in her face. Though her chin had come up, her teeth were worrying the inside of her cheek and a small vertical crease had appeared between her brows. Her breathing was shallow. Neither her shawl nor the hand closing over it could hide the rise and fall of her breasts.

He advanced on her slowly. Her eyes flashed as she glanced to the window as though it offered some escape. "It's too far," he said, his voice both quiet and intense. "And too far to the ground."

Elizabeth could not see that she had anywhere to go. She held herself very still, framed in the open doorway to her dressing room.

Northam stopped, a long stride still required to close the distance between them. "Come here."

She did not, could not, move. Tension running just below the surface of her skin pulled it tight. Anticipation was like a heated coil inside her. At the first touch of him it would unwind with such force as to make her cry out. She tried to pull into herself, shrink the feeling that was both dread and longing.

"Elizabeth."

Her name came to her as if from a great distance. She could not properly say whether it was his command, or rather the voice in her own mind, the one that chided her for hesitating. Without conscious effort she stepped forward into the room, caught herself, and once again resisted the urge to place herself in front of him. She looked down at the hand he extended to her, then back to his face, his beautiful face with the darkening eyes, both steady and patient, and she knew she was well and truly without defenses.

A bead of perspiration formed between her breasts and trickled along the curve of one. Between her thighs she was damp.

They moved at the same time. She let herself be backed against the wall. Her hand released the shawl. He caught the ends when they fell to the level of her waist, twisting them in one hand so that he could jerk her against him. She threw her hands to his shoulders and lifted her face.

The taste of him was splendidly satisfying. Salty. Sweet. Faint hints of brandy and mint. She opened her mouth for him before he pressed his entry. Her hunger was a thing unto itself, existing outside reason, outside shame.

Clutching his shoulders, she rose on tiptoe and arched. She ached for the weight of his palms on her breasts and the almost painful sensation of his thumbnails gently scraping across her turgid nipples. She accepted his chest as a substitute, and she rose and fell against him, rubbing, feeling his taut muscles shift and his breathing change. At her waist he gripped the shawl more tightly, yanking her hard, just once, and she felt the outline of his engorged penis against her belly.

He released the shawl but not her. His hands plowed into her hair, capturing her face and holding it still for his pleasure. In the midst of her ginger hair were strands of pure gold. They lay along the length of his fingers like silken shafts of sunlight. The pads of his thumbs pressed into the hollows just behind her ears. She moaned softly, a sound he swallowed, his mouth working hard over hers.

Elizabeth's hands slid under his jacket. She was almost frantic to touch him, pulling at the tails of his linen shirt. Her knuckles brushed his midriff and she felt his abdomen contract. His tongue was deep in her mouth, thrusting. Her fingers splayed across his skin, every fingertip isolated by a separate point of heat. She sucked on his tongue, his lips. She drove her hands upward to his chest and around his back. She scored the flesh of his shoulders lightly with her nails. This time it was his hips that thrust into her.

Northam's grip loosened in her hair and she jerked her

head back, breathing hard, and turned her face for the moment to the side. He bent his own head, his breath hot on the curve of her neck. His mouth opened over her tender skin and sipped on it with the delicacy of one drawing sweet cream from the top of the milk. All along the length of him he felt her shiver.

His hands rested on her shoulders while his fingers gathered the soft batiste of her gown into small folds. He slowly let his hands drift downward, pulling the fabric with them, widening the neckline until it slipped over one shoulder, then the other. The material was trapped between their bodies at the level of her waist. When he stepped back, it remained there, caught by the press of her buttocks against the wall.

For the first time he saw alarm cross her features. She was panicked enough that it penetrated the haze of her passion. She released him and made to grab her nightshift. He stopped her, covering her hands with his own larger ones.

"No," he whispered. He touched his forehead briefly to hers. "I want to see your breasts. I want to look at you."

A strangled sound came from the back of her throat, but she stopped trying to raise her hands.

Northam eased his grip and only circled her wrists with his thumbs and forefingers. His eyes never leaving her face, he slowly, deliberately, lifted her arms until they were just above the line of her shoulders; then he pressed her wrists to the wall. He laid his mouth over hers, teasing her lower lip with a single sweep of his tongue. He sucked on the lip so that when he released it there was the faintest sound of damp parting. She was trembling when he drew back.

His glance drifted over her features. She returned his gaze through eyes that were at once glazed and wary, as though she could not decide between passion or fear. There was only a hint of color in her cheeks. All the blood in her face seemed to have settled in her mouth. The line of her lips was swollen and cherry red from the pressure of their kisses.

A muscle jumped suddenly in her cheek. Her head jerked back again, bumping the wall as if he had pushed her with the heel of his hand. He still held her wrists in place. He hadn't released her or touched her cheek with anything save his glance; it was just that she felt it as something tangible, an index finger tracing her jaw or his knuckles brushing her chin. When she would have looked away, he caught her eyes, held them, and issued an unspoken challenge to watch him, to be as unafraid of his pleasure as she had been of her own.

Northam's lashes lowered as he shifted his study to the curve of her neck. He could make out the delicate beat of her pulse. A faint bruise had begun to darken her skin where he had suckled. She would have to cover it later with rice powder and a lace betsy, but he would know it was there, as would she. Its origin would also be no secret to them, the mark being as clear a stamp as his personal seal pressed in warm wax.

He felt tension return to her arms as his glance shifted again. A fine tremor moved from her shoulders to her wrists. Her struggle was confined to a single opening and closing of her fingers, and then there was surrender in her very stillness.

The position of her arms lifted her breasts toward him. They were full, achingly so. These were not the breasts of a young girl, but those of a woman, tipped with aureoles that were no longer a pale, blushing pink, but a deeper, and far more intoxicating, dark rose. The nipples were erect, thrust forward like twin buds and darker still than the corolla that circled them.

"You're beautiful." Then he heard her whimper softly as he lowered his head. He took one nipple into his mouth, drawing on it gently, rolling it between his lips and teeth, tugging, sucking. His hands on her wrists were holding her up now. The scent made his nostrils flare. He moved between her breasts and tasted the thin film of perspiration that made her skin glow. His tongue flicked the other nipple. He teased her, making her rise on tiptoe to try to offer herself up to his mouth. If not for the wall behind her, she would have thrown back her head. She tried to do it anyway, straining to arch, pushing up and out just once, only dimly aware that her legs were no longer supporting her, and that she owed her position to his strength and the brace of the wall.

Elizabeth's chemise began to slip. It hovered on her hips for only a moment, then slid over her thighs and calves like the trickle of warm water. The fabric pooled at her bare feet.

She closed her eyes. Her head rocked against the wall, the side-to-side motion not a negation of what was happening to her but an acceptance of it. His mouth was still on her breast, the tongue laving the sweet, dark aureole. When he sucked it drew on the slim fingers of fire in her belly so that they fanned out, leaping to places he hadn't yet touched, licking her skin in the hollow of her elbows and at the backs of her knees.

She cried out again, a soft mewling sound this time. It drew him away from her breast and brought him back to her mouth. He explored deeply this time, his tongue swirling around hers, hard and insistent, and he wrested another cry from her, this one a sob of frustration and tension. Her exquisitely silky skin pulsed with a static charge. The fine hairs on her forearms and at the back of her neck became erect.

With no warning he released her mouth and her wrists and dropped to his knees in front of her. He raised one of her legs and placed it over his shoulder, supporting her under the knee and then with his hands on her buttocks. He felt her stiffen and understood then that whatever her experience had been, this was new to her.

Her mons was covered with the same shades of gold and ginger hair as her head. The scent of her was intoxicating. He lifted his shoulder slightly, raising her knee higher and parting her moist flesh. He kissed her, lightly at first, nuzzling, preparing her by slow degrees for all the sensations of this most intimate caress. She was wet. He tasted her on his tongue. It was not the honey or ambrosia the poets were wont to describe, but the darkly sweet flavor that was woman, only woman, all woman, and had no real comparison anywhere else in nature.

He drew on her flesh here with the same pressure he had applied to her mouth. He sipped. Suckled. His tongue flicked her clitoris. Lapped it. Licked. He was greedy. He was patient. He took, took more, and then he gave.

Her hands fell on his bright thatch of hair. She could not bring herself to look down at his head. She would be lost. Even this short distance was too great a height. Her fingers curled in his thick hair instead, and she gave herself over to his mouth and his tongue, and his fingers pressing into the flesh of her bottom.

In time it would not matter that she never looked down, that she kept her eyes closed and the tears at bay, that she never watched him work his mouth against her, never saw his face buried in her thighs. She would fall anyway, and when she reached bottom she would shatter.

She came so hard that she *screamed*.

Northam uncoiled in a fluid motion and clamped one hand over her open mouth. He laid his own lips against her ear and whispered to her. The words were of no consequence. He gentled her with the tone and cadence of his speech. Her body thrummed against his. He slipped one arm behind her back, pulled her closer, and absorbed the tremors of her flesh. She trembled again when he let his hand fall away from her mouth. Her slender shoulders heaved once as she took a long, shuddering draught of air.

It was then that he raised his head, looked down on her face, and saw the tears pooling beneath her dark lashes.

He grazed her temple with his fingertips. Her skin was as smooth as porcelain. He kissed her closed eyes and tasted her tears on his lips. The dam burst and they fell soundlessly past her lashes, over her cheeks. One slipped into the corner of her mouth and he kissed it away.

He picked her up, and because she did not seem to know what to do with her arms he instructed her to put them around his neck. "Just like at the picnic," he whispered. She obliged him and made him smile when she pressed her face into his shoulder.

He carried her to the bed. She could not bear to be laid

out naked before him, so she asked for the sheet. It required some jostling, but he managed to get one corner of it in her hand before he let her go. She rolled herself into it when he put her down.

Northam studied her for several long moments. "I didn't think it was possible for a butterfly to return to the chrysalis."

Elizabeth stared at the ceiling. Tears dripped past her temples. "It appears you were wrong."

"So I see." He turned and crossed the floor toward the dressing room. Bending, he picked up Elizabeth's shawl and chemise and carried them back to her. He held them out, then dropped both on the bed when she made no move to take them. "Do you want an apology?"

With some difficulty, Elizabeth pushed herself upright, her movements limited by the cocoon. She wriggled one arm free, then the other, and made an impatient swipe at her damp cheeks. "Do you want to make one?"

"No." He reached out and let his fingers drift across her hair. She did not pull away. "Save for your tears, nothing happened that I regret."

She remained silent.

His fingertips continued to sift through her hair. He asked quietly, "*Am* I responsible for your tears, Elizabeth?"

The question shook her. It was as if he knew the bent of her mind. She would rather he had seen into her black heart and ravaged soul. She had not meant to expose her thoughts to him.

"Elizabeth?"

Their attention swiveled simultaneously toward the door. It was not Northam who had said her name this time, but a voice from the hallway.

The voice came again, familiar to both of them in its pitch and tone and insistence. The knob turned and the door rattled in place.

Chapter Five

"Libby? Whyever have you locked your door?"

"It's Louise!" Elizabeth grabbed her chemise and began pulling it over her head. From under a cloud of batiste she hissed at Northam, "You have to go!"

The earl was quite aware of whom was at the door and the necessity of leaving. Less clear was what route he might take. "Do you have some plan you would care to share?" He watched her continue to tug on her gown. She was making a hopeless muddle of it, but when he reached to assist her she batted his hands away.

"Have off!" Her head and one arm poked through the proper openings. "You must hide."

One dark brow kicked up. "I'm afraid I am no admirer of French farce. You will have to think of something else."

The door rattled again. "Elizabeth! Are you well? You will never believe what has happened not above an hour ago!"

Elizabeth threw her legs over the side of the bed and jumped to her feet. She shimmied out of the sheet, tossed it behind her on the bed, and when the chemise settled into place she shoved her other arm through the sleeve. "The dressing room," she whispered, pushing at Northam's chest. "You can stay there."

"Only if I do not have to squeeze into your armoire."

"Libby! Oh, never say you are sleeping so soundly. Did you take a powder last night?"

Elizabeth stamped her foot. She wanted to fling herself on the bed, have a thorough cry, and sleep until *tomorrow* morning. What she did not want was to have a lead role in this absurd comedy. "I am no enthusiast of farce myself," she told him.

"Then you understand what I mean about the armoire."

She blinked up at him, wondering how he could be accepting this so indifferently. He really was outside everything she had ever known.

"Good," he said. "Your tears have dried and you look as if you could do murder. Lest this take a tragic turn, you should point me toward the window."

Her eyes widened. "No, you cannot mean—"

"I'd rather take my chances on the outside than in. I have no liking for tight, cramped spaces." Since Elizabeth appeared unable to move as well as speak, Northam walked to the window without her escort. Pushing it open, he leaned out. "It does not look so terribly difficult. If the Gentleman Thief can do it, then it can be done."

"Elizabeth!" Louise rapped sharply on the door. "I am going to ring for Jennings and he will bring the keys. I fear for your safety."

Northam paused, one leg already dangling out the window. He looked to the door, then to Elizabeth, his question clearly communicated. *Perhaps he could sneak into the hall now?*

Elizabeth shook her head. "It will not be deserted. You can't risk—"

To prove the truth of her words the door shook again. "Elizabeth!" This time it was the baron's voice, his deep baritone only slightly muted by the heavy oak. "Elizabeth! You must come to the door!"

Elizabeth's eyes shot to the wainscoting that bordered the wall where her vanity stood. Northam followed her glance and suddenly knew what she feared. Lady Battenburn could access Elizabeth's bedchamber without ringing for Jennings. She turned back to him, her features imploring.

She did not beg him to go, however. She asked him to stay.

"You cannot do it," she said. "You will be killed. You must come back at once."

He smiled a shade recklessly. It probably should not have felt so very good to have her worried about him. "I'll be fine." He hoped it was true. Glancing at the ground below, Northam estimated the potential fall would involve several broken bones, some of them quite possibly in his neck. He took a deep breath and swung his other leg out of the window. This act drew Elizabeth closer.

"Please." She caught the sleeve of his jacket. "If you should be injured . . ."

Northam looked down at her slim hand. Her fingers bunched the material so tightly her knuckles were white. He raised his arm and brought her hand to his mouth, placing those bloodless knuckles against his lips. He glanced up at her, only to find her watching him with something akin to wonder. It occurred to him that he might have no need of a toehold in the mortar if he could walk on air.

His foot slipped. He was jerked downward. For a moment he dangled half in and half out of the window. Elizabeth's hand, the one that had been gripping his serge jacket so fiercely, now released him and flew to her mouth. Northam considered his predicament, most particularly the ignominy of his position. No, it seemed he would require those toeholds after all.

Northam's foot searched for a crevice between the stones. He blindly dug the toe of a boot into one such place and heard pieces of mortar crumble. He was able to raise himself up easily. Elizabeth, he noticed, appeared to be breathing again. His eyes darted past her to the vanity. His telescope still stood upright beside the key. "Fetch my scope, will you, Elizabeth? You don't want it found here."

He saw her hesitate, quite likely because she was considering braining him with it. He was certainly in no position to defend himself. Northam gave her what he hoped was a winning smile.

"Ooooh!" For all that the sound came from under her breath, it fairly resonated with frustration. Elizabeth spun around and retrieved the telescope. It was only upon holding it out that she realized he could not easily take it.

"Put it in my jacket."

Another inarticulate utterance passed her lips. She leaned toward him and managed to find the inner pocket without too much fumbling. It was all accomplished rather quickly, but for the time it took, it put her face very close to his. She was careful not to turn toward him, though she felt his eyes marking her profile. It was only when she straightened that she dared look at him again. He did not appear in any way to apprehend the danger of his own circumstances, but was watching her instead with something like concern. Behind her, the door was being rattled again.

"Go or stay," she whispered with some urgency. "But for heaven's sake have done with indecision."

Northam did not give full voice to his laughter. He did chuckle, though. "Very well. I'm leaving. Shut the window as soon as I'm gone." He found another toehold and began inching sideways. He cleared the window quickly and soon had his cheek pressed against the rough-hewn stone of Battenburn. He spared a glance for where he had just been and saw Elizabeth was leaning out the window, watching him. Her brown and gold eyes held the only color in her face. She looked as if she might be sick. Since that condition would do nothing to assist him, he ordered her back. "Now!" he said when she misjudged his command as a request.

Elizabeth was jerked out of immobility by that tone and ducked back inside. She pulled the window shut and dropped the curtains into place. A quick glance about the room assured her that everything was as it should be. She returned to her bed, pulled a few covers over her, and feigned sleep as the vanity began to inch its way across the floor.

Louise shoved the stand with enough force to make it

shudder. The stool tipped and thumped loudly. "Bother!" she muttered. It was impossible for her to see from her present position if the sound had awakened Elizabeth. Indeed, from where she knelt in the passage on the other side of the wainscoting, Louise was still not certain Elizabeth was in the room. When she was able to push the vanity a few more inches, she judged the space wide enough to squeeze through. She crawled out through the panel she had opened in the walnut wainscoting and used one corner of the vanity to assist her in rising.

Taking a moment to catch her breath, Lady Battenburn surveyed the rumpled bed and the figure sprawled across it. Elizabeth was most certainly present and she was not stirring. Louise's mouth tightened as she surmised Elizabeth had surely taken a sleeping powder. Her eyes fell on the bedside table for supporting evidence but saw only a book and two candlesticks. Odd, that.

"Elizabeth!"

Louise gave a start when she heard her husband's voice from the other side of the door. How much had Elizabeth taken to be sleeping through *that?* "It is all well, Harrison," Louise called to him. "She is merely asleep." *Out cold* was a more apt description. It occurred to her belatedly that some injury had been done to Elizabeth. She approached the bed to investigate before sending Lord Battenburn on his way.

Standing at the foot, Louise saw the steady rise and fall of Elizabeth's chest. Even as she watched, one of Elizabeth's feet burrowed under the covers. Satisfied, Louise went to the door. "You can return to your room, Harrison. Nothing untoward has happened to her." She did not offer to open the door for him. "Go on! Have her breakfast attended to."

Louise smiled to herself as he grumbled some reply. She waited for his footsteps to recede before she looked for the key. Since it was not in the expected place on this side of the door, she made a cursory sweep of the bedchamber and spied it on the vanity. Louise slid the wainscoting panel into its closed position and pushed the vanity back against the wall. She did not, however, return it to its previous place, where it had blocked the hidden entrance. She might have need to use it again and Elizabeth well knew that.

Louise glanced toward the bed and sighed. She could not remain annoyed with Elizabeth for long. This small act of rebellion was not entirely a bad thing. No one was harmed by it, and it afforded Elizabeth a measure of comfort that she was once again acting independently. "Poor darling," Louise said gently. She inserted the key in the door but did not turn it, preferring to wait for the arrival of the maid.

Elizabeth pushed at the hair that had fallen over her eyes. She raised the lashes of one when she felt Louise's weight depress the mattress. The tears she had shed served her now. Her eyes were faintly red-rimmed and swollen, and it appeared she was rising from the dregs of sleep. Elizabeth's soft groan only furthered this effect.

"Louise?"

Lady Battenburn laid her hand on Elizabeth's shoulder and patted it lightly. "Indeed it is. I have been considerably worried about you. Are you feeling quite the thing?"

"Tired."

Louise snorted. "I can see that for myself. Whatever did you take to make you sleep so soundly? You have missed the most incredible goings-on this morning. It is really not to be borne."

Elizabeth's response was reflexive. "I'm sorry."

"And I forgive you." Feeling rather magnanimous, Louise offered to help Elizabeth sit up.

"I can manage," Elizabeth assured her. "I am not so befuddled as all that." She yawned widely, hoping it would make her seem otherwise, and pushed herself up. She leaned against the headboard and took the pillow Louise plumped for her to place behind her back. "Tell me about the goings-on." She rubbed her temples, her eyes darting to the door. "How did you get in, Louise? I thought I locked the door."

"I came through the wall. Really, Libby, it was very bad of you to block it with the vanity. I had quite a struggle moving it from the opening. And I do not enjoy any time spent on my hands and knees." She paused, considering the import of those words. "That is to say, I do not enjoy just *any* time spent in that position." The sly slant of her eyes and the inflection in her voice imparted her meaning clearly. She laughed lightly when she saw Elizabeth flush. "However do you manage to affect such innocence, m'dear? You are familiar with the beast with two backs, are you not?"

Elizabeth stared at her hands. Her mouth was dry and she could not have responded to Louise's pointed and ribald humor if she had wanted to.

Louise patted Elizabeth's knee. "But I digress," she went on blithely. "As I said, I used the passage to arrive when you could not be roused to come to the door. Harrison waited in the hall. I do not believe we attracted attention. What with this morning's trying activities, nearly everyone has returned to the haven of their beds. I considered ringing for a key but decided the other route was faster. You won't block the panel again, will you, dear? As you can see, it was not entirely effective, and it did put me out with you."

Louise cupped Elizabeth's chin and lifted it. "I would have your promise, Elizabeth."

Elizabeth nodded.

"I would have you say it."

"I promise," she answered dutifully.

Louise did not pursue any response beyond these two words. She released her hold and stood. "I sent Harrison off to order breakfast for us. I shall tell you everything over toast and hot chocolate." Louise's eyes fell on the overturned vanity stool and she crossed the room to right it. "You have not told me what you took last night," she said.

Elizabeth did not mistake that the question was without purpose or that it had ever been forgotten. Louise had impeccable timing when it came to interrogation. "A sleeping draught," she said. "I prepared it myself."

Louise sat on the stool and turned so she faced the mirrored vanity. Beyond the image of herself she could see Elizabeth pulling at the covers. Was that a shawl she had in bed with her? "Perhaps in the future you would let Mrs. Fitz or your personal maid prepare it for you. You appear to have taken too much. There are stories of women who have died from swallowing too strong a dose. Some say it was that way for Mrs. Archer, though it is unclear if it was entirely accidental.''

"I will do as you ask."

"Will you?" Louise smiled at Elizabeth's reflection. "That is very good of you. There are other consequences besides death, you know. Laudanum has that peculiar quality of making one crave more of it. I do not like to think of you as one of those women who must drink the stuff to stay alive. It is a very sad existence."

"I believe it is."

Louise nodded. She turned on the stool and regarded Elizabeth directly. "It might be better if I took your powder. Where do you keep it, dear?"

Elizabeth's heartbeat tripped over itself. "I don't have any here."

"You don't? Then how—"

"That is, I used the last of it. So you see, there is no reason to concern yourself. It is only that I misjudged how much remained."

"Hmmm." Louise was thoughtful. "Well, if you're certain . . ."

"I am. Please, I'm feeling no ill effects now."

"Oh, my dear, that is only because you have not taken a full account of yourself." Her eyes dropped to the bruise on the curve of Elizabeth's neck but did not linger there. Neither did she comment on it, secreting the knowledge away instead. "Your hair is a complete tangle. Your eyes are red. The sheet has impressed its crinkles on your cheek, and I believe that is your shawl twisted in the covers. Did you take a chill last evening? I found it only tolerably cool for sleeping myself."

Elizabeth tugged at the fine woolen shawl only partially hidden by her blankets. She stared at it as if she had no idea how it had come to be in her bed. "I suppose I did forget to remove it," she said. "I must have fallen asleep while reading."

Louise's glance swiveled to the night table were Elizabeth's book lay, but she made no comment. She rose to her feet. "Shall I choose something for you to wear?" she asked. "I think I should rather enjoy playing your lady's maid this morning." Without waiting for Elizabeth to reply, Louise went to the dressing room.

Elizabeth pressed her fingertips to her closed eyes. The stirrings of a headache were very real. She listened to Louise rooting around in the armoire, knowing with certainty that the motive for the search involved something more than finding a morning gown. It was just as well that Northam had a discomfort of cramped spaces and no liking for farce, else Louise would have discovered him. Elizabeth did not permit herself to think ahead to the likely consequences of Lady Battenburn's *Eureka!*

Louise appeared in the doorway and held up a lilac gown. "Oh, do not rub your eyes so. You shall only make them redder. Here, look at this. Chintz is such a lovely fabric, is it not? And I have always admired this scalloped button closure. It sets off a very simple gown. Your modiste is to be commended." Louise looked down at the dress and frowned. "What is this?" She ran her finger over a small area of the bodice and sighed with some agitation. "There is really not enough light here."

Elizabeth's breath simply remained trapped in her chest as Louise opened the curtains and fastened them with the tiebacks. She almost expected to see Northam's face on the other side of the leaded glass.

"Oh, bother," Louise said, studying the gown's bodice more closely. "Who can see anything through these smudged windows? I will have to speak to Jennings. There really is no excuse." She flung open the window. "You have need of fresh air, by the look of it. I think a walk in the gardens would be just the thing this afternoon. You can carry that ivory parasol I gave you." She leaned closer to the opening and examined the morning dress again. "It is nothing after all; a mere shadow on the chintz. My, what a glorious view you have here. This is easily one of my favorite rooms.'' She thrust her head and shoulders out. ''Oh, what have we here?''

Elizabeth tasted blood on her bottom lip. The pain was not enough to make her stop biting it. She required this sharp focus to keep her from making a full confession.

Louise withdrew from the window, her smile at once cunning and content. She regarded Elizabeth with a great deal of satisfaction. ''Lady Powell is taking her constitutional with Mr. Rutherford,'' she said. ''That was my idea, you know. It should easily bring Lord Southerton around.''

Lord Southerton knew nothing about Lady Powell's defection. He had only just risen and was applying himself to cracking the crown of a soft-cooked egg. He pulled back the bowl of his spoon, preparing to give the shell a smart thwack, when a scratching at the window diverted him. The spoon flew out of his hand, missed the egg entirely, and skittered across the table. Somewhat annoyed by this, South waved Northam off.

''Go press your face to someone else's shop window,'' he said. ''I have no intention of sharing my breakfast.'' It occurred to him that North could not hear him properly but that he would get the idea eventually and move on. South picked up the spoon and considered the matter of his egg again. The scratching was more insistent this time. Southerton sighed, placed the spoon carefully beside his fork, and pushed back his chair. He watched North through the glass with decidedly more amusement than concern. Northam understandably returned his regard with less humor.

''Oh, very well,'' Southerton said, rising. ''You might have bothered East, you know. He's bound to have been up for hours.'' He crossed to the window and made a study of the situation. ''You'll have to get out of the way. You're on the wrong side of it opening.'' He watched Northam carefully inch his way clear of the window before he lifted the latch and swung it out. He stuck his head into the opening and looked straight down. "Not a comfortable landing, is it? I make it out to be at least fifty feet and a broken neck."

"That was my calculation as well," Northam said dryly. "Help me in, will you?"

Southerton extended a hand, which North caught at the wrist. "Easy," South said. "I've got you." He saw spots of blood on his shirtsleeve when North's fingertips slipped. Southerton put out his other hand, grabbed his friend by the scruff of his jacket, and heaved once, hauling Northam in through the opening with enough strength and momentum to make them both take a spill to the floor.

They lay still for several moments, breathing hard, then carefully disentangled themselves. Southerton looked down at his bloody shirtsleeve. "It's quite ruined."

"I'll replace it with a half dozen."

"That's very generous of you." He brushed himself off and stood. "But you'll have to use my shirtmaker. Firth's on Bond Street. No one else cuts the line of them to my liking."

"Firth's," Northam repeated. He sat up and pushed himself backward so he could rest against the wall under the window. His legs and arms were still trembling from the exertion. He was not at all sure he could stand.

Southerton eyed his friend critically. "How long since you took your turn at a few rounds in the ring?"

Northam merely grunted.

"I thought so." South went to the mahogany highboy on the opposite side of his bedchamber and opened the middle drawer. He riffled through the neat stacks of shirts before he found the exact one he wanted. He began to remove his linen. "I regret letting my valet wander away to whatever part of this damnable place he has his room. I didn't expect to require a change of clothes so soon."

Northam's voice was dry as dust. "How fortunate you can manage the thing yourself."

One of South's brows lifted. "I shouldn't adopt that tone if I were you. You don't look as if you can properly defend yourself." He tossed the stained shirt on the bed. "Not that

I would land you a facer for something so minor, but still, you cannot count on others being so even of temperament.''

"South." There was a hint of warning in the way Northam said his friend's name.

And Southerton ignored it. "Hmmm?"

Northam sighed. Southerton could not be ruffled. It was one of the very best things about him. "Nothing."

Southerton's mouth edged up in a rather ironic smile. "Do you require help getting to your feet?"

"Yes. But I intend to sit here a while longer."

"As you wish."

"Aren't you going to ask me how I came to be at your window?"

South smoothed the spotlessly clean shirt over his chest. "No. It would be a waste of my breath. You wouldn't tell me." He turned to the cheval glass and adjusted the chitterling until the frill on the neckline lay just so. He glanced at Northam's reflection and caught his friend's rather put-upon look. "Oh, very well. It's not as if I haven't sufficient breath to waste." He turned around, faced North, and asked dutifully, "How did you come to be outside my window?"

"You know I can't tell you."

South rolled his eyes. "Now that you have proven again how irritatingly discreet you are, I will return to my breakfast." On his way to the table he picked up his discarded shirt from the foot of the bed and tossed it to Northam. "Here, catch. For your hands."

Northam snatched it out of the air. "Thank you." He saw South wince slightly as he ripped the linen cleanly in two. "A baker's dozen," North said to placate him, more than doubling the promised replacements. "Firth's. I haven't forgotten." He wiped bits of mortar from his palms. Some of it was ground into the pads of his fingers. He would attend to it more carefully later. For now he merely loosely wrapped each hand in a piece of the linen.

Tipping his chair back on two legs, Southerton watched North fumble with the makeshift bandages. "Shall I ring for someone to find Brill so he can attend you?"

"No."

Southerton dropped his chair hard. "Oh, for pity's sake, let me do that for you. You never had any skill in the surgery and you're making a mess of it." The fact that North didn't protest said a great deal to Southerton. He hunkered down beside his friend and indicated that Northam should raise his hands. He unwound the strips and examined North's palms and fingertips for himself. "Christ. What a mess. Give me a moment. I'm going to get the basin."

"You don't—" He stopped because Southerton was already walking away.

South carried the bowl and pitcher from the washstand back to Northam's side. He poured water into the bowl and put the bowl on North's lap. "Wash up, and don't be gentle about it."

North plunged his hands into the bowl. In truth, the cool water felt good on them. It was only when he rubbed them together to remove more of the ground-in mortar that he winced.

Southerton couldn't quite tamp his grin. "Hands have gotten a little soft, have they?" He held up his own hands in a gesture of surrender when North shot him a sour look. "It's the same with me. Too many gloved functions." Neither of them were sure if he was complaining. "Here. Let me look now." He examined the heels and fingertips and nodded approvingly. "You'll live."

"Oh, good," Northam said. "I collect there was some doubt."

South ignored the sarcasm this time. "Would it be indiscreet of you to reveal how long you attached yourself to that wall?"

"An hour, I think. Perhaps a bit more. The going was slow."

"The terrain, my dear North, was *vertical.* You're not a bat, you know. What in bloody hell were you thinking?"

"Can't answer that, I'm afraid, circumstances being what they were."

Southerton shook his head. "I hope she was appreciative of your sacrifice."

Northam said nothing and gave nothing away.

Expecting no other end than this one, South did not pursue it. He neatly wrapped North's hands, then removed the basin. "Do you think you were seen?" he asked.

"I hope not. I certainly didn't notice anyone."

"Rather difficult for you to do with your nose to the grindstone, as it were."

North found that he still had the wherewithal to laugh. "Here. Help me up. My sticks are like willow branches."

Southerton pulled North to his feet. "Have you had breakfast?"

"Umm, no."

"You may as well dine with me, then." He pointed to the Windsor chair at the small table. "Sit. I'll pull this other around." He moved a ladderback chair from the hearth to the table and sat down himself. Taking a blueberry muffin from the silver tray, he cut it in half and spread a dollop of butter on one of the open faces, then handed it to North. "You don't look as if you can manage the thing properly, and you know how I cannot abide poor table manners."

Since they could both recall the time South had buried his face in a bowl of trifle on a dare from Marchman—and went on to lick the bowl clean—they shared a moment of comfortable laughter.

"You know," South said, "I don't believe I've eaten trifle since. Mother has it prepared every Christmas for me, unwavering in her conviction that I still like the stuff. And every Christmas I arrange for that trifle bowl to be delivered to Marchman's door."

North hadn't known that. He chuckled. "That's very good of you."

Southerton waved this off. "He must like it. At least he accepts the delivery and returns the empty bowl sometime early in the New Year. Mother, bless her, is none the wiser." He pushed aside his cold egg, his appetite for it gone, and buttered the other half of the muffin. "Have you seen East-lyn?"

"As a matter of fact, I have." Northam settled himself comfortably into the wide spindle-backed chair and began his account of the morning, starting with Lady Battenburn's bloodcurdling scream. Of necessity the entire interlude involving Lady Elizabeth was left out, and Southerton once again proved he was gentleman enough by not questioning certain holes in the story.

"So you think the Gentleman made his escape through the window," South said when Northam wound down his tale.

North didn't think any such thing, but it provided him with a reason for scaling Battenburn's stone edifice. "I needed to see if it could be done."

South made a sound at the back of his throat that was wholly skeptical. Still, he didn't pursue that perhaps there had been other reasons for North to take to the outer walls like an arachnid. "A shame you didn't catch the miscreant," he said. "I should have liked to have my snuffbox returned."

"It was uppermost on my mind, South."

A dark brow kicked up. "Uh-huh."

North was saved defending his white lie by Eastlyn's timely arrival. He opened the door without knocking, saw his friends in cozy conversation at the table, and let himself in.

"Eh? What's this?" he asked. "North, I've been looking for you. How'd you get here?" He picked up a muffin from the tray on his way to take a seat on the bed. Sprawling across the rumpled length, he bit into the muffin with obvious relish. "Should have liked to have had breakfast in my room myself. Couldn't though, could I? I was sent off on some cork-brained chase after a thief who was no doubt already enjoying breakfast in *his* bedchamber."

Southerton and Northam exchanged long-suffering glances.

"I saw that," East said. "Ill-mannered of you both."

South could not let that pass. "Pot calling the kettle and

all that,'' he drawled. ''I don't recall you waiting for an invitation to come in here. I might have been entertaining someone a great deal prettier than North.'' He glanced at Northam. ''Sorry, North. No offense meant.''

''None taken.''

Eastlyn turned on his side and propped himself on one elbow. He swallowed the last bit of his muffin. ''If you mean Lady Powell, you're sadly out of it there. She's wandering the gardens on Mr. Rutherford's arm. Saw them myself not above twenty minutes ago. Looking very enamored of each other, they were.'' He and North shared a chuckle at Southerton's expense and their friend's expression became perfectly disagreeable. ''I shouldn't wonder if they haven't lost themselves in the maze by now.''

Southerton merely grunted, which gave rise to more knowing laughter from the others.

''I suppose you'll have to find another partner for the baron's treasure hunt,'' Eastlyn said. ''Mr. Rutherford's not likely to pass on the opportunity to ask her. Shouldn't have let him steal a march on you, South.''

''You know, East,'' the viscount said pointedly, ''I'm not of a mind to take romantic advice from someone currently between Scylla and Charybdis himself.''

''He means Mrs. Sawyer and Lady Sophia,'' North said helpfully.

''Actually I meant it the other way around.''

Eastlyn flung himself back on the bed again. ''I *know* what he means.''

South warmed to his literary allusion. ''Mrs. Sawyer always reminded me more of a seething whirlpool, the kind of female monster that would suck a man into her vortex and—''

''I *remember* Homer,'' Eastlyn said, exasperated.

''And Scylla . . . wasn't she a nymph or something equally naughty before her appearance was changed?''

Northam nodded. ''It does seem more fitting that Lady Sophia should be Scylla.''

The Marquess of Eastlyn sat up, glared at both of them,

and said in clear tones, "I am carrying a pistol." He saw that had the immediate desired effect. "Deuced uncomfortable it is, too." He removed it from where he had tucked it in his trousers and laid it on the bedside table.

"Bloody hell!" South said feelingly. "There are other ways to extricate yourself from an amorous coil that don't involve shooting yourself in the ballocks."

"Have a care," Eastlyn said. "I still may shoot *you* there." Eastlyn propped the heels of his boots on the bed frame. His glance at his friends finally took in Northam's bandaged hands. "What happened to you?"

North told him, giving the same abbreviated account as he had given Southerton. Eastlyn was equally dubious about some of the particulars, but likewise he asked no questions. "I take it your search was also without results," said North at the end of his summary.

"Completely lacking," East said. "And I'm here to tell you I'm off for London. Damned convenient to find you both in the same place. My carriage is being readied now."

"You will inform us, will you not, how it goes with your ladybird and your lady?" South asked.

Eastlyn sighed. "I shouldn't be at all surprised if rumor reaches you before I do, but yes, I will take pains to keep you abreast of my love life, since yours is so sadly lacking."

South chuckled. "Give me a moment to find a jacket and I will see you off."

North held up his hands. There were pinpricks of scarlet at the fingertips where blood had seeped through. "You'll understand if I bid you farewell now."

Smiling, Eastlyn nodded. "I would not have it any other way."

Northam was not surprised when Elizabeth continued to avoid any situation where she might find herself alone with him. Her evasion was not so blatant as it had been and therefore did not invite comment from the other guests. At least no one felt obliged to remark on it to him. Elizabeth did not immediately absent herself from a discussion if he joined her group. On occasion, when he had been engaged in conversation with the baroness and her friends, Elizabeth came to the circle and participated in the discourse. She was seated beside him at dinner at two different times, once on his left and another at his right, and she proved to be an entertaining and relaxing companion, treating him no differently than she did her dinner partner on the other side.

Lady Battenburn's encounter with the Gentleman Thief was the subject of considerable speculation and a certain amount of exaggeration upon the retelling. She made much of the point that the thief was every bit the gentleman he was purported to be, and the fact that she had screamed should cast no reflection on his manners. It was just that he absconded with her favorite necklace and she had been overcome by the loss of it. There were those who quite naturally believed the Gentleman might have tried to be more intimate in his attentions than the baroness recounted, but they refrained from mentioning this within the lady's hearing.

There was conjecture about the possible identity of the thief, but an accusation was never leveled at anyone's head. Southerton's name was whispered about, a rumor that brought Lady Powell flush to his side again. Other names were mentioned in a good-natured way and no offense was taken. Indeed, the fact that the Gentleman Thief seemed to be among the invited guests at Battenburn did much to raise the social standing of the gathering. After all, it was reasoned, the Gentleman could certainly choose quality.

Other than starting the rumor about Southerton, Northam kept his theories to himself. The baroness's description of the thief was not helpful. In her overwrought state her accuracy was suspect. She sounded very certain of herself at one moment, then questioned her own memory of each detail. He was tall, certainly. But perhaps he was wearing lifts in his boots. His hair was dark, though she was not at all sure it wasn't a wig. He was broad of shoulder, yet because of the way his coat hung she could not say with confidence that it was not padding that made him seem so.

Tall. Short. Husky. Narrow. Fit. Fat. And so it went.

Northam sighed, reining in his horse. He let her slow to a walk along the stream and finally pick her way carefully through a shallow pass. On the other side he dismounted and allowed her to wander while he sat on the bank and chewed thoughtfully on a blade of grass. It was not his best thinking posture because he had nothing to lean against, but he reasoned it would serve him well enough.

Battenburn Hall stood like a fortress on the rise of land in the distance. Looking at her gray stone walls, nearly mirrorlike in the bright sunlight, Northam could hardly credit that he had managed to inch his way along them. The proof that he had done so rested on his fingertips, now protected by soft leather riding gloves. If the Gentleman Thief had been able to make a similar exit, then he had had the foresight to wear gloves. While taking pains to hide his own injuries, Northam had made a point to examine the hands of all the guests. It had proved no easy task, and he was reminded of the truth of Southerton's observation: They attended too many gloved functions.

Northam removed his gloves now and laid them at his side. His beaver hat joined them. Unbuttoning his frock coat, he leaned back on his elbows and crossed his Hessians at the ankle. Sunshine was pleasantly warm on his face. His mare snuffled in the tall grass nearby.

He applied himself once again to the consideration of the Earl of Rosemont's daughter. He could not recall the slightest hint of scandal attached to her name. Quizzing Southerton, after he learned of his friend's slight connection to Elizabeth through his sister Emma, had provided no more useful information.

Lady Elizabeth's first Season had not taken. She had had some admirers, but none of them had apparently come up to snuff in either her eyes or that of her father's. Northam reasoned that having to face William Penrose, Earl of Rosemont, would inspire sufficient terror in the breast of most potential suitors. Elizabeth's choices might have very well been limited to the desperate and the foolhardy.

Northam's own acquaintance with Rosemont was limited to passing him in White's or observing him in the House of Lords. The man took his responsibilities to provide leadership and rational debate in the Parliament seriously. His opinions were oft-quoted and he had the ear of the Prince Regent. It was said that he was in support of Wellington as the next Prime Minister, the inference being that he would not consider himself as a candidate for the same post. He was rather stiff of bearing, not stuffy, but invariably correct. Appearances seemed to mean a great deal to him.

From the colonel, Northam knew that Rosemont had been a widower for a number of years before remarrying. It had been his beautiful second wife, the former Lady Isabel Milford, youngest daughter of an earl herself, who had taken Elizabeth in hand and guided her through the balls and entertainments of that Season. Northam also knew Rosemont's much younger wife had delivered him an heir some six years ago.

The relationship that existed between Elizabeth and her father could not properly be categorized as an estrangement, the colonel had told him. Elizabeth was in residence at Rosemont twice a year and stayed for several weeks each time. Neither was she a stranger to his London home and had been known to visit his properties far to the north. She was unfailingly respectful and brooked no public argument with him, making Rosemont the envy of every father who had known the frustrations of a rebellious child. Because she was the very model of rectitude and good sense, the earl gave her his leave to spend a considerable time in the company of the most amiable and unexceptional Lord and Lady Battenburn. This was all well and good, the colonel had said, his tone indicating the very opposite, but over the years Elizabeth had also become less known to *him*.

Her letters were infrequent, her visits few. He was not fooled by Elizabeth's denials of a strain between herself and her father—it had existed at some level since the unfortunate death of her mother—but Blackwood would not countenance that strain when it began to unsettle his own connection with her.

Had her accident at Rosemont been the source of the odd cutoff with her father? The colonel had certainly placed no significance to the event. He had not even mentioned the fact of her limp, leaving it to Northam to discover for himself.

"Tell me what she is about," the colonel had asked instead. "I cannot shake this dread I carry on her behalf."

Dread. It was a good description, Northam decided. In spite of the pleasantness of the day, he felt considerable tension in his neck and shoulders. A muscle worked rhythmically in his cheek. He turned over on his stomach, discarded the blade of grass ground at one end between his teeth and plucked another, promising himself he would treat it more delicately.

He tried to imagine using Elizabeth's own words to explain how things were to the colonel. He could not. How would he say it? *"I regret to inform you, sir, but the daughter of your beloved cousin Lady Catherine has announced in no uncertain terms that she is a whore."* Northam could almost feel the pain of the pistol ball that would surely pass through his heart if he delivered that message. No, it wouldn't serve.

Even less palatable would be admitting his own intimacy with her. *"I have firsthand knowledge of that fact, sir."* But did he? Northam's experience with whores had been limited to camp followers. He had mostly made it a point to avoid them. In his early days in London he had set up a succession of mistresses, all of them intelligent, gracious, and skilled in bed, but ultimately found himself dissatisfied with the arrangement. He made each of them a generous settlement when he ended it, and inadvertently attracted the notice of a goodly number of other women with similar reputations and an eye for the main chance. He had bedded several but had never been moved to offer his protection, and he had never thought of them as whores.

Evidence to the contrary, he did not think that of Elizabeth

Penrose either. She had set forth her best arguments to send him on his way, had even charitably offered him an exit by staging her own retreat to her dressing room. He had ignored it all.

Northam knew there had been no force involved in what he had done to her, yet he believed the thing had been done against her will. She had not fought the battle with him, but with herself. Her surrender had caused no anger to be directed toward him. What he had seen in her eyes, the tears making them almost painfully bright, was self-loathing.

She had not spoken of a parade of men through her bed-chamber. She had made mention of only one. No, that was not quite true. He sought the memory of her exact words *. . . there was at least one other before you . . .*

He groaned, wishing his memory would have played him false. *At least one other* could mean *only* one or the veritable parade he now feared.

Northam sat up suddenly, feeling restless and edgy with ill-defined frustration. With little provocation he could smash someone's face in. He spit out the blade of grass and whistled for his mare. She sidled over while he jammed his hands into his gloves and put on his hat. He mounted, swinging his leg hard over the saddle. Every bit of his aggressive temperament was communicated to his mount and in moments they were flying across the meadow, trying to outrun the demons of doubt.

"I believe we are to be partners, Lady Elizabeth."

Elizabeth turned and found herself having to tilt her head up to Viscount Southerton. She smiled warmly. "Indeed, my lord, it appears so. I begged Lady Battenburn to place you with someone more quick-witted than myself, but she could not be swayed. I must tell you at the outset that I am not good with riddles."

"It does not matter," South said graciously. "I wager you have more familiarity with the twists and turns of this house than anyone but our hosts and perhaps a few of the servants. Since the latter haven't been invited to play and of necessity the baron and his wife had to excuse themselves, you are my very best chance to recover the treasure." His light gray eyes danced. "What is it, by the way? The baroness is being uncharacteristically closemouthed and his lordship would not divulge anything last evening, even when he was well into his cups."

"Do you mean you tried to get him foxed so he would tell you what it was?"

"I don't believe I encouraged him unduly."

Elizabeth laughed. "I should think not. Harrison enjoys his brandy." She tapped South's forearm with her closed fan. "As for the treasure, I haven't the least idea. I have not been privy to any of the planning regarding this hunt, else I would have had to excuse myself as our hosts have."

Southerton feigned disappointment. "Well, I suppose I shall have to endeavor to be brilliant. It strains the gray matter."

"It *strains* the imagination."

Startled, South's mouth clamped shut. When it opened again it was to let loose full-throated, hearty laughter that was not easily contained in the drawing room.

"Sshh," Elizabeth chided him, trying to temper her own smile. "You are attracting attention."

On the other side of the room, Lady Powell snapped her wrist and her fan opened with a flourish. She used it to hide her frown as she watched Southerton try to check another bout of laughter. "I shouldn't wonder that he injures himself."

"Indeed." Northam was also listening to his friend. His eyes, however, were on Lady Elizabeth. Her humor was in every way the opposite of his own, and the more she tilted her radiant smile in South's direction, the more he felt like breaking something, starting with Lady Powell's ivory fan and ending with his best friend's nose. If, somewhere in between he caught Lady Elizabeth's fine chin, all the better.

It was all a fancy, of course. He wasn't going to hit anyone. It wasn't done. Not by him. Not ever.

Lady Powell tapped his shoulder with the tip of her fan. "The best revenge is winning, don't you think? There is nothing for it but that we should take the prize."

Northam looked pointedly at the fan beating a tattoo against his arm. She removed it hastily. "Of course," he said. Turning his back on South and Elizabeth and blocking the same view from Lady Powell, he gave her his mostly undivided attention. The widow was an attractive woman, very much in her prime, with cocoa-colored hair and large brown eyes. Her figure was trim, her smile knowing, and her temperament was most politely described as mercurial. She wed young and had been, by all accounts, a faithful wife to her older husband throughout their marriage. After observing the requisite year of mourning in solitude in the country, Lady Powell had rejoined society at the urging of family and friends. Northam knew he could have drawn a much less desirable partner.

"I believe Lord Battenburn is about to give us the rules," he said, offering his arm. "Shall we step to the fore and have a listen?"

The baron cleared his throat and waited for quiet to settle over the gathering. He stood apart from the crowd, slightly elevated by a box that had been found for just this occasion. Rather nattily dressed in a lavender waistcoat, butter yellow breeches, and a pristine shirt with a chitterling and a casually tied cravat, he would have commanded a certain amount of attention without benefit of the box.

"It is really very simple," he began in his pleasant baritone. "And I promise you, as long as the Gentleman Thief does not arrive at the treasure first, your efforts will be rewarded most handsomely."

Chapter Six

The baron saw he had captured his audience and went on. "Her ladyship has secreted away a treasure somewhere within the confines of Battenburn. I mean the house itself, not the lands. You can be assured that it will not be found among anyone's personal possessions. Bedchambers most definitely should not be included in your search and no clues are meant to lead you there." He pretended not to hear the titters that ran through his listeners, though it took effort not to stare reprovingly at Lady Heathering. With every one of her giggles she was extending a rather blatant invitation to Lord Allen to find *her* treasure.

"Lady Battenburn is moving among you now to hand out the first clues. They are not, in all cases, the same, but will eventually lead the most clever of you to the right places. When you find other clues, leave them behind for those who follow you. There is only one treasure and you cannot mistake it for anything else. Have no doubt that you will know it when you find it."

"Is there a time limit?" one of them called out.

"Ah, yes, thank you. You have but until midnight." He made a point of lifting his fob and checking the time. "By my reckoning it is two hours hence. So that it is fair to everyone, we will mark the time by the clock in the great hall.'' His eyes swept over his guests and he paused in anticipation of more questions. ''Nothing else? Very well. You may begin as soon as you have your first clue.''

Their location near the back of the drawing room forced Southerton and Elizabeth to wait their turn. They both nodded politely as Lady Powell swept past them, her arm most possessively wrapped around North's sleeve. Elizabeth did not like the queer little turn her heart gave as she watched them go, or the fact that Southerton seemed to sense it. He was kind enough not to give her a pitying look and offered her arm a slight squeeze instead.

Their first clue was not terribly difficult. *A clergyman rises in the meadow and one to one, makes peace with his God.* Southerton asked Elizabeth to lead him to the library, where he instructed her that they were looking for a copy of Oliver Goldsmith's *The Vicar of Wakefield.* On page one hundred twenty-one, or one-*two*-one, they found their next clue.

Bright laughter, the odd shout, and much whispering could be heard echoing the halls of Battenburn. As the guests passed each other on their way from one solution to the next, they sometimes traded information and, on occasion, partners. Lady Heathering was able to finally corner Lord Allen, and they gave up any pretense of finding the treasure when they secluded themselves under the wine cellar stairs. Mr. Rutherford, finding Lady Powell to have switched her attentions yet again, began a dogged pursuit of Miss Caruthers, which resolved itself in some furtive groping in the lamp room.

The servants were required to absent themselves for this entertainment. They had a merry time of it in the village, making the most of the two hours with drink and dance, and being none the worse for it at midnight. They did not allow themselves to dwell on what might be going on in their own preserve. There would be time enough later to put things to right again.

Battenburn's guests were free to explore the kitchen and basements, the shoe room, the knife room, the quarters where the footmen slept three to a bed, the attic, the laundry, the folding room, and even the cubby rooms, so out of the way they could only be reached by ladder. This tour of the great hall's underbelly was greeted with a mixture of fascination and horror; some of the baron's guests had never seen their *own* kitchens. Still, as they tracked down clues in apple barrels, linen closets, and under straw mattresses, they were agreed it was an inspired idea.

The narrow passages that ran along the gallery and between the drawing rooms, the staircases that were hidden tightly in spaces shared with chimneys, and the panels that opened to closets and then to other rooms, were not found by everyone. Sometimes voices could be heard on the other side of a wall with no visible sign of how they had got to be there.

"You know, Lady Elizabeth," Southerton said as they sat on the servants' backstairs, contemplating their next clue, "North is not such a bad sort."

Elizabeth was silent for a moment. "I did not believe he was," she said carefully.

"It is just that I have a great regard for him. We were chums, you know, at Hambrick."

"He mentioned that ... about Hambrick Hall, I mean. As for the other, it appears to be mutual."

"Yes, well, we were a tight little group and did not invite outsiders. Called ourselves the Compass Club. Sworn enemies of the Society of Bishops."

She knew about the Bishops. Their association at Hambrick was legendary. This other was unfamiliar to her. "The Compass Club?" Her brow puckered, then dawning smoothed it again. "Oh. North. South. East. West. Though I don't understand about Mr. Marchman."

South shrugged. "He will grow into it."

"Lord Northam said much the same thing." She risked a glance at South. The candle he held illuminated his handsome face and softened the sharper edges of his features. "Did he ask you to speak to me?"

South's surprise was genuine. "Bloody hell!" The oath

was out before he could collect himself. He apologized immediately for his lapse and went on. "You can't know North if you'd think a thing like that."

"That's true," she said. "I don't know him. We have spoken perhaps on a dozen occasions since his arrival. About nothing very remarkable." *Oh, and he had me against a wall with one leg over his shoulder and his face buried in my thighs. Did he tell you that?* "I have had little opportunity to form an opinion." *Ask me about his tongue, though, and I will describe perfectly what it felt like thrusting in my mouth and between my legs. Has he described the same to you?* "He has made some judgment of me, I take it."

Southerton's brow lifted. "I don't know. He's very close-mouthed, North is. Doesn't chatter on about women the way East does." It was not strictly true that Eastlyn did either, but South felt a need to place Northam in the very best light. It was not strictly meddling, he told himself. It was his assignment from the colonel, and not one he particularly relished. He had tried to tell Blackwood that playing cupid was not his forte, but the colonel was having none of it.

Southerton was greatly relieved when he had not had to perform the introductions between North and Lady Elizabeth. The connection he had to her through his dear sister Emma was thin, and Northam would have seen through it. South had been content to observe things proceeding smoothly for a few days and then . . . He couldn't finish the thought because he had no idea what had happened, only that the course had most decidedly been altered. It was easier to navigate a skiff through the rough seas of the Channel than find the proper heading for true love.

South actually groaned aloud as he realized how hopelessly banal he had become. Raking back his dark hair in a somewhat sheepish gesture, silently cursing Blackwood, North, and, yes, even the lady at his side, Southerton gave the slip of paper in Elizabeth's hand his undivided attention. They had taken the time to copy what they hoped was their final clue, leaving the original in place for others to find. It was a long and rather difficult passage to commit to memory.

"What do you make of it?" he asked. "Are we to go up or down?"

Elizabeth barely heard him. Northam had said nothing ... *nothing* ... to his friend. She wanted to weep with gratitude. Hug herself. Shout. What she did was hold up the paper for Southerton to get a better view. It was a matter of some amazement to her that her hand was not shaking violently. In the aftermath of her fear, sustained over so many days, she knew the trembling that accompanied relief. "I think we should go down," she said, her voice reed thin but steady.

"But you're not certain."

"Yes." She laughed a bit self-consciously. "No. I mean, yes, I'm not certain."

"Then let's study it a little longer. Something will occur to us. We have done very well so far."

Elizabeth nodded. For the first time she felt completely comfortable in Lord Southerton's company. When Louise had informed her that she would be partnered with the viscount, Elizabeth had begged her to reconsider. Not, as she told South, because she had no head for riddles, but because she did not want to have to fend off his advances in corners and cubbies throughout Battenburn. She did not think her brief acquaintance with his sister—a friendship that had not endured beyond a single Season—would be enough to hold him at bay if Northam had shared the particulars of their lovemaking.

Northam was under no obligation not to do so. She had not asked for his silence. Indeed, she considered that her own insistence that she was a whore would lead him to believe it was an opinion shared by others. It was, but those others were confined to a very small number, and they had their own reasons for not speaking it aloud.

Southerton, however, had been naught but a considerate and congenial companion. Far from taking a single liberty, he had defended his friend, apologized for cursing, and summoned enthusiasm for a game whose outcome he could not have possibly cared.

Elizabeth regarded her escort in a new light. "You are very kind, I think."

South's head tilted to one side. "You don't intend to bandy that about, I hope. It would ruin me."

She solemnly crossed her heart.

"Good." He stood, took Elizabeth's hand, and helped her to her feet. "I don't mind if it gets out that I'm brilliant, though."

"You'll have to find the treasure first."

"This way, my lady. I believe we are almost there."

The gallery was a magnificent room designed during the time of James I by one Inigo Jones. Jones drew the plans for the Battenburn gallery some five years before he was named England's chief architect in 1615. Almost as tall as it was long, the gallery was the repository of the finest artwork acquired by the former Barons of Battenburn, as well as a history of the family in a succession of portraits, starting with the first baron in 1535.

Southerton recited the clue as he and Elizabeth stepped into the gallery. *"The Creator of church and chapel bids you welcome to His house.* What do you think? Was Lady Battenburn referring, perhaps, to this place?"

They had already been to the chapel and found nothing more in this clue to guide them to the treasure or another set of clues. The church in the village was beyond the limits the baron had set, so they did not consider it.

"I don't know," Elizabeth said. "What is the connection here to church and chapel?" She studied the portraits on the far wall. None of the former barons or their wives had ever struck her as particularly welcoming or God-fearing. "I can tell you, I've always found this to be a rather cold and godless place."

"Oh, it is," Southerton agreed, regarding the portraits with a critical eye. "But I don't think the creator in this clue refers to the Almighty. Didn't you tell me when we passed here earlier that this room was the work of Inigo Jones?''

"Well, yes," she said slowly. "But I don't see—"

Southerton interrupted her and expanded on this thinking. "Covent Garden *Church* in Westminster and the Queen's *Chapel* at Saint James's Palace each had Inigo Jones as their architect. He was their *creator.*"

Elizabeth could imagine South thought her truly simple-minded. "I warned you, I am very bad at riddles." She was surprised when this comment seemed to invite Southerton's protective instincts. He put his arm around her shoulders and gave them an affectionate, brotherly squeeze.

"You're a good'un, Lady Elizabeth." He examined the paper in her hand. "Now, what is next?"

"Quite the crush, would you not say, Northam?"

Elizabeth began to turn rather awkwardly in the direction of the distinctly feminine voice, but Southerton stayed her, his grip on her shoulder becoming more insistent than friendly.

Northam regarded the picture his friend and Elizabeth made with only a little less distaste than he had for the gallery of rogues on the wall. "I believe they are but two art admirers," he said evenly. "Come, we will have a better look ourselves." He escorted Lady Powell into the room, closing the great doors behind him. "If they are here, then we must also be in the right place."

Southerton's voice was cool. "As long as you remember that we were here first." He removed his arm from Elizabeth, folded it with the other in front of him, and feigned great interest in Baron Battenburn's ancestors. "Read the next part of the clue to me."

Elizabeth realized her hands were trembling now. She took a steadying breath, hoping Northam was paying as much attention to the portraits as his friend. "The line is, *A fall from grace in this place, removes a face without a trace.*"

Southerton grimaced. "The baroness is no Byron."

Northam cleared his throat to cover his small, strangled laugh.

"Well, what does it mean?" Lady Powell wanted to know. "My Christian name is Grace, you know. Does it have something to do with me?"

Southerton did not spare her a glance. "Only if you trip and flatten that pretty upturned nose of yours, my lady."

"Oh, that is very bad of you," she said, not at all mollified that he had called her nose pretty. To say it was upturned was a gross exaggeration of the pert appendage. "If that is an example of your wit, this hunt is a very dull entertainment, indeed." She left the trio standing in front of the portraits and flounced to the row of chairs on the carpet's perimeter, her nose angled several degrees higher than it needed to be.

Across the crown of Elizabeth's head, Northam and Southerton exchanged wry glances.

"Do you have a different clue?" Southerton asked North.

Northam shook his head. "I didn't have the foresight to write it down. Thought I could remember it all." His eyes darted back to Lady Powell, who was now sitting and making unnecessary repairs to her gown, a stubborn mien marring her features. "There were . . . er, distractions."

Southerton nodded, his own expression commiserating. "I think it would be wise if we join forces," he said. "What say you, Elizabeth? Northam is a great deal more clever than I am."

Her eyes looked to neither the right nor the left. She continued to stare at the slip of paper and made an effort at politeness. "Then we will be fortunate to have him helping us."

There was no mistaking Elizabeth's lack of enthusiasm, but Southerton would not be discouraged. "Wonderful." He reached around Elizabeth and clapped Northam on the back, shaking the cobwebs loose from his friend's brain. "Go on, North, take a crack at it. What do you think it means?"

Northam read it again. "*A fall from grace in this place, removes a face without a trace.* Well, if we're all agreed it has nothing to do with Lady Powell, then I think we should have a careful look at all the paintings. A fall from grace could signify a number of things."

"The archangel's banishment from heaven," Southerton said. He began to stroll the length of the gallery in search of an appropriate depiction of this event.

North followed. "It might be the destruction of Sodom and Gomorrah."

Elizabeth realized she was standing alone again, quite without a purpose now that two members of the Compass Club were working in tandem. She started to go to Lady Powell, hoping in some manner to soothe the woman's ruffled feathers, when Southerton called to her.

"Bring that paper here, will you, Elizabeth? I find it helps to look at the clue from time to time."

Elizabeth gave Lady Powell a small apologetic smile, feeling somewhat guilty that Southerton should single her out. "Excuse me," she said. "I will only deliver this into their hands."

The lady did not warm to this overture. "Do not concern yourself," she said airily. "I am resolved to observe the workings of such brilliant minds from afar."

Elizabeth accepted these words at face value, preferring to ignore the complete lack of sincerity in the delivery. Lady Powell looked as if she had swallowed something sour when she used the word *brilliant*. Sarcasm, Elizabeth decided, was ineffective when it was pressed too hard.

Northam paused in his observation of a landscape to wait for Elizabeth. "May I?" he asked, indicating the clue.

She held it out for him but he did not accept it, taking her wrist instead and lifting it and the paper into his line of sight. His hand was very warm on her skin. He was not wearing gloves and she could feel the roughened pads of his fingertips. Elizabeth's eyes flew to his face, realizing of a sudden how they had come to be abraded. He did not return her look, however, but continued to stare blandly at the paper in her hand.

At his end of the gallery Southerton observed the moment

with some satisfaction. It was too early to congratulate himself on bringing the thing about, but indications of a repair in the breech were promising.

Southerton continued circling the gallery in what he hoped was a nonchalant manner, leaving North and Elizabeth to sort out the last clues on their own. He stopped when he reached Lady Powell. "I believe I have taxed the gray matter enough for one evening. May I?" He indicated the vacant row of chairs.

To her credit the lady did not insist on a more eloquent excuse to take her company. "Of course," she said. She removed the part of her peach gown that had fallen onto the neighboring chair, giving Southerton a clear message as to where he was supposed to plant himself.

He obliged, lifting the tails of his coat as he sat. With one part of his mind still on North and Elizabeth, he found that what he had left was more than sufficient to entertain Lady Powell's conversation.

Neither North nor Elizabeth noticed Southerton's defection. "A fall from grace," North repeated, mulling it over. He released Elizabeth's wrist and watched her hand fall slowly away. He jerked his eyes back to the paintings and studied them anew.

"I wonder if it might have something to do with Adam and Eve," she said. "Their banishment was a fall from grace."

"There's nothing like that here. Still lifes, landscapes, scenes of medieval life." There were religious themes, most notably depictions from the New Testament. None, though, seemed to fit the clue. "Beautiful, but not inspiring a solution."

"Perhaps a garden."

North considered this. "That one," he said, pointing to a large oil depicting a spring garden a few yards from where they stood. He examined the face of it for clues and then stood on tiptoe to run his hands along the gilt frame. "Nothing."

Elizabeth frowned as North looked at his watch. "We

haven't much time left, have we? I don't think Lady Battenburn means to give anything away."

The same thing had occurred to Northam, but he was not discouraged. "There are some twenty minutes remaining. Time enough." He stepped back from the wall, taking up a place near the center of the gallery where he could better view the whole. He was pleased when Elizabeth joined him without any urging on his part. "Tell me what you see," he said.

"Talent far exceeding anything my poor hand has put to paper."

Northam smiled, remembering his comment about her watercolors. Apparently he was not entirely forgiven. "Still stings, does it?"

"Hmmm," she murmured noncommittally. She applied herself to the more important question. "That painting is by Hilliard. That one, a Brueghel. Those above them are the Dutch masters. The Battenburn collection is renown for its breadth of styles. Titian. Dürer. These works represent artists from all over the Continent and more than two centuries of history."

"Impressive."

"It is." She continued identifying the artists. "Raphael. Sir Charles Eden. Vermeer. De Troy."

North impulsively grasped her hand again. "Show me the Eden."

"What?" The jolt that had gone through her at his touch distracted her. She was looking at her hand, not the paintings.

"The Eden," he repeated. "Which one is it?"

It was then that Elizabeth caught his excitement. "Oh! The *Eden*. Of course. How clever!" She pulled him toward the oil of windswept cliffs and a turbulent sea. "This one. Shall I get you a chair? You can't reach it."

He shook his head. "Read me the clue following this one."

"*Removes a face without a trace.* I don't think I understand. The face of the cliff?"

"I think the baroness was simply enamored of her own poetry. Isn't there another line that follows?"

"Yes. *Below one finds a simpler time.* That doesn't mean very much to me either, I'm afraid. The last of it is this, *A treasure trove to end the rhyme.* That seems to promise that we have reached the end, wherever that is."

"Hmmm." Northam cupped his chin in one hand and considered the sum effect of the clues and the paintings. "I think better in a recline," he said when nothing came to him.

"Perhaps I could fetch a sofa instead of a chair."

He waved off the suggestion as if it had been made seriously. "Don't trouble yourself. It will come to me."

She wasn't certain if he meant the sofa or an idea. One seemed no more unlikely than the other. Rather than divert his thinking, Elizabeth let the comment pass.

Northam's eyes wandered to the oil painting under Eden's seascape. *Below one finds a simpler time.* It was a still life, the objects themselves unremarkable, as so they often were in such things. The surface of a scarred oaken table was the background for a partially open map, the edges of which were held down by a bottle of blue-black India ink, dividers, a sextant, and a sandglass lying on its side. It was the artist's rendering of these objects that made them seem far from ordinary. Light from an unseen window gilded the curved limb of the sextant, and where it was blocked by the ink bottle a shadow was cast across the map. Each grain of sand in the glass was perfectly realized.

"What do you think of this one?" Northam asked, pointing to the one that had caught his interest.

"Vermeer. You can tell by his exceptional use of light. It's called 'The Captain's Table.' "

Northam did not ask to see the clues again. He recited from memory, "*A fall from grace in this place, removes a face without a trace. Below one finds a simpler time. A treasure trove to end the rhyme.* Perhaps her ladyship was not so captivated by her poetry as I thought. She really meant it to be a clue."

"I am lamentably thickheaded," she said.

"That is certainly not true." Northam was not being gallant, merely factual. "I never would have thought of the Eden if you had not brought it to mind." He pointed back to that seascape. "*A fall from grace* is certainly referring to his work," he said. "But *removes a face without a trace* directs us elsewhere. To the one *below*." His hand dropped, index finger extended like a compass needle to the Vermeer. "The sandglass. A clock from an earlier *time*. One with no *trace* of a—"

"*Face!*" Elizabeth finished triumphantly. She laughed. "I believe you are done dragging this horse to water, my lord. I am prepared to drink."

He grinned. "Let's have a look at this painting more closely, shall we?" Northam carefully ran his fingers along the large ornate frame. "Nothing here. Do we dare remove it?"

Elizabeth leaned toward the painting and Northam eagerly. "I think that is perhaps the only way we'll know. Shall I help you?"

Nodding, he lifted the lower edge of the frame. "Take the other. Let's only tilt it away from the wall. That's it. Just ... enough ... to let me ... see. I do believe, Lady Elizabeth, that we have found ourselves a treasure." He slipped one hand under the frame and explored the wall. "Here it is." His fingers pressed and probed until they found the release. They both heard a spring uncoil. "Can you see? The opening is on your side."

Elizabeth ducked her head under the back of the painting. "I can reach it." Balancing her corner of the frame in one palm, she slipped her other hand into the opening. "It is not so very big."

"You sound disappointed."

Elizabeth's hand closed over the prize. It fit comfortably into her fist. "Do you mean I was the only one hoping for an enormous jewel or a bag of sovereigns?"

Southerton approached with Lady Powell on his arm. He noticed that at last her interest had been piqued. Southerton remained cynical. No doubt she was spending what she thought was her share. "What's this?" he asked. "Do you mean to say you've found a bag of gold under there?"

Northam's head came out from behind the painting. "I think you would do well to lower your expectations."

South smiled. Though North was speaking to him, he saw his friend was pointedly staring at Lady Powell. That avaricious gleam *was* enchanting. "What do you have there, Lady Elizabeth?"

North closed the panel, then eased the Vermeer back into place. "Go on," he encouraged her. "Show us the prize."

Elizabeth turned to face the trio and held out her fist. She unfolded her hand, her fingers opening like the petals of a flower. They all saw the treasure revealed at the same time.

At the center of Elizabeth's palm lay Lord Southerton's snuffbox.

Lady Powell was the first to speak. "Oh my, may I see it? It's exquisite, isn't it?" Without waiting for an answer she plucked it out of Elizabeth's hand. Holding it up to the candlelight pouring from the chandelier, Lady Powell could count the diamond chips embedded in the black enameled lid. The bottom was gold; not gilt over another metal, but solid gold. The box was not flat on its underside. It had a base that rested on the tiniest gold feet, each one shaped like a cat's paw. "This really is darling; quite unique. I've never seen the like before."

"I have," said Southerton. He took the box from Lady Powell before she could close her fingers over it. "It's mine."

Elizabeth's eyes shot to his face. "Yours? You mean the one that was stolen?"

"This is it?" asked Lady Powell. As if she should have been privy to everything concerning him, she made a small moue. "You never mentioned it was such an exquisite piece."

Southerton said nothing to that. "Was there anything else in the hiding place?" he asked.

Elizabeth shook head. "Nothing that I could feel."

Northam returned to the Vermeer. "Take the other corner, South. We'll have another look."

Pocketing the snuffbox, Southerton stepped forward to help. A second search of the interior proved futile. There was no other prize beside his own snuffbox waiting for them.

"Damn peculiar," Southerton said, running four fingers through his hair. "Battenburn has an odd sense of humor."

Elizabeth blinked. "Oh, you cannot believe the baron did this."

"Then Lady Battenburn."

"I refuse to countenance either suggestion."

Southerton shrugged. He looked at North. "What do you think?"

"I'd say the baron's warning about the Gentleman Thief was providential. He arrived at the treasure before us."

"That is not possible," said Elizabeth. "He had no clues."

"I confess to missing them myself," Lady Powell interjected. "Are you seriously proposing the Gentleman stole one treasure and replaced it with another he is also supposed to have stolen?"

Three heads turned on her and answered as one impatient chorus: "Precisely."

Lady Powell took the tiniest step backward. "Oh."

Elizabeth took pity on her. "It is difficult to believe," she said gently.

Northam leaned one shoulder against the wall, not at all concerned that he was sharing space with Titian and Brueghel. "I confess, if it is the Gentleman's work the purpose eludes me."

Southerton had been in deep study of the floor. His head came up as the clock in the main hall began to strike the hour. "I suppose we shall know soon enough if it is the work of the Gentleman or some odd whim of our hosts. It strikes me as a very peculiar manner in which to return something that was lost."

"Stolen," North reminded him.

"Just so. I mean, there was no way to predict that I would find the thing, was there?"

"But you didn't find it," Lady Powell said sweetly. "Dear Elizabeth did."

Now it was Elizabeth who felt the force of all those eyes upon her. Unlike the other lady, she did not quail in the face of it. Her chin came up. "Only because Lord Northam could not reach it from his side. And I was hopelessly muddled about the riddles." Her glance swiveled in both directions, from North to South. "You each know it."

"It's true," Southerton said, sighing. "She *was* muddled."

Northam wasn't so certain, but then he had only been her partner at the end. He decided to reserve judgment. His chin lifted toward the massive gallery doors. "If I am not mistaken, Lord and Lady Battenburn will be leading the parade."

He was not in error. The baron and baroness were at the forefront of the crowd that swept into the room.

Lady Battenburn pressed her hands together gleefully. "See, what did I tell you, Battenburn?" she exclaimed. "I just knew when they did not return to the drawing room at midnight that we would find them here. You have located the treasure, have you not? Oh, please say it was before the clock struck the twelfth hour. His lordship is being very much a stickler about the rules. One would think we were offering up the crown jewels instead of a mere watch fob and pendant."

Lady Battenburn paced the floor of her bedchamber from window to door and back again. Her husband sighed. "Come, dear, sit down. You will wear yourself out."

"I will not," she said stubbornly.

"Then you shall wear out the carpet."

This had no effect on her either. Her elbow-length gloves lay on the arm of a wing chair, her plumed turban at the foot of the bed. She was still wearing her evening gown.

"Will you not at least allow Fitz to assist you in preparing for bed?"

"I could not possibly sleep."

Harrison looked toward the fireplace where Elizabeth stood. He shrugged, turning over his hands in a gesture meant to imply that he had made his attempt and was done now.

Elizabeth drew a short breath. "Perhaps, Louise, it would—"

The sound of Elizabeth's voice did what Harrison had been unable to do. Louise stopped cold. "Do not speak to me, Libby. You are a wicked, *wicked* girl. I can only think that you are responsible for what happened tonight. The Gentleman Thief! The very idea that such a thing could be done under my nose is not to be borne."

Elizabeth met Louise's gaze but said nothing.

"Oh, I cannot imagine what you were thinking when you removed that snuffbox."

The baron leaned back in his chair. His valet was waiting in the adjoining bedchamber to help him out of his evening wear. He wondered what Pipkin did while he was waiting and amused himself with this line of thinking until Louise's spring wound down.

"Did you consider my humiliation? Did you think how it would appear to my guests? I shouldn't wonder if they don't believe I am in *league* with the Gentleman Thief! Was that your intent?"

There was a pause, but Elizabeth was not certain she was meant to fill it. Her chest felt as if it was being squeezed. Louise's anger did not seem likely to run its course quickly. She had had to contain herself too long in the gallery, first to recover from her own shock when Southerton held out his snuffbox, then to express her embarrassment that their game had been tampered with. Now Lady Battenburn's face was mottled with angry color and she looked very near tears.

"Say something, Elizabeth," she said. "Can you comprehend our complete mortification?"

Elizabeth glanced at the baron, since he had now been

included in the humiliation. For a time it seemed that Louise had no intention of sharing martyrdom. "No one blames you for the work of the thief," she said quietly. "When I reached behind the Vermeer I removed what was there."

"You certainly did."

"Lord Northam would have found it if I had not."

Louise actually stamped a slippered foot. "I am so out of patience with you."

"I defended you and Harrison," said Elizabeth.

Harrison came out of his reverie to cock his head at Elizabeth. "Did you?" he asked dryly, pinning her back with a cool blue study of her face. "That was good of you. Really, Louise, it was good of her to defend us."

"It was the least she could do. The very least."

The baron nodded slowly. "Yes, well, there is that."

Elizabeth's fingers curled at her sides. "It was a gracious gesture for the thief to return the snuffbox. Why can you not consider that?"

"Because I have no liking for interference in my plans!"

"Perhaps the fob and pendant will be returned."

"They'd better be," Louise said severely.

Harrison waved his hand, dismissing this notion. "They were trifles, dear. Not treasures."

Louise's satin gown rustled as she began pacing again. "Out of my sight!" she snapped. When Harrison and Elizabeth only exchanged questioning looks, she added, "Both of you. I am completely overwrought."

Harrison stood, caught his wife's proffered cheek as she passed, nodded vaguely in Elizabeth's direction, and left the room for the quiet and comfort of his own bedchamber. Elizabeth's hand was on the doorknob when Louise called to her. She only turned her head to regard Lady Battenburn.

"We are not finished," Louise said.

"But you said—"

"I am speaking of the future, not of this moment. You may go anywhere you like now, but you must know we are not finished. There *will* be consequences, Elizabeth. You may depend upon it."

Elizabeth's palm was damp on the knob. It required two attempts for her to open the door, an effort she was certain was not lost on her hostess, the Honorable Lady Battenburn.

Elizabeth lay on top of her rumpled bedcovers and stared at the ceiling. She wished she had even one of the sleeping powders she had pretended to take a few days earlier. *Restless* did not begin to describe what she was feeling now. Trepidation had given way to the proverbial ball of dread. It was indeed lodged heavily in the pit of her stomach.

She had not needed to hear Louise remind her things were unfinished between them. Elizabeth had never once considered this evening's harangue would be the end of it. But Louise did not do something without reason, even when she was in a rage, so her parting words had been intended to make Elizabeth know that the retribution would be stiff. It was this thought that was keeping Elizabeth sleepless. There were so many ways in which she was vulnerable. From which direction would Louise attack?

Elizabeth rose from the bed and went to the window. She pushed it open and leaned out. A cool breeze ruffled her hair and made her skin prickle. She forced herself to look down. Could a fall from here kill her? she wondered. Or would she only be maimed? And how could that be worse than what she contended with now?

But if she died . . .

She came in through the opening slowly, knowing full well she would never throw herself through it. An accident could accomplish what she was unable to bring herself to do, but she could not set about the thing deliberately. The hands she always felt pressing at her back, pushing her, guiding her, would have to be there in fact, not fiction.

Her stomach lurched when she heard the panel in the wainscoting sliding open. She had not expected Louise to have arrived at a plan so soon. In a way it would be a relief, Elizabeth thought, to have the matter between them over quickly, to have this terrible strain eliminated.

She turned, the words calmly leaving her mouth before she realized she meant them for someone else. "I was not expecting you."

"It never occurred to me that you would be." Northam stood, brushing himself off. He was dressed as he had been earlier in the evening: a black frock coat with tails, dark gray trousers, and a perfectly white shirt with starched collar points and an intricately tied stock; and he was none the worse for his journey through the passage. "But it begs the obvious question: Whom *else* were you not expecting?"

"Get out."

"I noticed the vanity is no longer a barricade to the entrance. I take it that was in anticipation of a visit by someone other than myself. I know Lady Battenburn uses the passage from time to time, but does her husband?"

As if struck, Elizabeth stepped backward. "Leave."

Northam's head tilted to one side as he considered her response. "Perhaps I was wrong about that. Forgive me." He bent, closed the panel, and straightened again. "Do you know, I'm not certain if I could have found my way here without tonight's entertainment? I stumbled upon a connecting passage while hunting clues with Lady Powell."

Elizabeth did not think for a moment that he had *stumbled* upon anything. If he had come to this part of the house during the treasure hunt, it had been by design, not because he misread the clues. Elizabeth glanced toward her dressing room. She had a fleeting thought of retreating there, barring the door with her armoire, and staying put until Northam had the good sense to leave her.

"I thought you had no liking for cramped spaces."

North glanced back at the close passageway. "Perhaps I overstated my discomfort. It is armoires I fear."

Gritting her teeth, she said, "You must go." With some part of her mind she recognized the very steadiness of her voice was a complete contradiction of her rising hysteria. When was the last time she had actually surrendered to her feelings?

The answer came quickly and was accompanied by a rush

of searing humiliation. She stood only a few feet from the wall where Northam had pinned her back with his hands and mouth and made her think of nothing but her own selfish pleasure. Yes, she had been all of a piece that morning, the same on the inside as out, and it had brought her no enduring calm. She was paying for it again now, was she not?

Northam nudged the vanity backward with his hip until it partially blocked the panel. He did not require Elizabeth to tell him if her door was locked; he crossed the room and did the thing himself. He pointed to the open window. ''I will not be leaving by that route tonight,'' he said. ''If the consequences of being here include a hasty marriage, I am prepared to repent at leisure.''

Elizabeth's mouth opened, but no sound emerged. She snapped it shut because even in the red haze that colored her consciousness, she understood that gaping would only serve to amuse him.

Northam pulled the padded stool away from her dresser and sat on it. He crossed his arms in front of him and extended his long legs. ''Will you sit, Elizabeth?'' he asked politely. ''I mean you no harm.''

She remained exactly where she was.

''Shall I get you a shawl?''

He was not so different from Louise, she thought. He extended a kindness to balance the cruelty. She refused his offer.

''Very well. I'm afraid I have started off rather badly.'' He did not expect an argument from her for the truth of those words, only one that pointed to their obvious understatement. She said nothing, however, but stood quietly, framed by the dark window behind her, candlelight from the bedside limning her features so he could detect the fine tremor of her figure. ''I could be your friend, Lady Elizabeth, if you would but let me. I cannot dismiss the notion that you may be in need of some help. I am offering mine. It is meant most sincerely and is extended without strings. You need have no fear I desire anything in return.''

Elizabeth drew a deep breath. Her delicate nostrils flared

slightly and her breasts rose. She let the breath leave her
lungs slowly. Her lashes fluttered closed, then opened, and
when her eyes settled on Northam they were devoid of all
emotion. Passion and pain, fear and resignation, were all
suppressed by a perfect blankness of expression. "Leave,"
she said. "It is all I require of you."

Northam considered his choices before he finally stood,
sighed, and began walking toward her. Her very stillness
made him want to shake her. Perversely, he also only wanted
to place his arms about her so that he might hold her. He
stopped a short distance in front of her. His hands remained
at his sides. In deference to the possibility of discovery, his
voice was low. There was no simple explanation for its
huskiness. "What did you say this evening to South that
made him laugh so?"

It was in that moment that Elizabeth understood physical
contact was not required to set her off balance. Northam
could make it happen on the strength of his words alone. She
reminded herself that he had been a soldier, quite possibly a
strategist, and that he was skilled in tactics as she was not.

She blinked, the absurdity of the question drawing an
immediate response from her. It never occurred to her to
dissemble. "I believe I disparaged his brilliance."

North considered that. "Really? And he laughed?"

"I think, perhaps, it was the *way* I said it."

He smiled faintly. "Aaah, that I can understand. You do
adopt a tone from time to time . . ." His eyes were thoughtful
as they slid over her face. He took no great pleasure in
exposing her vulnerability, but he could not let her pretend
that she was indifferent. "Southerton proved himself to be
very clever this evening, did he not?"

"Yes," she said quietly, wondering at North's direction.
"He did. He unraveled the meaning of each clue we found."

"I'm certain it seemed that way." The slight curve of
his mouth was enigmatic now. "I was referring, though, to
his placing us together at the end."

"I don't—" She stopped herself from making a rote
denial and thought back to the evening past. Her brows lifted

fractionally as the truth was borne home. She and North had been moved about the gallery like pieces on a chess board. ''My, he *is* clever,'' she said softly.

''He would say that was damning him with faint praise. He likes to think of himself as cunning.''

She could believe that. ''What piece were you?'' she asked. ''A bishop? The king?''

''Oh, nothing like that. South knows I'm a soldier.''

''A knight, then.''

''More likely a pawn.''

Elizabeth nodded, her own smile weak. She could identify with the piece herself. ''What was his purpose?''

''You would have to ask him. Perhaps his efforts were in aid of making Lady Powell his companion.'' He saw skepticism flash in her amber eyes. ''I know; it doesn't pass muster with me either. I spent most of the evening with her and cannot imagine South purposely seeking to do the same.''

''Lady Powell is a most congenial—'' Elizabeth stopped because Northam was shaking his head, not having any of it. ''No, she's not, is she?''

''Not in the least,'' he agreed. ''And that leads me to conclude that South suspects there is some attraction between us. I do not think the wager alone would move him to interfere.''

''There is a wager?''

''Yes.''

She swallowed. ''Concerning us?''

''I collect so. I do not know the details. You observed Eastlyn on the day of the hunt. They will wager on most anything.''

''You also?''

''I am not participating in this one.''

It was not precisely an answer to her question, but Elizabeth let it pass. ''Tell me, are we worth more than a shilling?''

''I believe I heard them indicate a sovereign was at stake.''

''My. An entire sovereign.''

"I know. It's rather humbling."

There was a tremor in her legs and Elizabeth realized her knees could not support her much longer. "I think I will sit down now." She did not resist the lift of his hand on her elbow. It was just the lightest touch and, against all good sense to the contrary, profoundly welcome. When she was seated in the wing chair Northam left her side, returning a very short time later with her flannel shawl. "Thank you." She let him put it around her shoulders. His knuckles brushed her skin just above the open neckline of her chemise. She shivered. They did not look at each other and nothing was said, agreeing by their silence to pretend it had not happened.

North carried the stool from the vanity and set it a few feet away, but directly in front of her chair. He disabused her of the notion he meant it for her own comfort by sitting on it. "Does your leg ache?" he asked.

"It is nothing." In truth, she hadn't given it any thought. She was actually grateful for his reminder. It served to help her keep her focus. "Is it because of the colonel?" she asked. "You know I wrote to him. You saw me composing the letter yourself. I communicated your greeting and assured him all was well with me. What more must be said to convince him?"

"Nothing at all. You must convince me."

The answer was not unexpected. "I don't see how I can do that. You do not believe me."

"I will when I hear the truth." He paused a beat, then struck. "Who did you think you were talking to before you saw it was me?"

She said nothing.

"Did the baroness tell you the treasure was behind the Vermeer?"

Elizabeth continued to stare at him.

"Why is it so important that I stay away from you?"

An eyebrow lifted in an ironic arch.

North drew up his legs and hunched forward, elbows resting on his knees, his hands forming a steeple under his chin. "How many lovers have there been?"

She could not quite swallow the moan that rose in her throat. Elizabeth's voice was only a thread of sound. "Do not do this, my lord."

"My name is Brendan," he said. "North, if you prefer. We have been intimates; we may behave intimately." He sat up and extended his legs again. The toe of one of his shoes brushed her bare foot and the touch sent a shiver through her. Fear? he wondered. Repulsion? Desire? Did she even know? He kept his eyes on hers, holding her in place with his quiet intensity. "I was jealous, you know. Last night. When I heard South laugh. And before that, days before, when you gave attention to so many others and only pretended to give me yours. It was a new experience for me. At first I thought you were right, and that the choice I'd made was to despise you, but upon reflection, I fear it is something else entirely."

"No," she said. "It is not. It is only that you want to fuck me."

Chapter Seven

North remembered how he had proved to her that she was still vulnerable. Now, with stunning accuracy, she had done the same to him. He had never heard any but the coarsest of women use that word. Even then it had seemed out of place to him, for he held the opinion that females were the gentler sex, and such rawness of language was unacceptable. He had, perhaps, adopted more of his grandfather's dinner-table platitudes than was strictly helpful to him now.

He drew a deep breath; let it out carefully. "If you knew the length and breadth of the lecture I am sparing you, you would thank me."

"You are a prig, my lord, whether you lecture me or not. You may as well lecture me."

North realized he was faced with another choice. He could allow himself to be offended, mayhap raise his hand against her, or he could give himself leave to be amused. He chose the latter because it was the least expected and more in the way of what he felt. A genuine smile flitted across his mouth and found its way into his eyes. "I *am* a prig," he said. "Though I do not believe taking exception to your use of that word is what qualifies me as one. There are other conventions I care more deeply about than whether one speaks in vulgarities. It shocked me, nonetheless. You may derive some satisfaction from that.''

He shrugged, his palms turning outward in a gesture that was at once sheepish and helpless. ''It was also true,'' he admitted. He saw Elizabeth's eyes widen the merest fraction. ''You were right, I *do* want to—''

She waited, watching him pause, almost choking on the word. ''Say it.''

Northam stared at her for a long moment; watched the rise and fall of her breasts, the catch when he let her read the intent in his eyes. He came to his feet in a fluid motion, and in two steps he had closed the distance separating them. He leaned over her, placing his palms on the curved arms of the chair. She had to tilt her head back to look up at him. There was defiance in the lift of her chin and her unwavering glance, but it was excitement that was darkening her eyes, and Northam could not mistake it for anything else.

She dared him again. ''Say it.''

He bent his head and touched his lips to her ear. He whispered exactly what he intended to do to her, in exactly the words she wanted to hear. Her arms came up and enfolded his neck and she bit back a soft moan when his mouth covered hers. He pulled her roughly out of the chair. Her body draped itself against his. One arm slipped behind her back, the other under her knees. He lifted her and carried her to the bed. She did not release him when he put her down, but kept her arms locked around his shoulders, her hungry mouth fast to his, and brought him down on top of her.

She released him only so she could cup his face. She pressed kisses to his cheeks, his brow, the line of his jaw. Her teeth caught his earlobe and her warm, damp breath seared his skin. She opened her mouth for him, accepted the hot suck of his own mouth. When he rolled to one side she turned with him and lay partially on her side, her nightgown rucked nearly to her thighs, one leg raised and thrown across both of his.

She breathed shallowly. Where his hand cupped her breast

he could feel the wild racing of her heart. He lowered his head, first to her neck, her chest, and finally to where he held her in his palm. His tongue laved her dusky rose aureole through a film of batiste. The fabric dampened and lay flat against her skin, perfectly outlining the puckered nipple. He rolled it gently in his teeth, tugged, dragged his tongue across it again so that she arched into him hard and he could feel every hollow and curve of her body and the place where there was nothing but the opening of parted thighs.

His hand slid under her nightgown from her knee to her hip. He palmed the back of her thigh, then higher, pressing his fingers into her buttock. She rode against him, rubbing his hip. Through his trousers she could feel the heat and hardness of his erection.

"Let me," she whispered.

He raised his head. A lock of bright hair fell forward. She reached up and pushed it back, raking her fingers through it as she had seen him do. She did not remove her hand completely. Candlelight flickered across his face and her eyes followed the movement, watching a golden glow chase the shadow. A smile, infinitely tender and somehow sad, changed the shape of her own mouth. He saw it and started to speak. She stopped him with just the slightest shake of her head. "Let me," she said again. Her fingertips smoothed his brow, touched the corner of his eye, slipped lightly across his beautiful mouth.

"You are astonishingly handsome," she told him, her voice husky. She saw his eyes dart away. "You are." She nudged his jaw with her nose, snuggling, teasing. "Has no one ever told you?"

Someone had, but he was wise enough not to invoke the name of the Dowager Countess of Northam now. More to the point, he did not mind being teased by Elizabeth. Her knee rose, brushing his erection. She placed her hands flat on his chest and pushed with light but insistent pressure. He lay on his back and she sat up. One sleeve of her nightgown slid over her shoulder. When she started to push it back, he stopped her with a single shake of his head. His eyes slowly traced the smooth, bare line of her body from the hollow of her cheek to the soft underside of her elbow. She left it there.

She undid the double-breasted front of his coat and lifted his shirt. He was not wearing a corset beneath it. He had a lithe frame; an athlete's tone ran through his muscles. His abdomen was firm and trim, the skin taut across his chest. She used her teeth to tug on his stock and undo the intricate fold. He murmured a name. Brill, she thought, and then heard him suggest murder might be done for those teeth marks. She found it odd that he could make her laugh. Odd, and dangerous. Frightening.

"What is it?" he asked her. He held the side of her face. His thumb made a trace across her trembling lips.

She only shook her head, glad when he let it pass. There was no answer she could give when she had so little understanding herself. She pressed her lips to the rough pad of his thumb instead, then his other fingers, and was reminded through each kiss what he had done for her. She drew his hand down and held it over her breast. A knot of tears lodged in her throat and still more made her eyes ache with the effort to hold them back. Leaning toward the bedside table, she blew out the candle, then returned to him and unerringly found his mouth with her own.

He sat up long enough to be helped out of his coat and shirt. She ran her fingertips across the breadth of his naked shoulders and settled her mouth in the curve of his neck. Later, she played handmaiden, removing his shoes and stockings and finally unfastening his trousers. Her hand slid under his drawers. He groaned softly, jerking his hips as her hand cupped his sac. His head was thrown back, his strong throat exposed. He reached for her wrist, but she stayed his hand and squeezed him gently. Her fingers lifted and wrapped themselves around his penis. He did not think he could be thicker or harder, but the touch of her hand, the scrape of her nails on the underside of his sensitive skin, seemed to make him swell and stiffen again.

She drew off his trousers, then his drawers, and he lay

perfectly naked on the bed. She had worn one article of clothing, her chemise, while he had had his coat, linen, collar, cravat, trousers, drawers, shoes, and stockings. She was still wearing her chemise, while he . . . he was wearing her.

"You're laughing," she whispered. Her mouth nudged his. She kissed the corner of it. It was as if she could taste his smile. "Tell me."

He twisted, rolling to the center of the bed until their positions were reversed. He heard her breath catch and raised himself on his elbows so she was not bearing all his weight. Only the thin film of batiste separated his skin from hers. "I was thinking you are still very modestly attired, while I . . ." He settled his groin more solidly in the cradle of her thighs and belly. His voice was like honey over sand. "While I . . . am not."

She stroked him from buttocks to shoulders. His flesh was smooth and warm and taut, and when he shifted he seemed to imprint himself on her. "No, you're not." There was some part of her that wished she had not extinguished the candle. She would have liked to see his features more clearly, to know the exact tilt of his mouth, to watch the muscle that leaped in his jaw. She knew he was watching her in turn, his cobalt eyes so dark that even in the light of day they would appear to be black. Darkness made her feel safe, protected from his stare.

This way she only had to shield herself from his laughter.

She stretched. There was something powerfully erotic about being clothed when he was not. Or perhaps, she thought vaguely, it was only something powerful. The chemise inched up at the hem while he lowered it across her breasts. When it was bunched up around her waist, they both forgot about it.

He kissed her bare breasts. She raised her knees. He suckled her. She cradled him. Her fingers wound in his hair. His fingers slipped between her thighs. Two went inside her. They both felt how ready she was for him, how slick and sweetly prepared her body was . . . and how tight.

He could feel her contracting around his fingers. He eased them out of her and thrust again. She moaned. Her hips lifted. He released her and raised himself up so he was kneeling between her thighs. His hands went to the small of her back, then lower. He cupped her bottom, lifted it. Her fingers curled in the tangle of bedclothes. At the first hint of his entry her teeth caught her bottom lip. She took a shallow breath, sipping the air as he pushed himself slowly inside her. She was tender and tight. It was true she was no virgin, but it had been a very long time.

Joined, he paused, leaning forward carefully, letting her get used to the size and pressure of him. He nuzzled her neck, the hollow of her throat. She was all around him, tight inside and out. Her breathing had slowed. It came evenly now, in a measured tempo. She was holding back, forcing herself to lie still and quiet and wait for his lead. He felt the pulse in her throat against his lips and the one that thrummed inside her against the length of his arousal. She contracted a little around him. The movement made him thrust upward. She gasped.

He pressed a hard kiss to her mouth, wrenching another cry from her. She took his face in her hands and held it when he drew back. "You must . . ." She forced herself to keep her eyes open as he began to move between her thighs. "You must not . . ." Her body continued to stretch and adapt to accommodate him. The pressure was insistent, the ache spreading from the tip of her womb all the way to her fingertips. Her hands left his face and she gripped his shoulders instead. "Promise . . ." she said on a thread of sound. "Promise you will not leave your seed in me."

Elizabeth felt rather than saw the change her words had wrought. Beneath her fingers his shoulders bunched. Every one of his muscles tensed. He did not strike her, though she suspected some part of him wanted to. He used all of his body to punish her instead, thrusting into her deeply, no longer mindful of her pleasure. He did not kiss her again, and she felt the absence of his mouth as keenly as she felt his presence elsewhere. His strokes were long and hard, jerking her back each time he ground himself against her. She strove to meet him, wrapping her legs around him, clutching his upper arms. She closed her eyes against what she imagined she saw in his face and caught the inside of her upper lip. On his next thrust she tasted her own blood.

It was fitting, she thought, that he should have found this way to make her bleed. The pain of it was not even unwelcome. She could not give him her virginity, but this, this small sharp stab of pain mingling with the warm metallic taste of her blood was easily made his. Reaching up, she grasped his head and pulled his mouth to hers, making him take what his anger had wrested from her.

She did not expect it to make a difference.

North stilled. The taste of her blood was on the tip of his tongue. His inarticulate groan was muffled by the pressure of her mouth on his. He raised his head slowly. Her hands fell away from his face and lay palm up on either side of her head.

His chest felt tight with the pressure of the breath he held. He let it out slowly. "I'm sorry," he said. "I've never . . ." He stopped because she was shaking her head from side to side. Her features were lost in the deep shadows of the room, but he could make out the movement, the refusal to allow his apology.

"It doesn't matter," she whispered.

But it did, to him. There was no denying that he had meant to hurt her. He could not excuse himself that it had been unintentional. It was a new experience for him, to set about trying to hurt a woman in any manner, but to do it in this particular way, with his mouth and his hands and his cock . . . It came to him then that he was fucking her, just as she had insisted he wanted to. Elizabeth had made him say it, then had set about proving how very true it was.

He started to withdraw, but her legs tightened around his hips. He was not proof against this or the contractions that held him more intimately.

She touched his face gently, brushing aside a lock of hair on his brow. Beneath his fingertips she could feel the strain that it took to remain so still inside her. "You forgot for a while, didn't you? Forgot there was someone else before you. I knew you had." She lightly touched his temple, then his cheek. "I cannot be a virgin for you, no matter how you make me bleed." Her hand slid to the back of his neck when he tried to pull away. "No. Don't leave me. Please. I want this."

He lowered his head and brought his mouth close to hers. "It should not be a punishment," he whispered.

"You cannot always have your way, my lord." Her hand fell lightly on his shoulder. "Sometimes it can be nothing else."

A growl was trapped at the back of his throat. He kissed her once, hard and deeply, and then his body began to move, lifting, stroking, taking her with the reckless force she wanted, her small cries urging him on.

He felt heat coil inside him, sparked by the liquid heat of her body around his. Tension skittered under his skin, drawing on his muscles, stretching them. His shoulders lifted, his back curved with the downward force of his hips. He strained to get closer, deeper, and felt her strain in exactly the opposite way, digging her heels into the mattress, arching her pelvis, throwing her head back and lifting her breasts and . . .

At the last Northam remembered what promise she had wanted. He had never given his word, but he knew, even as he had been angered by her asking, that he would do it. Still, he almost left it to too late. With a cry, and all the effort he could bring to bear, he withdrew from her and spilled his seed onto her flat belly and then into the tangled sheets.

Elizabeth lay quietly under him, listening to his breathing steady, comforted by the weight of him and the knowledge that his warm liquid seed was on her belly and not in it. For a time she was content to stroke his back. When he rolled away, she did not try to hold him to her.

Without a word she rose from the bed. She raised the neckline of her bunched nightgown to her shoulders and let the hem fall to her ankles. Her bare feet made no sound as she crossed the carpet to the dressing room.

Northam turned on his side and slipped one arm under the pillow at his head. He watched the door to the dressing room swing slowly toward him until only a strip of candle-light was visible along the frame. He heard her pour water from a pitcher into a bowl. Briefly there was a sound of splashing. He imagined her cooling her heated face, runnels of water slipping over her brow, cheeks, and then past her throat, dampening the neckline of her gown. He wondered if she was looking in a mirror, and what she would see if she did.

Satisfaction? Self-loathing?

He did not reflect on his own emotions as carefully as he considered hers, and he reasoned it might be no different for her. She might have no more desire than he to give much thought to what had passed between them and, more importantly, to what feelings were sustained in the wake.

There was silence in the other room. In his mind's eye he saw her lifting the gown and using a damp cloth to wipe away the last traces of his seed. She would raise one leg on a stool and touch it to her belly, her hip, and slide it between her thighs. Water would glisten on her skin and on the damp gold-tipped hair of her mons. She had been right, he thought, to insist on his withdrawal. He had done it before with one of the regimental whores because the thought of putting a child in her belly filled him with dread. After that he had used a length of sheep's gut, which he heard could also protect him against the pox. His mistresses had never demanded it of him. He knew they had ways of protecting themselves, and it was borne out over the years when none of the women he slept with presented him with a son or daughter.

He should have been relieved, he told himself, yet he knew there was a part of him that wondered if he *could* sire a child. His mother was certainly impatient for him to provide heirs. He was not sure she cared any longer if they were legitimate. And one son was not enough, she had reminded him, though this last admonition was unnecessary. He well understood the reasons for conceiving a second son. He was one. Not an afterthought at all, but insurance against tragedy.

Elizabeth stood in the doorway. She carried a candlestick in one hand, the light of which barely reached the bed. Still, it afforded her an unrestricted view of the golden god who lay atop it. Bright yellow hair fell across his forehead; some strands lay like gossamer threads on the pillowcase. He was naked. One knee was raised toward his chest, not in a self-conscious way, but in a manner that spoke of replete and sated senses. The taut curve of his hip and thigh glowed just at the edge of the candlelight.

Elizabeth walked to the bedside table and touched her candle to the one that was there, doubling the brightness of the light that caressed his body. She stared at his beautiful face, so youthful in sleep. She knew he was older than she in years, but it seemed he was younger in fact. Elizabeth did not think her own face was so untroubled when she slept. At least she hoped it wasn't. She had not earned the right to rest in such a careless web of dreams.

Elizabeth set down her candlestick and returned to the dressing room for the small basin of water and damp cloth. She placed them on the table, then eased herself gingerly onto the mattress. It was when she turned that she saw he was watching her, his eyes on the curve of her shoulder laid bare by the fallen strap of her gown. He reached for her, touching the nape of her neck with his fingertips, ruffling the fine hairs. His large hand curved around her neck and his thumb stroked the soft underside of her chin. She swallowed hard. He smiled as if he understood what she was thinking.

Lifting her hand to his lips, he kissed her knuckles. The tenderness of the gesture made her want to weep. She had promised herself there would be no tears this time. He did not deserve that.

"I thought you had fallen asleep," she said.

He lowered her hand and let it rest on his chest, still cupped in his. "Would you prefer that I had?"

"Only if you wished it."

One brow lifted. "So accommodating. And if I wished to make love to you again?" When she was silent he thought it was because she meant to dispute the words he had chosen, and he found himself holding his breath. Her eyes, however, went to the shadowed juncture of his thighs, where his penis lay soft and heavy and still, and her expression communicated so much doubt that he could not help but laugh. "I quite understand your lack of confidence," he said, grinning. "Perhaps in a little while."

She nodded, her eyes no longer on his thighs but on his face. His easy smile, his unselfconscious amusement, captivated her. "As you like," she said, hardly aware of her words or the fact that she was speaking.

"What are you thinking?"

She shook her head. "Nothing," she said. "It was . . ."

"Nothing. I know. Elizabeth, I think your nothings are more interesting than what most people regard as their deepest thoughts." He gave her hand a little squeeze. "Tell me."

She hesitated. "It is foolish, really. I was thinking that your smile is without any pain." She looked away for a moment, and when she looked back she saw it was gone. Perhaps that had been her real intent, she thought, in answering his question. She was no longer caught in the spell of it. "I wondered if life has always been so easy for you."

He studied her face. "Easier than yours, I think."

Elizabeth had not expected that his answer would turn back on her. She felt her insides twist and made to remove her hand from his. He did not let her go, pressing his fingers more firmly around it and keeping it in place just over his heart. How was it, she wondered, that he was the one naked and she was the one exposed?

"Do you not want to hear?" he asked gently.

She was not at all sure she did. She took the coward's route and said nothing, letting him decide if he would tell her.

"I spent my youngest years—how is it described?—aaah, yes, in the bosom of a loving family." He watched a slight smile lift one corner of her mouth. "There was my father, the fifth Earl of Northam, my mother, my older brother Gordon, named after my father, an older sister Leticia, and two younger sisters, Pamela and Regina. You see, already it is very different from you. You are an only child, I believe."

She started to nod, then remembered how things had changed. "That was true for a very long time. I have a half-brother now. Adam, Viscount Selden."

"Yes, I forgot." He went on. "We had all the usual rows. Fights over who should go first at duck, duck, goose. Who should cut the cake. Who should be the pirate leader. Gordon was very good about not always winning. He could have claimed the right as the oldest, but he never pressed that too hard. Leticia was more likely to be difficult—as girls often are—and Gordon and I were usually glad when she played with our younger sisters. Pamela and Reggie did not seem to mind in the least when she ordered them about.

"My father was very much connected to politics, rather like yours, I suspect."

Elizabeth suspected the senior Gordon Hampton had been nothing like her father, even in the course of his politics. She inclined her head, neither agreeing nor disagreeing, and encouraged him to continue.

"He spent a great deal of time in London and a great deal of that outside of our home, making speeches, attending to the business of government. My mother was also a favorite in social circles and she remains so to this day. Still, in spite of my parents' interests in the larger society, I believe we saw them a fair amount. They were there for the important occasions, and they always seemed to know when any of us had done something wrong." He smiled faintly at the memory of being marched into his father's study to explain how Regina's freckles had come to be connected by a narrow line of black ink. "They were not niggardly with their praise either. We knew when one or the other was proud of us. Certainly I spent more time with my mother and father than South did with his parents, for instance. Or East. Marchman did not know his father at all."

Elizabeth nodded. "I suppose that no matter what the circumstances of our growing up, we never think of it as being different from anyone else's. We end up believing that what we know is what *should* be." Her sigh was nearly soundless, and though she was thinking of herself and what had passed for usual in her home, she said, "You learned differently at Hambrick, I take it."

"Hmmm. When Gordon came of age he was sent to public school. Eton. It was where my father went. I missed him terribly, envied him almost as much. When it was my turn to go, I was sent to Hambrick. My grandfather, my mother's father, had come to live with us by then, and he had gone to Hambrick. He felt as strongly about sending me there as my father did Eton. Grandfather won, though, as he usually did when he set forth his arguments."

"Were you disappointed?"

"Not overmuch. I was old enough then to know that being at Eton with Gordon would have forever placed me in his shadow. I would always be compared to him in a way I had never been at home. From the very beginning our parents encouraged us on different courses. My father would have seen the wisdom of sending me to Hambrick earlier if it had not been proposed by my grandfather. They never agreed on anything, beginning with my father marrying my mother."

Elizabeth laughed. "But your grandfather did eventually agree. After all, your parents married."

One of Northam's brows kicked up. "They eloped," he said in a stage whisper, adopting the feigned secretive tone everyone in his family had used to discuss the event. "To Gretna."

"Really?"

He nodded solemnly. "It was a scandal." He smiled when Elizabeth laughed again. Releasing her hand, he sat up and drew a sheet modestly around his waist. He patted the space beside him and she left her place on the edge of the bed to sit in the crook of his arm. "Where was I?"

"The scandal."

"No, I wasn't. That's another story. I was going to tell you about Hambrick."

"Lord Southerton told me about your Compass Club. Sworn enemies of the Society of Bishops and all that."

"That's right."

"He said you were an exclusive club."

"He said that?"

She tried to remember South's exact words. "Well, he said that you wouldn't let anyone else in."

"He probably didn't mention that no one ever asked. We weren't exclusive, Elizabeth. We were excluded."

She frowned, unable to imagine such a thing. She remembered seeing them all together on the first day of the picnic, sprawled across a blanket, laughing so boisterously when Northam juggled peaches from her still life. Who would not want to join them? She had. Not even knowing them, she had wondered what it would be like to share their blanket and their laughter. "How could that be?"

"The simplest explanation is because of West," he said. "But that's only part of it."

"What is it about Mr. Marchman?"

"He's illegitimate."

"A bastard," she said softly. She felt Northam stiffen at her side. "No, I didn't mean anything by it. It's just . . . it's just that I was thinking how cruel the boys could be to . . . to someone like him."

"Someone like him," Northam repeated, not liking the taste of that phrase on his tongue, liking it even less that he heard it from Elizabeth. "It doesn't make him different from you or me."

"Oh, but it does."

Northam removed his arm from around her shoulders. "Explain that to me."

She knew he was unhappy with her but would not take back her words. It was better this way, she thought, better that he was reminded that her perspective could be at odds with his. "Illegitimacy does not make him intrinsically different," she said. "Not at birth. But soon after it changes him in some way. It could be because his mother is ashamed or his father is indifferent. It may be that someone responds more slowly when he cries or does not comfort him so easily when he is hurt. He begins to see himself as someone apart from others.

"You cannot say that society is kind to bastards, North, and in the end society has its way. An illegitimate son learns that what he wants he must take, that nothing will ever be given to him, and that sometimes even what he earns he cannot claim. He comes to believe one of two things about himself: either that he has no right to hold his head up or that he must hold it higher than everyone else. Whatever he chooses, it soon becomes visible to others, and they respond to what they see: a young man who accepts that he is everyone's whipping boy or one who constantly challenges the biggest and strongest and cares nothing for how badly he's beaten.

"I know nothing about your Mr. Marchman, but I suspect after meeting the rest of your little Compass Club that he falls into the latter category, and that you became his friend because he would have let you kill him before he would have stopped challenging you."

He was silent for a long time. Elizabeth turned her face toward him, expecting to see that derision or defense had changed the shape of his mouth. Instead she saw a sheen of tears. She found his hand under the covers and held it between both of hers. His decency made her want to weep. His kindness made her frightened for him.

North felt Elizabeth's head return to his shoulder. He collected himself, drawing in an uneasy breath at first, then another that came less painfully. "It was just as you said," he told her. "West kept coming at us. Me first. Then at East. Later South. We had to do something about him or it would never have ended." Northam shook his head, memory tugging at the corners of his mind. "He broke my nose. That's how this bump was fashioned." He ran his finger along the offending bridge. "He said I needed it. That I was too pretty by half and that without it I should be better off a girl.''

Elizabeth laughed softly. "I think it is safe to say that Mr. Marchman was a bit envious of your very fine looks."

He grunted, unappeased by this defense. "My grandfather said much the same thing. Told me it gave me character. Made a point of meeting Marchman at the next visitor's day and thanking him. My mother was less forgiving of West. She still brings it up from time to time. She is likely to think of him as a ruffian, though he has better manners than the lot of us put together."

"I imagine she's prejudiced in your favor."

"I suppose," he agreed reluctantly. "She's the other one besides you, by the way, to comment favorably on my looks. She thought it was a great pity about my nose. Said I had character enough without it."

Elizabeth pretended to study his face with great care. "I'm afraid, my lord, that without your nose you would *be* a character."

"Hah! I meant the bump and well you know it. You must think you're very amusing."

"No," she said. "But I should like to be."

"Why?"

"To make you laugh." She said it without thinking and, once said, could not draw it back. Her eyes darted away from his, knowing she had revealed too much. "You have a very nice laugh," she said lightly, as if it was of little significance.

"Do you think so?"

"Well, it is not so fine as Lord Southerton's, but it is a shade more robust than the marquess's. Though, now that I consider it, perhaps robust does not quite serve. Have you been to the zoo, my lord? There is an animal there that has a laugh—"

He kissed her. There was nothing else for it. If he let her, Elizabeth would spend the rest of the night trying to assign no importance to what had just spilled past her lips. It would be highly diverting, somewhat humbling, and certainly an invention from beginning to end. Far better to kiss her.

"Oh." She blinked at him widely when he raised his head.

"Indeed."

It was all she could do not to bring her fingertips to her mouth. It was something an ingenue would do, she thought. Something *she* had done once. She did not know what bothered her more: that she remembered being so innocent, or that he made her feel that way again. She heard herself ask in a tight little voice, "Do you want to take me now?"

She was like a cornered kitten, he decided. Back arched. Spitting. Tiny claws bared. He was beginning to know this aspect of her character better, not that he felt any assurance about the best way to handle it. Upon reflection, he suspected that it was something about the kiss that troubled her. Then again, perhaps it was only a wayward thought that had prompted this reaction. Whatever the source, she was clearly feeling threatened.

Northam ignored her tone and responded only to the words. "No," he said. He made a show of choosing a pillow, plumping it, and stuffing it behind the small of his back for his comfort. "Not just at this time. Perhaps later." Out of the corner of his eye he saw her mouth open, then close again. Good. Keeping her confused seemed to render her speechless. He filed this tactic away. He had virtually no doubt he would be presented with the opportunity to use it in the future.

Settling comfortably back against the headboard again, he said, "I believe I was telling you about Hambrick Hall. None of us was very popular with the other boys. I was too serious. South was too brilliant. And East . . . well, East was rather . . . how shall I put it? . . . well, *round* in those days."

Elizabeth was interested in spite of herself. "Do you mean to say he was a roly-poly?"

"Just so. Almost as wide as he was tall. His mother was forever sending him boxes of baked goods. Scones. Cakes.

Hot cross buns. He was fond of the icing and picking out the raisins. What was left he fed to the birds.''

"He doesn't sound the kind of person Mr. Marchman would have picked on."

"Oh, East had a reputation as a thrasher. He could knock anyone down. Had to. He was always being teased, and there were the cakes to protect, you know." Northam caught a glimpse of Elizabeth's smile. "So Marchman went after him. Never ridiculed him about his size, simply tried to remove his rep as the best thrasher."

"What happened?"

"You may have noticed that the marquess does not have a bump on his nose," he said dryly. "East won, of course. Several times. I don't know precisely how the fighting ended and the friendships began, but one day we noticed we were all sharing Eastlyn's feast from home and that was that."

"And you never thought to exclude Mr. Marchman?"

"Never."

"It seems he caused you all a good deal of trouble."

"He brought us together."

"The Compass Club," she said quietly.

"Mmmm. It was odd, that. None of us expected to inherit titles one day. It was one of the things that set us apart from many other students at Hambrick, most particularly the Bishops. Marchman's contention was that everyone in England was in line for a bit of land, a country home, and a title. It was only that so many people had to die first before one could claim it. To prove his point, he showed how each one of us could come by another name. Privately we took to calling ourselves by them."

"Rather ghoulish."

"It sounds so now. It wasn't at the time. Just a bit of silliness. There wasn't one among us who preferred a title. I was already determined to be a soldier. South intended he should serve in the Royal Navy. East fancied himself a diplomat, someone who could attend state dinners but still mend things."

"And Mr. Marchman?"

Northam paused, then answered carefully, "It is not so easy to say about West."

Elizabeth considered pressing him, then decided better of it. "It all came about though, didn't it?"

"Our titles? Yes. That all came about. Or will. There is still Marchman." He was quiet a moment, thoughtful. When he began again it was with more deliberation. "I was with the colonel in India when I received word that my brother had died. It was the influenza. I became Viscount Richmond. A month later a letter reached me in Delhi that my father had succumbed to the same illness. I did not even know he had taken sick."

"And so you became the earl."

He nodded. "Responsibilities to my family meant resigning my commission and returning home."

"Do you miss the soldiering?"

"Sometimes. I miss my father and brother a great deal more."

"I'm sorry," she said quickly. "I didn't mean—"

He found her hand, squeezed it. "I know what you meant. The truth is, I had lived in dread of them dying for years. When it finally happened there was almost a sense of relief, and then, of course, the terrible burden of guilt that settled on me. I thought I should have been able to *do* something."

Elizabeth was not surprised. Northam's nature remained unchanged.

"I was not much good to my mother or my sisters early on. It was not that I drank too much or gambled the family fortune away; it was simply that I was not *there*. It is considerably difficult to explain. I was going through each day, each week, because one knows it is expected, but feeling disconnected from it all, completing the routines of living without any sense of life."

Elizabeth thought he had explained it rather well. Or perhaps it was only that she had intimate knowledge of the very same. "What changed cicumstances for you?"

He shrugged. "Small things. Many things. My grandfather's lectures were compelling, if only because they were so unwelcome. My mother was able to see through her haze of pain to my own. Leticia married. Pamela had her coming out. Regina left the schoolroom.'' He stopped, considering all those things, then added one more. ''And the colonel sent for me.''

''He did? To see how you were getting on?''

''Something like that.''

''Oh,'' she said. ''He put you up to some intrigue, no doubt. Blackwood is known for that, or so I've heard my father say. He never discusses the same with me. I take it your meeting with him went a long way to piquing your interest in living again.''

''It damn near got me killed.''

She laughed as he intended she should. It was probably no exaggeration of the truth, she thought, yet she knew his put-off, sour expression was feigned. Northam had a great deal of admiration for her late mother's cousin. ''And so here you are. You will have something of extreme interest to report to Blackwood this time around, will you not?''

On this subject Northam felt no compunction to tell the truth. ''I was only asked to encourage you to write to him. I have done that.''

''My, you are a good soldier.''

''Yes,'' he said, with none of her lightness of feeling. ''I am.''

Elizabeth knew her tone had been misplaced, but it had not been without purpose. She did not apologize. ''It's very late,'' she said.

''It is. Do you mention it as a casual observation or as a prelude to asking me to leave?''

''You should leave.''

And that, he supposed, answered his question. He was tempted to ask if she had another liaison after him. He held back, dismissing it as unfair and unwise. ''How is it that no hint of scandal has ever touched you?'' he asked instead.

She made no reply, choosing to stare at her hands in her lap.

"It seems odd that I've never heard talk about your . . . your . . ."

"My promiscuous proclivities."

"Yes, that might be an apt description."

Elizabeth shrugged. "Perhaps you've heard nothing because you travel in different circles."

"The *ton* has but one carousel," he said. "Sooner or later everyone meets the same painted horses."

"That is a . . . umm . . . unique perspective."

"My grandfather's, I'm afraid. It's the strangest thing, Elizabeth, but you bring out his voice in me. I'm not thanking you for it, either. I am two and thirty, not two and eighty."

"And here I had been thinking how much younger than me you seemed."

Northam was fairly certain he should not accept that as a compliment. "How is that?"

"It's just that you seem so unaffected. I suppose, in light of what you've told me, that's not remotely true, yet I cannot shake the feeling that you are never worried overmuch, that you believe in a kind fate, and that if your wits fail you, your charm will carry the day. It keeps you young, I think."

Northam found that with Elizabeth, his first response was rarely the most considered one. He held back a moment. "You have been too long alone, Elizabeth. Family. Friends. They are what sees one through."

"I have friends," she said. "Louise. The baron. They have been very good to me."

He doubted she knew how much by rote her response sounded. She would have been more careful to make it seem otherwise. "Of course there is your family."

"Yes."

"I see." And he did. Elizabeth was every bit as alone as she appeared to him. "So you have no need of my friendship."

"Everyone can use more friends, my lord. It is your help I have no need of."

"You called me North a while ago."

"I did?" She thought back. "I suppose I did, my lord."

A chuckle rumbled at the back of his throat. She could be very provoking if he let her. "What happens after this rout?" he asked. "Will I see you again?"

"You said it yourself. The *ton* has but one carousel. It is inevitable that we'll meet from time to time."

"And will you share my bed?"

"I must needs point out that you are sharing mine."

"So I am. Will you permit me the same privilege in the future?"

Elizabeth was not at all certain she had permitted it this time. It just seemed to happen. "I think not."

"Then you would not consent to having me set you up in a house of your own."

She couldn't even pretend to be insulted. "Most definitely not." She moved from his side, putting some space between them on the bed. Far from turning her back on North, she faced him, drawing her knees up to her chest as she regarded him curiously. Her chemise fell around her like a cloud. "Did you think I might?"

"No, but it seemed that I should make the offer."

"Oh, then by all means, you may consider that you have done right by me."

"And marriage?"

She paled a little but went on gamely. "I see no reason why you should not do so. There is some pressure from your mother, I collect."

"Considerable pressure."

"And there is the wager."

"Yes. There is the Compass Club to take into account."

"Then might I again suggest Miss Caruthers? Or Miss Farthingale. Lady Anne also comes to—" She gave a little squeal as he caught her wrist and tumbled her forward. She fell into his arms still curled in a ball. Her voice was soft, a shade breathless. "They do not interest you? Then perhaps Lady Martha. She is, by all accounts, a most—"

"Marry me, Elizabeth."

Her mouth snapped shut. She stared at him, stunned, then found the presence of mind to attempt to push away. He held her fast, his fingers pressing firmly into the flesh of her upper arms. "Do not ruin everything," she said tightly. "You know what I am."

"No." His voice was gentle. "I know what you *think* you are."

She pushed at his chest again and got no farther from him than she had before. Continued struggle, it seemed, was not only undignified but futile. "I will *not* allow you to save me," she told him. "You have some notion that I require rescuing. It is not true, Northam. Have done with me."

He held her eyes, not missing the light of panic that brightened the shards of gold. "Why are you trying to save me, Elizabeth?"

"I am not. I—"

"You are. You think you present some danger to me. You said as much soon after I met you."

"I—"

He shook his head. "You cannot take it back now. You said my life would not be my own if you were in it. You were right about that, though I don't think you meant it in quite the way it has happened." He regarded her steadily. "My life is not my own any longer, Elizabeth."

Northam waited. She was so very pale. She seemed to shrink into herself. After a moment tears made her eyes liquid. Hurt? Fear? Pity? He didn't know and he didn't ask. He simply pulled her closer, released her arms so he could wrap his around her, and waited for her to unfold against him and sob out the misery she had no other way to express.

She cried at length. It was no soft weeping but shudders that racked her. She stuffed her knuckles against her mouth, embarrassed by the sounds she made reaching deep for another breath. He rested his lips against her hair, sometimes his cheek. He never tried to quiet her. His body became her sanctuary, the circle of his arms a place where she could know safety.

Northam found a handkerchief in the bedside table and handed it to her. She wiped her eyes and blew her nose. Over the top of her head he smiled to himself. He was

careful not to let her see it when he lifted her chin to look
at her face. Taking the balled up handkerchief from her fist,
he used it to erase the tracings of tears from her cheeks and
the corners of her eyes. He kissed her lightly on the forehead,
a tender, familial kiss. For reasons he did not entirely understand, she began weeping anew.

When she finished it was because she was asleep in his
arms.

In time, Northam joined her. They lay curled like spoons
in a drawer, heads on the same pillow, a sheet pulled over
them. He did not know how long they slept that way. It was
still dark when he woke. The candles had both been gutted
and only a sliver of moonlight slipped through an opening
in the curtains. He was lying on his back. At the first trickle
of something wet and warm on his belly he jerked up his
knees protectively.

Elizabeth's low laughter greeted him. "It is only I, my
lord," she said. "Come to assist you with your ablutions."
She twisted the damp cloth in her hands and wrung out more
droplets of water. His knees knocked hers as he tried to
escape. She snapped him smartly on the stomach with one
end of the cloth.

"Ow."

"Show some backbone."

"I have heard tales of a Chinese water torture."

"I do not think it is this one."

Northam tended to agree. He eased down his knees. "The
water could be a tad warmer."

"In a few minutes you'll be complaining it is too hot."

Real Chinese water torture couldn't have dragged that
admission from him, though he found it to be true enough.
Elizabeth used the damp cloth on him to erase all trace of
their last lovemaking. She was thorough, pulling back his
foreskin to trickle water over the head. Her touch was not
delicate but perfunctory. Darkness, he thought, made her
bold. What she did made him hard. His penis started to swell
long before she abandoned the cloth in favor of her hands,

and by the time she lowered her mouth to him, he was ready to come out of his skin.

The orgasm that shuddered through him had the same intensity as Elizabeth's sobs. He cried out so that she was forced to cover his mouth with hers, swallowing even the sound of her name. She held him, fingering his hair until his body lay quiet again and his breathing came easily.

His head rested on her breast. He curled one hand in the filmy fabric of her gown, pulling it tight across her waist and hip. She had had no real pleasure tonight, he knew. Their coupling had been for him; she had seen to that. And now this . . .

He lifted his head enough to reach the tip of her breast with his mouth. He heard her soft moan. She had earned something for herself, Northam thought, and giving her pleasure would be his best revenge.

Chapter Eight

Standing at the bank of arched windows in the gallery, Northam had an unobstructed view of the guests gathered on the lawn for the archery contest. Targets had been placed on bales of hay near a stand of trees so even the most wayward arrow would have little chance of doing anyone injury. There were five targets, three of them traditional concentric circles of varying diameters and colors. The remaining two, in honor of the anniversary of Wellington's victory at Waterloo, were rather skillful renderings of Boney himself, powerful and glowering in his commander's full regalia.

Northam noticed that the women invariably aimed their bows at the bull's-eye. The men, when they were not giving advice or making wagers on the women's shots, sent their arrows flying toward Napoleon's cocked hat.

The archery contest was the last outdoor entertainment planned for the Battenburn rout. Northam knew that some drawing room amusement would take place that evening, but he had no idea what Lady Battenburn had arranged. Even Elizabeth said she did not know. Earlier in the week that same response from Elizabeth would have been met with skepticism on his part; however he had observed a certain lessening of the amity between Elizabeth and their

hostess, a coolness that was not easily measured except by
what no longer occurred between them.

Northam had not seen Louise draw Elizabeth to one side
to ask her advice or whisper a bit of gossip. They were also
less likely to be together in the same clutch of laughing
women. Lady Battenburn had disagreed with Elizabeth on
two occasions, both of them very public and rather pointed.
What struck Northam was Elizabeth's good-natured acceptance of the rebukes. She neither defended her position nor
offered a witty reply. She took the sting out of Louise's
words by graciously accepting them. Except for the fingers
that curled into gentle fists at her sides, Northam might have
been fooled into thinking she had actually taken them to
heart.

To the best of his recollection, this shift in the relationship
between Louise and Elizabeth had taken place following the
recovery of the snuffbox. Northam could imagine that Lady
Battenburn was distressed that it had been found in such a
manner, but what she thought Elizabeth could have done
differently to avoid that end continued to elude Northam.

It was also that same night that he had visited Elizabeth's
bedchamber. He could not help wondering what Lady Battenburn knew about that evening. He was unable to convince
himself that Elizabeth had shared any part of that night
with her friend, but he recognized that his thinking was not
entirely clear where Elizabeth was concerned. She might
have been moved to tell Louise that he had extended a
helping hand in the mistaken belief she was in need of it.
It was more doubtful that she would have mentioned that
he had offered to place her under his protection, first as his
mistress, later as his wife.

Still harder to conceive was Elizabeth relating any of the
intimacies they had traded in her bed. Far less difficult was
the act of bringing those intimacies to mind. With very little
effort he could summon the fragrance of her hair, the feel
of it under his fingertips, the taste of her skin on his lips.
The back of his neck prickled with the sensation of her nails
making a tracing at the tip of his spine. He could feel the

weight of her as she lay stretched along his full length. There was a stirring in his groin as he once again recalled the sweet hot suck of her mouth.

His eyes followed Elizabeth now as she took her place at the line to make her shot. With efficient, expert motions she took an arrow from the quiver and notched it. Like all the participants, she wore gloves and a leather guard to protect her hands and the vulnerable inside of her extended forearm. Northam thought she looked far too fragile to accomplish the task she had set for herself, yet he had every confidence that she would succeed.

As fluid and graceful as the moon goddess Artemis, Elizabeth drew back the string and raised the bow and arrow in a single, effortless motion. She held it extended, taking careful aim, then released two fingers on the string and let the arrow fly. By the immediate applause of her admirers, Northam knew she had found the target squarely at its center. He did not confirm the arrow's flight; his eyes remained on the slight curve of her body while he imagined the tremor she had absorbed at the taut bow's final release. He felt it too, a rush of intense pleasure that had nothing to do with this lawn entertainment.

Northam took one step toward the window and for a moment laid his forehead against a cooler pane of glass. He closed his eyes. He could feel himself inside her again, buried deep, held tightly, her slender body under his in a curve as fine and taut as that bow's. And then the release. Her cry. His groan. Their mouths fused, still hungry, straining for the last remnants of pleasure.

As deeply as they had drawn from that well, nothing was changed by it. Elizabeth had sent him on his way, still refusing his offers of help, protection, or marriage. Their last intimacy, coming as it had in the first hint of dawn's light, only served to make Elizabeth more resolute. Though she said nothing to him, he knew she realized he had not withdrawn from her that final time. It was the only thing she had truly asked of him in exchange for that night's pleasure, and in the end he had willfully denied her that peace of mind. If she understood how purposeful he had been, she still leveled no accusations at his head, but appeared to be saving the recriminations for herself.

At the window, Northam straightened but did not step back. Elizabeth was giving up her place at the line for Lady Powell. They chatted briefly, then Elizabeth turned and walked back to the large blue-and-white canopy that had been erected to protect the guests from the sun. All of the splendid grace that Elizabeth had shown with her bow was absent as she limped toward the tent.

This awkwardness of gait struck him anew. It was easy to forget that she had any limitations when he observed her at archery or on horseback. And he had intimate knowledge that there was nothing at all hesitant or faltering about the way she moved with him and against him. He had massaged the small of her back while she lay on her stomach, her head turned to the side away from him. He thought her eyes were closed, but when he leaned over her and peered closely, he saw moonlight reflected in the gold shards. He had laid his mouth softly against her temple as his hand reconfigured its shape to match the curve of her hip. She said nothing, but her breathing had quickened.

It should have satisfied him, this immediate response to his touch, but then she had turned so that her face was bathed in sliver-blue moonshine, and he glimpsed such a stark look of aloneness in her features that it twisted his insides. Here he was touching her, sharing her bed, her body, savoring the very air she breathed, and she felt nothing so keenly as her own aloneness. It was perhaps in that moment that Northam appreciated the depth of Elizabeth's isolation. What had come afterward did nothing to ease it. When he left her room that morning he realized he had come to feel only a little less alone than she.

Northam watched Elizabeth take a seat in the same circle as Lady Battenburn. His view was only that Louise acknowledged Elizabeth's presence. There seemed to be no exchange beyond that initial greeting. Elizabeth laughed at something

Lady Heathering said to her and while it drew Louise's attention, it did not draw a comment.

What then, Northam wondered, was the source of Lady Battenburn's coolness toward Elizabeth? Certainly there had been nothing like it directed toward him. Harrison was also unchanged in either his dealings with Elizabeth or his wife. It was probably just as well. There could be nothing gained by stepping into the middle of a misunderstanding between two women. Invariably they quickly repaired their rift and the well-meaning but hopelessly ill-equipped meddler was left to lick his wounds.

Northam had had four days and nights to consider what Louise might have overheard in Elizabeth's room that evening, either from the hallway or from the other side of the sliding wainscoting panel. If Lady Battenburn knew for a fact that Elizabeth had been with someone, Northam told himself that her response, whether she approved or disapproved, would have but one outcome: overwhelming concern for Elizabeth's welfare.

He wondered why, then, it still felt as if he were trying to convince himself of the obvious.

Elizabeth hoped her laughter was not forced. She believed that Lady Heathering's observation was meant to be amusing but she was not entirely certain. She had been listening with only half an ear, and it was inevitable that sooner or later she would be caught out with an inappropriate response. Right now it seemed that she had been given a reprieve, for Lady Heathering was repeating her comment for others to hear, and they gave her the same amused approbation Elizabeth had.

Resolved to keep her attention focused, Elizabeth turned politely toward Lady Powell when she returned to her chair, and inquired as to her success on the archery field.

"Oh, but I have not seemed to acquire any skill at the thing, no matter how much instruction I receive," Lady Powell said. She opened her fan and languidly waved it in front of her face. "My last shot went into the woods and scattered an entire flock of birds from the treetops."

Before Elizabeth could respond, Lady Heathering noted slyly, "Perhaps, dearest Grace, it is because you so enjoy the instruction that your form does not improve. I have a suspicion that your arrows may fly off into the boughs again and again, but invariably you never miss your target."

Lady Powell did not deign to comment, but her flush was no longer strictly the result of her previous exertions.

"Southerton has been attentive, has he not?" Lady Heathering continued. "It is a shame that we all leave tomorrow, though I suppose there is every chance Southerton will be attending the Hulltons' ball in August."

The exchange went back and forth between the two ladies with occasional comments from others in their circle. Elizabeth felt her attention wander even while her head swiveled to acknowledge one speaker, then the other.

Northam's absence at this entertainment was both a relief and a distraction. She found herself looking for him at odd moments, glancing back at the manse as though she might spy him at one of the windows or striding toward them across the lawn. Southerton explained his friend's decision not to participate in the contest as an indication of his complete lack of skill with a bow and a desire not to embarrass himself in front of others. Although she had not asked for any such explanation, Elizabeth listened to it out of deference to South and accepted it for the same reason. She had no doubt it was a complete fabrication.

She did not blame North in the least for not wanting to spend the afternoon in her company. She did not want to be with herself either. In the last four days they had managed to find separate interests. She was reading while he was riding. She attended the musicale while he explored the boxwood maze at the center of the garden with Lady Heathering. She played whist partnered with Southerton. North played at more serious cards with Lord Battenburn and his cronies. Elizabeth wondered what was occupying his time while she pretended to listen to careless conversation and play at a pastime in which she had little interest.

She had hoped he would not occupy so much of her thoughts. That, it seemed, was the wishful thinking. In truth, it was difficult to let any other thoughts intrude. She fully appreciated how many functions in the course of living were accomplished without her conscious direction. If she had had to choose between breathing and thinking about Northam, Elizabeth suspected her lungs would not have drawn air.

Her response to him remained a source of discomfort. It could not be easily explained by the fact that she had held herself aloof for so many years. How much was Northam responsible for breaching her defenses and how much had she intentionally lowered them? She had never once considered that she could be so receptive to the intimate attentions of another man. For years she had wandered on the fringes of life, thinking herself not merely immune to pleasure but without capacity for it. Now she wondered if she had just been afraid.

It was not so simple an explanation as that. She was still afraid. Deeply so. Yet in spite of that she had once again allowed herself to know the joyous coupling and robust passion that was possible between a man and a woman, this time without the complications of love. She could not say if it was better or worse, only that it was different.

She liked Northam. She had from the first, and nothing he'd done changed that. Indeed, Elizabeth told herself that if she had liked him a great deal less she might have accepted his offer to be his mistress. She would have had to have no regard for him at all in order to become his wife. He was fortunate that she thought so well of him.

His offer to help her, even when he could not comprehend the nature of her difficulties, did not come as a complete surprise. The colonel's interest in her would have made Northam sensitive. She had anticipated that overture. The other offers were far more troubling. Elizabeth could feel her relief rising in steady increments as the time for their parting neared. Tomorrow morning Northam would take his leave. In spite of what she said to him, she knew she could avoid a second encounter. There might be only one carousel, but he would never meet her if she was at the center of its operation. She only had to convince Louise that was where she needed to be and the rest would take care of itself.

"I'm not at all certain you can trust Southerton," Lady Heathering was saying. "Have you ever noticed that he talks a great deal and says very little? I rather think it is by design, though what his purpose might be I cannot say."

"He likes to hear himself," said Lady Powell, not unkindly. "I hardly think it is the ruler by which I should measure his trustworthiness."

Lady Heathering waved her hand, dismissing this. "You do not take my meaning, Grace. It is . . ."

And so it went, just beyond Elizabeth's awareness, words flying like arrows over her head with an occasional strike at the center of her heart. She felt the impact now when the subject turned to trust.

"Trust me, Elizabeth." It was the last thing North had said to her before he left her room, and because he put it to her with such gravity she believed she could give him no response but the one she knew to be the truth.

"I do," she had said. She could have left it there, allowing him to complete the step that would have taken him beyond the door and out of her hearing, but she found herself unable to do that. She owed him one more truth whether he wanted it or not. *"But you must never trust me."*

He had looked as if he wanted to argue. Elizabeth had closed the door on him to prevent that and turned the key for good measure. Since those parting words they had traded less than a dozen sentences. Elizabeth had not suspected she could feel such a loss at a thing she knew must come about.

She lifted her head now as Southerton approached. Her smile was warm and unwavering. Only she knew that a pistol at the base of her skull could not have pushed words past the lump in her throat.

* * *

The guests at Battenburn gathered in the largest of the first-floor drawing rooms for the evening's surprise entertainment. There had been whispers about it all afternoon as Lady Battenburn let delicious hints drop like cake crumbs. Some said it was to be a special visitor, one invited just for this evening. Others believed it would be another game of twisted questions and enigmatic answers. There were those who wagered it would be charades and those who gambled it would involve cards.

When Lady Battenburn announced the entertainment all who had engaged in speculation discovered none of it was entirely without foundation. There was indeed a guest and an opportunity to pose questions. No doubt, Louise told them, there would be some charade among the assembly as it would be difficult for all of them to tell the truth. And, finally, cards would be turned over and fates revealed.

"We are very lucky tonight," Louise said to her hushed audience, "to have engaged the services of Madame Fortuna. I have it on the most reliable authority that her prognostications are without peer. She correctly foretold Napoleon's fall, exile, and subsequent assumption of power. She predicted it would be Elba that would hold him. It has occurred to me that with such successes in her background, the small matter of the Gentleman Thief should pose no problem for her."

She smiled gaily and without guile, as if the matter of using the fortune-teller to sniff out the thief had just occurred to her. Whether or not her guests believed that this was the case was of no concern to her. She had their complete attention, and it was this position at the center of everything that gave her such satisfaction. She glanced over the assembly and briefly acknowledged her husband's reserved smile, Lady Heathering's excitement, Mr. Rutherford's skepticism, Southerton's amusement, and finally Elizabeth's look of complete resignation.

Embracing her triumph as if it were a tangible thing,

Louise lifted her hand and indicated the rear entrance to the drawing room. At her gesture two footmen opened the doors and revealed Lady Battenburn's most lauded guest to the gathering.

Northam could not quite believe that it *was* Madame Fortuna. Expecting to see an old woman bent by time, he was confounded to see that while he had aged, she had moved forward through the years apparently unscathed. He was ten again, sitting across from her at the table inside her covered wagon, the crystal ball between them. Her graying hair was caught in a silk scarf. Copper earrings dangled from her long lobes and almost brushed her hunched shoulders. She wore a black dress and a purple shawl that was held in place by an enormous lapis lazuli brooch. Her hands were slender, rough-knuckled, and he remembered what they had felt like cupping his face.

It was only much later, after he and the rest of the Compass Club had left, that North realized she had never once touched him.

Southerton excused himself from Lady Powell's side and weaved through the guests to reach North. He stood just to one side and slightly behind his friend. His voice reached North's ear quietly. "She looks exactly as I remember her. How is that possible?"

North shook his head. He was still asking himself the same question. His glance shifted to Lady Battenburn, but she never looked in his direction. "What do you think of her plan?" he asked South.

"To catch a thief?"

He nodded.

"With any other fortune-teller I would say it had no merit." South shrugged. "But with Madame one never knows. She's a clever sort, as I recall. If the Gentleman is really among us, he should be afraid."

It occurred to Northam that perhaps fear was the real tool Louise meant to use to flush him out. Apparently Lady Battenburn intended to end her rout in a most memorable fashion. "Do you think she'll remember us?"

South grinned. "Only if you ask to see her quim."

North knew he should have expected the answer. It was the one he would have given if South had posed the same question. Still, he had to choke back his laughter, covering it with a hard cough that brought heads swiveling in his direction and gave South an excuse to slap him hard on the back.

"Sorry," South said when Northam winced.

"Don't pretend you didn't enjoy that."

Southerton merely chuckled. He looked around, saw that Lady Powell was turning about in a manner that would put him squarely off her port bow. "Excuse me, old chum, but the Lady Powell is tacking in my direction. I'm off." He moved smoothly away from Northam and into the crush around Madame Fortuna's table.

Out of the corner of his eye North saw the woman make a course adjustment. Poor Southerton. He was going to have to find himself another female. No other tactic was likely to divert Lady Powell's interest. As if Southerton could read his mind, North watched his friend slip one arm through Elizabeth's and lead her to the far perimeter of the eager onlookers. He noticed that Elizabeth did not hesitate to go with South. Sighing inaudibly as he watched their progress, he wondered if he would forever experience this odd little lurch in his heart. Elizabeth's words came back to him. *But you should never trust me.* It seemed that she meant to remind him.

The guests gave Madame Fortuna a wide stage on which to perform. They clustered in the shape of a horseshoe around her table so that everyone might see. Lord Allen volunteered to go first. He slipped into the chair opposite Madame Fortuna and smiled carelessly as she shuffled and cut the tarot cards. When she asked him to choose one he did so with a flourish and gave it to her. She studied it for several long moments, considering its meaning in the context of the question posed by Lord and Lady Battenburn, then fastened her dark eyes on Allen. Her thin lips were not set kindly and when she pointed her index finger at him his own smile vanished abruptly.

"A thief you are," she said. Years of smoking cheroots had lent her voice an authentic huskiness that she had only feigned in her younger days. She felt the guests lean toward her as she spoke. "But no gentleman. What you take has only the illusion of being freely given." She wagged the finger a little, cautioning him. "You have not mistaken me. You know of what I speak."

"So does most everyone else," South whispered against Elizabeth's ear. "She's as good as said Allen's making free with someone's wife. If he doesn't get up now, she'll tell us the details. Don't think she won't."

Elizabeth was relieved to see Lord Allen jump to his feet and hold out the chair for someone else to take a turn. He joked lightly with his rapt audience, but Elizabeth saw he never caught either Lord or Lady Heathering's eye. She also noticed no one was anxious to take up the chair. She certainly counted herself among the reluctant. Elizabeth knew Southerton's confidence in Madame Fortuna was not misplaced. Although she had no knowledge of his previous encounter with the fortune-teller twenty-two years earlier, she had little doubt that Louise had filled Madame's head with all manner of interesting tidbits about her guests. It only remained to be seen how judiciously they would be revealed. Madame's announcement to Lord Allen did not bode well for any of them.

Mr. Rutherford cleared his throat and stepped to the forefront. "I don't mind having a go. It's not as if I have any secrets." He had to grab the chair to keep Allen from thrusting it at his chest. His friend's eagerness to be away was most palpable. Rutherford lifted the tails of his frock coat and made a show of sitting down.

"Peacock," Madame said under her breath. She gathered the cards, shuffled them several times, then had Rutherford cut the deck and choose his card. It was from the Minor Arcana, that group of cards that represented the small dramas and concerns of living day to day. Here the Six of Pentacles,

showing that magical sign stamped on a coin, reinforced so
perfectly what the baroness had already told her about this
man. "I see here that great wealth may be in your grasp.
Your debts will be paid by the one you marry. Lest you
think you made the better bargain, beware that she will
also have her way." She glanced at him and caught his
astonishment. "But you said you had no secrets. I thought,
then, that everyone must know the extent of your debts and
your need to marry well and quickly."

Rutherford just managed to keep the chair upright as he
came to his feet. His face was flushed. Lady Powell pointedly
turned away when he glanced at her. Miss Caruthers stepped
closer to her parents. Once word of his impoverished state
became known among the *ton* he would have to cast his net
so widely his wife was likely to be an American. It made
his head ache to think on it.

A half-dozen guests took their turn in the chair before
Southerton boldly walked up to her. Not everyone who had
come before her had had the same experience as Allen
and Rutherford. Madame Fortuna predicted that shy Emily
Farthingale would find a publisher for her novel. Since no
one knew she had been penning one, it caused a favorable
stir. Sir Arthur Armitage heard that he could expect a boy
child in seven months. He leaped to his feet and found his
lady, lifting her and his unborn heir several inches off the
ground.

There was also favorable news for Lord and Lady Meri-
wether as they took their turns in succession, and finally for
Miss Stevens, who learned there would be an engagement
soon.

Even Lord Battenburn had cheerfully given in to his
guests' cajoling and sat in the chair. Madame Fortuna actually laughed when she saw the card he chose. His was one
from the Major Arcana, representing a powerful theme in
his life and describing the forces that moved him. She tapped
the Magician with her index finger. "We are not so different,
you and I," she said in her husky whisper. "Both of us are
arrangers of fates, both of us fond of a twist in the tale. You

play at cards yourself, my lord, though I think you have not been so fortunate to see in yours what I see in mine."

Nodding, Battenburn had pulled a deck from inside his coat and spread the cards across the table. He flipped them back and forth expertly before asking her to choose one. She did so and showed it to the guests. It was the queen of hearts, and when he pulled it from the deck a minute later, after shuffling and cutting and fanning the cards open and closed, he announced that the queen signified her and the heart she had taken was his own. Battenburn had further amused his guests by kissing Madame Fortuna's crepe cheek. His performance made her appreciate his skill; after all, it was not the seven of clubs he had forced on her.

When it was Southerton's turn, he spun the chair around and straddled it. His boyish grin was not lost on Madame Fortuna. "Rascal," she said, though there was no sting in her voice. She shuffled the cards carefully while he leaned forward. Rather than have him pick only one as she had had others do, she laid ten cards out in the ancient pattern of the Celtic Cross. "What do you see?" he asked when she fell silent. He felt a small prickle of alarm along his spine.

"You have a friend here," she said finally.

South had to strain to hear her. He doubted anyone else did. "Yes."

"There is a threat."

He frowned. "To my friend?"

Madame Fortuna hesitated. "Yes. But not only—"

Lady Powell called from the half-circle of spectators. "It is no good to us if you keep Southerton's reading to yourself. Tell us what the cards tell you." There was laughter, and murmurs of agreement. "Shall he be married before the year is out?"

Obliging her audience, Madame Fortuna pointed to the center of the cross where two cards were overlaid at a right angle to each other. She smiled and tapped it once, pulling South's attention to the Fool lying over the Lovers.

Southerton nodded. It was not difficult to interpret her meaning. "She says we're not suited," he told Lady Powell.

"But I am not inclined to believe her this time." He saw that Madame Fortuna meant to warn him differently so he stood. "I understand," he said quietly. "Completely."

When South rose he did not return to Elizabeth, but went to Northam instead. He drew his friend back from the other guests while someone else stepped up to take a turn.

North regarded Southerton with faint amusement. "I do not know how you accomplished it, but you have managed to alienate the affections of two women now. Lady Powell is so furious she's—"

"Stuff it."

Northam was immediately alert, the exact state in which South intended he should be. "What's happened?"

"She says there is some threat."

"Elizabeth?"

"No. Madame Fortuna."

North relaxed. Had Elizabeth given the warning he would have taken it seriously. He chuckled. "I doubt there is any need to worry. It is all part and parcel of her performance."

Southerton was less sure. "How can you forget that she predicted the deaths of your father and brother?"

"I haven't forgotten, but as I've told you before, she never said anything so straightforward as that. It was more of a feeling I got from her. Anyway, it was years and years after I saw her that they died." Northam remembered how much he had taken his brief exchange with Madame Fortuna to heart. Days and weeks, even months could pass and he would not think of what she had said to him; then it would come back and he would live long minutes and hours in absolute dread of the passing of his brother and father. It was a horrible manner in which to finish out his childhood. For a long time he actually considered trying to find her and make her recant her exchange with him, just to give him some peace of mind. "She is harmless," he told South. "It is a parlor amusement, nothing more."

"She knew I had a friend."

One of North's brows kicked up. "Oh? And did she give you a name?"

"You are not amusing."

North's laughter was low. Through a narrow gap in the spectators he saw that Lady Powell was being pinned back in her chair by the fortune-teller. He could not hear what was being said to her, but by the titters in the crowd they were taking some pleasure in her discomfort. He wondered at their lack of empathy when there was little doubt they would also find themselves facing Madame Fortuna. "Have done, South. It can give you nothing but worry to take her words too seriously."

Southerton considered the truth of that. "She showed me two other cards," he said quietly. "Lovers and a fool. What do you make of that?"

"Just what you told the salivating crowd. You and Lady Powell do not suit. It would seem Madame Fortuna knows it as well and is trying to warn you off."

In other circumstances Southerton would have laughed. Now his gray eyes simply narrowed. "That's just it, North. Your handmaiden comment aside, the romance with Lady Powell is in her mind, not mine, and we have certainly never been lovers."

North frowned. "What are you saying?"

"I don't think Madame meant the cards for me. They were a message for you." Southerton would not have been surprised if his friend had landed him a facer. He was at the very least prepared for a verbal blow, something that would land low and hard. When Northam made no reply but looked instead to Elizabeth, South knew he was the one who had hit the mark. "What does it mean, North?"

Northam shook his head, though he suspected strongly that he was the fool in question. Elizabeth had been standing off to the side of the guests ever since Southerton had deserted her. Her complexion was pale and her eyes were rather too large for her face. Far from enjoying the amusement Lady Battenburn had arranged for them, she looked as if she were going to be ill.

And well she might, he thought uncharitably. Elizabeth Penrose carried more secrets than Wellington's couriers at the height of the war. Which one, he wondered, did she most fear would be exposed?

North shifted his weight from one foot to the other, quelling the urge to go to her side. In spite of the fact that his presence would not be welcomed, it was still difficult to stay away. If there was some way he could spare her the agony of sitting in front of Madame, he would do it. Nothing occurred to him. Lord and Lady Battenburn had seemed to intend that everyone should participate, and North considered, not for the first time, that they were perhaps more serious about catching the Gentleman Thief than Louise's lighthearted introduction indicated.

"Return to Lady Elizabeth," he said, "while I take my turn with Madame. Be prepared to hear that I copied from your paper on the geography exam in our second year at Hambrick."

"You did? But I was a very poor student of geography."

"I know. I was resisting Grandfather's efforts to make a scholar out of me."

Southerton's shout of laughter brought a dozen heads around. He disarmed their censure with an apologetic grin. "Very well." He touched North's elbow, his features set with concern again. "But have a care, will you? I can't help thinking Madame Fortuna knows more than we do."

North was certain of it, though how much of the fortune-teller's prescience was real and how much had some other source was still a question in his mind. "Go!" He gave Southerton a small push forward when he saw Elizabeth was moving determinedly through the guests. "Stop her at least until I have had my chance."

South navigated through the throng with the agility and grace of a skiff, tacking first one way, then the other, until he was at Elizabeth's side. Once arrived, he glanced over at North and received a grateful acknowledgment for his efforts. Accepting no protest from Elizabeth, he linked arms with her and drew her back from the front line of onlookers.

"I was prepared to go next," she told him, her jaw set.

"Were you? Then I am not sorry. It is rather less amusing

to be in the fish bowl than watching the fish. Do you think
Lady Battenburn intended it so?''

''I cannot possibly know Louise's intentions.''

''Odd. I had come to think of you as her confidante.''

Elizabeth's tone was deliberately cool. ''Then you mistook the matter.'' She withdrew her arm from Southerton's
and stood on tiptoe, craning her head above Lord Heathering's broad shoulder to see who had taken her place at
the table. Her heart hammered in her chest. Northam. She
gripped Southerton's arm, this time twisting as much of her
sleeve as she could get between her fingers.

Southerton looked down at the fist clenched in the tight
woolen fabric of his frock coat. ''Lady Elizabeth?'' He said
her name quietly and made no mention of the fact that she
was badly creasing the material. He almost recoiled from
the accusation in her eyes when she raised her face to his.

''You planned this,'' she said tightly.

South did not pretend not to know what she meant. ''It
was inevitable that North should take a turn,'' he whispered.
''What difference can it make if he goes before you?''

All the difference, she wanted to say. But she could not
explain that to Southerton. With some effort she unclenched
her fingers from South's sleeve and let her hand fall to her
side. ''I want to see,'' she said. ''Take me to the front.''

Southerton had no good reason for not complying except
that it went against his instincts. Short of holding Elizabeth
in place himself, which would surely cause a stir, he really
had no choice but to assist her. He tapped Lord Heathering
on the shoulder and bid him make a place for them. In short
order he and Elizabeth were standing on the inner edge of
the onlookers.

Now that he was sitting so close to Madame Fortuna,
Northam saw that his first impression had not been entirely
correct. The fortune-teller had aged. The creases at the corner
of her mouth and eyes were deeper. There was a permanent
furrow above her brows. Liver spots dotted the back of her
hands. She seemed shorter, but he allowed that it might only

be that he had grown taller and straighter, while her posture was inclined forward, her slight shoulders hunched.

He smiled faintly as she shuffled the cards. After so many years and all the differences time had brought to his own features, North did not think it possible that she could remember him. He was, after all, but one of thousands she had seen over the years. Still, he had to temper his own sense of perverse humor. He was very much of a mind to ask her if he might see her quim. The subsequent uproar would effectively put a period to this amusement and make him a pariah in all but the most libertine of circles. He chuckled to himself as he considered there might be no unwelcome consequences to posing the question after all.

"Something amuses you?" Madame Fortuna inquired sharply.

Northam cleared his throat. "No, Madame."

"Your throat is parched. May we have some libation here?" She waved imperiously to Lord Battenburn. "Peach brandy, perhaps."

North blinked at her. "*Peach* brandy?"

Madame Fortuna's features did not change in the least. "Why, yes. You like the taste of a peach, do you not, my lord?" She paused as a footman brought a tray with a decanter and two glasses to the table. Putting down her cards, she waved the servant away and elected to pour the drinks herself. "You will see," she said, handing one of the small snifters to Northam, "if it doesn't do the trick."

North felt his fingers tingle as she passed the glass to him. At first he thought her hand had brushed his, but then he realized they were holding the snifter in two different places, she by the bowl, he at the stem.

"Just so," she said quietly. "It is as it ever was." Her dark eyes bore into his, communicating quite clearly that he was not alone in the memory of their earlier encounter. Since that afternoon at the fair more than a score of years in the past, Bess Bowles had been in anticipation of a second encounter. She knew neither where nor when, just that it would happen. "Only you," she told him. "It is only with you."

Northam frowned. "I don't understand."

Laughter cackled from her. She knocked back the peach brandy with the same careless appreciation she had for her gin. "Neither do I." For weeks after the fair she had lived in alarm of being visited again by the second sight. When it never came to her she was almost able to convince herself that she had imagined it. Almost. Sometimes there would be a tingling, a fine tremor that would move from her fingertips to her spine and trip lightly all the way down her back. When she put questions to the people who raised that sensation she inevitably discovered there was some connection to the man sitting across from her now. She could not explain it. She wasn't even certain that she believed it. Yet she could not deny the experience.

"Drink up," she said to him. She laid down the first card and nodded thoughtfully, not surprised to see that she had tapped into the powerful force of the Major Arcana. "A sacrifice . . ."

Northam stared at the picture of an empty gallows with the noose prepared. He had an urge to slip a finger under his collar and stock and loosen the fit against his neck. He was very much aware that all those looking on had ceased whispering. "It is not death?"

"Oh, heaven's no. You may ease your mind on that account. The Hanged Man can signify letting go or a reversal of current circumstances. Here I believe a sacrifice is to be made." She paused and added darkly, "Condemnation."

He finished raising the snifter to his lips and drank the brandy with as much disregard for the fine taste as Madame Fortuna had shown. He glanced over his shoulder at South. "I am only condemned," he said, grinning. "Not doomed." Southerton, he thought, could have made an effort to return more than a wan smile. Beside him, Elizabeth looked as if she might faint. North turned back to Madame Fortuna. "*My* mind is eased. Perhaps you could say something that would ease others. Who condemns me?"

Madame Fortuna took the top card from the deck and laid it over the Hanged Man.

North stared at the Empress, that card that related to motherhood, abundance, and nature. The voluptuous figure oddly reminded him of the baroness, and he looked to Madame Fortuna, a question in his eyes.

She said only, "A woman close to you."

Southerton felt Elizabeth's fingers claw his sleeve again. He placed his free hand over hers and willed her to remain silent and unmoving.

Though it pained him to do so, Northam asked with credible carelessness, "Are you being literal or figurative?" This had the desired effect of dispelling the pall that had settled over the drawing room.

In response, Madame Fortuna turned over a third card, this one a horned figure. She placed it on top of the lovers. "I believe it is the devil you know."

Northam had had enough. He started to rise.

"Sit down, my lord."

It was said so sharply and with such authority that Northam found himself firmly planted. This raised laughter from his audience, and he could not help but smile himself. "Very well. What else do you have for me, Madame?"

She held up the next card so that others might see it at the same time as he. It was the Seven of Pentacles. "This not only signifies reward," she explained to everyone, "but a change in direction. Wealth, I think. A treasure, perhaps, but one that is not your own."

Icy fingers began working their way up Northam's spine. He kept his voice even and schooled his features. "Explain yourself."

"You have something that does not belong to you."

A small vertical crease appeared between Northam's brows. "You will have to explain that as well."

Madame Fortuna put aside the cards in her hand and fanned out the ones she had already placed on the table. The Hanged Man. The Empress. The Devil. The Seven of Pentacles. There was no mistaking the signs, and she could not fault her own interpretation. She saw that when her hand passed over the cards it was trembling. The cause was not difficultly to know. She wished above anything that she could do differently by this man.

She remembered how very young he had been, the sweet innocence in his face when he had asked her that outrageous question. He was older, certainly, and his dark cobalt eyes had long since lost their guileless appeal, but Bess Bowles did not doubt his fundamental decency. That basic character trait had not been altered. She had known of its existence two and twenty years ago and she knew it now. She would have protected him if the cards had fallen differently, but here, with this man above all others, she knew they did not lie.

Against everything she would have wagered, Brendan David Hampton, sixth Earl of Northam, was the one known to all of the *ton* as the Gentleman Thief.

"It is Lady Battenburn's necklace," she said. "It can be found in your trunk. There is a small pocket in the lining for valuables. That is where it has been secreted away."

Northam's head snapped up. There was a buzzing between his ears that could not be solely explained by the frantic whispering going on at his back. "You are mistaken," he said with soft menace. But even before she shook her head and denied his words, he sensed that he was the one mistaken.

"Oh, but you must be," Lady Battenburn said. She clapped her hands together just below her rounded chin and left them there in an attitude of prayer. "Why, you have not spoken to everyone. I was sure Lord Northam would not even be among the suspects. He's as rich as Croesus. Everyone knows that."

Everyone did. While not one of the guests liked to think they were one of Louise's prime suspects, they let this small outrage pass and found their relief could mingle quite comfortably with pity for Northam's dilemma.

Lord Battenburn approached the table. "I must agree with my wife, Madame. It is not possible."

She shrugged. "Anything is possible."

Northam regarded Battenburn without emotion. The baron did not seem to want to suggest the obvious solution to their problem. Asking to search the trunk would be a serious breach of trust in itself and posed potential embarrassment for all of them. Battenburn's silence forced Northam to make the offer himself. "I invite you to look for your lady's necklace among my things."

Battenburn shook his head. "No. I will not have it."

Northam did not think he imagined the noose was getting tighter. He glanced down at the cards fanned out before him to see if the rope's circumference had indeed shrunk.

"Oh, but think of your reputation, my lord." It was Lady Powell, her hands steepled beneath her chin in a manner similar to Louise's.

Northam had not seen so much piety outside the framed painting of a Renaissance Madonna. "I think it can only be enhanced by this, my lady." He came to his feet. "Tell me that you do not think it quite thrilling that I may be the Gentleman Thief."

Lady Powell's scarlet cheeks gave her away. "That is very wrong of you, Northam," she scolded. She looked to Southerton for assistance. "Tell him. He could be transported for this."

Southerton wished she had not raised that particular specter before he'd had a chance to sort out what was happening. He tried to divine inspiration from Northam's expression and found it perfectly inscrutable. He had no idea what tack he might take to save his friend further embarrassment. In the end he decided to save him from transport. "That is only if the necklace is found," he said. "And I assure you, it will not be."

Northam sighed. He was not certain of any such thing, but he appreciated that South couldn't know that. Trust South to offer a spirited but wholly unreliable defense.

Battenburn fingered one of the crisp folds of his stock as he contemplated his options. "I suppose," he said finally, "that there is nothing for it but to have a look." He surveyed his guests and offered a tentative suggestion. "Perhaps we should have the trunk brought here."

No one save Northam responded. "By all means. But in the interest of fairness, send two men to get it."

"Of course. Southerton and Allen. Is that agreeable?"

"It is." North was more certain than ever that it would not alter the outcome. He gestured toward the door. "Gentlemen?"

South had gotten used to the pressure of Elizabeth's fingers against his arm. He did not realize at first what was halting his progress. He drew close to her long enough to surreptitiously disengage her fist. "It will be all right," he whispered, his lips barely moving around the words.

Elizabeth stared at him, unblinking, willing herself not to show the depth of her distress. "No. No, it won't."

There was no time to reason with her, even if there was a place. Allen was waiting. South gave her wrists a gentle squeeze, then turned.

The wait was interminable. The guests watched Allen and Southerton leave the room and no one seemed to be able to look away from the doors while they were gone. The footmen stationed on either side of the entrance grew uncomfortable under the scrutiny to which they were subjected, but like Praetorian guards of Ancient Rome, would have fallen on a sharp object rather than relinquish their posts.

Northam alone did not watch the entrance. He sat with one hip resting on Madame Fortuna's table and his other leg extended casually in front of him. It occurred to him that he was, perhaps, the most untroubled person in the room. Even the Gentleman Thief, unless he was entirely without conscience, would be having some qualms. Not that they would be enough to save him. He could not expect that the real thief would step forward to take his place, not when he had gone to so much trouble to put Lady Battenburn's necklace in his trunk. No, the Gentleman meant for him to take the blame.

Northam sighed, folding his arms loosely across his chest.

This was going to play hell with his mother's plans to marry him off.

There was a stir in the gathering as footsteps approached. The doors were parted, and South and Allen walked into the room carrying Northam's leather-bound trunk between them. They set it on the floor in front of Madame Fortuna's table.

"We haven't opened it," Lord Allen offered unnecessarily.

Lady Battenburn joined her husband. "I should certainly hope not, else what would have been the point?" She quieted when Harrison placed his hand soothingly on her shoulder. She bit her lip instead of adding to the tension with inconsequential chatter.

North gave a short nod to indicate to Southerton that he should open it. South lifted the latches and raised the lid. He stepped aside, offering the opportunity to explore the contents to Lord Allen. With some reluctance, Allen bent over the trunk and ran his hand along the lined lid. It was only a moment before he paused in his search, his fingers having dipped into a slit in the damask lining.

"You've found something?" North asked. When Allen nodded, Northam went on. "You may as well bring it out for everyone to see."

Three of Lord Allen's fingers slipped inside the lining and rooted for the object he had felt under his palm. It came out easily, and diamonds cascaded over his extended fingers like a sunlit waterfall.

Not surprisingly there was a collective gasp. Northam felt all the attention riveted on him. He said to no one in particular, "I don't suppose it matters that I neither took the necklace nor hid it there."

Batterburn cleared his throat. He plucked at his sleeve, removing an imaginary piece of lint as he considered how best to respond. "Can you prove it?"

The answer came from a most unexpected quarter, at least as the guests would report it in subsequent accounts.

Lady Elizabeth Penrose stepped forward. "Lord Northam

cannot be the thief,'' she said calmly. ''He was with me the morning it was stolen.'' In the event there was anyone who mistook her meaning, she added, ''And all of the night before.''

Chapter Nine

There was nothing for it but that they should marry. The details of the event were left up to others. Southerton procured a special license on behalf of his friend. The baron spoke to the vicar and made arrangements for the use of the village church. Lady Battenburn pressed the cook to make preparations for a lavish wedding breakfast, brought in her London modiste to attend to Elizabeth's gown and trousseau, and personally selected the flowers to be cut for bouquets and garlands. It was left to North and Elizabeth to inform their respective families. Of necessity this news came to the Dowager Countess of Northam and the Earl of Rosemont by express post. Lack of time, rather than cowardice, dictated that there could be no visits before the event.

The guests at Battenburn left on schedule, their regret at having to go somewhat mitigated by the fact that they were the advance guard of the most delicious *on dit* this year. They agreed to a person that the baron and baroness had provided a most diverting fortnight and were to be congratulated for so many memorable entertainments, particularly the revelations of the last night.

The prospective bride and groom were permitted little time in each other's company. Neither of them objected to this dictate, finding they were not at all eager to discuss how they had arrived at such an end.

Following dinner on the eve of their wedding, they walked side by side in the park at Battenburn. Behind them, at what he conceived was a respectful distance, strolled Southerton. He had raised mild objections to playing duenna, but no one thought his barn-door-closed-after-the-horse-was-out argument to be compelling.

The crushed stone garden paths were bleached white as the long twilight gradually gave way to moonshine. Standing torches lighted the crumbling corners of the abbey ruins that bordered the western edge of the park. There was virtually no breeze, but the air was not heavy. More than forty varieties of roses lent their fragrance to the evening; the scent was delicate, not cloying. Occasionally a pheasant stirred in the bushes or a plump rabbit darted for cover.

"I think I will make myself comfortable on this bench," Southerton announced. His voice echoed rather disconcertingly off the ruins. "In the event that anyone should want to know."

Elizabeth managed a faint smile. She kept her eyes straight ahead on the path. "Poor Lord Southerton. This cannot be but an onerous task for him."

"There are others more deserving of your sympathy than South." Northam meant for the words to be lightly spoken. Instead they came out stiffly, edged with reproof.

"Yourself, you mean?"

"You know I do not."

"I assure you, I do not know it at all. Why should such a thing about your character be evident to me? You must allow that we are not so very well acquainted." Elizabeth's shoes crunched the stones underfoot. She felt one work its way between her leather sole and the welt. "In any event, were you in need of sympathy I would be of no inclination to offer it."

Northam muttered something wholly unintelligible under his breath.

"Just so," she agreed.

He couldn't help it; he laughed.

Elizabeth was not proof against that sound. She suspected it would always be the proverbial chink in her armor. She felt the tightness in her chest ease so that the next breath she drew required less effort. "Have you received a reply from the dowager countess, my lord?"

"Will you not call me North?" he asked. "Or Brendan?" When she said nothing, he sighed and continued. "No, my mother is much too busy arranging for her visit to Battenburn to spare time for correspondence."

Elizabeth looked at him sharply. "You jest." But she could see that he did not. In profile his perfectly cast features were limned with moonlight. One corner of his mouth was tilted upward. "You do not mind that she is to come?"

"It would do no good to mind it. She will have her way." He turned his head in Elizabeth's direction and glimpsed panic that she could not quite conceal. "I should like to allay your fears," he told her, "but I collect I could not. South gets on well with her; perhaps you would believe you worry over nothing if you heard it from him."

"Lord Southerton did not force your hand in marriage. Your mother has no cause to think ill of him."

Years under the command of Colonel Blackwood had taught Northam to choose his battles. He was not willing to engage in this one, at least at this time. "And your family?" he asked. "What have you heard?"

Elizabeth felt the stone wedge its way under her foot. The discomfort gave her a point of focus and helped her answer with credible indifference. "My father has written to the baron. He will not be coming."

"I see."

"No, I don't think you do, but it is kind of you not to inquire further." She pretended interest in her silk shawl, adjusting the loose knot at her breasts. "Harrison has agreed to give me away."

Northam had to strain to hear her. "Is that agreeable to you? Or to your father?"

Elizabeth shrugged.

Northam paused on the stone path. Elizabeth came to a halt a half-step in front of him. Her head was bowed and she did not look back. "No matter the circumstances of our wedding," he said, "I would not have you agree to anything that causes you discomfort."

"Have a care, my lord. You cannot know the half of what causes me discomfort."

He reached out and lightly touched her elbow. "Look at me, Elizabeth." He waited, aware of the scent of roses, the flicker of the torchlight in her hair, and the slow thud of his own heart. He wondered what he would do if she did not turn and was glad he did not have to answer that now. The stones shifted softly as she slowly pivoted. "If you mean in bed, know now that I would have nothing from you that is not given freely. I want you to tell me that you know it will be your choice."

She stared at him. His sincerity wrenched her heart and his naïveté made her want to scream at him. She said quietly, "You know nothing at all of my choices."

"Then tell me."

"I cannot explain it to you. Suffice it to say, I will accommodate your every whim in our bedchamber. You need not concern yourself."

Northam found he was actually entertaining the thought of striking her. He could see himself drawing back his hand and letting it fly, laying his palm smartly across her cheek. She would reel backward, probably stumble and fall, but he never once saw her drop her chin or raise an arm to protect herself. She would stare at him, not precisely defiant, but not resisting.

She made him afraid sometimes. For her. For himself.

"I don't hear anything," Southerton called from his position in the garden. He was stretched out negligently on the bench, his back wedged in one corner and his long legs extended diagonally into the path. He used an index finger to tip back the brim of his polished beaver hat and made a peripheral assessment of the sudden quiet. "What is toward? If it is kissing, one of you must demonstrate the presence of mind to kick up the stones a bit, as if you were still walking. I assure you, I can be fooled.''

He felt rather than saw one of those stones whiz inches from his nose. South was also certain he heard the word *fool* uttered in disagreeable accents. His mouth twitched. He let his hat drop back into place and folded his arms across his chest. Stones once again crunched underfoot as he settled in for the duration.

Northam found pitching that stone served as an effective release. He fell in step beside Elizabeth. He could not help but notice her limp was more pronounced. Good manners dictated that he should at least offer her the opportunity to rest. He remained silent, certain that he was with the one woman who required no invitation from him to do as she pleased.

Elizabeth stopped fiddling with her apricot shawl and let her hands fall to her sides. ''I daresay I will provoke you again,'' she said quietly.

''The same has occurred to me.''

She nodded. ''Shall you beat me?''

Put before him so very baldly, Northam felt like something less than a man for having even imagined such an end. Almost as troubling was that he had been so ineffective in concealing his thoughts from her. ''I will never raise a hand to you.''

Given in the manner of a solemn pledge, Elizabeth did not question his sincerity. Rather she considered he did not know how sorely his honor would be tested. ''I will give you cause,'' she said.

Northam did not smile. ''Of that I am certain.'' He raised his elbow. ''Will you not take my arm?''

Elizabeth recognized the subject was closed. Having said what she considered most important, she was also not eager to belabor her point. She slipped her arm through his. ''South is a good friend, is he not?''

Northam supposed her comment was not a complete non sequitur. Even though he would not have struck her, she must have realized that South's intervention was timely. "He is the very best of friends."

"And Eastlyn and Mr. Marchman?"

"The same."

"You are indeed fortunate."

"I am."

"You must not think that our marriage will change the nature of your alliance with these men."

Northam frowned slightly as he considered her words. He decided to be honest. "At the risk of shattering what remains of your good opinion of me, I confess that it never once occurred to me."

"I suppose that is because you have had mistresses before, and their place in your life was set and interfered little." When she glanced at him she saw his frown had deepened. "Clearly I have done much to raise your concerns when my intention was quite the opposite. I wanted to assure you that I shall not mind if you choose to spend a great deal of time in the company of your friends."

Northam's tone was dry. "Am I to suppose from this that you wish to be treated as my mistress, or that you shall be content to see me as little as possible?"

She averted her face and fell silent.

"Are you thinking or merely speechless?" When she made no response he let it pass. "I believe it is quite likely that with you in my London residence the Compass Club will choose to meet there instead of White's."

"Do you mean to flatter me, my lord?"

"Is such a thing possible?"

Elizabeth found herself smiling. "I had not thought so."

Taking a turn on the park's inner path, they fell into a companionable silence. The sound of their footsteps kept South from inserting a caution.

"At the risk of raising Lord Southerton's suspicions," said Elizabeth, "I find I must sit down."

"Of course." Instead of leading her to the stone bench, Northam guided Elizabeth off the path and toward an old apple tree where a swing was suspended from a thick knobby

Take A Trip Into A Timeless World of Passion and Adventure with Kensington Choice Historical Romances!
—Absolutely FREE!

Let your spirits fly away and enjoy the passion and adventure of another time. Kensington Choice Historical Romances are the finest novels of their kind, written by today's best selling romance authors. Each Kensington Choice Historical Romance transports you to distant lands in a bygone age. Experience the adventure and share the delight as proud men and spirited women discover the wonder and passion of true love.

Take **4 FREE** Books!

We created our convenient Home Subscription Service so you'll be sure to have the hottest new romances delivered each month right to your doorstep — usually before they are available in book stores. Just to show you how convenient Zebra Home Subscription Service is, we would like to send you 4 Kensington Choice Historical Romances as a FREE gift. You receive a gift worth up to $23.96 — absolutely FREE. You only pay for shipping and handling. There's no obligation to buy anything - ever!

Save Up To 30% On Home Delivery!

Accept your FREE gift and each month we'll deliver 4 brand new titles as soon as they are published. They'll be yours to examine FREE for 10 days. Then if you decide to keep the books, you'll pay the preferred subscriber's price. That's all 4 books for a savings of up to 30% off the cover price! Just add the cost of shipping and handling. Remember, you are under no obligation to buy any of these books at any time! If you are not delighted with them, simply return them and owe nothing. But if you enjoy Kensington Choice Historical Romances as much as we think you will, pay the special preferred subscriber rate and save over $7.00 off the bookstore price!

We have 4 FREE BOOKS for you as your introduction to KENSINGTON CHOICE!

To get your FREE BOOKS, worth up to $23.96, mail the card below or call TOLL-FREE 1-800-770-1963 Visit our website at www.kensingtonbooks.com.

Take 4 Kensington Choice Historical Romances FREE!

YES! Please send me my 4 FREE KENSINGTON CHOICE HISTORICAL ROMANCES (without obligation to purchase other books). I only pay for shipping and handling. Unless you hear from me after I receive my 4 FREE BOOKS, you may send me 4 new novels - as soon as they are published - to preview each month FREE for 10 days. If I am not satisfied, I may return them and owe nothing. Otherwise, I will pay the money-saving preferred subscriber's price plus shipping and handling. That's a savings of over $7.00 each month. I may return any shipment within 10 days and owe nothing, and I may cancel any time I wish. In any case the 4 FREE books will be mine to keep.

KN092A

Name _____

Address _____ Apt No _____

City _____ State _____ Zip _____

Telephone ( ) _____ Signature _____

(If under 18, parent or guardian must sign)

Terms, offer, and prices subject to change. Orders subject to acceptance by Kensington Choice Book Club. Offer valid in the U.S. only.

‖‖‖‖

PLACE
STAMP
HERE

||.||..||.|||...||||||||.|.||.|.|.|||.|.||.||||..|

KENSINGTON CHOICE
Zebra Home Subscription Service, Inc.
P.O. Box 5214
Clifton NJ 07015-5214

branch. He tested the strength of the ropes and the security of the seat. Finding both satisfactory, he indicated she should sit. The alacrity with which she complied told him how much she was pained by her hip and leg. "Is there some way I can assist you?"

She hesitated, her eyes darting toward Southerton's bench. She could only make out the dark shape of his beaver hat in the torchlight.

Northam followed the direction of her gaze. "I believe he is sleeping. He can do so most anywhere. Something he learned in His Majesty's Royal Navy." He looked back at Elizabeth. Her head was tilted at a sweet angle, her lashes lowered as she studied the toe of one shoe. Moonshine glanced off the curve of her neck. He would have liked to place his lips there, just in that gentle curve, and see if he could taste the moonlight. As if feeling his eyes on her, Elizabeth lifted her hand and placed it in the exact spot he wanted to kiss. She brushed aside a fallen tendril of hair.

Before she caught him out, Northam dropped to his knees in front of her and raised the foot she was regarding so seriously. He placed it on his thigh, holding it between his palms when she would have pulled back. "Is it a stone?" he asked.

Elizabeth nodded. "I must have a hole in my shoe."

Northam ran his fingers along the edge of her sole and found it in short order. "Here it is." He began unlacing her shoe.

"Oh! I do not think—"

"Elizabeth." Northam said her name pleasantly enough, but in a manner that brooked no argument. He removed the shoe and shook out the stone. The slight weight of her stockinged foot against his thigh was pleasant. She had understood the intimacy of this small task better than he. He put down the shoe, picked up her foot, and began to massage her arch with the balls of his thumbs. He watched her lips part, first to mount a second protest, then simply to offer up a sigh that was the very definition of contentment. "The park is pleasant in the evening, is it not?"

"Yes."

"Hampton Cross has such a place. The swing, though, is large enough for two."

Elizabeth thought it did not bode well for her that she immediately wondered with whom he had shared it. "Is Hampton Cross your country home?"

"One of them. It is where I prefer to spend my time when not in London."

"Your mother lives there?"

"No. She enjoys town. With my sisters all settled, the house is much too large for her, or so she says. When she retreats to the country she likes to stay in Stonewickam with my grandfather. You do not have to worry that she will interfere with your running of Hampton Cross."

Elizabeth could not quite credit it. "A mother who gives up her son *and* the chatelaine's keys? She must be the best of all mothers-in-law."

"I believe you will find her so," Northam said blithely.

She regarded him suspiciously. "You are pulling my leg."

He chuckled, giving her foot a little tug. "Indeed."

Elizabeth found she was smiling again. How did he manage it? she wondered. No doubt he disarmed his mother and sisters in just such a fashion. They probably all spoiled him. It was little wonder that he thought the dowager would accept her.

Northam glanced up in time to see Elizabeth's quicksilver smile vanish. "What are you thinking?"

"You make things seem as if they can be accomplished without effort."

"Do I? I work very hard at it."

"I am serious."

"So am I." North stopped massaging her foot and picked up her shoe. Stretching the heel slightly, he helped her slip it on and began tying the laces. When he was done he let her remove her foot from his thigh. The scalloped hem of her gown fell into place around her slender ankles. He sat back on his haunches and brushed off his trousers, then rested his forearms casually on his kneecaps. "It cannot have escaped your notice, Elizabeth, that as scandals go, ours is not much of one.''

Elizabeth's brows puckered. ''Have you been involved in a great many?''

''This would be my first.''

''Mine also. It does not seem without consequence.''

One corner of his mouth lifted. She sounded a shade disappointed that this might not be so. ''Oh, it most definitely has import,'' he said. ''Certainly for us, but in the end you may discover it falls a week short of a nine-days' wonder.'' He straightened and placed one hand on each of the ropes holding Elizabeth's swing. ''Perhaps it would help to examine the particulars.''

Elizabeth had to tip back her head to look up at him. His shoulders blocked the torchlight, throwing his face into shadow. If she had thought about finding herself in just this position, she would have anticipated a certain amount of wariness, even discomfort. The reality was quite different. Unwise as it seemed, she could not deny that she felt safe in the shelter of his large frame, protected. ''I should like to hear,'' she said. ''What are these particulars?''

''Well,'' he drawled, ''in spite of Madame Fortuna's reputation for accurate prognostication and the irrefutable fact that Lady Battenburn's necklace was found in my trunk, I don't believe most people present at the discovery credit me with being the Gentleman Thief. As the baroness noted, I'm as rich as Croesus, and while it is not a solid defense, it takes issue with my motives. Regarding Southerton's snuffbox, it hardly seems the sort of thing I would take, given the fact that South is my friend and also that I've had so many previous opportunities to finger it. It begs the question: why now?''

''Yes, indeed,'' she said with a certain wryness. ''I asked that very question myself.''

Northam gave the ropes a little jerk, shaking the swing and a bit of Elizabeth's complacency. He felt her grab the ropes to steady herself. ''Have a care, my lady. It would take but a small effort to send you backward, head over bucket.''

He would do it, too. Oddly enough, the threat cheered her more than raised an alarm. It had been such a long time since anyone played with her. ''Go on,'' she said. ''I find myself enthralled by your discourse.''

Northam thought Elizabeth would not be quite so full of herself had she been able to see his smile. He had it on good authority, namely from a well-known French opera dancer, that this particular smile could cause a frisson in a woman's breast. At Hambrick Hall there had been an unfortunate incident with the headmaster's wife because of this smile, but that was before he understood about frissons or the importance of exercising caution in the use of the smile. He had been twelve and rather thoughtless. Elizabeth could only benefit from what he had learned since then.

Before she suspected the bent of his mind, Northam went on. ''The gold watch fob and ruby pendant that were meant for the winners of the treasure hunt have not been recovered. They weren't in my trunks and they have not appeared anywhere else. By Lady Battenburn's own admission, neither item was highly valuable, yet they had some worth. Not, though, as much as South's snuffbox. Battenburn's other guests do not think I am so cork-brained as to have returned a snuffbox in order to take something of less value.''

North saw that Elizabeth was still staring up at him, her shadowed features attentive. Steadying himself and the swing by holding on to the ropes, he raised one leg and placed the toe of his boot on the wooden seat beside Elizabeth. ''It remains true, however, that while I am not the Gentleman Thief, I could not prove I did not take Louise's necklace, possession being nine-tenths and all that. . . .''

''Oh, excellent,'' she intoned dryly. ''You will appreciate I was becoming fearful that my confession was not only ill-timed but ultimately unnecessary.''

His chuckle was deep and edged with playful menace. He rocked the swing seat lightly with his boot so that she gave a sudden small cry and gripped the ropes more tightly.

"Regarding your confession that we spent that particular evening—and morning—together, it appears that most of the guests did not believe you."

"What?" Elizabeth planted her feet firmly on the ground to keep the swing from bobbing. She found this information astonishing. "That cannot be right. You must have misunderstood. Why would anyone think I would say such a thing if it were not true?"

"But it is *not* true," he reminded her.

"Of course it is not. Still, I cannot like it that people would doubt my word."

Northam considered that if he were to refine on her logic for the rest of his life, he would not be able to make sense of it. "I must have your promise that you will never try to make me understand that. I believe the effort would kill me."

"You make it very tempting," she said after a telling pause. "Oh, very well, perhaps I can be made to understand your thinking. Explain yourself."

Northam felt compelled to point out, "It is not precisely my thinking."

When he fell silent waiting for her response, Elizabeth gave the swing a small shake to urge him to continue. He could be most frustrating in his desire to reason things out.

Grinning, Northam went on. "It is just that a number of guests have remarked that your announcement was a highly romantic gesture. Apparently it is their conclusion that you made the confession because you are deeply in love with me, not because any impropriety actually took place." Even in the deepening shadows, North could see Elizabeth's mouth open, then close. "You must allow that your own rather sterling reputation supports this reasoning. It puts them all in a bind. On the one hand they must accept your story because it was most sincerely confessed and it absolves me of stealing the necklace. On the other they are inclined to assign you pure motives."

Elizabeth simply shook her head, not quite able to believe

what she was hearing. "Why should they extend me such benefit of the doubt? It is not at all the usual thing."

"I agree. I imagine it is because you are so well regarded. And, if I may be immodest, I also have supporters." The one that was sleeping soundly in another part of the garden gave an abrupt little snore. North saw Elizabeth put one hand to her mouth to stifle a laugh. He sighed. "The fact that we are to be married helps to mitigate the circumstances surrounding it. The *ton* is apt to be more forgiving when things have been made right, or what they consider right. If either one of us were to cry off . . ."

Elizabeth's smile had disappeared, along with her urge to laugh. She wished he had not said the last. She required no reminder that things could not be changed. "I understand," she said quietly.

Northam felt her stillness and wondered at it. He looked longingly at the apple tree. If only he could stretch out beneath it, rest his back against the trunk, cross his arms, his ankles, generally assume his finest posture for contemplation, then perhaps he could conceive the theory that would explain Lady Elizabeth Penrose. It was not as if he were proposing to understand *all* women. He wanted only to understand this one.

North drew in a deep breath and let it out slowly. Comprehension, if it was possible, was not likely to happen tonight. "Lady Powell has a slightly different view of your confession."

That garnered all of Elizabeth's attention. "Oh?"

"She thinks you placed the necklace in my trunk and made the confession in order to trap me into marriage. She was highly complimentary of your efforts. Called it Machiavellian, I believe."

"Lady Powell doesn't know Machiavelli from my left foot."

"Perhaps I misunderstood that part."

"Hmmm."

"But she was complimentary."

"I have no doubt. Lord Southerton should be concerned she will follow my example."

"His valet has already gone through his trunks—twice."

She felt her lips twitch. "A perfectly reasonable precaution."

"Fear makes him cautious."

Elizabeth laughed outright. "Have you considered South's role in all of this? Perhaps he put the necklace in your trunk in the hope that I would rush to your rescue. There is the wager, after all. A man can be persuaded to almost any end for an entire sovereign."

"West won. South wagered we would *not* marry."

"Oh."

"Indeed."

She sobered and asked carefully, "Do you think I meant to trap you?"

"I seem to recall proposing marriage and being rejected in no uncertain terms. If you changed your mind about it, I think you would have come to me, not gone about it in this havey-cavey fashion." Northam absently nudged the swing with the toe of his boot. It rocked slightly, causing Elizabeth to dig in her heels to steady it. When he felt her resistance, he realized what he had been about. "I'm sorry."

"Mmmm." She waited patiently for him to continue. Her grip on the swing relaxed and she lowered her toes.

"I wondered if perhaps you thought I had meant to trap you."

A slight smile lifted the corners of her mouth. "It wasn't a very certain trap, was it? I think you could have made a better job of it than hinging the outcome on the mere hope that I would rescue you. What is it you truly wish to know?"

He laughed quietly, not at all uncomfortable with the idea that she knew something else was on his mind. "Do you think I'm the thief?"

The question startled Elizabeth. After a moment she said, "It never once occurred to me."

"Really? Never once?"

She shook her head.

"I confess that surprises me."

"Do you mean you should like it better if I had entertained the idea? You will have to explain that to me, I'm afraid. Most men would not want their honor impugned. Unless it is because you believe that drivel you said to Lady Powell."

"Oh? And what drivel is that?"

"About your reputation being enhanced by the suspicion that you are the Gentleman Thief."

One of his eyebrows lifted. "I take it your heart does not beat more wildly at the notion."

"It does not even flutter." She felt North's low chuckle as a vibration through the swing. "Why did you think I should suspect you?" she asked seriously.

He considered the question before he answered. "Several reasons, I suppose. The first evening I stayed at Battenburn I came upon you in the library."

"I thought you were in want of a book."

"I was. But there was no reason you should suppose that to be true."

"I see." She was glad for the darkness. It covered her poor efforts to temper her amusement. "So I should have supposed you were in search of items to steal. Pray, go on."

"I see you mean to have fun with me, Lady Elizabeth."

"Yes, I think I do."

North did not mind at all. That she could feel such comfort with him boded well, he thought, even if she did not realize it. "Well, then, for your continued merriment, let me add that you witnessed my athletic grace in leaving a bedchamber by a window route. According to Lady Battenburn, that is how the thief left her room."

"True," she said. "But I quite miss the point. I thought your experience with scaling walls the result of a great many near encounters with suspicious husbands, not that you were stealing from the *ton*."

"Is it your intention to flatter or wound me?"

"Neither. I am still having fun with you."

He grinned. "As you like. There is also the fact that I helped you find the treasure."

"Odd. I thought I helped you."

"Do not split hairs."

Elizabeth laughed. "Very well. You present some compelling points and I have been remiss in not suspecting you. You must return the gold fob and ruby pendant immediately to Louise and make amends to society."

"And you will stand by me?"

"I will write you faithfully in Australia."

North responded to her butter-wouldn't-melt tone with a shout of laughter.

Elizabeth placed a finger to her own lips to shush him. "You'll wake Lord Southerton," she whispered.

Laughter continued to rumble. "Now that would indeed be unfortunate."

"Why is that?"

"Because I could not so easily do this." He swooped quickly, catching her while her face was still raised. His mouth slanted across hers. North felt her momentary resistance, part surprise, part uncertainty, then her sweet response, the parted lips and breathy little sigh, the tentative press of her mouth and the damp edge of her tongue. It was with some reluctance that he drew back. He could not properly take her in his arms and he had no wish to start something he could not finish. Tomorrow night was another matter entirely.

Elizabeth felt him remove his foot from the swing seat. His hands slid up the ropes again. She lowered her head, then her eyes. Her own hands dropped to her lap. She could still feel the outline of his mouth against hers. She wanted to resent him for her response but knew there was no fairness in it. He could rouse nothing from her that she was unwilling to give. "May I speak frankly?" she asked.

North thought she had certainly done so in the past. "I hope you always will. I would not have it otherwise."

"You only think that now," she said softly. Elizabeth shook her head. "It is of no matter. I do not mean to make that argument again. What I want to say is—"

"Can you not look at me?"

Her chin came up predictably. She saw that North had shifted just enough to one side to allow the torchlight to bathe her face. While he still stood in shadow, she was exposed. It did not make her shy away from what must be said. "I think you imagine some tender feelings toward me. Am I correct?"

"I would only take issue with the word *imagine*. The tender feelings are quite real." North could not tell if this small concession make it easier or more difficult for her to continue. Even in full light, Elizabeth's features gave nothing away. "Does this present an impediment to our marriage?"

Uncertain if he was making light of her, Elizabeth frowned slightly. "That is for you to say. You must know I return no feeling other than a kind regard for your good character." She peered up at him, trying to gauge his reaction. It was impossible to tell what he thought, or if he was moved in any way. "I would not have you fall in love with me."

Northam released the swing and let his hands drop to his sides. "Surely that is not up to you."

"I realize that. In truth, I do not know if such a thing is possible. Whatever the nature of your feelings for me now, it will come to change. I should think it very likely that someday you will hate me. Indeed, I do not know how it can be otherwise. You probably believe I am saying this for your sake, but it is not so. I say it for my own. I find I am selfish enough to hope that you will hate me less if you never love me at all."

Northam was quite without words. He watched a sheen of tears overlay her implacable eyes. She continued to regard him steadily, unblinkingly, as if willing them not to fall, and he wondered at the cost to her pride to put this matter before him. Did she think so little of herself, or so much?

"There is no need for you to marry me," she said gravely. In spite of her wish for it to be otherwise, there was a catch in her voice. Elizabeth drew a shaky breath. "I want to be very clear on that account. It is not too late to withdraw your proposal. You could choose to set me up as your mistress and I would accept. We need only keep the arrangement a few months, live through the scandal, then go on with our lives. Your reputation will not suffer unduly, and since I never had any intention of marrying again, what they say about me does not matter. Divorce is a much more difficult end to achieve.''

"There will be no divorce," North said. "There is no—" He stopped, frowning. His fingers raked his hair, then came to rest at the back of his neck. He massaged the knot of tension that was forming there. "What do you mean you had no intention of marrying again?"

Now Elizabeth blinked. "I beg your pardon?"

North did not believe for a moment that Elizabeth had not heard him. For the first time in their short acquaintance he suspected she was preparing to dissemble. "You said you had no intention of marrying again. It suggests that you have been married before. Is that true?"

She shook her head forcefully. "No. No, I have not."

North's eyes narrowed. "Then explain yourself."

"There is nothing to explain. I believe you misunderstood or I misspoke. I was making reference to our possible marriage. I simply meant that I never had intention of marrying again after *that*."

North tried to bring to mind the whole of her little speech and found he could not. He was left only with the impression that all was not as it should be. "You were no virgin," he said.

Elizabeth's laugh sounded a trifle hysterical to her own ears. She recovered quickly, covering her mouth with her hand until it was swallowed. She said evenly, "I believe that is explained by the fact that I am a whore."

Northam knew he could easily lose patience with her. As a defense, what she offered was unconventional. "But if you were married—"

"And I have said I was not."

"Then you have had a great many lovers."

Unable to help her response, Elizabeth flinched. "I believe that is the very definition of a whore."

Which, again, was not precisely an answer. Northam

thought he had accepted that there had been someone else before him, but now he had cause to wonder. Was it the vision of that damnable parade of men to her bed that troubled him, or this new suspicion that there had been but one man, a very special man . . . a husband?

He stepped back from the swing entirely and extended his hand. "Come," he said somewhat stiffly. "I will escort you back to the house."

Elizabeth stood without accepting his assistance and made to walk past him. His hand on her elbow stopped her. She looked at it pointedly.

"I will escort you," he said again.

She thought better of pulling away. Come tomorrow she would have no right to do so. She might as well accustom herself to it now. Northam seemed to have already reconsidered his promise that nothing should be done that would cause her discomfort. Elizabeth looked up, startled, when his hand fell away. Torchlight flickered across his face and she saw he had not changed his mind at all; rather there was a hint of regret in his dark blue eyes that she found most unsettling.

"This way," he said. "The path is less circuitous."

Elizabeth had never fainted and she willed herself not to do so now. She wished that it was appropriate for North to take her arm. She would have been grateful for his support. Instead he stood beside her, seemingly at his ease while her entire body thrummed with the strength of nerves pulled taut.

She lifted the small bouquet she held just enough to catch the delicate fragrance of lilies-of-the-field. Better that Louise should have placed smelling salts among the greenery. That at least would have assured she remained upright, if not entirely coherent.

What was the vicar saying? She caught fragments of his opinion on the purpose of marriage, the sanctity of the vows, and the rights and privileges of the contract they were making with each other and with God. Elizabeth had no idea if she agreed with any of it. She kept her focus on the vicar's spectacles. They winked in the sunlight coming through the stained-glass windows and cast a reflection that prevented her from seeing his eyes clearly. It was more difficult not to imagine his censure.

She found no relief by considering what those sitting behind her might be thinking. Lord and Lady Battenburn sat alone on her side of the church, the only people in attendance who were known of long acquaintance. Northam's contingency was scarcely larger. The Compass Club was there, infinitely more sober than the first time Elizabeth had seen them together, and in the first row was the dowager countess. Elizabeth could not know if Northam's friends were on their best behavior because of respect for the occasion or fear of his mother. Elizabeth had only glimpsed her ladyship as she limped past her pew on her way to stand with Northam. What she saw did not ease her mind in the least.

Lady Northam had eyes a few shades lighter than the cobalt blue of her son's, and infinitely more in common with a frozen lake than a halcyon sky. For a moment Elizabeth had not been able to breathe. She still had not fully recovered when it was time to say her vows.

She heard Reverend Rawlings address her inquiringly. His spectacles flashed a spectrum of color at her and broke her concentration. Panicked, she found herself looking to Northam, never questioning but that she would find something in his face to quiet her.

His smile was more than kind; it was understanding. His eyes simply held hers, making neither a demand nor offering judgment. She could change her mind, he seemed to say, but his was set.

The vicar began again, and this time Elizabeth heard herself repeat the vows, her voice clear and steady, the intonation almost heartfelt. She never looked away from Northam, and for this brief passage of time she forgot that anyone save him was with her. Then she was hearing the words again, this time with more resonance and not the slightest hesitation. North made his promises as a knight might express fealty to his lord, pledging not just his loyalty but his life, and the manner of his spoken word left Elizabeth profoundly shaken.

The ring he slipped on her finger did nothing to change Elizabeth's impression that he had become hers. She was humbled by the depth of his trust even though she had begged him not to give it.

The vicar cleared his throat, a less than subtle prompt to encourage Northam to kiss his bride. Elizabeth's nod, more a fine lowering of her lashes than a movement of her chin, was imperceptible to everyone but her husband. He inclined his head toward her, his lips hovering just a hairsbreadth above hers. It was then that she entirely understood the extent of his patience and the cleverness of his strategy. In front of his mother, his friends, Lord and Lady Battenburn, the vicar, and before God, Brendan David Hampton, sixth Earl of Northam, waited for her to kiss him.

Elizabeth closed the distance between them and kissed him full on the mouth. There was a raucous cheer from the second pew, something more suited to a Covent Garden entertainment than a wedding, and it died so suddenly that Elizabeth imagined Northam's mother must have delivered a quelling look. She felt North's lips change shape against hers and knew he was smiling, probably thinking the very same thing as she. Her arms came around his shoulders as he slipped his around her back.

It would be so very easy to fall in love with him.

That thought was enough to steel her heart and make her stiffen in his embrace. Northam felt the change in Elizabeth instantly and let her go. Without a word and no alteration of their expressions, they turned simultaneously and faced their audience for the first time as husband and wife.

Lady Battenburn reached Elizabeth first and hugged her to her ample bosom. "I am so happy for you, my dear. You will see how splendidly a married state suits your temperament. Already you are glowing! Is she not, Battenburn?"

She kissed Elizabeth on the cheek. "Yes, you are warm. Your joy must be evident to even those who cannot see."

Northam spared a glance at his wife's face and thought Louise a bit lavish in her assessment of Elizabeth's mood. While Elizabeth no longer looked as if she might faint, to characterize her as glowing was far from the truth. What color flushed her cheeks was most likely there as a result of Louise's enthusiastic embrace and the determined advance of his own mother.

Battenburn bowed his head toward Elizabeth as his wife stepped out of the way. "You are indeed looking very pretty, my dear."

Northam thought this was damning Elizabeth with faint praise. She was extraordinarily lovely this morning. Even in her most uncertain moments, her beauty was undiminished in his eyes. She wore a gown of white bombazine, trimmed with a tier of lace ruffles at the hem and bands of satin ribbon on the sleeves and bodice. Matching ribbon was threaded through her coiled hair and great pains had been taken to curl gold and ginger tendrils so they framed her oval face. She looked like nothing so much as an angel, but when he stopped to consider that perhaps this was a mere fancy on his part, he saw that his friends' regard was a similar blend of admiration and awe, and came to conclude that his own perception was not a mere bias of affection.

The Dowager Countess of Northam was a full head shorter than her much-beloved son. She noticed this disparity in their heights around the time of his fourteenth birthday and promptly dismissed it as unimportant. For his part, North pretended he never noticed at all. In the figurative sense, at least, he was inclined to look up to her.

She was an attractive woman, well-regarded, and remained influential among the *ton*. Northam suspected she had taken lovers in the years since his father's death, but she was discreet, and he had no desire to know the truth of it. There were a few steady companions and many hopefuls. Her interests in fashion and fashionable entertainments concealed a clever mind, occasionally even from herself. Northam knew his mother did not always appreciate how astute her political observations were, and he was loath to encourage her too much in this arena. He had read Mary Wollstonecraft's *Vindication of the Rights of Women* even if she hadn't. The implications of his mother taking up the cause of women's rights always gave him pause. She never did anything by half measures, even when she did not know quite what she was doing.

"Mother," he said, bending to kiss the cheek she offered. "It was very good of you to come."

"There is that saying about wild horses," she said. "I fancy you know the one."

"Indeed I do."

She tapped him on his shoulder with the tip of her sandalwood fan. "You must not simply stand there welcoming me—though I have had a most difficult journey and despaired of a timely arrival—pray, introduce me to your bride."

Northam turned to Elizabeth and gave her what he hoped was an encouraging smile. "Mother, this is my wife Elizabeth, Lady Northam. My lady, my mother the Dowager Lady Northam."

Elizabeth made a careful curtsy that did not expose any awkwardness. "My lady," she murmured. "It is a pleasure to make your acquaintance."

"I don't know how that can be," announced Celia Worth Hampton. "It cannot have escaped your notice that I am most vexed. Whether it should be with you or my son, I have not yet decided. At this moment I am inclined to be more put out with you, but that could change." She leveled North with a clear blue glance that was only moderately thawed. "Is that not so?"

"Indeed it is," he said.

"You're being impudent."

He chuckled. "Mother, I just agreed with you."

"That is precisely how I know you're being impudent," she said tartly. She addressed Elizabeth again. "It is all in his tone. I collect you will know what I mean."

"Oh, yes," said Elizabeth. "I do."

Celia nodded approvingly. "Good. That is a beginning." She indicated the three men hovering behind her. "You see these three, my dear? When a mother knows her son chooses to befriend such as these, what hope can she have that he will make a better match in his marriage?"

Elizabeth looked at each of North's friends in turn. They had come to stand by him, wish him happy, regardless of what they thought privately about the manner of his marriage. In spite of losing the wager, South was looking inordinately pleased with himself, while Eastlyn and Mr. Marchman were hardly more reserved. Elizabeth had to believe they would not be of such like minds if Northam himself were not satisfied with the arrangement.

At the risk of offending the dowager countess, Elizabeth said quietly, "I should count myself fortunate to have friends such as these. I think a mother would be glad if her daughter-in-law proves she is but one-half the good companion to her son that these men have been."

Complete silence greeted Elizabeth. She fought the urge to lift her chin, suspecting this nervous gesture of defiance would not be looked on kindly.

Celia Worth Hampton inclined her head and smiled in a most conciliatory manner. "Just so, m'dear." With that, she turned her back on North and Elizabeth and held her palm out to the Compass Club. "One hundred pounds each," she said. "I will graciously accept your markers. I told you North would not choose a bride who could be cowed by his mama."

North groaned slightly, while Elizabeth looked on in astonishment. Lord and Lady Battenburn exchanged startled glances. Leaning toward Elizabeth, North whispered, "My mother enjoys a larger wager than we usually allow among ourselves."

"I heard that," Celia said. "I am not yet in my dotage. None of you have the least sense of how to manage a proper wager." She nodded to Southerton, Eastlyn, and Marchman in turn as they dropped their markers into her open palm.

She closed her hand around the markers and placed them in her reticule. "Thank you, gentlemen. I always enjoy taking your money."

Southerton shook his head, a sheepish grin making him seem a score of years younger. "How could we know she wouldn't be afraid of you? *We* are."

Celia patted his cheek. "Just as I intend you always should be."

"Yes, ma'am."

She turned back to her son and new daughter. "Oh, do not be so disapproving, North. If you are not careful, you will soon be as priggish as your grandfather, and you know how unbecoming that is." She glanced at Elizabeth, whose mouth was still parted and missed being a full gape by only the narrowest fraction. "And you, dear, you really must not blame North. He knew nothing about this. You can see for yourself, he doesn't have the sense of humor for it. I am going to trust you to see that he doesn't become a complete dullard as I can only boast modest success on that account." She ignored North's long-suffering sigh and raised her smooth cheek for Elizabeth's kiss. "Come, I should like something more affectionate than a curtsy. It was very nicely done, infinitely respectful, and just the thing my father will find to his liking when you meet him."

Still somewhat bewildered, Elizabeth placed her lips on Celia's proffered cheek. "May I take it that you are not so vexed as you first appeared?"

"Oh, it was not entirely an act, though I could see immediately that you were not faint of heart. I am still inclined to be unhappy with my son. However, it will pass. It always does. Though generally much too soon, as I cannot help but dote on the boy."

Elizabeth pressed her lips together to tamp down her smile. Beside her she felt Northam shift his weight from one leg to the other as he heroically tried to bear the burden of his embarrassment. She slipped her arm around his and gave it the slightest squeeze. He looked down at her and smiled. For a moment it was just as if there were only the two of them.

Eastlyn cleared his throat. Southerton grinned. Mr. Marchman coughed politely, while Reverend Rawlings studied the embossed cover of his Bible. Lord and Lady Battenburn exchanged another glance, this one self-congratulatory, and Celia Worth Hampton blinked to stem a sudden tide of tears.

No one noticed the doors to the church opening until an authoritarian voice boomed out, ''Am I come too late to deliver the bride to her groom?''

Chapter Ten

The arrival of Colonel Blackwood delayed the newly-weds' departure from Battenburn until evening. It was necessary to light the lanterns by the time North and Elizabeth were able to make their farewells and climb into the carriage. There had been some discussion of remaining at Battenburn for their wedding night, but they both privately agreed they wanted to be away.

Northam's elegant carriage had been brought up from London that morning, outfitted with a team of four matched grays. Brill, Northam's dour valet, sat with the driver and groom, and the driver's young son rode standing at the rear, quite happy with his new status as tiger. He kept his eye on the tower of trunks piled high on the carriage roof lest any one of them should take a bad bounce to the road.

Elizabeth sat beside North on a comfortably padded leather seat. She was very much aware of the luxury of her surroundings, from the beautifully etched windows to the polished brass sconces that lighted the interior of the carriage. By Northam's own admission, as well as information shared by others, Elizabeth knew he had substantial lands and at least Ł18,000 per annum, but she had never given a thought as to how he might use his wealth.

"You're very quiet," North said. He was leaning back

into one corner of the carriage, his long frame already assuming a half-reclining position across part of the seat. He had removed his hat and tossed it on the opposite bench. Now he ran one hand through hair that was made gold by the lantern light. "What are you thinking?"

Elizabeth raised one hand, turning her palm over in a graceful gesture to indicate the interior of the carriage. "This," she said. "I was thinking that my father's income is easily as large as yours and he would never deign to spend so much money on his equippage. Lord and Lady Battenburn have several fine carriages but none so enormously handsome or comfortable as this."

"Are you concerned I will spend your allowance?"

Embarrassed, Elizabeth prickled defensively. "I assure you, the matter of an allowance had not—"

"Elizabeth," North said calmly, "I am teasing you."

She glanced at him uncertainly and saw that the corners of his mouth were turned up ever so slightly. Even the slumberous, heavy-lidded look of his eyes could not quite hide his amusement. Her insides turned over queerly. Elizabeth quickly looked away. She tried to think of some clever riposte, but the best she could come up with was, "Oh."

He chuckled quietly. "I dislike traveling by any means save horseback. Since it is not always practical to do so, I find it helps if the carriage is of the finest construction. The seats are wider than is the norm, and the heavy springs in the undercarriage protect us from jouncing with every rut in the road. I believe I've had this equippage for a year and I've ridden in it but half a dozen times. I lend it out more than I've used it." He casually folded his arms across his chest. "Does it satisfy you that I am not a spendthrift?"

"You are teasing me again."

"Yes, I am."

Elizabeth found she did not mind overmuch. She settled back against the soft leather squabs and smoothed her gown over her lap. It was tempting to close her eyes, but she was afraid she would sleep and her mouth would fall agape. It could not be an attractive pose. When she knew North better perhaps she would let him see her in such a state, but not on their wedding night. "How far do we travel tonight?"

"As far as Weybourne. There is an inn there that was recommended to me."

"I know the one. I have stayed there on my way to—" She stopped, struck by a possibility that had never once occurred to her in the days leading up to this one. "Where are we going?"

"I suppose I have ruined the surprise. Your father has invited us to Rosemont."

Any thought of sleep fled. Elizabeth sat up straight. "You are teasing me."

One of North's brows lifted. "No, not this time."

"But—"

"You are distressed?"

"Yes ... no ... I am ..." What? she wondered. Confused? Frightened? Surprised? Perhaps all of those things. "It is most unexpected," she said finally, inadequately. "My father does not often call for me."

"I am not certain he has called for you this time," North pointed out. "I believe he wants to inspect me."

Elizabeth nodded slowly. He was right, of course, at least as far as he could understand. "He will not be so pleasant as your mother, and much less likely to find something to recommend you."

"No one is as pleasant as my mother when she has determined to be so. As to your second point, I am unconcerned by your father's opinion in any matter, including his judgment of my character, so I suspect we will get on fine."

Elizabeth did not know whether to be worried or grateful. North had hit upon the very thing that would ensure the peace. The key was not to care overmuch. By caring not at all Northam might actually be conferred a grudging respect. It was more than she had received these last ten years.

Drawing a steadying breath, Elizabeth pressed two fingers to her temple and rubbed gently. "If I said I do not want to go, could we not?"

"Do you not want to go?"

"I wish you had discussed this with me. I suppose I assumed we were going to Hampton Cross."

"Lord and Lady Battenburn suggested this invitation was better presented as a fait accompli."

"Did you never wonder why?"

He had, but he also wanted to visit Rosemont, so he had not asked any questions that would persuade him to think better of it. "I believe their intention was to surprise you. They confided that you were disappointed when your father could not be in attendance today, which was already as I suspected. When the invitation arrived separately they spoke to me. Battenburn made the arrangements for our stay at the Weybourne inn and sent a rider ahead to make certain your father knows we have accepted."

"They are very . . . thoughtful." Elizabeth turned her head toward the window. The carriage's interior light made the etched glass a dark mirror, reflecting her pale image. "I suppose it was meant as a kindness." Somehow she managed to keep from choking on the words.

"You have not answered my question," said Northam. "Do you not want to go?"

"Would it make a difference?"

As much as he wanted to meet the earl, North knew his conscience would not allow him to force this trip on Elizabeth. "Yes," he said. "It would make a difference."

Elizabeth eyes lifted to his reflection in the glass. Before she thought better of it, she said, "I believe you."

"You should."

She made a faint nod, distracted by her own admission. It made her feel somehow vulnerable, as though he could use it against her. She realized that in an odd way, it was already happening. Drawn by a force outside her good judgment, Elizabeth heard herself say, "I want to go home."

Northam was struck by her description of Rosemont as home and the hint of longing in her voice. He commented on neither, suspecting that attention to these details would only persuade her to change her mind. "Then that is what we shall do," he said quietly. He held out his hand to her.

She caught the movement in the glass and turned to him. "Come." North moved his legs and made room for her beside him. "It would not be at all amiss for you to rest your head here." He indicated his shoulder. "It is more comfortable than even the squabs."

It looked as if it might be. He was so very handsome in his black tails and dark gray trousers. His hair shone almost as brightly as it had this morning when he waited at the altar. She remembered with singular clarity that a sunbeam had glanced off the crown of his head and for a moment hovered like a halo. She had almost stumbled badly on Battenburn's arm then, but he had steadied her and she kept going, unsettled by this vision of Northam as her guardian angel but unable to dismiss it as mere fancy.

Elizabeth carefully removed her bonnet and placed it beside North's polished beaver hat. The white ostrich feather swayed hypnotically as the carriage rolled on. North raised his arm and beckoned her to the shelter he provided in the crook of his shoulder. He found her hesitation touching because it was clearly borne of shyness. She presented a surfeit of contradictions that he sometimes wondered if even she understood. For the time being he was content to let them rest.

"It was so very kind of the colonel to come today," Elizabeth said. "I confess I wanted him to be there, but I thought the journey too arduous for him to make. Thank you for writing to him."

"Your gratitude is misplaced. I didn't write him for the same reason as you."

She frowned. "Then who—"

Northam considered the suspects. "Most likely it was South."

"Lord Southerton? But why would—"

"You will have to ask him. I'm sure he extended the invitation with Battenburn's pemission."

"I didn't mean—"

"You may have noticed that South is well acquainted with Blackwood."

"I did, but I—"

"As are East and West."

Elizabeth sat up, turned, and pressed her index finger sharply into North's chest. "Am I never to be allowed to finish a sentence again?"

Both his brows lifted. He looked from her to the finger, then back to her. "I apologize."

"It lacks sincerity when you smile so."

He made an effort to appear more contrite. "Is this more the expression of remorse you were looking for?"

She sighed. "It will have to do, though I believe the gleam in your eye is what is widely known as unholy."

"Really?" North bent his head quickly and kissed her. "And now?"

Elizabeth was forced to revise her earlier assessment. What she was looking at now in those dark cobalt eyes was certainly unholy. She removed her finger from his chest. "Perhaps I was mistaken."

"I thought you might have been. You must allow there is a fine distinction between merely wicked and unholy."

"I am learning it is so." She found herself held rapt by that distinction now. "I . . . umm . . . I should . . ."

North waited patiently for Elizabeth to finish her sentence, then he made certain she couldn't by adding that smile. It did indeed seem to induce a frisson. Infinitely pleased with himself, he bent his head again to kiss her and collided with her forehead instead when the carriage hit a deep rut its springs could not manage.

He grunted and touched one hand to his mouth to inspect for blood or a broken tooth. Elizabeth had a palm across her brow. "Are you injured?" he asked.

She lowered her hand so he could see for himself. "Am I?"

There was a small red mark that would fade quickly. "No. The skin is not broken. And me?" He flashed her a boyish grin.

She pretended to be unimpressed. "Every tooth accounted for." She settled back in the crook of his shoulder again.

"You must have had some success with that gleam and that smile." Elizabeth felt laughter rumble pleasantly in his chest.

"A modest amount."

"Hmmm."

"I gather the mood is broken."

"We are fortunate that is all. I might have smashed your nose." She tried to stifle her own smile with one hand and ended up yawning widely. Embarrassed, she ducked her head.

Northam gave her slender shoulders a light squeeze. "Rest, Elizabeth. You have certainly earned it."

She resisted closing her eyes for a few minutes. In time she could not help herself. She remembered nothing of the remainder of the journey to Weybourne, not the passing of the villages and pastures, not the moment when Northam covered her with his own coat and let her head rest in his lap.

When they reached the inn Elizabeth stirred only long enough for North to help her from the carriage. He carried her across the courtyard and up the stairs of the inn. Brill ran ahead to open the door to their room but was glad to be immediately dismissed after pronouncing the lodgings adequate. The valet did not fancy himself performing the functions of a lady's maid, though he could not imagine his employer providing those same services.

Northam did so quite competently, helping Elizabeth out of her spencer and gown without the smallest protest from her. She lay back on the bed that Brill had turned down and allowed him to raise first one leg, then the other, and remove her kid slippers and white stockings. She actually sighed when he unhooked her corset.

He undressed himself with similar efficiency, washed his face at the basin, and finally snuffed the candles before he slipped into bed beside Elizabeth. She was curled on her side facing him. Without the slightest compunction, he turned her over and fit himself comfortably against her. The full roundness of her bottom settling against his groin stirred his blood. His smile was somewhere between sleepy and rueful.

"It is not the wedding night I imagined," he whispered against her hair. He thought his bride's breathy little response sounded very much like a snore.

Elizabeth stood at the window of the small bedchamber and looked out on the fog-shrouded courtyard. The mist was so thick that the stable was barely visible at only forty yards away. A figure left the inn from the door below her and all but disappeared into the fog on his way to the stable. She blinked as the first raindrops fell and left their etchings on the windowpanes.

A knock at the door tore her away from the window. She hurried to answer it before North was awakened.

"Your breakfast, m'lady," the serving girl announced. She bobbled the heavy tray as she made her curtsy. "His lordship's valet says I was to bring it up directly."

"Thank you." Elizabeth opened the door wide enough to take the tray but not to admit the bearer. The girl was much too interested in the sprawled figure on the bed for Elizabeth's tastes. "There is nothing else." She turned, closed the door smartly with her heel, and placed the tray at the foot of the bed. A chill had crept into the room and Elizabeth set about laying a small fire with the kindling and logs available. Satisfied with her efforts when she had the flames crackling, she stood back to appreciate the warmth.

Northam appreciated the view. Elizabeth's thin chemise was like a sheer curtain, permitting firelight to suffuse it with color and silhouetting the entire length of her slender legs, gently curving hips, and the lines that tapered from her shoulders to her waist.

She turned and caught him out. He did not even attempt to look repentant. He held out his hand and she came immediately to his side, haste making her limp barely noticeable. Elizabeth placed her fingers in his and sat on the edge of the bed.

"You're awake." She blushed a little at the insipidity of this remark. "Breakfast has arrived." That was hardly any better. She could not seem to keep from stating the obvious. "Shall I serve you?"

"Mmmm." He released her hand and reached behind her neck, cupping it in his palm. Applying but the slightest pressure, he pulled her toward him. "What are you serving?"

Her mouth was sweet. He kissed her at his leisure, nibbling on her bottom lip, taking his fill of her lips before making the first foray past them. He sucked on her tongue, wresting a small cry from her as he pulled her down on the bed. The covered dishes at the foot of the bed rattled, but neither North nor Elizabeth heard them. He opened her mouth wider, sweeping the ridge of her teeth with his tongue, then teasing her, advancing, retreating, drawing on the same air as she so that when they broke apart they were both breathless.

He recovered first, leaning over her, kissing her just below her ear, touching the tip of his tongue to the hollow. He imprinted the heat of his mouth on her temple, her cheeks, and the corner of her mouth. When she raised her chin, he kissed the exposed line of her throat from her jaw to the hollow at its base.

Elizabeth wondered that she could feel such pleasure. It was not so much that he stripped away her defenses but that she had none where he was concerned. Was there anything he could conceive of doing to her that she would not allow? Elizabeth did not think so.

She closed her eyes as his fingers lightly traced the rounded neckline of her chemise. A vague memory teased her. North undressing her. North taking such care with her gown, easing it over her shoulders, kissing her softly on the cheek when she murmured how very tired she was. North's hands slipping over her breasts, her waist, letting the gown spill to the floor before he plucked her out of the center and sat her on the bed.

Elizabeth turned her head toward the fireplace and saw her gown lying neatly over the room's only chair, just where she had imagined he'd placed it. She smiled, slipping her fingers into his silken hair, feathering it at the nape of his neck.

"You undressed me last night," she whispered. Her smile deepened as North hummed his assent against her collarbone. It was as if his voice was coming from inside her. "Do you intend to finish what you began?" His low growl raised a flush across her skin. Elizabeth was glad for the gray skies and the cloak of fog pressing against the windows. It was enough that he could feel her heat; she had no wish for him to see it clearly.

North's foot bumped the breakfast tray. The lid covering a plate of bacon slid to one side and the aroma raised an instant response in his stomach. It rumbled loudly.

Laughing, Elizabeth slipped her hand between their bodies and pressed her palm to the outline of his erection against his nightshirt. "Which hunger will you satisfy?" she asked.

God help him, he thought, if it had to be one or the other. He sat up quickly, caught the tray before it slid off the bed, and lowered it to the floor. He inhaled deeply of the bacon's piquant aroma and resolutely covered the plate. Levering himself up again, he stretched out beside Elizabeth.

"I take it you have made your choice," she said, arching one brow.

"It was a narrow thing."

"I cannot like it that my rival was a pig."

"A dead pig."

"A cooked pig."

"Do you want to eat?"

Elizabeth pushed herself upright. "I thought you would never be persuaded."

North did not let her get as far as the edge of the bed. He caught her by the shoulders, pulled her back, and trapped her legs with one of his own. His hands slid up her arms to her wrists and secured them on either side of her head. "Later," he growled, nuzzling her neck. "If I can wait, so can you."

"Hurry."

He nipped her skin with his teeth. "You really wouldn't want me to."

Elizabeth discovered he was right. North took her slowly, deliberately, drawing out each sensation so that she was balanced delicately on the narrow line between pleasure and pain.

He showed none of the care for her chemise that he had reserved for her gown the night before, pulling it over her head and pitching it to the floor. A moment later his nightshirt followed. When she tugged at the sheet, he yanked it back. He touched her, first with his eyes, then his hands, and just when she thought she would sob with tension, he used his mouth.

At times his touch was almost insolent, without regard for her person, and she found it wildly exciting rather than the opposite. It was but one part of the trust he had asked for and she had granted. His casual manner frustrated her, made her hot and wet and denied her release. She moved under and against him, stretching, digging her heels into the mattress, and still it was not enough.

"Please," she whispered.

North levered himself over her body. Her thighs cradled him warmly, and it took all his willpower not to bury himself between her legs. It was what she wanted. It was what he wanted as well, but not just at this moment. There was something else first.

"How is that again?" he asked. His voice was husky and teasing, but there was also the edge of something serious framing the words.

"Please."

"That is not the word."

Elizabeth actually whimpered then. She pushed at his shoulders with the heel of her hands and arched under him, trying to make him take her. What did he want from her? She would not say she loved him. *She would not.*

"Look at me, Elizabeth."

She turned her face and stared up at him. The arousal that

had darkened the center of her eyes was giving way to defiance. Her mouth was set mutinously.

North kissed her anyway. Slowly. Patiently. With infinite care he worked at her mouth until it parted for him again and his tongue could sweep the sensitive underside of her lip. He drew back when he felt her breathing catch. His groin settled more heavily against her; his pelvis gave an involuntary thrust. He groaned softly, almost painfully. He did not want to come against her belly.

His rasped demand was intense, urgent. "Say my name."

Elizabeth heard the words but not the sense of them. That came to her more slowly, and when she realized it was only this that he wanted relief made her very nearly shout it. "North!" She clasped her hands behind his head and pulled him closer. She kissed his chin, his jaw, the corner of his mouth. "North." More softly this time in both word and deed, she nudged his lips with her own. "Brendan." She gave up this last small intimacy as he entered her.

She started to come on his first stroke, and by the time he reached his own release she had come again. Noisily. Happily. Her passion in these moments was unfettered by inhibition. It was left to Northam to swallow her cries and he had not the least desire to.

They both lay unmoving, replete. The perspiration of their bodies mingled. For a few moments, at least, it mattered to neither of them if they never stirred again. When North finally made to move, Elizabeth stopped him, giving her head a slight, quick shake and trapping him with her legs. The damp inner walls of her vagina contracted around him as well.

"For just a little longer," she whispered. "I can feel all of you."

He could feel her, too. This was a novel experience for him, this wanting to remain joined in the aftermath of love-making. Sometimes it was he who wanted to quit the bed quickly; sometimes it was the woman who was eager to have him gone. Though they were loath to complain of his weight or the stickiness, he occasionally was amused by wagering how long it would be before they hurried to the bathing room to make their ablutions. With Elizabeth there was no such urge to leave quickly. It seemed to be the same for her.

"Stop that," he fairly growled as she contracted around him again.

"I didn't do anything." His skeptical glance raised her own leisurely smile. "I didn't. Not on purpose. It just happens sometimes. There. Like that. I cannot help it. My insides are still aquiver."

One dark brow was lifted a fraction higher. "Aquiver?"

"Well, yes. All tingly."

He chuckled softly. "It sounds—" Elizabeth's stomach chose that moment to rumble most disagreeably. Both of North's brows rose this time. "It sounds as if my lady still has certain appetites."

She sighed. "It's true. I do." She did not try to stop him when he eased out of her. While he retrieved the breakfast tray, Elizabeth picked up her chemise and slipped it over her head. When she came out through the opening she found Northam was watching her with something like disappointment on his face. "I am not going to partake of my breakfast naked," she told him tartly. Her features softened when he managed to look even more pitiful. "At least not this morning."

He grinned. "Then I have hope to live for."

"Fool."

"Probably. Hand me my nightshirt, will you?"

Laughing, Elizabeth scooped it up and tossed it at his head. He slipped it on and they proceeded to tuck into their breakfast with ill-disguised relish.

"I have been thinking," Elizabeth said as she plucked another strip of crisp, if cold, bacon from the plate, "that perhaps it would be wise if you did not mention the colonel's attendance at our wedding to my father."

"Oh?"

Northam's noncommittal response forced Elizabeth to go on. "It is simply that there is no love lost between them.

My father will be disagreeable about it, and it cannot make the visit easy for either of us."

"Then I will not bring it up."

"Thank you." Elizabeth knew she was not entirely successful at keeping the full measure of her relief to herself. North was watching her very closely. "What is it?" she asked.

"You did not really want the colonel at our wedding, did you?"

His perception did not surprise her, only his willingness to put it into words. "No," she said after a moment. "I did not." She slowly placed her uneaten bacon strip on the plate. "It is not what you think."

"What do I think?"

"That I don't hold him in the same affection he holds me. Nothing could be more ill-conceived. I love him dearly. It is only . . ." Elizabeth shook her head, not so much unable to continue as unwilling. She wondered if Northam would know the difference.

"Only . . . ?" When she did not answer he said, "Pray, do not tell me it is because you thought the journey too difficult for him. That was my reasoning, and I am heartily glad South considered it not at all when he extended the invitation."

"Are you really certain it was South who invited him?"

"Yes." He hesitated, frowning. "Who else would have done so?"

Elizabeth said nothing. She merely stared at him for the length of several heartbeats, then ducked her head and applied herself once more to her meal. She should not have raised the question; she knew that now. He would be like a hound on the scent of a fox.

Her scrambled eggs were cold and almost tasteless, but hunger and a need for diversion pressed her to continue eating them. "He got around very well, I thought. This wheeled chair is an immense improvement over the last."

Northam did not like that she was shifting the subject,

but he permitted it just the same. "I think the colonel would prefer his crutches. The chair is a defeat for him."

"You are right, of course. I spoke without thinking. I believe you have come to know him better than I."

He did not miss the hint of both melancholy and wistfulness in her voice. "Perhaps that will achieve some balance now that we are married. I have cause to visit him quite regularly. I hope you will come with me."

"I suppose I will," Elizabeth said quietly. In spite of her wish to the contrary, she had failed to inject any enthusiasm into her agreement. She tried again. "It is kind of you to suggest it." Ignoring his narrowed, watchful glance, she went on. "I could not help but notice that you spent a good deal of time in each other's company yesterday."

"Odd," he said. "I was about to comment that my observation of you and Blackwood was quite the opposite. It appeared you went out of your way to avoid him."

"Your perception is inaccurate."

"Perhaps I should have said that, unlike me, you avoided being alone with him."

"It does not matter how you put it. You are still wrong."

North did not think he was, but once again he let it pass. "I believe he regretted he was not present in time to give you away."

Elizabeth set down her fork hard and refused to give in to the ache squeezing her heart. She said coldly, "It would have been a pathetic display: He in his chair, I with my limp. I could not have borne it."

As if she had struck him, North's head jerked back. He stared at her without moving again, reeling all the while on the inside. He imagined his face was as pale as her own and that his eyes were just as icy. Setting down his plate, he moved to the edge of the bed and stood. "You will excuse me."

Elizabeth's fingers curled in tight fists around the sheet. Her mouth was dry and her tongue could not manage an apology even if she knew how to frame it. She watched him pick up his trousers and put them on, shoving the tails of his nightshirt under the waistband. He made equally quick work of his stockings and shoes and eschewed a brush in favor of raking his hair with his fingers. He did not take the time to put on his jacket, choosing to toss it over his shoulder instead. The door was closed quietly behind him. It was only in Elizabeth's heart that she felt it slam.

The ride to Rosemont was accomplished largely in silence. They sat side by side without touching. Elizabeth suspected that North chose proximity as the lesser of two evils. He did not want to sit opposite her and be faced with her countenance every time his eyes strayed from the window. She found herself wishing he had arranged for his mare to make this journey with them instead of sending her with a groom to Hampton Cross. He could be outside their carriage now, riding in solitary splendor and leaving her to lick her wounds in private.

Elizabeth concentrated on smoothing the pale pink fabric of her muslin gown across her lap. Her head snapped up when North spoke in impatient tones.

"Pray, have done with your fidgeting. Sit on your hands if you must. You have pressed your gown four times over since we left the inn. There is not a wrinkle in want of your attention."

Fingers frozen, Elizabeth turned quickly to the window. The countryside passed in a blur, though it was not entirely the speed of the carriage that caused it to be so. She willed herself not to allow a single tear to fall.

At length Northam sighed. "It is only that you spoke so cruelly, Elizabeth. Not only of the colonel but of yourself." Out of the corner of his eye he saw her nod. "I love him, you know. I loved my father, but I came to know the colonel better. I admire and respect him, and when you—"

"I understand," she said on a thread of sound. "I . . . I love him, too."

North said nothing for several minutes, hoping she would say more. When she didn't he took a linen handkerchief from his pocket and pressed it into her hand. She accepted it without acknowledgment, making a ball of it with her fingers while she continued to stare out the window. She held it so long that North thought he was mistaken about her need for it. "Will you say nothing at all, Elizabeth?"

She shook her head. The small movement was enough to break the dam of tears. They dripped over the rim of her lashes and fell down her cheeks. She raised the balled hand-kerchief and impatiently wiped them away.

Oh, my poor Elizabeth, he thought sadly. *How am I ever to understand?*

Northam lifted his feet and placed his boot heels on the opposite bench, careless that the blacking would leave marks on the fine leather. Tipping his hat over his brow, he slouched comfortably forward, resting his head against the squabs and crossing his arms and ankles. In just this position he passed the remainder of the journey, sometimes in contemplation, sometimes in sleep.

Rosemont was a grand structure, though not of the proportions of Battenburn. The Penrose forebears appreciated elegance and design but not strictly for its own sake. There was simplicity to the manor that other country homes would have done well to emulate. Northam was struck by how much it reminded him of Hampton Cross.

Five towers rose above the main stone structure, three at the front and one each at the end of the east and west wings. The house was perfectly situated for a southern exposure and a large pond at the front required that a bridge be used to make the approach.

North was sitting up now, looking out with interest. "Hampton Cross has such a pond," he said. "But no bridge, I'm afraid. It has never been practical, since the pond sits more to one side and it is easy enough to go around."

"It is probably just as well," Elizabeth said, outwardly calm. "The bridge requires much in the way of attention." The fact that her palms were damp had nothing to do with the state of the bridge, but with the state of her nerves. She was loath to press her palms against her dress for fear Northam would accuse her of ironing it again. "I hope you will not regret coming here," she said suddenly.

There was no time for Northam to reply. The carriage was stopping in front of the main entrance and Elizabeth was alighting without assistance from anyone. He watched her lift her gown and hurry up the stairs, only her limp preventing her from taking them two at time. Someone who knew her less well might have mistaken her haste for eagerness. Northam suspected that it was only her desire to forewarn that gave her such speed.

He followed at a slower pace while servants began to spill from other parts of the house to deal with the horses, carriage, and tower of trunks. It was not Elizabeth who greeted him when the immense white doors were thrown open.

Here was a woman singularly poised and of exceptional beauty. Isabel Penrose, Countess of Rosemont, stood just under five feet. Even on the lip of the entrance it was impossible to mistake her as any taller. Everything about her was dainty. Her delft blue eyes and smooth, almost translucent complexion only added to the impression that she had more in common with a china figurine than a flesh-and-blood woman. Her blond hair was covered by a lace cap, and the curls artfully arranged across her forehead might have been sculpted, so constant were they in the face of the breeze that flattened her gown against her petite figure.

"Lady Rosemont," Northam said, making his bow. It should have been Elizabeth making these introductions and he vowed he would not spare her his grandfather's lecture this time. "I am not mistaken, am I?"

"La! There is no mistake." Isabel Penrose threw out both of her small hands. Her charmingly bowed mouth widened to what passed as a broad smile for her. "And you are Lord Northam. Elizabeth described you so perfectly in her letter I would know you in any circumstances." Her curtsy was precisely preformed, as fine and graceful in form as she was. "Please, forgive me, will you not come inside? It was not my intention to leave you standing." She raised her perfectly heart-shaped face to the sky. "It looks to begin raining again."

Northam was ushered inside. His hat was immediately taken by the butler, who was waiting patiently in the hall for the moment he could be of some use.

"Elizabeth is already with Rosemont," Isabel said. "She is not usually so ill-mannered, but I suspect you know that."

"She has been in great anticipation of seeing her father, I believe."

Isabel merely smiled. "Come, I will take you to them. Everything has been made ready for your visit, though I confess I had not expected you so soon."

"And I was concerned that we were come too late. We were delayed in our departure from Battenburn and have recovered only a fraction of that time." Northam watched Lady Rosemont's brow furrow. Even this was done with delicacy. Her natural reticence kept her from questioning him or revealing what had come to her mind.

"Here we are," she said when they reached the darkly polished pocket doors at the end of the great hall. "My husband's study. You may want to admire his collection of old weaponry. He holds it in high regard." She grasped the handles and parted the doors wide. They slid soundlessly from their runners. "Elizabeth, dear, you cannot leave your husband just anywhere. It is not done."

Northam felt the tension in the room before he had fully entered. Judging by Lady Rosemont's unaffected air, North surmised she was either unaware of it, which seemed unlikely, or used to it.

Lord Rosemont was standing beside the green-veined marble mantel. He was a tall man, not so commanding in his height as North, but considerably taller than his wife. He was also powerfully built, with broad shoulders and a robust chest, so that Isabel was made even more diminutive in his presence. His hands were as large as paddles. One of them rested on the edge of the mantel, the other held an iron poker.

Isabel walked straight to her husband's side, lightly

touched his forearm, and took the poker from him with her other hand. She stabbed at the flames once, then set it with the other tools. "My lord," she said, addressing her husband, "may I present Elizabeth's husband, his lordship, the Earl of Northam."

"I know who he is," Rosemont said with some impatience. His voice had a deep bass timbre, rising as it did from a barrel chest.

"Of course you do," Isabel said, unperturbed. "You have met before, have you not? At White's, I think you said. And in the conduct of your government work. I will not carry on, then. I shall ring for tea instead." Excusing herself, she deliberately crossed between them and went to the bellpull.

"Northam," Rosemont said tersely.

"My lord," Northam returned. Out of respect for Elizabeth he made a slight bow.

William Penrose looked his son-in-law up and down in the manner he used to inspect horseflesh. His brown eyes, so dark they might have been black, added to the inscrutability of his expression. "So you have married her."

"I have."

Rosemont grunted. "Have you bedded her, then?"

"Father!" Elizabeth was out of her chair as though shot from a cannon.

Isabel was even moved to use her husband's Christian name to admonish him. "William!"

Only North remained silent, his eyes fixed on Rosemont's. They stared in such a fashion while the women held their breath. Finally it was Elizabeth's father who broke the contact by looking to his wife.

"It is just that he seems to prefer the company of other men," he explained. "They even have some fool name for themselves. The four of them together don't comprise gray matter enough to make a half-wit." His glance swiveled back at Northam. "Well, sir? Are you a sodomite?"

"William! That is quite enough."

"Please, Father."

Northam, when he clearly understood what had prompted his father-in-law's first question, burst out laughing.

Rosemont grunted a second time. He gestured toward Northam as though no further confirmation of his judgment was needed. "A bedlamite, then."

This comment actually brought tears to North's eyes as he laughed harder. He held out his hand to Elizabeth, who promptly found the handkerchief he had lent her earlier and placed it in his open palm. He used it to quickly dab at his eyes. Finding the wherewithal to sober took considerably longer. "My friends will enjoy your wit as much as I have," he said at length. "I look forward to telling them how fortunate I am in learning of my father-in-law's good humor."

"Hhmpf."

"And in his articulation of the finer points of his opinion."

"Now you go too far."

Isabel threw up her hands. "Enough. Rosemont, you will sit over there." She pointed to the large wing chair that was comfortably worn in the exact impression of her strapping husband. "Elizabeth. My lord. You will please sit on the sofa."

Northam found it interesting that none of them argued. They were all taking their orders from the one who looked least likely to give them.

Lady Rosemont nodded, satisfied with the arrangement. The scratching at the door distracted her. "Aaah, here is tea. We shall all be made composed by it." She turned her back on them and said sotto voce, "Or I shall lace the next pot with tincture of opium."

If it fell short of composing them, the tea did lend civility to the proceedings. There were no more pointed exchanges, and Isabel guided the conversation skillfully, pressing Elizabeth to describe her wedding dress and the flowers in the church. She went on to talk about the ceremony, omitting any mention of the colonel's presence and the dowager countess's wager with North's friends. Northam was still puzzled about the former but grateful for the latter. He could accept anything Rosemont said outright about him. Comments about his mother would of necessity require that he choose something from Rosemont's wall armory of lances, maces, and battle-axes and strike him with it.

Unaware of North's lingering interest in a Celtic broadsword, Isabel drew him into the discussion, encouraging him to recount details from the Battenburn rout. While she appeared entertained by the discourse, Northam doubted the same was true of her husband. He contributed when asked a direct question—always by Isabel or Northam—and otherwise sat in judgment.

When the pot of tea was empty and the plate of cakes still remained largely untouched, Isabel made excuses for herself and Elizabeth to retire to another room and discuss things that were the prerogative of women.

The doors had barely closed when Rosemont stood. "I know I want a drink. Will you have one with me?"

North reflected it was less of an invitation than a command. "Very well. Scotch."

Rosemont nodded. He went to the ornately carved liquor cabinet and removed a decanter of whiskey. He poured two fingers in twin cut-glass tumblers and handed one to Northam, who remained seated on the sofa. Hovering for a few moments longer, continuing his assessment through remote eyes, Rosemont sipped his drink.

Northam lifted one brow and regarded his father-in-law coolly. "Is there some other name you wish to call me?"

"Fool."

"I see I rise in your estimation after only a single hour. I am no longer a buggerer or even a lunatic."

Rosemont returned to his seat. "You will have observed that I allow my wife a good deal of latitude in her dealings with me. Do not mistake that I will allow you the same."

Northam made a slight nod, acknowledging what was said. "You will likewise never seek again to embarrass me in front of my wife."

The earl gave no indication of his intention one way or the other. "Why have you married my daughter? And, pray, do not tell me it is because you have compromised her. I know Elizabeth well enough to know that she cannot be compromised. Her correspondence intimated that she acted to protect you from a false accusation. Is that true?''

''Yes.''

Rosemont closed his eyes briefly and rubbed his index finger along his hooked nose. He felt infinitely older than his forty-eight years. ''God's truth, but she is a willful child.'' He lowered his hand and looked at North again. ''You will have to take her in hand. I left her too much on her own before and after her mother died. Catherine spoiled her, I fear, and I paid it little mind. When I saw what she had become it was too late. I remarried, but Belle was too young to properly discipline Elizabeth. I came belatedly to that realization also. They were fast friends before I understood it.''

That was easily explained, Northam thought, by the closeness in their ages. He estimated there were but six or seven years separating Elizabeth from her stepmother, and some fifteen between Isabel and her husband. Still, he did not question that if Isabel had borne no love for Rosemont at the beginning of their marriage, the same was not true now. As for the earl, he did not extend latitude to just anyone— he apparently had none for his daughter—so North supposed that he must hang the moon by his wife.

''I find Elizabeth to be . . .'' Northam considered his words carefully. ''. . . determined and deliberate.''

Rosemont nodded. ''Willful.''

North chose another tack. ''What did you mean when you said Elizabeth cannot be compromised?''

''Bloody hell,'' Rosemont said roughly, taking another swallow of his drink. ''I was not speaking of her principles. I thought you bedded my daughter. If you did, you know she was someone else's whore before yours.''

Northam came to his feet slowly. It occurred to him that Rosemont was not having his first whiskey of the day. Isabel's tea had been a mere hour's respite. It perhaps explained his behavior, though it fell considerably short of excusing it. "She is my wife," he said quietly. "Whatever else you think she is, know that she is that. You will never speak of her as anything else in my presence or I promise I will hurt you. And you will never speak to her thusly in or out of my presence, else I will forget the promise and kill you instead. There are several pieces in your weapons collection that I have come to admire."

He set his tumbler down on a side table and walked to the doors. "I will talk to Elizabeth and decide if we mean to stay."

In the hall North caught a servant on her way to the dining room and asked to be shown to Elizabeth and Lady Rosemont. He expected to be taken to one of the drawing rooms, or perhaps the quiet conservatory. Instead he was led upstairs, not to Isabel's private sitting room as he then anticipated, but to the west wing, where he was informed the young lordship's rooms were.

It was natural, North realized, that Elizabeth would want to see her brother. Knowing how short their time might be at Rosemont, she had not lost a moment.

North politely rapped on the door and was called in, announcing himself as he entered. The sight he came upon arrested him.

His wife lay unmoving, sprawled on her stomach on the floor. The skirt of her gown, wrinkled and quite possibly soiled, was rucked as high as her knees. Her head lay at an odd angle on her forearm. Her other arm was flung outward, the fist lightly curled. At the corner of her mouth the pink tip of her tongue was visible. Her eyes, open wide, were also expressionless.

North's breath caught. His feet remained rooted.

Elizabeth flicked the cloudy blue marble in her hand and knocked two of her opponent's marbles from the center circle. Her head bobbed up, her smile gloriously unrestrained. "Oh, Northam, did you see? I am undefeated!"

Chapter Eleven

"Good for you," Northam said dryly. He helped his wife to her feet, then Isabel, who had been similarly sprawled on the floor. Adam Penrose, Viscount Selden, had no difficulty springing to attention. He unfolded sturdy legs from their crossed position and hopped up in a fluid motion, making a formal bow to North.

"I am Selden," he said. "I am very pleased to meet you, my lord."

"As I am you," North said. Aware that he was still under grave study by the boy, North returned the same. The child's manner was inordinately confident for one of only six, but not precocious, and he supposed that was Isabel's influence, rather than Rosemont's. As for the look of him, he was much more his father's child. There was a robustness to his small form that Northam imagined Rosemont had had in his youth. He had not yet grown into his hands and feet. They still fit him badly, like a puppy's oversized paws. His eyes were every bit as penetrating as his father's but without the remoteness. They were saved from the illusion of being black by the same shards of gold that favored Elizabeth's eyes.

As far as North could see, the only feature that Isabel's son took from her was the fine flaxen color of her hair.

He saw that the boy had finished his assessment also. "Well?" he asked.

"Our Elizabeth has done very well for herself, I think. We despaired that she would. She is willful, you know."

"Adam!" Elizabeth and his mother spoke at once.

North ignored them, as did his young lordship. "Is she?" he asked politely. "How so?"

"Do not encourage him," Elizabeth said. "Why do you think he says such things if not because our father has countenanced him to do so?"

North continued to regard Selden, awaiting explanation.

"Well," the boy said in confidential tones, "my sister has been forever climbing trees when she is expressly forbidden to do so. To the very top, too. And she hunts, my lord. Oh, she is a bruising rider, but it puts gray in our hair."

"I see," North said solemnly. "That is very wrong of her. Is there yet another example of her willful nature?"

Selden thought for a moment, then his eyes brightened. "She has promised to teach me to do both."

"Elizabeth!" Isabel fairly wailed. "What can you have been thinking to promise him such? And after I expressly forbade your interference in both."

"I believe that is the very definition of willful," North offered.

Elizabeth bent down in front of her brother and tapped him on the nose. "You were not supposed to tell," she scolded. "Now I am in trouble with your mother, quite possibly Northam and, if word spreads, certainly with our father."

Selden took a commanding stance, shoulders back, feet planted. They all recognized it as identical to the posture Rosemont used when he wanted to assert himself. "But he asked straight out," he said. "It is not right I should lie."

"Yes . . . no . . ." She sighed. "But it was a secret, and it is in the nature of secrets that sometimes one must tell an untruth to keep them."

Isabel came up behind her son and placed her hands firmly on his shoulders. "That is quite enough," she said in disapproving accents. "What can you imagine you are teaching him now?"

"Life." She straightened slowly and regarded her stepmother without emotion. "I am teaching him life."

Silence followed. Northam suspected there was still a great deal being said between Isabel and Elizabeth that was outside a male's normal range of hearing. This was borne out when he glanced at Selden, who was certainly feeling the tension between his favorite women, but as lacking in insight as North was himself. North crooked his finger toward the boy and Selden wriggled out from under his mother's grip.

"I noticed the large pond upon our arrival," he said. "Is it stocked?"

"Yes, sir."

"Then perhaps you will fish with me."

The boy cast a doubtful glance out the window. "But it's raining."

"That won't bother the fish. Will it bother you?"

Selden's eyes darted to his mother and sister, who had only marginally relaxed their postures. "No, sir," he said feelingly.

Casting a significant look at both women, Northam took the viscount under his wing and made their escape.

Northam learned in the course of their fishing outing that Elizabeth had already informed Selden they would be at Rosemont for a sennight. It was not in the nature of a promise, but Northam decided against suggesting a change in plans as unfair to Elizabeth. She had fallen in with his wish to go to Rosemont; it would have been churlish of him to alter those plans after one unpleasant exchange with her father. North had to allow that Rosemont's manner of conducting himself was not entirely unexpected.

Lord Selden proved himself to be a boon companion during the course of their stay. He could sit in relative silence while he fished with Northam or chatter at length when they walked through the gardens. He was knowledgeable about the history of Rosemont and made certain North visited all five towers. He related the darkest tales about each one, quite frightening himself in the telling of them. One story, Northam realized, sounded suspiciously like the plot of *Castle Rackrent*.

It was but a small example of Elizabeth's influence on her brother. North had only seen her so easy with herself when she had been flying across the fields on Becket's powerful back. Whatever the rift between Isabel and Elizabeth, it was quickly mended. Nothing was said about the time Elizabeth made for her brother. Northam found her on two more occasions in Adam's room on her hands and knees, teaching her brother the finer points of shooting marbles. North was persuaded to join them, and under Lord Selden's keen supervision he was soundly defeated.

"It is of no matter," North had explained coolly. "I can still take her in arm wrestling."

Elizabeth had been wryly amused, first by North's feigned indifference to his loss, then by Adam's worshipful stare at her husband.

North also came upon them climbing trees in the apple orchard. He was about to inquire as to the wisdom of Elizabeth going against her stepmother's express wishes when he caught sight of a dainty foot dangling from an upper branch. Isabel, it seemed, had been persuaded of the fun of it herself.

The fly in the ointment continued to be the earl. Though Elizabeth's father was scrupulously polite in every exchange following their first one, Northam could not mistake that it was his wish that he and Elizabeth were gone from his home. It begged the question of why they were invited in the first place. North no longer believed Rosemont had been desirous of making an inspection of his daughter's new husband, and the invitation had certainly not been extended for Elizabeth's sake. What remained in his mind were two possibilities: one, that Isabel had been the one set on having Elizabeth home, or two, that the request for their company had not originated from Rosemont at all.

Northam propped himself on one elbow and studied Elizabeth's face. She was staring at the damask canopy, her bottom lip caught just a bit between her teeth. He recognized the expression on her still features as one of contemplation. Candlelight flickered across her brow and the slim bridge of her nose and highlighted the gold in her hair. He was not certain she was even aware he had awakened until she spoke softly.

"Will you be very glad to leave on the morrow?"

"I am anxious for you to see Hampton Cross, but no, I shall not be very glad to leave. I find there is much about Rosemont that I will miss."

She nodded. "It is the same for me." There was the manner of a confession in her tone. "I resist coming and when I am here I do not want to leave so easily."

"It is your home."

"No. It hasn't been that for a long time."

"Will you hear me out?" he asked.

Elizabeth did not answer immediately. Such a question usually presaged some unpleasantness. She did not doubt that was the way of it now. "If you wish."

"I have come to believe your father loves you, Elizabeth." He saw a muscle jump in her cheek as she pressed her jaws together. To her credit she did not clamp her hands over her ears. "Not in the way you deserve to be loved, but in the only way that he can. He does better, I think, with Selden." He watched Elizabeth's mouth part and staved off her reply by continuing quickly. "Pray, do not say it is because Selden is a boy and the heir. Men are not all disposed to favor one child over another because of the vagaries of biology."

Elizabeth could not let that pass without challenge. "Do you mean to say you would accept a daughter as readily as a son?"

"I mean to say I would accept our *child*."

She pressed her lips together and swallowed with some

difficulty. When Elizabeth was certain she could speak with
no catch in her voice, she said, "Do you remember what I
said to you on the eve of our wedding?"

He recalled many of the things she said that night, but
he suspected he knew which one she referred to now. *I find
I am selfish enough to hope that you will hate me less if you
never love me at all.* "Yes," he said. "I remember your
warning that I should develop no tender feelings for you."

She nodded, grateful she did not have to explain it all
again. "It is rather like that with my father. I have been a
great disappointment to him, North. You said he does not
love me as I deserve to be loved, and for that I am grateful,
because neither has he come to hate me enough to cut me
entirely from his life. I would never be able to see Isabel
again . . . or Adam. I think I should die if he kept me from
them. They are my anchors." Her smile was a trifle watery
and she quickly knuckled away tears. "Forgive me. I fear
I am being melodramatic. Of course I would not die."

But she would grieve, Northam thought. That was what
she had been doing tonight, mourning the separation that
must of necessity occur on the morrow. And not just from
taking leave of Isabel and her brother, as she would have
him believe, but also from leaving her father. Nothing was
so black and white in that uneasy alliance between Rosemont
and his daughter. Each nuance of their kinship was shaded
gray.

North rested his hand on Elizabeth's shoulder. His thumb
made a gentle pass across the curve. "Who was your lover,
Elizabeth?" He felt her stiffen, but she did not jerk away
from him. "There was only one, wasn't there?" She nodded
almost imperceptibly. "And your father found out." This
time there was a more noticeable assent. "This is how you
think you hurt him. He was angry with you."

"He was enraged," she said tonelessly.

Now Northam nodded. Rosemont's reaction was understandable. No matter how the relationship with his daughter
had already been strained, he was still her protector. "What

did he do, Elizabeth? Send your lover away? Challenge him? Arrange for your marriage?''

She shook her head. ''None of those things. He did nothing.''

This was not in keeping with Rosemont's character. It seemed to North that the earl's own considerable pride would have demanded some sort of satisfaction. His eyes glanced over the flat line of Elizabeth's mouth, the stubborn tilt of her chin. *Willful.* The earl would have done something. *Willful.* Unless . . . ''You never told him who it was,'' North said as the truth was borne home to him. ''In spite of all the pressure he brought to bear, you never told him.''

''And I will not,'' she said with implacable calm. Her head turned to the side to regard North. ''As I will not tell you.''

North lifted his hand from her shoulder and cupped the side of her face. He traced the lower edge of her lip with his thumb, his touch infinitely tender. ''It has been very hard for you.''

''No more than for my family.'' She caught his wrist and stilled his hand. ''Do not pity me. I had choices then. Perhaps I was not so very wise in the ones I made, but I am responsible for them.''

Nodding, he withdrew his hand. ''Have you never told anyone? Isabel? The colonel?''

''No!'' She amended her forceful response more gently. ''No. They would have told my father.''

''I understand.'' Whether misguided or necessary, Elizabeth's silence had been predicated on the belief that she was protecting her lover. ''You were in love.''

''Yes.''

It was the admission North expected, but he had been unable to prepare for the pain of it. He inhaled quietly, deeply, and let the breath out very slowly. Before he could think better of it, he asked, ''Did he love you so well as I?''

A small, strangled sound came from Elizabeth's throat. She looked away and stared at the canopy again. Tears

welled in her eyes and the act of trying to blink them back
made them slip from the corners and fall past her temples.
"You will think I am a waterworks," she said shakily,
attempting a laugh.

Northam ignored this. He had made himself vulnerable
to her. He thought he deserved an answer, even if she meant
to trample him with it. "Did he, Elizabeth? Did he love you
so well as I do?"

She closed her eyes, stemming the flow of tears. "No."
Her answer was hardly more than a puff of air. "No, I do
not think he did."

Something eased inside Northam's chest. He nodded. "I
am selfish, too," he said. "I would know that I have some
special place in your life."

He'd had that for some time. It was the other place he
was making for himself, the one in her heart, that kept her
silent.

Elizabeth turned to him, her eyes luminous. "Will you
love me?"

His smile was gentle. She had never asked him before,
and it seemed to North that her voice caught on the single
word he said so easily and she said not at all. He reached
for her, drawing her into his arms, and kissed the tear stains
at the corner of her eyes, her temples. She shuddered a little
in his embrace. He stroked her hair and waited for her to
quiet, then he set about loving her.

And he did it so very well.

In the morning a post arrived for Elizabeth as she was
finishing her breakfast. She used her butter knife to lift the
baron's distinctive seal. "It is from Battenburn," she told
Isabel and North. Her eyes skimmed the neatly penned missive once, then a second time to make certain she had missed
no detail. When she was done she folded the letter carefully
and placed it on her lap under the table. She held it there,
not because she was afraid it would fall, but because it gave
her a place to hide her fidgeting hands.

"He writes from London," she said. "Louise has suffered some ailment of the heart. The doctors have seen her and she is resting comfortably." Elizabeth's view no longer encompassed her stepmother; she looked only at Northam. "She has asked for me."

North nodded once but said nothing. He schooled his features in anticipation of what was coming.

"May we go to London?" Elizabeth asked. "I am heartsick to ask it of you, North. I have so been looking forward to seeing Hampton Cross."

He held up his hand before she threw herself prostrate at his feet. "Of course we must go. Louise is your friend, is she not?"

Emotion knotted Elizabeth's throat. She nodded once.

"Very well. Then we go."

Isabel leaned toward Northam and touched him lightly on the forearm. "You are very good to our Elizabeth. Rosemont has confided the same to me. I know I should not speak in his place, but it has been said and I would share it."

Because Isabel meant it as a kindness, Northam said nothing that would spoil her giving spirit. Had Rosemont been present, instead of visiting tenants on his daughter's last morning at home, North would have said that his goodness to Elizabeth was no more than she deserved. It was probably just as well that Rosemont was out. The comment would have in no way been warmly received.

Northam added cream to his coffee and stirred. "Does Battenburn say how he came to write us here?"

"He also sent a letter to Hampton Cross in the event we had already left."

"I see." He lifted his cup and tasted the coffee. "The baron leaves little to chance."

Elizabeth frowned, uncertain of his meaning. "I believe he wants to do whatever is necessary for Louise's comfort. My presence will ease her mind."

"And his."

"Of course."

North's suspicions were too ill-conceived to be put into words. There was nothing to be gained by continuing the discussion until his own thinking was clear. "It will be tomorrow night before we can reach London. The horses cannot go so far without a rest, even if we can."

Northam's London home was in Merrifeld Square in the St. James district. The houses all sat behind impressive iron gates and faced the small center park, where nannies could sometimes be seen with their young charges. It was a comfortable residence, distinct from others on the square because of North's insistence that the outside lanterns be brass instead of iron.

"It is for prevention," he explained to Elizabeth when she noted the difference. "It prevents me from ending up in Lady Morgan's bed on the right or in Mr. Whitley's on the left. It is only when I am into my cups, you understand. Otherwise I have no trouble finding my room."

"I am so relieved to learn of it."

Elizabeth's experience managing so many concerns for Lady Battenburn came to serve her in good stead, for events seemed to conspire to keep the newlyweds in London.

In the beginning it was Louise's heart palpitations that occupied Elizabeth. Northam commented that Lady Battenburn's wants seemed to be vastly different than her needs, but he never considered asking Elizabeth to attend to her friend less often. He watched his wife set out in the morning, sometimes for several hours, and then again in the late afternoon. On occasion he went with her but found the visits strained his good humor. It was little wonder, he reflected, that tension was quickly visible in Elizabeth's features. When he inquired solicitously as to whether she was perhaps taking on too much, he received such a sharp lecture concerning the responsibilities of friendship that he wondered if she had been in correspondence with his grandfather.

As Louise's health improved Northam's own mother found ways to occupy Elizabeth's time. He did not begrudge

Celia's attentions to his wife, for Elizabeth was eminently worth showing off to London as the new Countess of Northam, but their own private hours together were too brief. There were days when he only saw his wife alone as she tumbled into bed.

Complicating Northam's desire to leave London for Hampton Cross was a succession of robberies, all of them pointing to the Gentleman Thief. The items publicly acknowledged as stolen were always jewelry. Lockets. Pearls. Earbobs. Rings. The Gentleman usually selected one interesting item from a jewelry box and left everything else untouched. Since it was never the most valuable piece available, the victims often felt some relief mixed with their sense of violation. Many times the theft went unremarked upon for days because it was not noticed or was considered to be trifling.

"It's the damnedest thing," Northam told his friends, "but I'm beginning to suspect myself."

South chuckled and pointed to the cards in the middle of the table. "Your play, North. Don't hold up the game."

North threw down a two-spot that trumped the play and South happily collected the trick for their side. "As best as I can work it out, many of the robberies have occurred during entertainments where I have been present."

Mr. Marchman considered his next play. "Do you think you're being set up? After what occurred at Battenburn, it must be tempting for the thief."

" 'Course he's being set up," South said. "Play your card." He glanced over his shoulder at Elizabeth, who was reading a book near the fireplace. "I say, Lady North, if these fellows can't talk and concentrate on the game, would you consider two-handed whist with me?"

Elizabeth looked up from her book, her smile vague. "Were you speaking to me, Lord Southerton?"

South grinned. "No, m'lady. I was, as usual, speaking to myself. Please, go on with your reading." He turned back to the game and found all three of his friends staring at him with real impatience. "Oh? My turn, is it? Well, what do we have here?'' He pretended to study the cards already down and then the ones in his hand. Southerton made his play a moment before the others prepared to cheerfully strangle him.

Eastlyn tossed his card down and took the trick. ''Bad play, South. You keep this up and North will invite his lady to take your place. Come to think of it, the idea has merit whether you play well or not.''

The game went on with decidedly more focus until Eastlyn and Marchman won the final tricks. They left the table to enjoy a glass of port. Southerton seated himself beside Elizabeth and stole a look at her book. ''Highly edifying,'' he commented. ''Malthus's *Essay on the Principle of Population*. Bloody hell. North? Do you know what your wife is reading? You must take her in hand quickly else she will get *ideas*.''

Everyone laughed, including Elizabeth. She closed the slim volume around her index finger and placed it on her lap. ''My lord suggested it to me. He is working to repeal the Corn Laws and thinks Malthus's work may be used to present his argument. I am to help him by debating the opposite side, so I must be familiar with the principles myself.''

South rested his head against the back of the sofa. ''If this is an example of modern marriage, then I am for all time a bachelor.''

Northam came to stand behind the sofa at his wife's back. He touched her shoulder lightly. ''You will remain single, South, because no one of any sense will have you.''

''Hhmpf.''

Elizabeth raised her face and basked a moment in her husband's kind smile. She reached up to her shoulder and laid one hand over his. From the perspective of Eastlyn and Mr. Marchman, modern marriage had a great deal to recommend it.

Marchman settled himself comfortably in a chair across from them and propped his feet on a stool. ''How serious were you, North, about being suspected as the thief?''

He shrugged. "I don't know. I don't want to believe that people would seriously credit me with the robberies, but I've heard snippets that make me think the *ton* is wondering."

"Then they should wonder more quietly," Elizabeth said sharply. She saw that her quick defense brought a smile to the others. "Oh, do not patronize me. It is quite right that I should assert my husband's innocence. Someone might say the same of any of you and I would take up cudgels on your behalf."

"Cudgels," South murmured. "Now, what exactly are those?"

The Marquess of Eastlyn smirked. "Have a care, South, or she'll level one at your head and none of us shall stay her hand."

"Thank you, my lord," Elizabeth said politely. She tapped North's hand. "I do not understand your interest in the Gentleman. And, pray, do not tell me it is because you have been suspected of being the thief. I believe your interest began before that unfortunate incident."

One of North's brows lifted. "Unfortunate? As I recall, that incident led to a most public proposal."

Elizabeth blushed as his friends chuckled. "I did not mean ... that is, it was not precisely unfortunate ... it is simply that ..."

South shook his head slowly. "I hope you can defend the Corn Laws better than your marriage, else you will be no help to North's debate."

"I may forgo cudgels, Lord Southerton, and hit you with Malthus."

That threat made South sit up straight and push himself into the corner of the sofa. He kept a watchful eye on Elizabeth over the rim of his glass.

His smile in check, Marchman sipped his port. "Do you still think the thief is among the guests, North? Or someone who takes advantage of the rout to slip unnoticed abovestairs, perhaps from the outside?"

"Either is possible. I remain undecided."

"You still have not explained your interest," Elizabeth

said. When the question was met with silence from all quarters, she nodded. "Oh, I see. It is the purview of the Compass Club and I, being without a direction of my own *and* a female, cannot have it explained to me. Very well, gentlemen, I shall excuse myself and let you carry on privately, but if you care to remove my husband from among the suspects, you will encourage him attend some entertainments without me. I cannot always be his alibi. Now that we are married, no one believes that he is ever with me."

Northam kissed Elizabeth's cheek when she came around the sofa to bid him good night. "And they would be right," he said. "I saw very little of you at Lady Dover's assembly three nights past. Or the Wilmonts' party before that. Your admirers and my mother conspire to keep you away from me."

"That is false, my lord. It is only that you are so concerned with catching a Gentleman that you fail to notice your lady."

"Oh, ho!" South regarded them, one dark brow cocked. "What is this? Do I hear the inklings of a quarrel?"

North and Elizabeth both looked at Southerton, their expressions a mixture of amusement and disapproval. Elizabeth handed the Malthus to her husband. "You hit him with it, my lord."

The entire Compass Club was grinning as they watched her exit the drawing room.

"You are vastly lucky, North," Eastlyn said when the door closed behind Elizabeth. "I own that I find much to admire about your lady."

Marchman raised his glass in agreement. His voice was a shade wistful. "If only she would have walloped South. Now, *that* would have earned my undying favor."

North set the book aside. "I had the same thought."

Southerton's tone was serious. "You've told her nothing about the colonel's assignment?"

"I told you nothing either," said North. "You simply arrived at it on your own."

"I don't see what can be the harm of explaining it to Elizabeth."

"The harm," Eastlyn interrupted, "is that ladies talk." He went to pour himself another glass of port. "I know it for a fact. I would not be in such a coil if Mrs. Sawyer had not spread it about that I had attached myself to Sophie."

"Sophie, is it?" Marchman asked. He blithely ignored Eastlyn's sour look. "Still, you cannot paint all women with the same brush. You must allow that Lady Northam is someone very fine."

"I believe I'm the one who said I find her most admirable. Can't trust 'em not to talk, though. That's the thing."

North held out his own glass and was silent while Eastlyn topped it off. *But you must never trust me.* Elizabeth's soft voice echoed in his head. He wanted to trust her. It pained him that he could not answer her questions. "It has nothing to do with her talking. She would say nothing, not even to my mother, and you all know what pressure can be brought to bear from that quarter." There were immediate murmurs of agreement. "She would, however, involve herself, and that could have no end but a bad one."

South considered that his friend was right. He remembered how impulsively Elizabeth had stepped forward to help North at Battenburn. "She had an interesting point, though. As far as your rep goes, North, you should consider going about without your wife—"

"Bloody hell," North interrupted. "I am in want of seeing her now. She is out driving with my mother or sitting with Lady Battenburn. There are the afternoon teas and literary circles. Morning promenades. Charities. Lectures. I had no idea women could find so much nothing to occupy themselves."

Southerton cleared his throat to prevent his laughter from spilling out. A glance at Eastlyn and Marchman assured him that they were equally amused. Poor, neglected North. He was pitiful. They independently assured themselves the same would never be thought of them. "Surely you can see her point," South pressed on. "If you attend every evening assembly with her, she becomes less effective as your alibi. The Gentleman Thief seems to be taking some care to steal from the very homes in which you are an invited guest. Perhaps by permitting one of us to escort Lady North while you—"

"Certainly not."

"While you stayed home would allay suspicions."

"And what if there is no theft that night?" asked North. "That will certainly make the *ton* wonder."

Southerton raked his dark hair. "Well, then, I'll steal something. Just a trifle, nothing valuable, and I'll have it arranged to be returned as my snuffbox was returned to me. What can be the harm of that?"

"The harm," East was compelled to point out, "is that you could be caught. It would be deuced difficult to explain how you were not really stealing but assisting a friend. Let me or West do it. At least we have some experience with thieving."

Marchman sighed. "I wish you would allow me the honor of volunteering my services myself."

"Enough," North said. "It is not going to happen."

It was quite late when North came to bed. In spite of his adamant opposition to their plan, the rest of the Compass Club would not leave off. No matter what other subjects were offered up for discussion, the conversation always came back to the problem of the thief. Finally North simply let them talk on, neither approving nor objecting to their scheming. Had it not involved Elizabeth he admitted to himself that he might have been amused.

She turned over sleepily as he raised the covers and slipped into bed. Her arm curved around his chest and she snuggled closer, pressing her lips to the nape of his neck. "They kept you up far too long," she murmured. "I could not stay awake."

North raised Elizabeth's hand and kissed her fingers. No matter what the circumstances of their days and evenings, the nights were their own. Elizabeth never turned away from him when he turned to her. She let him love her, and loved him in return, without ever saying the words. North never pressed her to speak them, though sometimes he thought they hovered there, just outside her consciousness, waiting for her to open up to the idea of them.

"We did not mean to exclude you this evening," he said quietly, returning her hand to his chest. Her fingers splayed in the soft mat of blond hair that covered him.

"Yes, you did. You cannot help it."

"Then I am sorry for it."

Her smile was a trifle sad. "I know. It is the same for me." *You must never trust me.* The words hung between them. Elizabeth did not know how or when it had come to pass, but North had begun to take her at her word. Sometimes she felt his distance even when he was deep inside her, her body held in his most intimate embrace. She saw a remoteness in his eyes even when his smile was most gentle, a restraint in his touch even when it made her shudder with its tenderness. "I think I am a trifle jealous of them." The words surprised her. She had never dared admit as much to herself and now she had said them aloud. "You are all so very close."

Northam would not allow himself to assume he understood the sentiment behind her words or what compelled her to express it. "Perhaps they should not visit so often."

"No," she said quickly. "Oh, no. I would not have it. I like them very much, and I know they keep you company when I am otherwise occupied."

"Then perhaps you should not be so often otherwise occupied."

Elizabeth realized too late the trap she had laid for herself. "Please. Let us not argue. I am with you now." She kissed his shoulder. Tension ran through the line of his back. "Brendan?"

He turned and unerringly found her mouth. The kiss was hard and hungry, impatient with need, confident of no refusal. She moaned a little at the pressure of his lips, then opened her mouth and gave herself over to him. This, at least, had not changed. She took solace from the fact that she could please him here, that she responded to him in a way that was necessary for his own arousal. He always seemed to know if she was holding back, and it was the one thing he would not allow. His own pleasure required hers; it was the price he exacted for loving her. He would have her surrender.

North's fingers curled in Elizabeth's nightshift, pushing the hem to her thighs. He pressed her knees up and apart. Beneath the covers he found her hand and guided it to his groin. Her fingers closed around his erection. Her hips lifted and then she was drawing him inside her. In spite of her willingness, she was not quite ready for him. She bit her lip when he thrust deeply, but no sound, not even one at the back of her throat, escaped.

"Why do you do that, Elizabeth?" North's whisper was husky. He settled himself against her, not moving, waiting for her body to accommodate his entry. She held him so tightly, it was an agony of pleasure. He leaned forward, levering himself on his elbows. Elizabeth legs immediately wrapped around him. "Why do you let me hurt you?"

"It is nothing."

"It is *not* nothing, dammit." He felt her wince, this time from the harshness of his tone. "Do you think I mean to punish you?"

She did not answer immediately. When she did, her voice was almost inaudible. "Sometimes. Yes."

"God." He closed his eyes and lowered his head, pressing his forehead for just a moment against hers. "Maybe I do. Perhaps it is only that you are more honest than I am." He started to withdraw, but she held him, clasping his hips with her thighs and knees. "Elizabeth, I can't—"

"No, it's all right. I'm ready now. Please. Please don't—" She lifted her bottom a little, pushing into him. "See? I only needed a—" She felt him stir. "A moment," she finished, almost on a sigh. Her hands settled on his shoulders. She caressed him. His skin was smooth, warm. Above her his shadowed features were taut. "Love me," she whispered.

Her punishment was that he did.

* * *

Her Grace, the Dowager Duchess of Calumet, had planned
a splendid ball. It was easily November's most hoped for
invitation, and the Earl and Countess of Northam were
among those who received one. It was on this crisp evening,
with a hint of snow in the air, that North was finally persuaded to remain home and permit Lord Southerton to escort
his wife. He had second thoughts before they were out the
door, and nearly charged after the carriage when it began
to roll away. Somehow he managed to stay his ground and
finally return inside to wait.

Eastlyn and West kept him company. The marquess had
declined to attend the ball in favor of staying with North,
even though the duchess was a great friend of his own
mother's and his refusal had caused some friction there.
"Sophie could not go," he told North. "So it is no real
sacrifice to stay away."

North and Marchman exchanged glances. They both recol-
lected that at one time Lady Sophia had been considered
unexceptional company. Apparently something had
changed, at least in Eastlyn's mind if not in Sophie's character.

No invitation had been sent around to Mr. Marchman's
residence, which neither surprised nor displeased him. It
would have been a sore trial to his stamina to have attended
the thing. "Does Lady North know anything about South's
plan?"

North's eyes went heavenward. "I can only hope that is
not the case. Of course she knows why I am not going; that
was her own idea. But as to what South will get up to at
the ball, she has been told nothing. She would certainly try
to talk him out of it—as we did—and failing that—as we
did—she would most assuredly get in the way."

"Or give him away," Eastlyn said.

North shrugged, not certain this last was true. He did not
want to share with this friends that Elizabeth was very good

at not giving things away. "Shall we play cards? I collect it will be a long evening."

Southerton told Elizabeth he was going to find a card game while she made repairs to a tear in her hem. She warned him to be careful as Battenburn was among the guests and was always looking to reclaim what South had won from him. Unconcerned, since he had no intention of playing cards, South waved Elizabeth off. Laughing, she went in search of a maid who could assist her.

Southerton wandered in and out of several rooms until he found the entrance to the backstairs. He was quite certain that the guests milling in the hall paid no attention to his exit. The music from the ballroom faded as he climbed the stairs. He counted himself fortunate not to encounter a servant. While they would have said nothing to him, they would have certainly remembered his use of these stairs later, especially when it was learned that a piece of her grace's jewelry was missing.

South was aware that he could not know if the Gentleman Thief would strike this evening, but he also could not leave it to chance. In order to clear Northam of suspicion, a robbery had to take place when he could not have committed it. It was most aggravating to the colonel that North's investigation had been compromised and, in the end, North had had little choice but to accept his friends' help.

It was too bad that Elizabeth could not be informed. South considered that she would have made an admirable lookout.

South had litte difficulty locating the dowager duchess's suite. It was only a matter of opening and closing a dozen doors on the way to the right one. Finding her jewelry case was an even simpler matter. It was open on her vanity, the dark blue velvet bed almost hidden by the coiled strings of pearls on top. Among the pearls were rubies, sapphires, and emeralds. Pear-shaped and square-cut. Necklaces. Rings. Hair ornaments. Earbobs. Her grace's careless regard for even this small portion of her collection took South's breath away. An eddy of cool night air from an open window circled the room and gave it back. South spared a glance for the billowing drapes before he studied the jumble of jewelry again and wondered at it. In light of the recent robberies it was really inexcusable that the duchess would leave such an open invitation to the thief. . . .

Unless it was a trap.

It was on the heels of that thought that Southerton realized he was not alone.

"You will not credit it," South told his audience, "but the Gentleman Thief is entirely misnamed. I can state unequivocally that he is no gentleman. A gentleman would not have dived through her grace's open window without so much as a by-your-leave."

"Yes, well," Northam said ironically, "that cuts it. He certainly did not attend Hambrick Hall."

Eastlyn and Mr. Marchman nodded in agreement, their own good humor barely kept in check. Only Elizabeth was more subdued. "You might have been run through," she said. "It was very dangerous for you to confront him. Why did you tell me nothing of this plan of yours? I might have stood in the hall and warned you of . . . of . . . well, of *something*."

"Which is precisely why you were not forewarned," Northam said. "As for South being run through, that is doubtful. No one has ever accused this thief of carrying any weapon, let alone a sword."

South nodded. "But it is very good of you to be concerned."

Elizabeth snorted. "You can rest assured I will not be so again. Go on, finish your tale. It is outside everything that you accompanied me back here without saying a word of this."

"I dislike twice-told tales," South said, perfectly sincere. With a cheerful smile, he picked up his snifter of brandy and sipped. "I wish I had had a better look at the brigand.

He is on the smallish side, North. And agile as a monkey. He wore a black frock coat and trousers much like I had on, though I do not think they fit him so well. There could have been no hat else he would have lost it diving through the window as he did. In any event the drapes did much to hide him from my view."

"You ran to the window, didn't you?" East asked.

"Of course. But I expected him to be below me and I spent valuable seconds looking for him in that direction. When I allowed myself to consider another possibility, it was too late. My last glimpse was of a leg dangling from the lip of the hip roof. He pulled it up quickly enough. I could not see anything at all after that. I have to assume he crossed the roof and found another avenue to the street, no doubt across a succession of rooftops."

"At least you had the good sense not to pursue him," said Elizabeth. She moved closer to North on the sofa and slipped her arm through his. It was as if she thought she could ground him, knowing as she did that he would not have been so cautious as Southerton if he had been in his friend's place. "You might have been killed."

"It was not the possibility of dying that kept him from giving chase," Marchman said. "It was the certainty that he would ruin his new coat."

"Just so," South said, unoffended. He brushed an imaginary mote of lint from his sleeve. "I was also thinking that I needed to exit quickly myself, and a door suited my purposes better than a window. I left everything as it was and took my leave. The hall was deserted and I returned to the ballroom by the main stairs. I was not even missed. I can tell you, North, what I learned is how surpassingly simple it has been for this thief." He cleared his throat when he saw the others were very nearly gaping at him. "Er, that is, if one discounts his rather inspired and skillful method of escape. What I mean is that there was virtually no problem moving in the house. The duchess cannot easily close off the upper floors to her guests. Why, Elizabeth herself required some privacy to make repairs to her gown."

Elizabeth felt all eyes on her for a moment. "Lord Everheart stepped on my tunic and tore the embroidered band."

"Clumsy fellow," Eastlyn said. "I would have run him through."

Elizabeth gave him a quelling look. "Go on, South. You were saying that it has been surpassingly simple for this thief."

"A small exaggeration, perhaps," South allowed. "Still, it was easy enough for me, and I have no practice thieving."

"Did you take anything?" asked North.

"No, but not because it wasn't there to be taken. At first I thought the duchess was unconscionably careless with her baubles; then I considered that she had laid some sort of trap. When I understood who was with me in her room I realized that I had interrupted him. He was the one who had found her jewelry and was going through it."

North felt Elizabeth's arm tighten against his. He suspected she was going to take him to task for what South had done tonight, or at least for not telling her of his plan. "Did you know if anything was taken?"

"Not then. Naturally, with no decent explanation for my own presence in her room, I could not go to the duchess myself. I was forced to wait. It was nearing midnight, poor Lady North was making rather pitiful noises about wanting to leave, and I was providing sad excuses as to why we should stay. I was finally witness to a general disturbance in the circle of people around the duchess and in minutes the rumor of a theft reached my ears. I escorted your wife out immediately and came here. I understand it was a sapphire and diamond necklace that was removed from her case. The gossip could have it wrong, the duchess could have mistaken the missing piece, but it was a certainty that the thief did not leave her grace's room without something that belonged to her."

Southerton lifted his brandy snifter in a salute. "It has all been accomplished," he said, supremely satisfied with himself. "North can no longer be entertained as a suspect by anyone with a modicum of intelligence, I can provide a

modest description of the thief, and I managed the thing
without getting caught." He eyed his three friends shrewdly.
"So tell me, who wagered against my success?"

Without a word, the three other members of the Compass
Club leaned forward and dropped coins into South's raised
glass.

Elizabeth was brushing out her hair when North entered
their bedchamber. "You dismissed your maid?" he asked.

She nodded. "Brill is waiting for you in your dressing
room."

Northam crossed to the adjoining room, where his valet
helped him out of his coat and boots. He tugged at his stock
himself, gave the length of cloth to Brill for laundering, then
sent him on his way. North padded back into the bedroom,
his shirt open at the collar and the tails no longer tucked
neatly into his trousers. He ran one hand through his hair
as he came to stand behind Elizabeth.

She looked up, finding his face above her in the mirror.
He looked tired and vaguely disreputable. Neither diminished his extraordinarily handsome features. The tiny lines
at the corners of his eyes and mouth only brought her attention to them. "It was wearing for you this evening," she
said. "I understood it was difficult for you to let us go to
the duchess's home, but I mistook the reason for it. I wish
you had told me what South intended."

He took the brush from her hand and began to run it
through her hair. Strands of ginger and gold spilled over his
fingers when he lifted her hair and pulled the brush through
on the underside. "What would you have done?" he asked.

"I told you I would have lurked in the upper hall and
warned South of imminent discovery, but it was only pique
that made me say it. In truth, I don't believe that I would
have gone at all."

North waited patiently while Elizabeth rearranged the per-
fumes and creams on her vanity. He recognized the scents
he had chosen for her by their uniquely designed crystal

bottles and stoppers. She moved a plain brown bottle he had not seen before from the forefront to the rear, tucking it away so it would not detract from the artisanship of the others; then she lined up several small pots of cream and powders on the opposite side. When everything seemed to be ordered, North felt her draw a breath and prepare to go on.

"I realize it was my idea for us to attend separate functions. I believed that sooner or later the thief would make a call while you were elsewhere. I would not have countenanced South taking matters into his own hands."

"I did not agree to that part either. None of us did. South could not be reasoned out of it."

"Something terrible might have happened." For a moment the brush paused in her hair. Elizabeth was very aware of North's study of her reflection. Her hands were flat on the vanity top and she pressed her fingers against the wood to still their fine tremor. There was nothing she could do to keep it out of her voice. "It was unfair of you not to tell me. You gave me no choice."

North let the brush make one more slow pass through her hair before he placed it on the vanity. "And you gave me none," he said quietly. "*Do not ever trust me.*" He let the words hang a moment between them.

Elizabeth's head bowed and she stared at her hands, unable to look at him any longer.

"Then you have not forgotten," he said.

She shook her head.

"I was only taking you at your word, Elizabeth."

She felt his hands rest lightly on her shoulders. His thumbs brushed the nape of her neck. "I want to go to Hampton Cross," she said on a thread of sound. "I want to leave London."

Chapter Twelve

North's eyes dropped away from Elizabeth's reflection and stared down at her bowed head. He removed his hands from under her hair and let them fall to his sides. "I should like nothing better than to go to Hampton Cross." Even though he was no longer touching her, her immediate relief was palpable. "But I cannot."

Elizabeth's head came up quickly, her eyes stark. "Of course you can. Have you not been the one saying we should—" She stopped because he was shaking his head, his features implacably set. "Please."

The single word was like a lash striking his skin. It cut him not to be able to do this thing for her, though he little understood her desire or urgency to have it done. "There are matters that keep me here."

"The colonel's matters." When he did not answer immediately it was confirmation enough for Elizabeth. "This thief has somehow become his concern and yours." Again North remained silent and let Elizabeth think what she would. Her laughter was brittle. "I thought it was only your Compass Club playing at some game. . . . I didn't understand it was more than . . ." Her voice trailed off and her hands fell into her lap. "But it is no game at all, is it? This is not four Hambrick boys advancing on the Society of Bishops. God help us all, you are quite serious about apprehending that man.''

''Elizabeth.''

His calm sounded vaguely patronizing to Elizabeth. Her hands curled into fists. ''I am writing to Blackwood in the morning. No, I am going to write to him now.''

North stepped back as she stood, but he caught her arm when she would have walked by him.

Elizabeth looked pointedly at the hand on her elbow. ''Do you really mean to stop me?''

''No, not if you are determined to spend your time on such a futile endeavor. I only wanted to make certain you know that's what it is. You can change nothing.''

She lifted one brow. ''We shall see.''

Colonel Blackwood's reply arrived in the afternoon post three days later. It was filled with details about his horses and his plans to refurbish his study. He wrote that cooler weather had provided relief for his illness and that he was in anticipation of no further weakness at this time. He recommended books to her from among the ones he'd recently read. There was an amusing account of his foray into painting landscapes and he ended with inquiries into her health and that of North's and a gentle request that she would correspond more often.

Nowhere in the letter was there a reference to London's Gentleman Thief or any of the concerns Elizabeth had raised about her husband's involvement.

She was grateful for North's silence on the matter. He knew of the letter's arrival and asked for no confirmation that he had been correct. Her own silence let him know that he was.

Elizabeth was helped out of her redingote and bonnet as she entered the house. Raindrops had made spiked tufts in her fox muff and she brushed them out before she gave it to the housekeeper. "Where is my husband?" she asked. Even to her own ears her question sounded peremptory. Only she knew that it was weariness that made it so. Louise had been particularly contentious during this morning's visit. There was no reasoning with her, and even Battenburn could not calm her. The baroness had been in a mood to have her way in everything.

"My husband?" she asked again, less imperiously this time.

"In the library, my lady. He is in receipt of two letters delivered not one half hour ago. He asked not to be disturbed."

"I am certain he did not mean to include me." Elizabeth had no idea if that was true or not. North had been cool toward her these last few days. His good manners kept him from being anything less than polite, but she felt his remoteness nonetheless. He had expressed no interest in making love to her since the night she wrote to Blackwood. She felt him slipping away from her, just as she had known he would someday. Knowing it would happen and living through it were not the same thing at all. "I will be with him," she told the housekeeper. "Please bring tea."

Elizabeth entered the library quietly. North was slouched in his favorite reading chair. He looked up, acknowledged her presence with a slight nod, but made no attempt to stand. The letters, she noted, were not in evidence. A decanter of brandy was. "Are you foxed, my lord?" she asked. It was not at all what she had expected.

A faint smiled edged his mouth. "I am. Have you some objection?"

"No. None at all, though I am not accustomed to it. I have asked Mrs. Wallace to bring tea. Will that suit?"

"I don't care what you drink."

Elizabeth could see that North's mood was every bit a match for the one she'd encountered in Louise. She did not know if she had the patience for it. "May I enquire as to the reason you are drinking at this hour of the day? Mrs. Wallace mentioned a post."

North nodded. ''Marchman sent word 'round of his father's death. It was not entirely unexpected, though one is never properly prepared. The old bastard left a will that recognizes Marchman as his son. He would never publicly admit to it during his lifetime. It makes Marchman the elder, you see. The heir over his younger half-brother.''

Elizabeth sat down slowly. ''Then Mr. Marchman is now . . .'' She could not quite comprehend it. ''Why, it is just as you said it would be. He has come into his name after all this time.''

North raised his glass, his eyes unfocused and vaguely slumberous. ''Found his direction, if you will forgive the pun.''

She ignored this. ''So he shall be the Duke of Westphal now. Poor West. I believe he has never wanted that.''

''Never.'' He drained his glass and set it beside the decanter. ''West only ever wanted one thing from his father. It was not his title.'' With none of his usual grace, North pushed himself to his feet. ''Would you like a drink? No, that's right. You asked for tea.'' He walked to the fireplace, chose the poker from among the tools, and prodded the logs to give up more heat. ''You will attend the services with me,'' he said.

''Of course.'' Elizabeth was surprised he even mentioned it. A feeling of dread began to unfold in her stomach. She pressed her hands protectively against her midriff.

''Afterwards . . .'' North carefully leaned the poker against the marble jamb. He turned on Elizabeth, his gaze steadier than it had been minutes earlier. ''If you want to go to Hampton Cross or to Rosemont, I will arrange it.''

''I don't—'' A lump lodged in her throat, making speech impossible.

''It will not cause much comment when I remain in town, especially if you visit your family.''

Elizabeth swallowed with difficulty. ''Is this because of my letter to the colonel? Mrs. Wallace said you received two letters this morning. Was one from Blackwood?'' She disliked brandy, had only tasted it a few times in her life, but just now it seemed very appealing.

"One was *not* from the colonel." North reached into his pocket and withdrew a small brown bottle. Watching Elizabeth, he idly played with the stopper, removing the cork and replacing it. For a time the faint sound that action made seemed louder than the crackle of flames in the fireplace. North placed the bottle on the mantel with a delicacy usually reserved for porcelain. Elizabeth's stricken eyes were drawn to it, just as he'd known they would be. She did not want to look at it and she could not look away.

"You recognize it," he said without inflection.

"Yes."

"I saw it for the first time the night you returned from the duchess's party. Do you recall? We were at your vanity. I was brushing your hair."

It seemed a lifetime ago, and yet less than a week had passed. Elizabeth nodded faintly. She thought she would embarrass herself by being sick.

"You lined your little jars and bottles up like soldiers, flanking the troops on either side of the mirror. This one stood out, so different from the rest. You pushed it to the rear. I thought it was because it was not as pretty as the others. It did not occur to me then to wonder what was in it." He watched Elizabeth's head drop. "I wish to God it had not occurred to me later."

A knock interrupted the silence that lay thickly between them. North went to the door because Elizabeth could not seem to move. He took the tray from Mrs. Wallace and declined her offer to serve. The cup and saucer trembled when he placed them in Elizabeth's hands.

Taking neither tea nor brandy for himself, North returned to his chair across from Elizabeth. "The letter I received was from the apothecary," he explained. "A formality, really. I knew what was in the bottle when I found it again. You hid it in your wardrobe. Is that where you usually kept it?"

Her lips only moved around the word *yes.*

"I sent only a sample for confirmation. I did not want

you to miss the bottle. I took it again when Mr. Goodall's letter arrived.'' He glanced at the bottle on the mantel and then back at his wife. His face was pale, his voice taut. ''Is it only my child you do not want, Elizabeth, or any man's?''

Tea sloshed over the rim of her cup as her hands jerked. Her head came up. She thought it curious that her eyes were dry. The ache behind them, though, was almost intolerable. ''I will only say it once, my lord. There is no one else.''

God help him, he knew it was true, had known it even as he asked. What he did not know was if it was better this way. Sorrow. Hurt. Disappointment. Frustration. Each emotion was forged hot and honed razor sharp with rage. He delivered it in the cutting edge of his voice. ''Then you weren't in fear of presenting me with a bastard.''

Elizabeth merely stared at him, offering nothing else in her defense.

North's arm shot out to the side, sweeping the brandy decanter and glass off the table. The glass shattered against the fireplace apron. The decanter thudded heavily and overturned. The glass stopper fell out and brandy spilled onto the carpet. ''Leave it,'' North said when Elizabeth started to rise. He repeated the words more wearily a moment later. ''Just leave it.''

The odor of the brandy soaking into the carpet made Elizabeth's stomach roil, and the simple act of lifting the teacup to her mouth did not seem possible. She held it between unsteady fingers and waited.

''You do not want a child,'' North said flatly.

''No.''

Northam wondered that he did not reel from the blow. ''I once had a mistress who used the same thing. She soaked a sponge with it and placed the sponge inside her. Is that how you used it?''

''Yes.''

''Yes, of course. It was an inane question.'' His half-smile was rife with self-mockery. ''I find I do not know what to say to you. Perhaps I am too drunk to manage the thing properly.''

"I should leave."

He nodded. "That would be best, I think."

Elizabeth set the cup and saucer on the tray and stood. She took a tentative step in North's direction, but he quickly turned his head. It was not that action but what she glimpsed in his eyes that stopped Elizabeth cold. She pressed bloodless knuckles to her mouth to stifle her own sob and fled from the room before she heard his.

Elizabeth dreaded going to West's home to pay her respects. In her mind it brought her one hour closer to the time North would ask her to leave. There had been no mention of her going to Hampton Cross or Rosemont since he suggested it the first time. She doubted he had changed his mind. It was more to the point that he had spoken very little to her since the confrontation in his library. While she spent the afternoon and evening in her sitting room, he had gone to the club with Southerton and Eastlyn. She supposed the new Duke of Westphal met them there.

He had come home none the worse for wear. He was quiet. Pensive. Elizabeth found herself wishing he had returned drunk and reeking of a whore's perfume. Instead he set the small brown bottle among the others on her vanity and disappeared into the dressing room to change. Elizabeth feigned sleep when he came to bed. He pretended to believe her.

There were shadows under Elizabeth's eyes the next morning. North's own complexion had a gray cast. They both wore black, a color dictated by the occasion of the funeral and wholly suiting their mood. Her gown was bombazine and his double-breasted frock coat was wool. The dipping temperatures and icy rain forced them into heavy outerwear. North's caped greatcoat and Elizabeth's fur-trimmed pelisse shielded them from the elements and did nothing at all for the chill in their bones.

Colonel Blackwood was not present at the service honoring the old duke, but he was at West's residence when a cadre of friends gathered there after the interment. Elizabeth knew she should have expected to see him. It said much about the state of her mind that she had never once considered crossing paths with him today.

Unlike her wedding day, when, contrary to what she told North, Elizabeth had made a point not to be alone with the colonel, she sought him out now. She wheeled him down the hall and into West's empty study.

"Am I to assume this is an abduction?" he asked.

Since she had asked for a moment of his time in front of North and had taken him away in full view of West's invited guests, it was hardly that. "If it pleases you to call it such."

"Butter does not melt in your mouth, Elizabeth." He pushed himself closer to the fireplace where a small fire had been laid. "Hand me that rug, please. It is too chilly in here, even for me."

Elizabeth took the wool blanket that was folded over the back of a wing chair and opened it across the colonel's lap and legs. She stepped away quickly and turned to the fire herself, holding her hands out to warm them.

"It pains you to look at my poor sticks," Blackwood said.

"Yes."

"More than it pains me, I think. I am used to it. You must not feel pity for me, Elizabeth. What is, is." He studied her profile. Her complexion glowed in the reflected heat of the fire. "Come. Do not stand there so. The price of begging a moment of my time is that you must look at me."

Elizabeth knew he meant it. He would leave if she could not give him this one thing. She turned and faced him.

In many ways he had been little changed by his illness. It was change made by the passage of time that she noted first: the shock of black hair that was thinning at the crown and seeded with gray throughout; the pronounced creases at the corners of his eyes; the way the line of his mouth was pulled down on the ends so that its relaxed state was also a faint frown; the gold-rimmed spectacles that rested below the bridge of his hawkish nose. Unchanged by illness or time was the clarity of his dark brown eyes and their challenging, appraising glance. Neither was he different in his attention to his clothing. Though he would have been shocked to hear her say so, he was as fastidious about his manner of dress as Battenburn and unlikely to accept the good-natured teasing about it that Southerton did.

Elizabeth finally made herself acknowledge the more disturbing changes wrought by the colonel's wasting illness. Most obvious were the thin, flaccid legs that kept Blackwood in his chair when his desire was to be anywhere else. His shoulders and chest were no longer robust. The exercise forced on him by propelling his chair was insufficient to keep him broad and firm. His complexion was sallow, having long ago lost the healthy infusion of color that so much time out-of-doors had brought him. There was a tremor in his hands more often than not, and a gravity to his manner that was there by virtue of his slowing reflexes.

He was but four years older than her own mother would have been had she lived and he was her last link to that person she had loved so dearly. There were subtle reminders of Catherine Blackwood Penrose in the way he tilted his head at just a certain angle, the perceptiveness of his gaze, and in the gentleness of his smile when he offered it up.

"You're very much like her, you know," the colonel said.

Elizabeth gave a small start, surprised to hear her thoughts spoken by him. "I was thinking the same of you."

"Me?" Blackwood snorted, the sound both derisive and amused. "I am nothing like Catherine."

"You snort exactly like her."

"Your mother never made a sound such as that in her life. Unladylike."

Elizabeth snorted.

The colonel chuckled appreciatively. "Tell me, your father and Isabel . . . how do they fare?"

"All well."

"And young Selden?"

"Well also." Elizabeth gave him an account of her wedding trip to Rosemont, some of which she had written in previous letters. She knew that North had also corresponded with him, but she recognized the colonel's interest was genuine and answering him helped put her at her ease. She finally sat down, perching on the edge of her chair at first, then gradually sliding backward, pressing herself more deeply into the smooth, aromatic leather upholstery.

"Would you like a glass of Madeira?" Blackwood asked when Elizabeth finished. "I know where West keeps it."

"Nothing, thank you. May I get it for you?"

"No."

Elizabeth learned quickly that the colonel was not refusing libation, only her help. It required some effort for him to push his chair to the sideboard, but it was accomplished without her assistance. It was only when he had poured his drink that he realized he could not easily return without spilling it. Not permitting him to refuse her, Elizabeth got up and pushed the chair back. "So you will not ruin your fine cravat," she said. "South would tease you mercilessly."

The colonel smiled. "He would." He sipped his wine. "So what is it that has prompted this tête-à-tête?"

"The question is beneath you, sir."

"Aaah. Then it is our last correspondence that you wish to discuss."

"You answered none of my questions."

"I will not answer them now, Elizabeth."

To be turned down so out of hand took her breath away. She felt herself flush with embarrassment. "I . . . I do not understand."

"Don't you?"

Her fingers tightened on the curved arms of her chair. "No, I don't. Why can you not tell me if you are directing Northam to apprehend the Gentleman Thief?"

The colonel remained silent.

"You order all of them about," Elizabeth persisted. "The Compass Club. You are their commander."

"Elizabeth," he said calmly, "nothing can come of this discussion."

"But you do not deny it."

"I give no credence to it."

Elizabeth stood. Without conscious thought, she approached the colonel's chair and knelt beside it. She stopped his immediate protest by placing both palms on his forearm. "Look at me now," she said quietly. It was both a directive and a plea. "Tell him to stop. *Make* him stop. I know it is within your influence to do so."

Blackwood held Elizabeth's eyes for a long moment. She would not look away; neither would she allow him to look in. "If I could do it, Elizabeth, *why* should I do it?"

"Because I have never asked any favor of you."

He raised an eyebrow. "I can bring a score of people in here within the hour who have never requested a boon from me. Shall I then grant whatever favor they ask?"

"But you care for me."

"I love you."

Elizabeth felt the instantaneous welling of tears. Her hands tightened on his arm. "Then will you not do this thing to please me?"

"No."

"Then to make me happy?"

His small smile was gentle. "Will it, Elizabeth? Will stopping North make you happy?"

"Yes."

"Why?"

Elizabeth opened her mouth to answer and no sound came out. She closed it slowly, coming to her feet a moment later. Her height presented no advantage. The colonel's question had set her completely adrift. Knowing it was an inadequate response but having no other at the ready, Elizabeth said, "He is my husband."

"So he is."

"I want no harm to come to him."

"Harm? Do you imagine the Gentleman Thief could make you a widow?"

"Yes . . . no. You are missing the point. It is only that he could be hurt. He is very brave, you know. Dedicated and loyal. He admires you greatly and he will follow your lead because he believes you are in the right of things.''

Blackwood raised one hand and rested his chin on his knuckles. ''I know what North is and why he does what he does. I am much less certain of you, Elizabeth. By my reckoning it's been a little more than six years that I've been left to wonder at your character. You made a tour of the Continent then, remember? With Isabel and your father. I expected to hear so much of your adventure . . . your impressions . . . descriptions . . . all of it with your fresh eye. You wrote very little during that time. Even less later. Selden was born in Italy, was he not? I recall one correspondence about your fears for Isabel's health, your concern that she would not survive childbirth as your dear mother had not. You were so frightened that you would lose her. Rosemont was distant, wrestling with his own fears for his wife. You could not turn to him and Isabel only reassured you that everything would be fine—a platitude you could not accept because you knew its falseness. You came to me then, dear Elizabeth, with what was in your heart. Can you not do the same now?''

Elizabeth actually took a step backward. Nothing at the beginning of the colonel's speech prepared her for the end. She stared at him, her hands falling to her sides as hurt was quickly suppressed by anger. ''I have come to you, Colonel, and you have rejected me. As for what is in my heart, I showed it to you and you will not believe.''

Blackwood frowned. ''But you have shown me nothing.''

''Then I have shown you everything.'' Without waiting for a reply, Elizabeth fled the room.

Liar. Elizabeth flung the word at herself and it stung. She had lied. Another lie. Another bead on a string of lies. *Liar.* There was no other word more accurately descriptive of what she had become.

And now she was lying to herself.

Then I have shown you everything. She had meant, of

course, that she had nothing in her heart to share with anyone. In the moment it took to say the words Elizabeth knew she had been most sincere. It was only in the aftermath, in hearing them for the first time, that she finally understood something had changed and what it was was inside her.

Elizabeth did not return to the drawing room with North and the other guests, and nothing could induce her to face the colonel and admit her lie. She walked to the rear of the house, ignoring the disapproving clucks from the cook and her helper, and kept on walking until she was outside on the small back stoop.

It was too chilly to be out for long without a coat, yet Elizabeth had no proper sense of the elements. She leaned back against the cold brick and closed her eyes, unaware that the wind whipped her gown about her legs or that icy shards of rain lashed her bare arms.

Did it matter how or when it happened? she wondered. Or was the fact of it all that was important? She loved him. Loved North. She loved Brendan David Hampton, sixth Earl of Northam.

The revelation was not welcome. It did nothing to improve her mood or lighten her heart. Just the opposite was true, in fact. This knowledge was an immense burden to her and the source of her immediate panic. Her chest hurt and it was difficult to draw a full breath.

None of it was how she had experienced love the first time it came to her, but then circumstances had changed. *She* had changed. Elizabeth was afraid of the very thing she had once embraced so completely.

"Elizabeth?"

She heard the voice as if from a great distance. It swirled in her head, not quite making sense to her. She did not recognize her own name or the fact she was being spoken to. Without opening her eyes, Elizabeth tried to raise one hand to ward off the intrusion.

"Elizabeth!"

Her knees started to fold. The back of her gown was snagged by the bricks as she began to slide against them.

Darkness pressed on her from all sides. Falling into it seemed the only sensible thing to do.

North sat beside Elizabeth on the chaise longue in West's rear parlor. He tapped her cheeks lightly and pushed aside a damp lock of hair that had fallen across her forehead.

"Shall I send someone for a physician?" the colonel asked from the doorway.

"No. She has only fainted." North glanced at Blackwood. It would have been difficult to miss the colonel's concern. Every line in his face was deeply etched now and he looked considerably older than he had a single hour ago. "Will you leave us?" he asked. "And please tell no one. Elizabeth would not like to call so much attention to herself."

The colonel nodded and began to back out of the room. He stopped, a thought occurring to him. "Is she going to have a child?"

North kept his eyes on Elizabeth's pale face. He collected himself before he answered, not wanting to give voice to the bitterness that welled inside him. "No, sir," he said. "There is no need to concern yourself on that account." He felt Blackwood's pause and knew his reply had not been as neutral as he might have wished. Hardly aware he was holding his breath, he waited for the colonel to close the door. The quiet click prompted Northam to draw air again.

Brushing Elizabeth's chin lightly with his knuckles, North repeated her name. This time he felt the first stirrings of a response. A moment later her dark lashes fluttered open. The centers of her eyes were wide and unfocused. She did not seem to recognize him or have a sense of her own situation. Her brow puckered and the corners of her mouth turned down ever so slightly.

"You fainted," said North, withdrawing his hand from her face. "You were outside. Do you remember?"

Elizabeth's nod was uncertain. She had never fainted before, and the memory was not entirely clear.

"I am persuaded your private meeting with the colonel did not go as you would have liked."

North's words brought it all back to her and waves of embarrassment flushed her cheeks. She started to sit up, but North pressed her back by putting his hand on her shoulder. "Please," she said. "I want to get up."

"In a moment." He could feel her tension under his palm. "What happened? Why did you go outside?"

"It was as you said," she told him. "My meeting with the colonel did not go at all well." She saw that North was in no way appeased by her inadequate explanation. "He would not agree to ask you to stop pursuing the Gentleman Thief."

One of North's brows kicked up. "Really?"

"He would not admit that he had any influence in that regard."

"Aaah. That sounds very much like him. He gives little away, our colonel."

Elizabeth was not certain she understood North's tone. There was an edge of unpleasant sarcasm that sharpened his words. His features, though, were without any hint of the same. "I should like to leave," she said.

Nodding, North released her shoulder. "Of course."

She sat up without help, but she felt North watching her closely. "I shall not faint again."

"The colonel asked if you were *enceinte*." He did not miss Elizabeth's sharp intake of air. "I assured him this was not the case."

Elizabeth turned to the opposite side of the chaise and stood. Her mouth was dry.

"It is not so, is it?" he asked.

She shook her head. Her hands remained at her sides and her fingertips twisted in the fabric of her gown. The fidgeting was necessary. It kept her from folding her hands protectively in front of her empty womb.

North stood also, his rise weary. He regarded Elizabeth's back for a moment. "Will you want to speak to West before we go or shall I make our farewell alone?"

Elizabeth had already started for the door. "I will go with you."

Once they were home in Merrifeld Square Elizabeth went immediately to her room. She requested a hot bath and within the hour she was sitting up to her shoulders in lavender-scented water. Her head rested at the back of the copper tub, supported by a folded cloth. Steam rising from the surface of the water curled her hair and made her skin glow in the lamplight. Outside rain continued to pelt the windows and draw a dark gray cloud over the late afternoon. As though pulling a comforting blanket over her, Elizabeth sank a fraction lower into the water.

North thought she had fallen asleep. He entered the room quietly when he saw she didn't stir and crossed to the bed. Loosening his stock, he lay back.

"When do you mean to send me away?"

He did not look in Elizabeth's direction. "If the weather is improved I thought tomorrow. Have you considered where you want to go?"

"If I have no choice in leaving, then—"

"You don't."

"Then I would prefer to go to Rosemont."

"As you wish."

Elizabeth opened her eyes and stared at the fingers of flame snapping and twisting in the fireplace. "It is not as I wish. Nothing is as I wish it. Please do not pretend it is otherwise."

North said nothing, but his head turned in her direction. He watched her rise from the bath slowly. Water slid in glowing rivulets across her arms and down her legs. She placed a hand at the small of her back as she stepped out of the tub. Her other hand was held away from her body to provide balance. There was just the slightest hint of awkwardness in the movement.

"Are you in pain?" he asked.

Elizabeth reached quickly for her robe and shrugged into

it. Without answering him she limped into the dressing room. She stirred a packet of powder that Louise's physician had prescribed into a glass already filled with water.

"What are you doing?" North asked his question from the doorway. "What is that?"

Elizabeth's fingers curled around the glass and she raised it halfway to her mouth. "Something that will help me sleep."

North had an urge to knock it from her hand. What he did instead was close his fingers around her wrist. "Let me see it." He was vaguely surprised when she did not try to fling it in his face. He bent his head and smelled the preparation. "Who gave you this?"

"Lady Battenburn's physician."

"It has laudanum in it."

"I suppose it does."

North's grip on her wrist tightened so that her fingers loosened on the glass. He allowed that it might have been an unnecessary tactic. Elizabeth did not resist when he lifted it from her. He opened the window just enough to toss the contents, then he set the glass on the commode. "Come. I know something that will help you sleep." He extended his hand palm out but made no move to touch her.

Elizabeth looked first at his hand, then his face. He simply stood there, infinitely patient, giving so little away that she could not know his intentions. A week ago she would have thought he meant to make love to her and she would have gone to him willingly, even eagerly. She did not do so now.

"Do you trust me, Elizabeth?"

The words caused tears to well in her eyes. The question in Elizabeth's mind wasn't if she trusted him still, but whether she had ever trusted him. "I'm afraid," she whispered. "You can't know how afraid I am."

North raised his hand a fraction. His fingers moved almost imperceptibly, beckoning her. His cobalt blue eyes never left her face.

"Don't send me away," she said. Elizabeth blinked back tears. "I'll do anything you—" She reached out blindly for his hand and brought it to her breast. She cupped it against her heart as she took a step toward him. "Please. I can learn to trust you. I can—"

"Sssh." North used his free arm to draw her to him. He could feel her heart pounding against his palm. She was damp and trembling and just moments shy of breaking down completely in front of him. "Sssh. Come. Let me take you to bed." Her hair and skin held the fragrance of lavender. Her thin robe clung to her. He felt her warmth; her body heat outlined her slender frame. North gently removed his hand from between them and lifted her. He carried her to their bed and put her down on top of the thick comforter.

Sitting at her side, he tugged at her loose sash. Elizabeth's arms remained at her side. Her fingers tightened on the comforter as he opened the robe across her belly and breasts. Candlelight from the bedside table fell across her skin and she had an urge to cover herself.

As if sensing it, North told her to turn over. Elizabeth complied with what she thought might be misinterpreted as indecent haste. The truth was more complicated than that. She buried her face in a pillow to keep from revealing it and closed her eyes. He removed her robe. She heard the whisper of silk as it slipped off the edge of the bed.

North left her side for a moment and returned with a warm towel. He dried her shoulders and back and lifted each arm in turn to dry them as well. He used the towel to rub her buttocks and the back of her thighs. Tension tightened her muscles at first and then slowly seeped out of her as his touch remained impersonal and undemanding.

North left the bed again to put the towel aside and remove his shoes and jacket. Elizabeth's head now rested on its side, no longer elevated by the pillow but by the back of one hand. She watched him place his jacket over a chair, then unwind his cravat. He did so with an economy of motion that was a pleasure to watch. His hair gleamed in the firelight. That brightness was in perfect contrast to the shadow that overlay his features.

He came to the bed still dressed in his shirt and trousers.

His knee made a deep depression in the mattress as he climbed on and straddled her thighs.

Elizabeth's head shot up and she craned her neck to see him. "What are you—"

North leaned forward and pressed her head back. "Close your eyes. You want to sleep, do you not?"

She did. Not just for a few hours. But for days and days. She was not at all certain that she wanted to wake from wherever a sleep like that could take her. The thought of what she was really considering did not overly frighten her any longer. Was she braver, then, or more of a coward?

Elizabeth emitted a soft sigh as North's hands pressed gently on the small of her back and worked their way up her spine. His fingers kneaded her naked shoulders with tender but firm pressure and slowly traveled down the sides of her back. He repeated the path three more times, each time dipping a little lower so that he was finally pressing the heels of his hands into her hips and taut buttocks. He adjusted his position so that he was over her calves and then massaged the backs of her thighs. By the time North returned to her back, Elizabeth was sleeping deeply.

North rose from his chair as Elizabeth entered the dining room. "Forgive me," he said politely. "I did not anticipate that you would join me. You were still abed when I inquired of your maid not an hour ago."

Elizabeth nodded. A servant held out a chair for her and she took her seat at the table. She had dressed with some care in spite of the speed with which it was accomplished, choosing a lavender gown with a wide neckline that she could accent with pearls. It seemed important to Elizabeth that she look her best this evening. It was a matter of pride.

A fine powder covered the shadows beneath her eyes and a touch of rouge put color in her cheeks and lips. She hoped that if he noticed her application of cosmetics he would say nothing of this small deceit. It paled in comparison to so many others.

North waited while Elizabeth was served consommé. He noticed she made a credible effort to pretend she was hungry at the beginning of the meal, but with each subsequent course her enthusiasm flagged. In the end she could only manage a few bites of the flaky steamed trout before she asked for her plate to be taken. Matters were not helped by the fact that he could think of little to say. Engaging her in conversation for its own sake seemed pointless, and the things he wanted to tell her were perhaps better left for another time.

For her part Elizabeth was satisfied with the silence. She had not come to dinner to sate any hunger save the one that demanded she spend these last hours in the company of her husband.

"Will you join me in a glass of wine?" North asked when the table was cleared.

She nodded. "Yes . . . I'd like that."

"In my study, then." He stood, waving back the servant who stepped forward to help Elizabeth from her chair. He assisted her himself, then escorted her on his arm to the study. "You are looking very fine this evening," he said. "Your sleep was restful, I collect."

"Indeed it was."

"Good." He released her arm and dismissed the butler, who had arrived to serve them. North poured them each a glass of Madeira. Elizabeth was standing in front of the fireplace and he carried hers to her. "You're cold?" he asked.

"A little." She took the glass. "This will warm me."

"Do you want a shawl?"

"No." Elizabeth sipped her wine. It sent immediate heat coursing through her veins. Her laugh was a trifle shaky. "You will not want to refill this for me, even if I ask."

North smiled. "Very well." He placed his glass on the mantel while he poked at the fire. Elizabeth thanked him for his thoughtfulness and then they fell silent again. It was not wholly uncomfortable. She slowly walked the perimeter of the study, taking note of North's books, while he remained standing at the fireplace, content to watch her.

"I see you have added some Gothic novels," she said. "You have certainly broadened your reading interests."

"Actually I purchased those from the bookseller for you."

She glanced over her shoulder, surprised. "You did?"

"Yes." North was already regretting the admission. He had made the purchase the day before he found the bottle on Elizabeth's vanity. The books arrived after the confirmation of the bottle's contents. In light of more important concerns, he forgot about them. One of the servants must have shelved them. "You may take them with you to Rosemont."

Elizabeth's hand tightened on the stem of her wineglass. "No, thank you," she said stiffly. "My father does not approve of romantic twaddle. If it will not improve me, then I should not read it."

"Hang your father."

She made no response to that. Turning away, she continued to regard the books but with only the pretense of interest. Her circle of the study concluded when she reached the fireplace again. In spite of what she had told North about drinking more, she topped off her glass. He made no move to stop her. "I should like a day to manage my affairs," she said quietly. "There has been no time to visit Louise and explain that I am to leave London."

"That can be accomplished by post," North said.

It was what she expected him to say. She nodded, not offering any argument. If the weather was not improved she would have time. "There is also your mother. I did not speak of it at West's. Did you?"

"No. It would have been ill-timed."

"That is what I thought." Elizabeth sipped her wine. "You would prefer to tell her, I imagine."

"Yes."

She nodded slowly. "And what will you say?"

"That Isabel has asked for you, I suppose. I have not given it much thought."

"Just so," she said. "It is understandable. You are anxious to have me gone." She watched a shutter close over his features. "Do not worry that I will beg you again to reconsider. I have no wish for any unpleasantness this evening. I would ask that you explain to your mother that I was called away suddenly. I have a great affection for her and would not have her think I cared so little that I would say nothing."

"Of course."

"And I'm certain that in time you will be able to find some reasonable explanation for the divorce."

North frowned. His cobalt blue eyes darkened and pierced her. "Divorce? Why do you assume there will be a divorce?"

Elizabeth blinked. "I cannot stay at Rosemont forever, my lord. And I cannot very well live in London apart from you, though I am certain Louise will allow me to stay with her in spite of the inconvenience and scandal."

Anger mingled with disbelief. "You would live with the baron and baronness?"

"I just said I could not, didn't I? I would have to establish my own residence."

This did little to appease Northam. "That's absurd. You will live here when you return to London."

"Not if we are divorced."

North sucked in a breath and forced himself to let it out slowly. "There will be no divorce, Elizabeth. We will not discuss this further."

His arrogance made her chin come up. "I would know what your plans for me are. I thought I was being banished to the country. I cannot live there forever, my lord. I will not."

"You will stay until I send for you."

"And when will that be? A fortnight? A month? A year from now?"

It pained North to admit, "I do not know."

"Then, pray, do not be surprised when I am not there to receive your summons."

"Are you threatening me, Elizabeth?"

It shocked her that he could think so, yet it was pain that filled her eyes. "No, my lord. It is no threat." Elizabeth set her wineglass down on the tray. "This was a poor idea. Coming downstairs, I mean. Forgive me." She started for the door and was halted halfway by North's quiet entreaty.

"I require time," he said. "How can you not know that?"

Elizabeth waited, her back to him, in anticipation that he would say more. When he did not, she nodded once, then let herself out.

She did not turn away when he reached for her. Elizabeth had wondered if he would and she made up her mind then that she would deny neither of them this bittersweet union.

His large hands caressed her breasts, her thighs. He pinned her wrists to the bed while his mouth captured hers. He sucked on her lips, ran his tongue along the ridge of her teeth. He buried his face in the curve of her neck, biting gently on her skin, worrying it, raising a mark that she would see in her mirror for days to come. His fingers made brief prints in her flesh as they trailed from her wrists to her shoulders. He caught the lobe of her ear and tugged and then kissed the hollow just below. His whisper was soft and husky and tickled her skin.

Elizabeth moved restlessly. Nothing he did satisfied her, yet it was all of a piece, leading her toward that end. His mouth closed over her breast. Her nipple grew hard. He took it between his lips and teased it with the damp edge of his tongue. Her fingers slipped into his hair. She held him close, arching as he drew a response from deep in her womb.

It was the first time she made love to him knowing that she loved him. She wondered if the difference in her response was only inside her, or if North felt the hesitation and uncertainty that loving him introduced. There was a certain amount of awe in her touch, a need to remind herself that he was flesh and blood, and to know it by the weight and heat of his body on top of hers.

Loving him made her aware of herself. She learned the shape of her breasts in the cup of his hands and the curve of her hip against the taut plane of his thigh. And more profoundly, she understood the breadth of her own heart when she laid her palm over his.

She opened her thighs at his urging and cradled him with her hips as he thrust into her. Her heels pressed into the mattress, lifting, driving him deeper inside. Her fingers rested on his shoulders, lightly at first, then with more pressure. He moved slowly and deeply, and she felt herself being drawn inexorably toward the same end as he, giving as much as she was given, surrendering herself in a manner that was no defeat. Though he could not know it, the terms North had finally wrested from her included her heart.

She thought she might cry. His release was powerful, thrilling. She shattered a moment later, every line of tension in her slender frame vibrating under him. Elizabeth held him to her as she always did, slipping her arms around his back, not wanting him to leave her too soon. She hoped that she alone understood the desperation that made her want to keep him with her now.

A full minute passed before North eased himself out of Elizabeth's embrace. Without a word he slipped out of bed and padded naked to their dressing room. She heard him washing, and a little later he appeared carrying a small basin of water. She bit her lip, willing herself to remain outwardly indifferent as he set the basin down and prepared to wash every last trace of himself from her body.

Candlelight bathed her skin. A thin sheen of perspiration made her flesh glow. North's remote glance was drawn to the mark on her neck and another on the soft underside of her arm. Her breasts were still slightly swollen, as was her mouth. He pulled his eyes away and touched the damp cloth to her flat belly. He felt her abdomen retract as she sucked in a breath.

North looked down at his hand. The cloth in the cup of his palm made it curve over her belly. It was as if she were rounded there, growing large with their child. He removed his hand quickly and dropped the cloth back in the basin. Droplets of water splashed her and she twisted a little as she went to flick them away.

Candlelight. Her movement. Beads of water. They came together in perfect concert to reveal the faint web of silvery striations that marked the taut flesh of her abdomen and hip.

North's eyes were riveted, first to her belly, then to her stricken face as she saw what was in his. He understood clearly in that moment what had never occurred to him before: His wife did not want his baby because she had already given birth. "What happened to your child, Elizabeth?"

Chapter Thirteen

Elizabeth realized immediately that he had no intention of listening to her answer. He was stalking toward the dressing room before she had pushed herself upright. Grabbing her nightgown, she yanked it over her head and followed him.

"Stay away from me," North said. "You cannot depend on me to keep my promise not to strike you."

Elizabeth shrank a little against the doorjamb, but she did not move away. "Where are you going?"

"Away." He jammed his legs into a pair of trousers, turning away from Elizabeth as he fastened them. "Endeavor to remove yourself from this house before I return."

"I warned you," she said hoarsely, her throat thick with unshed tears. "I told you how it would be; that I would give you disgust of me. Now I am to hide myself away like a leper because it has come to pass. I will not do it, North. Do you hear me? I will not do it!"

"Everyone in Merrifeld Square can hear you." He shrugged into his shirt and moved to stand in front of the cheval glass to tuck it in. His eyes were drawn to Elizabeth's reflection. She looked like a wraith, her complexion almost as pale as the shift she wore. Her arms were caught behind her back as she leaned against the doorjamb. He supposed she kept them there to prevent herself from attacking him. She seemed to think she had reason. He spoke to remind her that she did not. "There *is* a child somewhere, isn't there?"

She hesitated. Years of denial had made it almost seem otherwise. "Yes," she said softly, finally.

North carefully released a long breath. "Why could you have not told me?"

The question did not entirely surprise her. It went straight to the heart of his hurt. "I cannot explain why."

He turned on her. His voice was calm, weary. "Get out, Elizabeth. I swear I cannot tolerate the sight of you just now."

It was what she saw in his eyes that made her go. She had felt the sting of that look before. Her father had once regarded her with the same disillusion and it still had the power to lash her. No matter how often she had imagined coming under North's similar regard, she was not prepared for it.

Elizabeth sat on the edge of the bed until North was gone. When she heard the front door close, she methodically dressed herself and made arrangements to leave Merrifield Square.

It was noon of the following day before North arrived home. The evidence that he had passed the last twelve hours in some activity other than sleep was in the faint gray shadows beneath his eyes and the limp folds of his cravat. If that was not enough to convince his valet that he had been out, there was also the unmistakable odor of tobacco smoke, gin, and sweat clinging to his clothes and his skin.

Brill had a bath drawn immediately upon witnessing Northam's slow ascent of the stairs. "Shall I prepare a morning-after drink for you, my lord?"

"God no," North said feelingly. He leaned forward in the tub as Brill tipped the kettle and sluiced his back with warm water. "Hate that stuff you concoct, Brill. What do you put in it?"

"That would be a carefully guarded secret, my lord."

"Probably just as well." North fell back, resting his head against the towel Brill hastily inserted against the lip of the tub. "Lady Northam is gone?"

"Yes, my lord."

North did not miss the note of disapproval in Brill's tone. Though he had no need to explain himself, North decided he should discover how the lie set on his tongue. "She goes to Rosemont at her stepmother's request."

"So she said."

There it was again. That disapproving edge. North glanced up at his valet. Brill's thin features were no more pinched than was usual. From North's angle he was a sharp chin, two finely cut nostrils, and an overhanging brow that was honed like a blade. "She told you?"

"Yes, my lord. I assisted her packing."

North rubbed his temple. "Surely her maid could have done that."

"Her ladyship did not want to wake her maid since she had no intention of taking her. She came upon me in the hall and asked for my help. I obliged, of course."

"Of course," North said absently. He wasn't at all certain he understood what Brill was saying about Elizabeth's maid. Why would she have to be awakened at all? She was invariably up before Elizabeth, ready to lend her services within moments of Elizabeth ringing for her. "Brill?"

"Yes, my lord?"

"What time did Lady Northam leave this morning?"

"I believe it was shortly after one, my lord. I sent young Tipton to find a hack on the half-hour. It took him some time to locate a suitable driver as I insisted on sobriety as a requirement."

Fat droplets of water slapped the floor and fell back in the tub as North hauled himself out. He grabbed the towel Brill held out to him. "What do you mean she took a hack?

And she left while it was still dark? In the middle of the night? Why did you not send someone for me?''

Brill patiently offered another towel when North's first one flew from his hands as he hastily rubbed his hair. ''Her ladyship specifically requested a hack. I reminded her of the carriage that could be brought quickly from the livery for her, but she declined that conveyance. As for the hour, Lady Northam was adamant that there was some urgency. And to the last, I asked if I could send someone for you, as I knew you had quit the house only a short time before . . .'' Brill cleared his throat, an action that drew attention to his censure rather than covering it. ''Lady Northam assured me it was unnecessary. She said you were not only aware of her departure but had encouraged it.''

North snorted. ''Do you think I'd permit my wife to leave London at that hour of the night in a hack?''

Brill made no reply and blandly handed North a third towel.

North tossed it back. ''Riding clothes, Brill. Did you hear what direction Lady Northam gave the hack?''

''The post road, of course. I believe she means to take a coach from there.''

North actually shuddered, though it was not entirely due to the thought of Elizabeth crammed in a coach with London's rough trade. ''My clothes, Brill. Before I expire of cold.''

The conservatory at Stonewickam was a most pleasant room. The air was faintly humid and rich with the scent of black earth and lush greenery. Large ferns in stone pots served as sentinels just inside the doorway. Ivy climbed the interior stone wall, and the high domed ceiling made entirely of glass let in winter sunlight.

Elizabeth reclined on a chaise near the south-facing bank of windows. Light streamed over her shoulder and high-lighted the pages of her book. She felt her eyes drifting to the row of orchids on the floor just beyond her reach. Their delicate lavender and pale blue petals were an exotic wonder at this time of year and she enjoyed looking at them. It made her feel as if she were not in England at all, but in some remote jungle, or at least how she imagined a jungle might look.

"Here you are."

Elizabeth started to sit up as Lord Worth stepped into view between a neatly trimmed bush of miniature roses and the offshoot of a palm tree he had received some fifty years earlier as a gift from the great explorer Captain James Cook. He waved her back in place with the hand that was not leaning heavily on his cane. "Please," she said, moving her legs to one side and closing her book. "Will you sit with me?"

"If it pleases you," he said gruffly.

She smiled. North's grandfather was really a very sweet man. Elizabeth could easily conceive that he had intimidated his grandchildren with his fiercely drawn countenance and willingness to pontificate upon a variety of subjects, but Elizabeth found him to be a most tenderhearted soul. One only had to watch him working in the conservatory, puttering among his orchids and roses, talking to them, encouraging and admonishing them, to see that his gentleness ran deep to the bone.

"What are you smiling at, gel?"

"You. Your grandson is very much like you, do you know that?"

"Eh? You wouldn't insult your host, now would you?" He used his cane to point to the potted palm. "That tree has more in the way of good sense than Brendan. Still, it's hard to credit the boy hasn't found you by now."

"I told you not to expect him. He is not looking for me. He has a thief to catch." Elizabeth watched Worth consider this, stretching his long legs in front of him and crossing them at the ankle. It was exactly the same posture that North had adopted for contemplation. She felt a wave of sadness and longing that quite took her breath away.

"What is it?" Cecil Worth demanded. "Are you not well?"

"I'm fine."

"You don't look fine. Look like you mean to lose your breakfast."

"I mean to do no such thing."

He continued to regard her suspiciously. "You are not gravid, are you? I told you I could not be persuaded to hide you here if that was the way of it."

"And I told you I am not."

"Not what? Hiding or gravid?"

"Both. Neither."

"Well, what's wrong with my grandson that he ain't got a child by you?"

Elizabeth sighed. "You will not bully me, my lord. If that is your pleasure, I shall quit the conservatory and go to my room."

"Hah!" He gave the tip of his cane a sharp tap on the stone floor. "You are certainly an impudent gel."

"You cannot deliver a set down when you are laughing, no matter how hard you snap that cane. It is not effective."

"Hhmpf. I was not laughing."

"Your eyes were."

"Hhmpf."

Elizabeth covered her smile with one hand. She was fortunate indeed to have thought of North's grandfather as a possible refuge, more fortunate still that he had embraced her with so few reservations.

Arriving in the village of Stonewickam a full two days after leaving London, Elizabeth had been bone weary and without many resources left. She used almost half the money she had remaining to hire an open carriage to take her to Lord Worth's. The two-seater was just large enough for her and the driver. Her trunk rested on a rack behind them and she carried her valise in her lap.

It was dusk when she came upon the manor. The sun was slipping behind a hill in the distance and the stone absorbed the pale pink color that trimmed the horizon. The driver helped Elizabeth alight from the carriage and unloaded her trunk, but he waited only long enough to make certain she was invited into the house. He did not know there was a possibility she might not remain there.

Her interview with Lord Worth came to the point very quickly. She introduced herself and offered such particulars as to affirm her identity. Once that was established to his satisfaction she asked simply for sanctuary.

He appeared to like her choice of the word. Safety. Solitude. Refuge and protection. He invited her into his conservatory and asked her if this was what she had in mind. She had only to breathe the air, redolent with fecund soil and tropical flowers, and knew that for this time at least there was no other place so suited to her needs.

Now it was one day short of a fortnight and Elizabeth no longer thought it odd that she and Lord Worth got on so well. His care of her vacillated between badgering and coddling. He always seemed to know which she required. Occasionally he lectured but learned that she was immune, having already heard some version of his favorite discourses from North.

For her part Elizabeth showed a real interest in his passion for growing things. Her questions, her genuine curiosity, endeared her to Cecil Worth as nothing else could have. She appreciated his reminiscences, listening with pleasure to the stories from his own youth but even more gladly to those that were about North. Lord Worth's memories of Hambrick Hall were most telling about himself and his grandson, and Elizabeth began to understand how the bonds of friendships made in those days could endure for a lifetime.

North sat with his friends in his Merrifield Square home. It was more correct that they sat and he stood. They exchanged concerned glances when he turned his back on them and continued pacing toward the window. None of them knew how he was still upright. He looked as if he had not slept since Elizabeth disappeared.

In spite of their long abiding friendship, or perhaps because of it, almost a week had passed before North asked the Compass Club for help. By that time he had already learned that Elizabeth was not at Rosemont and that there was no one there with any expectation of seeing her. Neither had she remained in London with his mother or the colonel.

Each time he had to approach someone and raise the question of Elizabeth's whereabouts he was initially met with puzzlement. When they realized he was in earnest, their confusion gave way to apprehension and eventually to fear. He was left to calm their worries when he felt nothing so much as sorrow himself.

Rosemont had been scathing in his opinion of North for not taking his wife in hand, but nothing he said cut so deeply as the things North said to himself. Isabel's sympathy was much more difficult to accept. The look she graced him with was at once understanding and helpless. He came to the slow realization that no matter what she knew, he could depend on no aid from her, that even if he found Elizabeth, she could already be lost to him in ways that could not be changed.

Elizabeth's brother had charged after North as he was leaving Rosemont, calling after him in his high-pitched, youthful voice and finally catching him on the bridge. Out of breath, excited, Selden was nonetheless able to make himself understood. "You will find her, my lord," Adam had said, part command, part hopeful question. "She is the best of all sisters and you must find her." There was nothing for it but for North to promise that he would.

Southerton leaned forward in his chair and rested his chin on his folded hands. He raised one brow as North pivoted at the window and began walking toward his friends again. "What do you hear from Battenburn and his wife?"

"Louise was here a few hours ago," North said. His steps slowed, then halted. "Didn't I tell you that?"

South, East, and West shook their heads in unison. They were careful not to look at each other.

North rubbed his brow. "I thought I told you."

Without a word, the Marquess of Eastlyn rose from his chair and rang for the butler. "Coffee," he said succinctly.

West invited North to sit beside him on the divan. "You have exhausted yourself, North. You can no longer be certain of the day or time."

It was very nearly the truth, North thought. Trust his friends to point out what he would not admit. He did not think he could sit, however, and chose to rest his hip on the corner of his desk.

South looked up at him. "Lady Battenburn," he prompted. "What did she want?"

"Yes," North said, more to himself than to the others. "Yes, Louise." He came out of his reverie and spoke more strongly. "You all know I could not approach Lady Battenburn. I believed that if Elizabeth had indeed gone to her, the baroness would have denied it."

"Probably taken some delight in it," South said as an aside.

North managed a meager smile. "No doubt. She is protective of Elizabeth. I believe she approved of the marriage, but I think she does not like having Elizabeth away from her side. Perhaps it would be more fair to say that she would not encourage my wife to return to me."

"Well," Eastlyn said, "it is a point of no account. I have made a study of the baroness's London residence and she and her husband have no guests. Elizabeth is certainly not there."

"And I've been back to Battenburn," South said. "In fact, the chill of the journey still permeates my clothes. Elizabeth is not there."

Eastlyn heard the approach of the butler and opened the door. He took the tray, gave the door a push closed with the heel of his boot, and carried the coffee to the desk. "How could you know, South?" he asked, pouring a generous cup for North. "The place has a history of hiding the most disreputable characters, and I suspect our dear Lady North could not be found there if she wished it so."

Southerton waved Eastlyn's question aside. "I know because of my acquaintance with a certain chambermaid."

"My, you are a deep one," East said dryly. "Did you know about the chambermaid, North?"

Northam shook his head. He held his cup between his palms and raised it to his lips. It was hot, almost scalding, but precisely what he required to center his thoughts. "Louise came to confront me about Elizabeth's whereabouts."

One of West's brows lifted in a perfect arch. "Then Elizabeth has not corresponded with Lady Battenburn?"

"Apparently that is so," said North. "I confess, it surprises me. Louise was agitated that Elizabeth left London without a word to her. She does not believe that Elizabeth is at Rosemont, which is what I told her."

South accepted coffee from Eastlyn and leaned back in his chair. "Called you a liar, did she?"

"I *am* a liar."

"Well, yes. But she need not have called you one."

"She was not quite so direct as that, but she made her point." North paused, recalling the unpleasant meeting with the baroness. "The odd thing was that she was more upset with Elizabeth than with me."

Eastlyn considered that, nodding slowly. "That is odd. Women like to rally around this sort of thing. Blame all of Adam's descendants for biting the apple. Never mention tempting us. Never mention how miserable they would have made our lives if we hadn't bitten."

Southerton rolled his eyes. "Trouble with Sophie," he announced to the others. "We take your point, East."

"I hope so," East said. "Because something is havey-cavey, I tell you. Your mother blamed you, didn't she, North?"

"I don't know that I would characterize it as blame," he said carefully.

East snorted. "We all know your mother. She is very fond of Lady North and would not think twice about assigning responsibility for her departure to you. Doesn't make sense that Lady Battenburn would do otherwise. Bloody hell, North, we're your friends and *we* think you must have done something to chase her off."

North's short laugh was without humor. "And you would be right," he said after a moment. "All of you."

The Compass Club fell silent for a time, each member's pensive features reflected back in those of a friend.

South's cup and saucer clattered as he set them down. "Coffee's fine for bringing North around," he said to no one in particular, "but tea leaves are what's called for now."

They all stared at him.

"Tea leaves," South repeated. "Fortune-telling, you know." He sighed. "A poor attempt to lighten our mood. Forgive me."

What they did, though, was congratulate him. No matter that it pained them to admit it, there were times when South was bloody brilliant.

Flakes of snow melted on the conservatory's glass dome, but just inches beyond the bank of windows they began to accumulate on the frozen ground. Elizabeth sat on a wooden bench a few feet from the windows, watching the full moon turn each dancing, twirling flake into a pinpoint of light. Outside, on this crisp December evening, it was as if all of heaven's stars were falling to Earth.

Elizabeth adjusted her fine woolen shawl around her shoulders and loosely tied the tails at the level of her breasts. Beside her on the bench was an unopened drawing pad, charcoal, and a lamp she had blown out in favor of watching nature's ever-changing tapestry.

She sat very still in the moonshine, her complexion as coolly colored as marble, her lashes tipped by blue-silver light, the centers of her eyes wide as she took in as much as was possible of the glittered, frozen landscape.

Elizabeth did not turn when she heard the doors to the conservatory open. It was not unusual for Lord Worth to sit with her here in the evening before they retired. She anticipated his familiar step, distinctive because of the cane that inserted a tap between the placement of his right and left foot. What she heard instead was a step also well known to her: steady, strong, and confident. The back of her neck prickled with alarm and she felt her shoulders and spine stiffen.

Elizabeth's eyes changed their focus from the exterior landscape to the vague reflection in the windows. She could just make out his ethereal outline in the glass. She could almost believe she was imagining him behind her. It would not be the first time.

Elizabeth stood and turned to face him slowly, glad that she had blown out the lamp, glad there was nothing but moonshine to highlight his features or hers. Her eyes drank him in. "My lord," she said quietly.

"My lady."

There was silence. Neither of them moved.

Elizabeth took in a ragged little breath and said, "So you have found the Gentleman Thief."

Of all things she might have greeted him with, North had not been prepared for this. "Why do you think so?"

"Because you are here."

"Bloody hell," he said under his breath. "I am here for you. I haven't given a thought to the thief since you disappeared."

She smiled faintly. "Truly?" It was less a question than a subtle mockery.

"Truly." North's fingers raked his thick hair. "I do not want to talk about the thief, Elizabeth."

Neither did she. Not now. She made a small nod. "Does your grandfather know you're here?"

"Yes. He called me a great fool for taking so long to find you."

Elizabeth pressed her lips together to keep from smiling.

"And an ass for letting you leave in the first place."

Her mouth parted in surprise.

"I told him he was right." A glimmer of a smile lifted one corner of North's mouth. "I have found that agreeing with my grandfather is the shortest route to reconciliation. In this case, however, I agreed because he was right. In these last weeks I have called myself much worse than a fool and an ass. Grandfather's assessment of my character was most complimentary.''

"North."

"I should not have demanded that you leave, Elizabeth."

Elizabeth said nothing for a moment, searching out the right words to follow this overture. "I am sorry for many things," she said finally. "But not for leaving you when I did or as I did. I needed to be gone, North, and you needed me to be gone. You said as much."

He fought the urge to close the distance between them. "But to leave no word . . ." His hands lifted in a helpless gesture, then fell slowly to his sides. "You agreed to go to Rosemont."

"I know." She glanced down at the floor. "I could not."

"I went there," he told her. "I knew from the manner of your leaving that it was unlikely that I would find you, but I went to Rosemont anyway. I went to the colonel and my mother. I even went to Hampton Cross. I followed your trail to the inn where you spent your first night away from Merrifeld Square. No one could tell me where you had gone after that. You had quite disappeared." North's throat closed. He swallowed hard and kept going; his voice rasped with emotion. "I thought you had gone to him, you see. I thought that's what I had done. Pushed you away from me and sent you flying to him."

Elizabeth's head came up slowly. "Him?"

"The man you allowed to give you a child."

Her knees actually wobbled. She put a hand out to steady herself, but her fingers only closed over a fistful of air. She dropped to the bench like a stone. "I'm sorry," she said. The words were given hardly any sound. "I'm sorry. I am so very sorry."

North quickly moved to the bench and knelt in front of her. He took her hands that were pressed so tightly against her midriff and held them in his. His thumbs brushed against her white knuckles. "Elizabeth. Please. I do not mean to cause you such pain."

She was cold everywhere except where his hands lay over

hers. She wished he would take her in his arms. She wished she could ask him. "You are not the cause of any pain," Elizabeth whispered, her voice thick. "The pain is always there. I live with it. Sometimes better than others. And because you have lived with me, you have lived with it, too." She managed a shaky breath. "That is why I left the way I did, North. Or part of it. It was wrong to make you share what you could not even understand. You were right to want me out of your life." Elizabeth tugged on his hands, not to be free of them but to urge him to stand. "Will you not get up?" she asked. "Please. It is not right that you should be on your knees."

The stone floor was cold and uncomfortable and if he was to stay there much longer he would need his grandfather's cane to help him rise, yet North had no intention of moving. "Tell me about him, Elizabeth. Just once. Allow me to understand and allow yourself to heal. Life is not meant to be experienced as an open wound."

Elizabeth searched his face. The pale moonshadow was insufficient to close off his features to her and she could not mistake the sincerity of his expression. His eyes were not implacable but patient. He was like an army laying siege to the keep. He did not storm the front gate or try to climb over the walls. He would gain entry simply by waiting her out. She was vulnerable because he was infinitely more tolerant and restrained than she was.

Was he right? she wondered. Could her life, at its very core, be something other than pained?

"You won't get up?" she asked softly.

He shook his head, his smile rueful.

"I won't tell you his name," she said after a moment.

"You don't have to. It is the least important thing. Tell me about him."

Elizabeth took a quick shallow breath and began. "You will be disappointed, I'm afraid. There is really very little to tell. I did not know him so well as I thought." She laughed a bit self-consciously, without humor. "My father's perspective of my childhood is quite different than my own.

For all that he believes I was most imprudently spoiled, I was also sheltered. That changed ever so slightly when my mother died and the colonel became an important figure in my life. He was rarely around. My father would not have him at Rosemont and his duties kept him away, but he opened another world to me through his letters. You will find it perhaps odd that I understood so little of what was beyond the boundaries of my home. Oh, I was a good student in the schoolroom. I knew of other places, of course. I had read about them avidly. But reading the colonel's letters made things different somehow. Everything seemed more real. Someone I knew was experiencing what I had only marginally grasped from the pages of a book.''

Elizabeth squeezed North's hands. ''Can you understand that?''

He nodded, returning the slight pressure. ''Go on.''

She caught her lip a moment, worried it, then continued. ''You will have probably already surmised that he was a soldier. An officer, as you were. I met him during the Season. That I was allowed to make a London debut at all was Isabel's doing. She made that argument to my father on my behalf. I like to think that she does not entirely regret winning her point. It has not all turned out badly for her . . . or him.''

''Selden, you mean,'' North said quietly.

Elizabeth gave an involuntary start. She would have pulled her hands away from North had he not been holding them so firmly. ''How did you—'' She stopped. ''Did they tell you?''

North shook his head. ''No. I don't believe I should have ever discovered it that way. Your father and Isabel are as committed to the secret as you. It was young Selden himself who gave it away.''

Elizabeth's brows rose. ''But he couldn't have. He doesn't—'' She stopped because North was already confirming this with another tolerant shake of his head.

''I'm sorry,'' he said. ''It was not my intention to alarm you. You're right, of course. Selden doesn't know he is your son. Unless someone tells him, I can't imagine that it will ever occur to him.''

''Then how did you come to know it?''

''He ran after me as I was leaving Rosemont. I imagine he must have overheard your father tearing a strip off me, or perhaps it was Isabel's imploring me to find you that he heard.'' North shrugged. ''It does not matter how he came to know that you were gone from London, only that he did. He would have run me to ground if I had not stopped for him. He demanded that I find you. He just stood there on the bridge, blocking my path, hardly tall enough to reach my mare's nose, and ordered me to bring you back safely.''

Elizabeth had been holding her breath. Now she let it out slowly. ''Did his chin come up just so.'' She lifted her own.

''Just so,'' said North. ''And his eyes flashed. And his hands rested on his hips. His head cocked to the side. It was all there for a moment. *You* were there, in him, just for a moment. The precise inflection in his voice. The tension in his frame. I knew. It came and went in the space of a heartbeat, but I knew. Viscount Selden is your son.''

''Viscount Selden is my father's son,'' she corrected gently. Tears filled her eyes. ''I gave birth to Adam.''

''Aaah, Elizabeth.'' He released one of her hands to cup her face. His thumb brushed her cheek. ''Of course. Just Adam. Your beautiful little boy.''

She nodded. A tear spilled over the edge of her lashes and North wiped it away before she could do the same. She drew a shaky breath. ''Adam's father . . . my soldier . . . he didn't know about my pregnancy. He was already gone by the time I realized I was carrying his child. I sent him away, you see. He was . . . he was married.''

North swore softly.

Laughter, rife with self-mockery, trembled on Elizabeth's lips. ''I said that very thing from time to time,'' she told him. She accepted the handkerchief he pressed in her hand and wiped her eyes. ''I did not know he had a wife. I did not even imagine that such a thing was possible. Not that he could not have been married, but that I could have been

fooled. It was only in retrospect that I could comprehend
my own naïveté. I suspected nothing. Presented with the
same circumstances again, I still would not suspect. He loved
me, I think. As much as it was possible when he was already
committed to another. I say that now, but it felt boundless
at the time. I was sure I understood his feelings then.''

Elizabeth's fingers crushed the handkerchief. Her eyes
were dry and the press of tears was gone. She spoke clearly,
softly, with little inflection, the raw edges of the open wound
less red and angry than they had been only minutes before.
''I was just as certain that I understood my own. I loved
him. I've told you that. I could not have lain with him had
I not, not then. It would not be fair to say he seduced me.
I wanted to be with him. I believe I demanded it.''

A faint smile touched North's mouth. ''You would.''

Elizabeth marveled that there was no censure in his tone.
''You will not be surprised that our . . . our affair . . . was
conducted in secret. My father met him several times early
on and judged him wholly lacking in character. Since this
was my father's assessment of most people, particularly
those who expressed any interest in me, it seemed of little
consequence. Knowing that there would be no approval from
that quarter, we saw each other in only the most casual way
publicly. I had suitors to fill my dance card—none of whom
came up to snuff in my father's eyes—but they served their
purpose in diverting his attention.''

Elizabeth bent her head, finding it too difficult to look at
North. He did not admonish her, but remained just as he
was and allowed her to let the story unfold in its own way.
''I met him late at night. It was quite simple for me to
leave the house. No one suspected at all, you see. Father's
imaginings of my disobedient nature did not extend to what
was surely my most outrageous behavior. I always returned
before anyone was awake. I came and went as I pleased.''

Something nudged North's thoughts. A tiny prompt. A
little niggle. He frowned, trying to bring it to the surface,
but could only grasp the vague alarm that accompanied it,
not the thing itself.

Caught in her confession, her head still bowed, Elizabeth did not notice North's slight frown or his momentary distraction. "When the Season was ended I returned to Rosemont. My debut was unsuccessful by the *ton's* standards, but I had my own measure. Naturally, I saw him less frequently once I was in the country. It was infinitely more difficult for him to get away than it was for me, but I was content with what time we had together." Her voice softened. "We spoke of marriage. I thought we would elope. It was to be Gretna for us."

North felt a measure of selfish relief that was tempered with an appreciation for how Elizabeth's own dreams had been met with disappointment. "It was wrong of him, Elizabeth." At the risk of raising her hackles, North could not be silent on this matter. "He had no right to hold out that hope."

Her face lifted and she acknowledged the truth of North's words with the sadness in her own eyes. "In my mind we were husband and wife. I was with him for six months when I learned the extent to which I had created my fantasy. I found a letter from his wife in his coat. He was not at all contrite. Rather, he was angry at me for going through his pockets." She raised the hand that held the crumpled handkerchief, her smile more wry than rueful. "I was looking for one of these."

North nodded, understanding very well that she never seemed to have her own at the ready.

"Perhaps I should not have read the letter." She shrugged. "But I did. When he gathered his wits he would have had me believe that his marriage did not matter. It says something about the state of my mind that for a moment or two . . . or three . . . I wanted to believe it was so."

"I think it speaks more eloquently of how much you loved him."

She nodded weakly. "I told him I would not see him again and he took me at my word. I think it helped that on occasion I resented him for that, sometimes more for that than the fact of his marriage or his lying about it. You will understand that I am not proud of this. I mention it only because you deserve to know the person I am. Petty. Unfair. Unreasonable.'' The corners of her mouth lifted in a slight smile. ''A fool and an ass.''

''Not in my grandfather's estimation,'' North said, a hint of laughter in his tone. More gravely, he added, ''And not in mine.''

Elizabeth laid her hand over the one North had resting lightly on her knee. ''Almost two months passed before I realized I was carrying his child. Actually I never accepted it consciously until Isabel confronted me. My admission was more for my own benefit than hers.'' She paused, remembering how quickly events had transpired after that, and sorted them out in her own mind before she went on. ''There were few choices left to me. I could do exactly as my father wanted or I could leave Rosemont to make my own way. Leaving meant I would have no support. My father was firm on that. I could expect nothing from him. I would not see Isabel again and I would not be allowed to return to Rosemont. I had no reason to doubt that he meant it. I could have applied to the colonel for help, but I was too proud. In any event, the colonel could not have kept me from becoming a pariah. Once my pregnancy became known I would not be accepted. That mattered little to me, North. I hope you will believe that. What mattered is that my son would be a bastard.''

North had a sudden recollection of Elizabeth's fierce response to him when he revealed West's illegitimacy. She had adamantly argued that the fact of West's birth made him different from others. *Not intrinsically different*, she had said. *Not at birth. But soon after it changes him in some way. It could be his mother is ashamed or his father is indifferent . . . He comes to believe one of two things about himself: either that he has no right to hold his head up or that he must hold it higher than everyone else.* He had heard the passion in her voice as she spoke; what he had not understood was the source.

"You might have married," he said. "It is done more often than you think."

"Perhaps. But I could not do it. To marry someone I did not love and ask him to accept my child . . . or worse, pretend my child was also his . . ." Her voice trailed off. She could not leave it there. She had not been so principled that the thought had not crossed her mind. Elizabeth wanted him to know that. "It occurred to me, North. I cannot let you believe otherwise. It was simply not as satisfactory a solution as the one my father presented."

North nodded. His hand slipped over hers and he gave it a gentle squeeze. He watched her take a steadying breath and prepare to go on.

"My father arranged for the three of us to tour the Continent. Before we left he placed a few hints about physicians and Isabel's inability to present him with an heir. He was careful to make it seem that there was an underlying reason for our trip. And of course there was, though not quite the one he would have his confidants believe.

"We saw very little of the Continent, but went immediately to Italy. Adam was born in Venice. The midwife placed him in Isabel's arms and they left the room before I was delivered of the afterbirth. I was not allowed to hold him. My father insisted on that. I cannot even say that he was wrong. I might not have been able to give him up had it been otherwise. They left Venice for Rome that same evening. I did not cradle my son to my breast. I did not hear him cry. My milk dried because I could not feed him. From the very beginning he was nourished by a wet nurse."

Elizabeth glanced past North to the curtain of falling snow beyond the windows. "After a time it did not seem quite real. While I remained in Venice my body returned to a form more familiar to me. My breasts lost their fullness. The ache in my back disappeared. My belly flattened." She looked at him again. "You saw for yourself the only proof that remained. No matter how often I rubbed oil into my distended belly I could not erase those marks. They have faded over the years, but nothing save my own denial could make them disappear. It is not how I meant for you to find out that I had conceived and carried and delivered a child.''

''Did you ever mean for me to know?'' he asked.

Elizabeth could not deny him the truth. ''No.''

North let out his breath slowly. It was not an unexpected answer.

Her heart ached for him. He deserved so much better than what she had been able to give him. ''It is not what you think,'' she said. ''At least not what I imagine you think.''

''Oh? Then what is it?''

''It is not that I did not trust you.'' She saw one of his brows lift skeptically. ''It is that I did not trust anyone. I could not.''

North's brow lowered and he schooled his features. ''I'm listening.''

''From the moment Adam was born my father relied on my silence. Isabel's also. It was the only way in which our deception could proceed. In order for Adam to be accepted as Lord Selden, my father's heir, there could be no one who knew otherwise. I have already explained that it was not so difficult for me to believe. It was almost two months before my father sent for me from Rome. Adam was in every way Isabel's son by then. At least I told myself it was so. I denied the ache that tore at my breast when he cried and she comforted him. I would not acknowledge the tears I shed when my own father coddled his son and had so few words to spare for me. Can you appreciate how selfish I believed myself to be, North? They were giving my child everything and I was as resentful as I was grateful. I did not know how to reconcile both things inside me.''

Elizabeth's amber eyes softened as she implored him to understand. ''When we returned to London, then to Rosemont, it was simply too difficult for me to continue to live under my father's roof. I chose to return to London and . . .'' She hesitated, her courage failing her. North did not press, but she knew he would die right where he knelt rather than allow her to leave off now. ''And I think they were relieved. It was then that I met Lord and Lady Battenburn.''

She saw him nod faintly, as if he had expected this direction and understood its import. She found it easier to continue. "Louise befriended me. I enjoyed her company and she was everything kind. Harrison did not seem to mind that I was forever a guest in their home.

"I do not know precisely how it came about. It seems so disingenuous to say that I lowered my guard. I do not think I properly had one where Louise was concerned. She did not badger me. She did not even seem to know I had a secret to share, yet one day that was precisely what I did. I told her everything."

North said nothing. He rose stiffly to his feet while Elizabeth stared at her hands. "She has been blackmailing you since that time?" he asked.

Elizabeth's head shot up, giving the truth away even before she asked the question. "How did you know?"

"A guess," he admitted. "One you have now confirmed." Things at the periphery of North's mind suddenly moved front and center. "Your father? He knows what you did."

She nodded, her shoulders slumping as she did so.

"Louise blackmails him as well."

"Yes." The answer was barely audible.

"I take it Louise is not alone in this endeavor."

"Battenburn is fully aware. In some ways he tempers her. In other ways he provokes it."

North closed his eyes and rubbed the bridge of his nose with his thumb and forefinger. "Christ," he said softly. "What a mess." He dropped his hand and regarded Elizabeth again. "I imagine they threaten you all with exposure."

"Yes. My father and Isabel would be humiliated for having put forth the deception, but that is of little concern. It is that Selden would know they are not his parents that distresses them."

"They could adopt him."

"Of course they could. And they would. We have talked about it. But it is that he would know that keeps us all silent. Perhaps some day we will determine that he can have the

truth, but not now. It remains a fact that none of us want
others to know.''

''So you are no longer keepers of your secret but prisoners
of it.''

''Yes. Exactly.''

North considered this in silence for a time. ''This is at
the root of your father's anger toward you?''

She nodded. ''He considers the fact that I told someone
about Adam more grievous a sin than my having had him
in the first place.'' She saw an objection rise to North's lips
and she stopped. ''He loves Selden. You know that's true.
You observed it yourself when we were at Rosemont. He
can't find it in himself to despise me for giving birth, only
for wanting to relieve myself of the burden of hurt and grief
that surrendering my son caused me. That is what he cannot
forgive.''

North leaned against the cool panes of glass at his back.
''It would mean he has to accept some responsibility.''

''But he did nothing wrong. He was—''

''He took your child, Elizabeth. He wanted an heir and
he took your son. Have you never wondered how it might
have been different if you had delivered a girl?''

She had. ''Isabel would have insisted he keep his word,''
she said quietly.

North suspected that was true. ''Of course,'' he said at
length. ''It is of no matter now. Selden has proved to be a
very good son to his father and Rosemont a good father to
his son.''

Elizabeth fiddled with the knot in her shawl. ''I would
see that it remains so. Do you understand why I said nothing
to you? Why I would have kept it a secret?''

''I understand that people you trust have betrayed you,''
he said. ''Adam's father. Louise and Harrison. In some
fashion it is even true of Isabel and your father.'' He heard
Elizabeth's sharp intake of breath. ''You do not like to think
of the last, do you? Or rather, it is acceptable if you think
it and keep it to yourself, but unacceptable if I say it aloud.
Were they the ones who convinced you that your son's life

would be beyond the pale if he were acknowledged as a bastard?''

''I . . . they . . .''

''And you? Did they say that you could have no place at all in society, make no match, have no chance at any happiness if you—''

Elizabeth shot to her feet. ''Stop it! My decision was made! I made it! I—'' Her voice was caught on a sob. She said the words again, this time with hardly a sound. ''I made it.'' Her shoulders shook once and a second breath rattled through her slender frame. ''I have to live with it.''

North closed the space between them in a single stride. He took Elizabeth in his arms and held her, pressing her head against his shoulder. Every tremor that shook her body he absorbed into his own. ''You don't have to live with it alone,'' he whispered against her ear. ''And you don't have to fear betrayal or reprisal from me. I love you, Elizabeth. I married you because I loved you. Nothing has changed that.''

''You . . . you told m-me to l-leave,'' she said brokenly. ''You s-said I sh-should go.''

''Because I was hurt. Not because I no longer loved you. I needed time to decide if I could live with you, knowing it was not the same for you, knowing that I would be hurt again and again by your inability to trust yourself to love me or trust me to love you.'' He caught her by the shoulders and held her back from him, his shadowed face close to hers, his dark eyes intent. ''I cannot do it, Elizabeth. These last weeks . . . not knowing where you were . . . it was an agony. Loving you without having it returned would be an agony stretched over a lifetime. I know that now. I am prepared to leave you, tonight if I must, if you can offer me no hope that it might be different.'' He could not help himself. His hands trembled, then his arms, and when it reached his shoulders he shook hers. It startled him so much that he pulled her to him again, wrapped his arms close about her as though he could cleave her to his heart. ''Can you, Elizabeth?'' he asked, his cheek pressed to her hair. ''Is there hope?''

''There is love,'' she said. She lifted her face and cupped his. ''Do you hear me, North? There is love. I was certain of it when I left London and I am no less certain of it now. I love you. God help us both, but I hope it is enough.''

He kissed her then. For the moment, at least, it seemed that it was.

Chapter Fourteen

The chaise was more comfortable than the stone floor, wider than the bench, and met the critical criterion of being handy. Outside the conservatory the snowfall had stopped. Moonshine glanced off the white landscape. An occasional wind lifted sparkling eddies of snow and reshaped the pasture with drifts like cresting waves. A silver-blue ribbon of light marked the path to the chaise, and the palm tree—that South Seas gift from Captain Cook—shaded the lovers with its feathery fronds.

Hunger born of abstinence, eagerness born of love, sent them tumbling on the chaise. Arms and legs tangled. Mouths fused. Impatience made them ignore clothing except as it presented a barrier to their furious coupling. They filled the air with moist heat until crystalline frost flowers appeared on the panes of glass. Their breathing came in small gasps, surprised and satisfied in turn as they pleasured each other and themselves.

He came when he was deeply inside her. She held him there with legs that were wrapped around his hips and arms that circled his shoulders. She embraced his shuddering body as if it were an extension of her own and then marveled that it wasn't. Her own cry mingled with the last threads of his and he supported her, whispering against her ear, ruffling her hair with each soft expulsion of air.

They lay quite still at the end, too replete to move except for the movements they could not help. Her fingers twitched. His calf jumped. Their heartbeats slowed with more delicacy. Their laughter mingled, low and rich, more of a rumbling than an eruption. They said inconsequential things that at the time seemed to have the weight and import of philosophical tenets. Discomfort aside, in fewer minutes than they realized, they slept.

The second time they made love it was in Elizabeth's bed. Frantic behind them, this union was lingering. Sweet. Sometimes playful. Sometimes gentle and grave.

Their clothes were scattered on the floor from doorway to bed. The heavy drapes were closed, blocking moonshine. It was the warmer glow from the candles that lent their perspiring flesh a sheen of gold and orange.

Lying back on the bed, her head resting on North's shoulder, Elizabeth lifted one arm and turned it so the soft patina of candlelight was visible along its length.

"Beautiful," North said, watching her. "You should always wear light."

"But—" Then she realized what he was saying. Elizabeth let her arm drop and she turned slightly, for a moment wearing only her smile. North noticed that looked very good on her, too. "You're a very sweet man," she told him. "But as careful with a shilling as your grandfather. I suppose I shall have to be content with the wardrobe I have."

North chuckled. "Then you've heard his lectures on the virtues of thrift and the vices of gambling."

"The entire repertoire." She laid her hand flat on North's chest. "He's not going to be pleased that you overturned two of his orchid pots. He's very proud of them, you know." Elizabeth's breath caught as North shut her up with a thorough kiss. When he raised his head she was smiling up at him. "If that is your idea of a consequence for my idle chatter, I doubt I shall ever find anything important to say again." She welcomed his rumbling laughter. Her fingers ran along the edge of his jaw and touched the corner of his mouth. Raising herself up on one elbow, Elizabeth's eyes searched his face. The toll their separation had exacted was still visible in his features; a deep weariness that was only partially ameliorated by their lovemaking was still there.

Elizabeth's index finger traced the line of his cheek from his mouth to his temple. Her own expression was both solemn and curious. "How did you find me?"

"Madame Fortuna." He smiled as Elizabeth's mouth opened and closed. He had actually rendered her speechless. He recalled that surprise had the same effect as kissing her. "I wish I could say that I was clever about it, but you left virtually no trail. No one remembered seeing you after you arrived at the inn. When pressed, the innkeeper could not even recall you leaving. Eastlyn watched the baroness's London residence and determined you had not come back to London to stay there. South went to Battenburn. West questioned innkeepers and coach drivers along the most traveled roads. There was no hint of you at any turn."

"But Madame Fortuna?" Elizabeth asked. "How ever did you—"

"The Compass Club's involvement with that lady goes back twenty years." North enjoyed himself immensely, watching Elizabeth's blush creep from her breasts to her neck and finally suffuse her face as he told her about his first encounter with the fortune-teller.

"A peach!" she said, perfectly astonished. "You asked to see her . . . her . . ."

"Her quim."

"Yes. *That*. And she showed you a peach?"

"Well, yes," he said calmly. "They're very much alike, you know." Under the blankets, North's hand found the inside curve of Elizabeth's thigh. His fingers began to walk up her leg toward the fruit in question. "And you wouldn't expect that she would show a schoolboy like myself her actual nether parts, would you? I was only ten."

Elizabeth pushed his hand away. "And a perfect devil.

Entirely too forward even then. Did the Bishops suspect the truth?''

"Never. Didn't let us join them, though. Madame Fortuna warned me they were villains—and so they were.''

"I cannot believe you stole my still life to indulge in naughty reminiscences with your friends.''

North laughed. "I really am never to be forgiven for taking those peaches.''

"Never.'' She managed to maintain a stern mien for a few moments more, then added accusingly, "You *juggled* them.''

His eyes crinkled and tears gathered at the outside edges. Having no handkerchief, North accepted the corner of the sheet Elizabeth tartly handed him. It took him a little longer to catch his breath. "I did, didn't I?'' he said with rather more pride than regret.

Elizabeth sighed and waited patiently for him to collect himself. "Was it your idea to ask for Madame Fortuna's help?''

'South's.'' He anticipated Elizabeth's next question. "And I asked her to find *you*, not your . . . peach.''

She rolled her eyes. "A small mercy.''

North plumped the pillow under his head and lay back again. "She sent me here,'' he said. "I had never once considered that you might go to my grandfather.''

"It only occurred to me at the last moment.''

He fell silent, remembering all too well the fear that had eclipsed his drunken glow when he realized Elizabeth had most likely *not* gone to Rosemont. North stroked her hair, absently assuring himself of her presence now. "Elizabeth?''

She immediately recognized the gravity of his tone. "Yes?''

"You said earlier tonight that I was only partly responsible for you leaving. Who was the other influence?''

"I think you already know the answer to that: Louise and Harrison.''

He nodded slowly, considering the implications.

"Madame Fortuna said that I would find everything I sought when I found you."

"Did she?"

"I thought she was waxing romantic."

"Perhaps she was."

North regarded her closely, noting that Elizabeth's smile did not quite reach her eyes. "Perhaps," he agreed. "It's true enough in the romantic sense."

"I'm glad for that."

He smiled faintly at her wry tone but would not be diverted by it. "I wonder if it might not also be true in another, more literal sense."

"Oh?"

North felt Elizabeth's stillness in the single thread of tension that ran through her slender frame. He sensed anticipation in her quiet. "Do you know why finding the Gentleman Thief has been so important?" he asked.

"Is not that obvious? He steals the *ton's* valuables."

"He steals their secrets." Though Elizabeth did not move, North felt the subtle change in her as tension became rigidness. "That is why the colonel became involved. The matter of missing diamonds and rubies is of little importance to him, but missing documents, state papers, private correspondence that details policy and parliamentary affairs, that is something else again. You can understand, I think, how it would concern him."

Pressing her lips together, Elizabeth nodded.

"The stolen documents are not common knowledge. It is easier to admit the loss of jewelry that can be replaced than private papers, which cannot, but these people are loyal citizens and eventually a few come forward, some angry, some embarrassed, all of them worried, and report what has been taken that makes them and the Crown vulnerable."

Elizabeth's eyes had been widening slowly as North spoke. When he finished, looking at her somewhat expectantly, she blinked. "Do you mean to say the Gentleman is responsible for these thefts?"

"It's one possibility," North said carefully.

"But you make it sound treasonous."

"Given the contents of some of the stolen documents, it is exactly that."

Elizabeth pushed herself upright, dragging the sheet to cover her breasts. "You must be mistaken. The Gentleman has only ever been interested in baubles."

"Or clever enough to make it seem so."

"Oh, I doubt he is so clever," she said, shaking her head to emphasize the point. "Thieves are not, you know. He has a certain style, I think, but you must not assign him too much wit in the upperworks."

"Truly?" he asked with a certain dryness of tone. "Do you think so?"

"I am sure of it."

"It does not reflect kindly on me, though, does it? After all, I was given this assignment to find the Gentleman almost a year ago. He has eluded me and those who came before me."

Elizabeth frowned. "You mean there were others who were looking for this thief?"

"Half a dozen over the years, I should think. Frustration at the highest levels led to the colonel getting the unenviable task of ending the Gentleman's career."

"But he has passed it on to you."

North shrugged. "My success or failure will ultimately be his. That is the nature of his work. He is known to his superiors. I am not."

It was a great deal for Elizabeth to take in. "The colonel would not tell me any of this."

"No, he wouldn't."

"Neither would you," she reminded him. "You wanted me to think the colonel had nothing to do with you finding the thief." A vertical crease appeared between Elizabeth's brows as the obvious question occurred to her. "Why are you telling me now?"

His cobalt blue eyes mocked her gently. "Elizabeth," he chided her, "do not dissemble now."

"Dissemble?" Her voice cracked a little on the word.

Yanking the sheet, Elizabeth tore it from under the blankets and wrapped it around herself as she twisted and rolled out of bed. The tail dragged behind her like a train as she stalked off in the direction of the dressing room.

"Is that what is famously known as a high dudgeon?" he called after her.

"Yes!" she called back.

He nodded, impressed. "Am I supposed to infer from it that I have offended you?"

Elizabeth appeared in the doorway wearing her robe. She tossed the sheet toward the bed. "You said I was dissembling."

"Aren't you?"

"Yes, but I have no wish to have it remarked upon."

"Aaah." North reached over the side of the bed, caught the edge of the sheet where it had fallen short of its mark, and pulled it back. Rising, he tucked it around his waist. "Then it is being caught out that you do not like."

"I suppose."

"Then you will not like this," he said, regarding her steadily. "You forgot to limp on your way to retrieve your robe."

"Hah! I did not forget. I had no use for it. There is a difference, you know."

North's brows lifted a fraction. The expression was more of an amused salute than one of surprise. "I am learning that. Is there something else you want to confess?"

"Do you mean I must say it again?" she demanded.

He smiled, knowing quite well what she meant. Her first words to him this evening had been a confession, yet he had not heard it in that vein. *So you have found the Gentleman Thief.* "Are you the Gentleman, Elizabeth?"

It was the sympathetic timbre of his question that was her undoing. She caught her lower lip, swallowed hard, and managed a single nod of assent. Drawing a deep breath, she crossed the room to stand before him, graceful, lithe, her step unfaltering and not at all tentative. "I do not know how you can believe me, North, but I have committed no treason. I am guilty of so many things but not that. Never that.''

He took her hand. It was cold. His thumb brushed the back of it. ''I do believe you.''

She felt breath return to her body. She closed her eyes briefly, thankfully. Then a thought occurred to her. ''Is it because you know I am not so very clever?''

Laughing, he pulled her to him. ''I do not think there is any answer that will not damn me.'' Hugging her, North kissed the crown of her head.

Elizabeth's arms went around his back. ''They never asked it of me, North,'' she admitted. ''You understand, don't you, that stealing was never fully my choice?''

He nodded. The fragrance of her hair enveloped him. He rubbed his cheek against the silky strands.

She hugged him more tightly. His skin was warm against hers. She could feel the beat of his heart and took confidence from its steadiness. ''It was Louise's price for her silence. Harrison's, too. I only had to steal for them once before that very act became part of all that I needed to keep secret.''

North stroked her back. ''Does your father know?''

''Yes. And Isabel.'' Elizabeth's hands became fists. ''Battenburn insisted on them knowing. Their complicity was required to further assure their silence.'' She leaned back in North's embrace and lifted her head. ''Does my father know about the stolen documents?''

''I don't know. It is very likely. He is in a position to.''

Elizabeth's eyes communicated her distress. ''He will think I am the one responsible.''

''It has been going on for years, Elizabeth. If he knows, then he has long ago assigned you the responsibility.''

''But he has said nothing!''

''Protecting you. Protecting himself. Pretending none of it is happening.'' He touched her cheek with the back of his hand. ''We cannot be certain what he knows.''

''He's no traitor, North.'' Her stomach turned uneasily. ''He's *not*.''

Northam said nothing for a moment. ''Let us hope that

is so." He led her back to the bed and bid her sit, then he stoked the fire before he returned to her side. She held the covers up for him and he crawled in beside her, dragging the sheet wrapped around his waist with him.

North leaned back against the headboard while Elizabeth leaned against him. "Have you suspected for a long time?" she asked. "About me, I mean?"

"I should be embarrassed to admit it, but when I suspected you, I said so immediately. In hindsight I can see that you gave me any number of hints—all of which I completely ignored. Blinded by love, I suspect." He paused. "Or every bit the village idiot your father accused me of being."

"Oh, North. He said that?"

"It was one of his kinder observations when I went looking for you at Rosemont. In light of what I understand now, his anger was born of fear and his fear encompassed much more than your immediate welfare. He told me I should apply to Lady Battenburn for information, that is where you would most likely go."

"Did you?"

"No. Not overtly. I mistook her motives, but I was aware that she would not be helpful. She eventually came to me. I already knew that you were not at her London residence or at Battenburn, but it was the first I realized you had not written her. That surprised me. Why didn't you?"

Elizabeth considered her answer. "I suppose because when I knew I was not going to Rosemont I realized I had a chance to get away from her and the baron, too. You can't imagine how much I wanted that."

One of those niggling thoughts that had been plaguing North for some time came back to him now. "Neither your father nor Isabel invited us to Rosemont, did they?"

"No," she said quietly. "It was the baron's idea we should go there. A reminder, I believe, to my father and me that we were still under his control."

North recalled the letter that had arrived as he and Elizabeth were ready to leave Rosemont for Hampton Cross. "Louise never experienced a heart ailment, did she?"

Elizabeth shook her head. "Her health is fine. It always has been. It was naught but a ruse to bring me back to London. Louise wanted me to marry you, North, but I think it was because she was afraid of you in some way. Her intention, I believe, was that I should compromise you, just as I had my family. Perhaps she and Harrison have some knowledge of your efforts to find the Gentleman. Everyone but West was invited to the rout at Battenburn. Louise may have suspected something even then. She asked a great many questions about your association with one another."

North was thoughtful. "That would explain why Louise claimed her necklace was stolen."

"Yes. She hoped it would divert any gossip that she and Battenburn were somehow responsible for South's stolen snuffbox, which, of course, they were." There was a brief guilty pause. "Indirectly, I mean. I took the snuffbox. South-erton thoroughly trounced Battenburn earlier that evening at cards and I was required to recover the loss."

"My God," North said softly, shaking his head. "They are a pair."

"It was something of a game to them. A chess game comes to mind. Certainly I was a pawn. My father and stepmother also. There are probably others, although I cannot begin to suppose who they are. Until you told me about the stolen papers I believed Louise and Harrison were only guilty of practicing the worst kind of cruelty: amusing themselves at the expense of others. I never guessed at this other side, even when Louise began to place more pressure on me."

"Pressure? In what way?"

"To attend more functions. To steal more often. From your mother. Your friends. I never told her you were looking for the thief, but I have to believe now that she knew it very well. I think she wanted you to catch me . . . to save me . . . to make certain that you were also complicitous. Louise did not understand that you are more honorable than that. She did not realize you would not be compromised by your affection for me."

North's short laugh held little humor. "Louise is a better student of human nature than you are. Perhaps if all I felt for you was affection, I might not defend you so vigorously. Loving you, though, presents challenges I could not have anticipated."

Elizabeth turned her head to look at him. "Does this mean I shall not be transported?"

He could not help it. Her question was everything sincere, but he reacted too quickly to take that into account. The sixth Earl of Northam laughed long and hard. It required Elizabeth's elbow in his ribs to encourage him to take a different tack. "I'm sorry," he said, wiping tears from his eyes. "It struck me as humorous."

Elizabeth, who had always been attracted to North's laughter, was now wondering why that was. "I was quite serious," she assured him.

"I know." His laughter almost broke through again. He managed to confine it to a rumbling in his chest. He gave her an apologetic smile when she looked at him sharply. "Forgive me."

Sighing, Elizabeth settled back into the crook of his shoulder. Now that he was no longer shaking with mirth it was a comfortable shelter. "I am a thief," she reminded him. "It was a perfectly reasonable question. Many people guilty of far less than me have been sent away. I should consider myself fortunate if I am not hanged."

That sobered North. "It is not a possibility," he assured her. "Trust me."

Elizabeth realized then that she most surely did.

They shared a bounty of breakfast in bed. The maid informed them that Lord Worth would see them in their bedchamber if they were not inclined to remove themselves by the noon hour. North told her to assure his grandfather they would see him in his library, but when she was gone he locked the door in the event they were otherwise occupied at the appointed hour.

"What hints?" Elizabeth asked, seemingly out of no-where. In truth, she had been mulling over the puzzle for the better part of the morning, or at least the part of the morning that was not made better by North's lovemaking. "Last evening you said I presented you with hints about my identity as the thief. Do you think I meant to give myself away?"

"It has occurred to me," he said. "Perhaps it was not your willful intent, but rather a more subtle wish. There was the matter of the snuffbox, for instance. Not only did you take an immense risk stealing it back from the baron, but you skillfully maneuvered the treasure hunt so that either Southerton or I would find it. It settles the question of who helped whom on that occasion. You led South and me around by the nose, I think. I imagine Battenburn was furious."

"More so Louise. I returned the gold fob and ruby pendant to her, but she would not be placated. I suppose it was then that she conceived of the plan to place her diamond necklace in your trunk. I knew nothing about that."

North nodded. "So I gathered." Over the rim of his teacup, he watched Elizabeth brush out her hair. It crackled with each long stroke. "You also climb trees."

Her hand paused mid-stroke. "What?"

"It was another clue," he explained. "At Rosemont you were climbing trees with Selden. He said you promised to teach him. I should have thought that your injury would have prevented you. Indeed, when we were at Battenburn you made some remark about a fear of falling. It was all so much smoke and mirrors. Very effective, though. I did not see through it."

Elizabeth resumed brushing. "There is no satisfaction for me in having fooled you," she said. "It was done of necessity."

"I know that."

"My infirmity was Louise's idea. She was persuaded that a limp would make me an even more unlikely suspect. I suppose the fact that I was a woman was not enough." Elizabeth set down the brush gently and turned on her stool to face North. "My back began to ache from the pretense. Even now, after weeks of resting here at Stonewickam I find there are times when my hip stiffens. The longer I practiced the deceit, the more it interfered with my ability to climb. At Battenburn no such skill was required of me. I could use the secret passages to move about, but once we returned to London ..." Elizabeth could only shake her head at the position in which she had found herself. "As difficult as I found spending time with Louise, it also offered some respite. When I was with anyone else I had to maintain the sham of my physical limitations. The night South escorted me to the duchess's ball I was very nearly caught out because I was so stiff."

"Bloody hell," North said softly. He banged the back of his head lightly against the headboard. "That was you."

Elizabeth looked at him oddly. "Of course it was me. Isn't that what we've been discussing?"

"Yes, but ..." Closing his eyes momentarily, North ran his fingers through his hair. "Bloody hell," he said again. In his mind's eye he could see her just as South had described, hanging off the lip of the roof, pulling her leg up at the very last moment so she could escape over a succession of rooftops. "You might have been killed."

"It was not such a narrow thing as South would have you believe," she said quickly.

North grunted, not so gullible as that.

"I admit my situation would have been improved if someone had confided South's plan to me. I don't think you can properly appreciate my surprise when he appeared in the duchess's bedchamber."

North simply banged his head again.

Elizabeth fought down a smile. "Perhaps it would be better if we said no more about that particular evening, though I suppose you must wonder how it was all accomplished."

"Believe me when I say I wish it were otherwise."

"Then I shall say it all quickly." Elizabeth proceeded to do just that, racing through her explanation with barely a breath while she ticked off the major points on her fingers. "Battenburn arranges a change of clothes for me if we believe one will be necessary. The location of the jewelry is known beforehand because Louise always discovers it. Sometime during the evening I excuse myself from the dancing, usually completely unnoticed, and find the host or hostess's valuables. At the duchess's ball I did not go to another rooftop as South suggested. I merely dropped to the other side of the house, entered by a window I had left open for just such a purpose, and—"

North held up a hand. "If you have any feelings for me, you will stop this recitation. I am still seeing you hanging by your fingernails from Lady Calumet's hip roof."

"It was not—" She cut herself off because he lifted his hand a fraction higher. "Very well." Under her breath she added, "Not so very different from what you did at Battenburn."

He pretended not to hear that. "What about the times jewelry was taken from necks, ears, and wrists that were wearing them?"

"I am afraid you will think me immodest, North, but it is not so difficult after one learns the way of it."

"I take it there was a great deal of practice in the beginning," he said dryly.

"Hours and hours."

"Louise and Harrison taught you?"

"They hired . . . tutors, I suppose you would call them."

"I would call them thieves."

"They were that. Very accomplished."

North was finding it hard to credit he was having this conversation. He realized he was shaking his head a lot. "The baron and baroness are not always present when the thefts occur."

"That is true. Over the years I would say perhaps a third of the time."

"I will have to share my information regarding dates with you, but that would likely correspond closely to those events where documents were stolen. Who is the more probable thief? Battenburn or his wife?''

"I could not say. You must allow that it may be neither. There could be yet another person engaged by them.''

North considered it possible, though not likely. The nature of the stolen papers was such that the thief would have to be astute and discriminating in order to make the correct choices. It was not the sort of thing well left to others. "We have to return to London,'' he said, watching her carefully.

"I know.'' Her voice was wistful. She was already missing Stonewickam. "I should like to visit your grandfather again soon.''

He smiled. "I am not certain which one of you is more enamored of the other. He likes you immensely.''

Elizabeth rose and walked toward the bed. She held out her hands to North and when he took them, she pulled him to his feet. Standing on tiptoe, Elizabeth slipped her arms around his neck. "I like him also,'' she said, her mouth just a moment from his. "But I love you. No one will ever love you so well as I do.''

He remembered saying much the same thing to her once. She was tipping her head back, watching him, the sweetest emotion there in her eyes. She remembered it, too. "Aaah, Elizabeth,'' he whispered. He kissed her then. Their mouths lingered tenderly, and when the kiss dissolved they did not move apart. North's cheek rested against her hair. Her fingers ruffled his.

"I do not know if there will ever be a right moment to say this,'' he said, "so it may as well be now—while you are feeling charitable toward me.'' Before she could guess at what it might be, he continued quickly. "There was a time not so long ago that I thought the colonel had been your lover.''

Elizabeth's head reared back and she looked up at him, eyes wide, her mouth gaping. "You are quite serious,'' she said.

"Well, yes.'' When she simply stared at him, he felt compelled to explain. "You love him. You've said so. And he is only your mother's cousin. The difference in your ages is not so great and he was credited to be quite handsome when—"

"He is still handsome," she said.

North reluctantly acknowledged that was so. "It seemed that you wanted to avoid him. You were not pleased to see him at our wedding, and then—"

Elizabeth set one finger to his lips, halting him. "He is like an uncle to me. It was always that way, nothing more. I began writing him less when I became involved with Louise and Harrison. I did not want them to know he was important to me because they would have tried to compromise him also. They are trying to do it anyway, in spite of what I've done to protect him. It is likely they were the ones who encouraged him to come to our wedding. South may have penned the invitiation, but Louise or the baron, or both together, prompted it." She moved her hand to North's shoulder. "But that is not the only reason I have not wanted to see him. He confronted me with the other truth at West's. He knows that my reluctance has been because he is ill. He is more like my mother than you can imagine, and being in his company is as extraordinarily sweet as it is painful."

Elizabeth touched North's cheek, tracing the line of his jaw. "I am not sorry you told me this, for I plan to see much more of the colonel in the future, and I would not want you to have any doubts about the place he has had in my life." She lowered both her hands and took his, drawing them toward her heart. "Adam's father is dead, North. In January it will be five years. It was in a place called New Orleans. There was a battle there. A senseless thing, really. The war with the United States was already ended, but word had not reached either side."

"I am sorry, Elizabeth." And he was. He meant the words most sincerely. "How did you learn of it?"

"Louise. My naive confession to her left out nothing, not even . . . not even his name. She made inquiries and eventually found what had become of him. It was not a kindness that she did this. She would have used him in some way if he had not been killed." Elizabeth's eyes darkened. "I hate her, North. I hate her and her husband and I hate what she has encouraged me to become. I hate that I did not say no to them, that I have always believed I could not." Her voice dropped to a mere whisper, yet remained intense and clear. "Sometimes I think I could kill them both."

It was only partially to comfort Elizabeth that North held her close. He did not want her to see that he shared this same thought.

"So you are returned." Louise looked Elizabeth up and down. She made her assessment as if from a superior height, although it was Elizabeth who stood and she who reclined casually on the chaise. "Open the drapes, dear," she said. "It is rather gloomy in here, is it not? I fear the day will not be improved by sunshine."

Without a word Elizabeth crossed the sitting room and fixed the dark green velvet drapes with tiebacks. Fog pressed against the windowpanes. The houses across the square were visible only as a vague outline. Immediately below she could see her driver hop down from the carriage to tend to the grays. When she turned away, Elizabeth was unsurprised to find Louise still watching her closely.

Lady Battenburn idly smoothed the fabric of her robe over her lap. "I confess I am surprised by the hour of your arrival. Am I to assume that you are eager to see me?"

"I thought it was you who were eager," Elizabeth said without inflection. "My husband said you came to Merrifeld Square to inquire after me."

"And a most unsatisfactory interview it was. Northam would have had me believe you had gone to Rosemont. I told him that could not be true as I had reason to know differently. He was quite unpleasant about it."

Elizabeth's brows lifted fractionally but she said nothing.

Louise picked up her teacup. "Do not express yourself so to me, Elizabeth. I assure you it is the truth. I can excuse his behavior because I believe he was not well. He certainly

did not look well. I remarked to Harrison later that it seemed
to me Northam did not know where you were and that
accounted for his surliness.''

It was difficult to imagine that Northam had been surly.
Elizabeth considered it said something about the state of
Louise's nerves that she thought it was so. ''I am here now,''
she said.

''And feeling a bit too full of yourself. I cannot like it,
Elizabeth. You must set the matter straight. Were you running from your husband or from me?''

Elizabeth had known the question was coming. She managed to look surprised while still giving the answer she had
practiced on her way over. ''Both of you, Louise. And
neither of you. I required time for reflection and I could
only find that by leaving London. Northam, however, knew
precisely where I was. I imagine his decision not to tell you
had to do with his respect for my privacy.''

''And where were you?'' she asked suspiciously.

''At Stonewickam visiting Lord Worth, Northam's grandfather.''

Louise was not at all mollified. ''It was wicked of you to
leave with no word.'' Her rounded chin was thrust forward.
''What is it that you needed to reflect upon? Am I to assume
you have had doubts about the wisdom of continuing our
arrangement?''

Elizabeth sat in a Queen Anne chair near the foot of the
chaise. ''I have always had doubts. I have never been quiet
about those. Now I also have doubts about my marriage.''
She raised one slim hand to ward off Louise's interruption.
''You can set yourself easy, for I see no way out of either
short of leaving this life altogether. Yes, I considered it, and
no, it does not appeal. I am well and truly caught, Louise, you
and the baron on one side and my lord husband on the other.
That is what I had to come to terms with. And I have.''

Louise regarded Elizabeth closely, weighing her words
and her sincerity. ''Then there will be no more of this nonsense,'' she said finally. ''You will not leave again without
a word. I must be able to depend upon that, Libby. It was

most distressing that I could not find you. Even your father
and Isabel could give me no word, and I know they would
not have withheld it. Pray, do not look so startled. Naturally
I sent someone to Rosemont. How else could I have known
Northam was lying? I cannot like it that you would tell
Northam your whereabouts and he would conceal this fact
from me. He must be brought in, Elizabeth.''

"Brought in?" she asked.

"Included.''

"Oh, I cannot believe that is necessary. It has worked
well thus far. You know it has. I have been so careful to
give no hint to him of our arrangement.''

Louise's generous mouth thinned for a moment. "Do not
be disagreeable, Libby. I assure you, I am quite set on the
matter. Harrison is of a similar mind. If, indeed, you have
given nothing away, it is only a matter of time before North
learns the truth. I should rather it be on my terms, not yours.
You can understand that, can you not?''

She could. It was precisely what she and Northam had
expected of Louise. "I do not think it is a good idea, Louise.
He is not so easily caged as I was. You cannot hope to
control him.''

"You caged him, m'dear," Louise said sweetly. "What
is marriage if not that? He may pace from time to time,
chafe against his confinement like some great tiger, but he
is satisfied with his lot. All men are. They do not manage
very well when they are left to their own devices. Gambling.
Affairs. Intrigues. War. You must see that. Your husband
is no different.''

Elizabeth was sincerely happy to be sitting down. She
felt an urge toward hysterical laughter and managed to quell
it by not looking at Louise directly, but at a point just past
her shoulder. "I do not think Northam knows he is caged,''
she said after a moment.

"Of course he doesn't. Not now. That is what must be
changed.'' Louise reached for the teapot, poured Elizabeth a
cup, and held it out to her. She warmed her own cup after
Elizabeth was served and contemplated the problem Northam

presented as she sipped her tea. "Your absence from London caused us to miss an opportunity at the Langham rout. The countess has a sapphire bangle I have long admired." Louise sighed dramatically. "But it is not to be mine."

Elizabeth said nothing. If the baroness was anticipating an apology, she was sadly out of it there.

Louise raised one eyebrow. "So that is to be the way of it. No remorse for your behavior."

"My presence here speaks well of me, Louise. Depending on your point of view. Northam would be appalled to know the nature of our discussion."

"Then it will be all the more delicious when he is included. I confess, I look forward to it."

"I take it you have a plan." Elizabeth imagined Louise had had one for a very long time, probably conceived when she first saw the direction of North's interest at the picnic. "I must warn you, Louise, Northam is not so easily led about."

Louise waved this concern aside, confident that what she had in mind could be accomplished. "It is only that you must not be too clever. It would not go at all well if you were to choose your husband's side against me. There is Selden, after all. And your dear papa."

Elizabeth felt herself pale. She nodded shortly. "What is it I must do for you?"

"For yourself," Louise reminded her. "Protecting a secret such as the one you have becomes a complicated affair, does it not?" Not requiring a reply, Louise went on. "You are aware of the French ambassador's winter ball?"

Careful to give nothing away, Elizabeth nodded.

"It has every indication of being a most coveted invitation. The prince will surely be there. And Wellington, naturally. There is no better way for the *ton* to show our goodwill to the French than by our attendance at the ball. Why, your own father will certainly be invited."

"And you, Louise? Have you and Harrison received your invitation?"

"I am certain it is to arrive any day." She paused, lifting

an eyebrow to be sure Elizabeth understood. When Elizabeth nodded, Louise continued, "Good. I am hopeful you have already responded favorably."

"Northam did."

Louise did not trouble to hide her pleasure. "I thought that he would. How very good of him. You will see, Elizabeth, how well this turns out for all of us."

Elizabeth tossed her bonnet and gloves onto a chair as she marched into Northam's study. North looked up from his writing and saw the butler hovering in the doorway while Elizabeth removed her own pelisse and threw it carelessly aside. Her agitation was so high that she did not notice North dismissing the man or hear the doors close behind her. Her cheeks were flushed and her eyes were bright. Had she not just come from Lady Battenburn's home, North would have been moved to comment that she looked quite pretty. Such an observation now would likely be met with pointed silence.

Elizabeth went to the fireplace and held out her hands. "It is not warmth I crave, North, but cleansing," she said quietly. "I suppose I did not truly want to believe that you could be right about Louise or, more correctly, that I had been associated with the theft of private papers." She paused, glancing in North's direction. "That seems to be the way of it, though. Louise requires an invitation to the French ambassador's ball."

North pushed back from the desk and turned slightly in his chair. "That can be arranged easily enough."

Elizabeth's hands fell to her sides. She turned and looked at him fully, gauging his response. "You are not surprised."

He did not deny it. "You and I both knew she would want you to prove your loyalty to her quickly. The ambassador's ball is precisely the right affair. In her place I would have chosen the same."

"She means to draw you in."

"That was to be expected," he said. "You did not give it away, I hope."

Elizabeth bristled a little at the suggestion. "I am a more accomplished liar than that." Her flush returned as she realized the full import of her words. "It is a rather incriminating defense, is it not? But there you have it."

"Indeed." Chuckling, he held out his hands to her. She did not hesitate to take them and allow herself to be drawn onto his lap. "What have you been told to take?"

"The ambassador's daughter has an emerald necklace that Louise covets."

"More likely she covets what is in the ambassador's private study."

"That is what I was thinking," said Elizabeth.

"There is some suspicion that the French are not as subdued as they would have us believe. If there exists proof that certain members of our own government are working in concert with them—for personal gain—that proof would be valuable to Louise and Harrison. People would go to great lengths to keep it from becoming public."

"Should you like to have such proof?"

"Most certainly, though the truth is, it is hard to say what might be uncovered at the residence. I imagine Louise and Harrison's forays do not always yield what they anticipate. There must be times when they are disappointed . . ." North's voice trailed off as he became more thoughtful. A slow, secretive smile eventually transformed his face. "Do you know, Elizabeth, I believe I think better when you are on my lap. It is the fragrance of your hair, I am certain of it."

"Do not think I can be diverted with flattery, North, though it was a very pretty compliment. Tell me what you are thinking." She saw his decidedly wicked smile. "Not what you are thinking at this precise moment," she amended. "I can divine that well enough. Tell me the other."

Persuaded that she could truly not be distracted, North surrendered. "It occurs to me that if on occasion Battenburn and his wife are disappointed with what they find, then the opposite is also likely to be true."

Elizabeth waited to hear more. "And . . ." she prompted.

"And I will have to speak to the colonel," North said.

"To see if the ambassador's ball might not be one of the latter occasions."

"You are being deliberately vague."

"Yes, but not because I think you would give anything away to Louise."

"Hhmpf."

"You are a very accomplished liar."

Elizabeth was not amused by his teasing. She set her teeth.

"I cannot tell you what I do not know," he said. "Let me speak to the colonel. He will know what can be done. If I acted on my own, I could very well make a tangle of someone else's assignment."

"But then he will have to know about me," she said. "What I am . . . what I've done. And Selden . . ." Elizabeth considered all that had been done in aid of keeping her own child from knowing the truth of his birth. "I want to tell the colonel myself. I cannot let you say it for me."

"If that is your wish."

She nodded solemnly. "It is." Elizabeth could not keep the concern out of her eyes or the question out of her voice. "I think he will forgive me."

"There is nothing to forgive, Elizabeth."

"He will be hurt that I did not apply to him for help."

"He will understand. If not immediately, then in a short time. He knows your father. He will understand the pressures that kept you silent. As for Selden, you can depend upon the colonel saying nothing. He will respect your decision to see that Adam's birth had legitimacy."

She had to believe he was right. "So many times I've wished I told him about Adam's father. I would not have felt so alone when I discovered I was pregnant. He might have sent for me. I might have gone to India and met you there."

North's smile was gentle. "Perhaps. Some things are meant to happen no matter how we try to avoid them."

"Are you speaking of yourself as well? Of marriage?"

"I was certainly not of the same mind as my mother on the subject."

"Really?"

He nodded. "She was determined that I should be wed. I argued with her just before I arrived at Battenburn. South was there to witness some of it, though he had the good sense not to take sides."

"I imagine he has a gun to his head also."

"A cannon. That is what his mother wields."

"Mothers are wont to see their sons settled." She cupped the side of his face, touching the corner of his mouth with her thumb. "They are wont to see their sons with heirs."

North's eyes narrowed. "Has my mother said something to you? I told her I would not brook her interference."

"You will not credit it, but your mother has been tight-lipped on the matter. However, you neglected to say something similar to your grandfather." Beneath her hand Elizabeth could feel warmth suffuse North's cheek. "He meant well," she said. "And I did not mind. It was reasonable that he should wonder about an heir."

"Yes, but did he have to wonder aloud?"

Elizabeth smiled, then pressed it against North's own lips. She felt the shape of his mouth change slowly, warming to the touch of hers. Drawing back slowly, she looked at him, her eyes darkening in response to what she saw in his. "Will you give me a child, North?"

He could say nothing for a moment. "Are you certain?"

She nodded. "Very. It is one of the things I came to understand when I was with your grandfather. I thought I was afraid to carry another child, afraid that I could not be a proper mother or afraid it would be taken from me, but it is not fear, North, or rather it is not *only* fear. I realized at Stonewickam that I have been punishing myself, and that I have been doing it for a very long time."

North's own smile was tender. He pressed the heart of her palm against his mouth and kissed her there; then he held her hand in his. "Let us see what we can do about this matter of an heir," he said. "Among all the people who care for us, there is sure to be a wager."

Chapter Fifteen

Elizabeth glowed. Guests of the ambassador remarked on it as North led her onto the dance floor. The Dowager Countess of Northam heard rumor repeated as gospel that her daughter-in-law was *enceinte*, which she neither confirmed nor denied, though she suspected the truth was merely that Elizabeth was most sincerely happy.

North turned Elizabeth in the first wide arc of the waltz. Her face was lifted toward him, bathed beautifully in prisms of candlelight from the crystal chandeliers. The gold shards in her amber eyes flashed, making the smile she communicated there more wicked than the demure placement of her lips would suggest. "You should not look at me in quite that manner, my lady. This evening might well be over before it is properly begun. The ambassador is a Parisian, do not forget. He will understand perfectly our hasty exit from his ball."

Elizabeth's smile was not reduced in any manner. "And you should not have encouraged me to have a second glass of wine before we left our home. I have no head for drink."

North's own smile did not waver, though there was no accompanying teasing light in his eyes. To the throng of guests crowding the edge of the ballroom, nothing had changed in his demeanor. To Elizabeth, he communicated something different. "Are you clearheaded enough to continue?"

She nodded. "I was having fun with you, North. Do not concern yourself that I shall not be able do everything as you and the colonel have planned."

"Bloody hell, Elizabeth."

"You're glowering. People will talk."

North's fingers tightened around her hand and at her waist, but he managed to look less threatening. "I should have had a second glass," he said under his breath. He glanced with some longing toward the crush of people around the punch bowls. Elizabeth's light laughter garnered his attention and her beautiful smile kept it there. There was a pale flush to her complexion, a hint of roses in her cheeks that might have been the wine, but he doubted it. Excitement and anticipation put some of the color there; he could not say what accounted for the rest.

The strains of music rose and fell as they danced the length of the ballroom. The ostrich plume in her ivory turban dipped each time Elizabeth was turned. Metallic gold threads in her tunic and gown sparkled with her every step. The ivory fan dangling from her wrist swung lightly to the stringed accompaniment, and in spite of the limp she affected, she was light and lithe in his arms.

"What are you thinking?" he asked.

She did not hesitate. "That I shall be free," she said simply, gravely. "That if all goes well, I shall finally be free."

North nodded. This, then, accounted for the remainder of her glowing complexion and the brightness in her eyes. The worry, even fear, he had seen earlier at Merrifield Square, the dread that had prompted him to give her that second glass of wine, seemed to have been left behind. It gave him pause. In his experience a certain amount of anxiety was not entirely a bad thing. It served to keep one's wits sharpened.

Elizabeth searched North's face when he remained quiet. "It will all go well," she said, though it was unclear from her tone whether she was giving assurance or seeking it.

"The colonel. You. So much planning this last fortnight. Everyone is agreed that nothing has been left to chance."

"Something is always left to chance," he said. "A foregone conclusion only achieves that distinction in hindsight." North felt her stumble a little, the first misstep she had made in his embrace. Until now she had been light in his arms, the limp she affected all but vanishing as she moved with the music. He inclined his head toward her and whispered just below the lilting strains of the waltz, "I say it not to shatter your confidence but to hone your awareness."

Elizabeth nodded once. What she became immediately aware of was the rush of blood from her head to her feet. "You will understand if I do not thank you for it," she said shakily.

"Chin up," he directed her. "Better. Now smile. Very lovely. Do you know I mean to make love to you tonight? Perhaps in the carriage before we reach home. Think about that."

She trod on his toes. "Think about *that*."

Grinning, he recovered easily. "Is it your intention to give me a limp to match your own?"

Elizabeth considered taking aim at his stockinged shins. "It is fortunate for you the waltz is ending."

His grin merely deepened. He spun her to the edge of the ballroom floor just as the last notes faded and they were immediately welcomed into a clutch of glittering guests. North skillfully steered Elizabeth to one of the unoccupied chairs at the edge of the room. For once she seemed grateful for the pretense of her limp. "Shall I get you something to drink?" he asked.

"Ratafia." She laughed when North made a face, showing his distaste for the sweet, fruity liqueur. "I don't really like it either," she admitted. "Therefore, I am certain not to indulge myself."

Making a slight bow, he left her. Out of the corner of his eye he saw Lady Battenburn immediately withdraw from her circle of friends and begin to wend her way toward Elizabeth. He had to resist the urge to return to Elizabeth's side. He wished there had been no part for her to play in tonight's game, but from the outset he knew nothing could be accomplished without her. If she had been Lord and Lady Battenburn's pawn in the past, she was now the colonel's queen.

Elizabeth's fear that Blackwood would find fault with the choices she had made were unfounded. The colonel had drawn her to his side, holding her cool hand as she told him all and spared herself nothing. There was no condemnation, no reproach. Just as North had said, the colonel told her there was nothing to forgive. His regret was that she had borne the burden alone, that the betrayal of her trust had left her afraid to trust even him. North had left the room quietly, giving them privacy and time to come to terms with the circumstances and revelations that had separated them.

And when he returned they began plotting the end of the Battenburn terror.

Watching Northam disappear in the crowd, Elizabeth fanned herself absently. Lavender silks and pink satins intermingled in the ballroom as guests positioned themselves for the next dance. A gap in the onlookers allowed Elizabeth to have a narrow view of the floor. She glimpsed Lady Powell in a cloud of rose silk and Lord Heathering making a fine leg to his wife. Silver threads in his waistcoat caught the light and the buckles on his pumps gleamed.

The ambassador's winter ball was every bit the squeeze Lady Battenburn had predicted. Carriages lined the street in front of the gated residence for blocks on either side and filled the circular drive leading to the main entrance. Drivers, footmen, and young tigers, all wearing their livery beneath heavy woolen capes, waited stoically in the cold January night to be of service again. More than a hundred torches illuminated the snow-covered grounds, lending the illusion of perpetual twilight to an evening with no moon's grace.

Inside the ambassador's palatial residence, noble guests had the muted rainbow hues of their silk gowns and satin coats reflected back to them from polished marble floors. The grand entrance was brightened with gilt-framed mirrors that added dimension to the extraordinary size of the room and multiplied the attending throng.

Guests crowded the perimeter of the ballroom and spilled into the hall and up the elegant curve of the wide staircase. Laughter mingled pleasantly with the music. One simply could not be heard separate from the other. Chatter was endless; gossip was rife. Good humor forgave the occasional slight, and there was general agreement among the assembly that the French ambassador was a most generous host—this last praise being given by those imbibing freely of the French ambassador's brandy.

Caught in the infusion of color and candlelight, Elizabeth only saw Louise when the lady was upon her. She could not help the tension that drew her back straight, but she hid it with a graceful gesture, indicating the vacant chair beside her and asking Louise to join her.

Lady Battenburn surveyed her immediate surroundings and judged there to be sufficient privacy to engage Elizabeth in conversation of consequence. She sat, her generous smile for the benefit of anyone watching her. At a distance no one could see that it failed to soften her dark eyes. She opened her fan and waved it idly in front of her, lifting her face to expose her throat as she did so.

She was elegantly attired in an ice blue gown with matching slippers and draped satin cap. The white ostrich plumes that adorned it were frosted pale blue at the tips. The delicate ends fluttered as Louise made another pass with her fan and the similarly colored diamonds adorning her neck winked as light alternated with shadow. "It is a pleasant gathering," Louise said. "Do you not find it so?" Her words were not intended as absent chatter. She watched to see if any heads turned in their direction when she spoke. "I was right to expect it would be an important event, although it is too bad of Prinny to make so short an appearance. I suspect it was that corset he was wearing. He looked abominably uncomfortable."

Elizabeth knew the Prince Regent's abbreviated attendance had nothing to do with his corset, though Louise's observation that he had looked uncomfortable was accurate enough. "I believe Princess Caroline is unwell," she said. "That is what I have heard."

Louise shook her head. "Mark my words," she said, testing the waters by raising her voice just a bit. "It was the corset." Satisfied when no one turned to regard her, Lady Battenburn went on in more confidential tones. "Our plans have changed."

Elizabeth blinked. She gripped her closed fan in both hands to steady them. In the past Louise had occasionally presented her with some alteration of the plan as it was first laid out, but tonight she had hoped it would not be the case. "In what way?" she asked.

One of Louise's russet brows lifted. "Have you not seen what the mademoiselle is wearing this evening?"

Knowing that Louise was referring to the ambassador's daughter, Elizabeth nodded. "The emeralds," she said. "It is of no matter, Louise. I can easily take them."

Louise shook her head. "No. Battenburn and I are agreed it is too dangerous. They would be quickly missed. I had not expected her to wear them this evening. I was led to believe it would be pearls. Indeed, they would be a better complement to her gown than the emeralds." She sighed. "There is no accounting for the whims of young women." Casting a significant look in Elizabeth's direction, she continued. "The ambassador keeps all his daughter's jewelry in his private library."

Elizabeth's eyes widened fractionally. "Private library? But you told me I could expect to find them in her room."

"And so you could have until recently." Her smile twisted ironically. "The Gentleman Thief has made everyone cautious."

"Is the library on this floor?"

"Yes. That is agreeable to you, is it not?"

"It will have to be," she said with credible calm. "I will require some direction. I have no notion where to go."

Lady Battenburn quickly explained how Elizabeth could find the private library. "I understand the ambassador has a fine collection of rare books," she added with a brief smile. "You must tell me if that is so." Louise tapped her fan lightly on Elizabeth's wrist. "You will go quickly, m'dear. Battenburn has engaged the ambassador in conversation and will see that you are not interrupted." She stood, preparing to leave.

Elizabeth had no liking for the urgency with which Louise presented herself, but experience had taught her that raising objections was pointless. She came to her feet. Beyond Louise's shoulder she could see Northam approaching but could risk no expression of any kind that might serve as a warning. She smiled coolly at Louise. "You have not told me what I am to bring you."

"The pearls, I think. The ones *la jeune fille* should have worn this evening."

Elizabeth turned and slipped between the press of bare shoulders and glittering throats. She could see neither the ambassador nor Battenburn, but it made no difference to the purposefulness with which she moved through the crowd. With her back turned to Louise she risked a small smile, pleased that the deviation to the baroness's plan was precisely as she and North had expected.

Calling no special attention to herself that would make someone think she required assistance, Elizabeth continued unescorted into the entrance hall. She was narrowly caught in conversation by Northam's mother but managed to avoid eye contact and went on as if she had not seen the dowager countess.

The library was best approached through the gallery rather than the hall. This had not been Louise's instruction, but the advice of the colonel and North. For once the opposing influences in her life were guiding her toward the same destination, albeit with different ends in mind.

Elizabeth did not expect to find the long gallery deserted, and it was not. The Marquess of Eastlyn was there with Lady Sophia. His head came up over the back of a sofa;

hers popped up a moment later. Elizabeth averted her eyes, but she was spared neither East's devilish grin nor Sophie's flushing features. There was a small squeak—surprise? protest?—as East ducked behind the sofa and pulled Sophie with him.

Elizabeth hurried to the opposite end of the gallery and through the double doors that led directly to the library. The room was a third the size of the gallery but consisted of two levels. A narrow spiral staircase led to a balcony that ran along the perimeter of the room and allowed every inch of the walls to be given over to shelves. It was indeed an impressive collection of books, but Elizabeth did not stop to admire them. Louise had been particular to stress that it was the ambassador's private library that she was to find, and now she ran her hands along the shelves to the right side of the ambassador's desk.

The spring that opened the concealed door sounded very loud to Elizabeth. There immediately followed another sound, but whether it was her own stirring or an echo of the spring she couldn't say. Still, she paused, glancing over her shoulder, half-expecting to see that Eastlyn and Sophie had followed her into the room. There was no one. No head appeared from behind the sofa that faced the fireplace. No one moved on the balcony above her. She slipped inside the smaller room but did not close the shelving behind her. The ambassador's private library had no windows. The only light she had came from the lamps burning in the adjoining room.

The cases of jewelry were just where Louise had told her they would be. Lady Battenburn's sources were accurate in this regard, and Elizabeth wondered anew at the number of people Louise had at her disposal to take on an enterprise such as this one.

Among the velvet bags and cases, Elizabeth found a pearl rope, a choker, and a necklace consisting of three strings, all perfectly matched. She chose the choker, laid it on the arm of the room's sole chair, and returned the empty case. She began to reset the books in place in the same order in which they had been removed. Curiosity niggled at her as she ran one finger along the embossed leather spine of the book she held. She resisted at first, rather pleased she could do so, then surrendered to the impulse because she knew the opportunity would never present itself again.

She opened the book randomly and held it up so the shaft of lamplight allowed her to view the page. Expecting to struggle with her schoolroom French or worse, Latin or Greek, Elizabeth was amused to see that she had opened the book to a pair of illustrations. It took another moment to recognize what she was seeing. Her mouth parted on a soundless *O*. She turned the book a little to the right, tilting her head at the same time. Then the left. The two cleverly entwined couples seemed to rock with the motion. Elizabeth's eyes widened fractionally. Were such positions even possible? How did the woman get her leg . . . ? And the man . . . surely no man was so . . .

She slammed the book closed and hastily replaced it. Why, the ambassador from France was . . . well, he was . . . *French*. Heat flushed her complexion and when she dropped the choker between her breasts and felt it settle there, the pearls were decidedly cool against her skin.

"Elizabeth?"

She stilled, her hand raised in midair. Her heart slammed hard in her chest, and for a moment she could only hear a steady roar of blood thrumming in her own ears. *Please*, she thought, *let this all not be for nothing*.

"She's in there."

Northam's head swiveled in the direction of the voice. Battenburn stood beside the fireplace, his elbow resting on the mantelpiece. His index finger was raised rather negligently and pointed toward the narrow opening in the shelves. "In there?" North glanced at the odd angle of the shelves. "That's a door?"

"Of sorts," said Battenburn. "There is such an arrangement in my own library. Did you see it when you were my guest this summer?"

North shook his head distractedly. "Elizabeth?" he called

again. There was no answer. "Are you certain she's in there?"

"Very. I watched her go in."

Walking toward the wall of books, North said Elizabeth's name a third time. The shelves began to swing toward him and North stopped. Elizabeth appeared in the opening. Her face was remarkably pale, and he did not miss the tremor in her hands before she hid them by crossing her arms in front of her. "What is that place?" North asked, trying to see past her.

"A book room," she said, shrugging. "The ambassador's private reading room, I imagine. There is a room like it at Battenburn. Did you—"

Raising his hand, North cut her off. "So I've heard," he said. "And no, I haven't seen it. What were you doing in there? Louise said you were not feeling the thing and came this way to find quiet."

"I—I was . . ." She touched her temple, closing her eyes a moment. "A headache. Nothing more. The ballroom was crowded. I could abide the chatter no longer."

Battenburn chuckled deeply. "Elizabeth, m'dear, he does not look convinced. In his place, I would be the same. Perhaps the truth will serve you better."

Her eyes swiveled to Battenburn. He was tugging lightly on the sleeve of his satin frock coat so that the material was smoothed along the line of his arm. Fastidious, she thought, even now. It lent him an aura of unconcern. She could not find the wherewithal to present the same demeanor. "Why are you here?"

"To stop you," he said. "Louise said I was foolish, that you would not risk so much by attempting anything tonight, but I entertained certain doubts."

North looked from Elizabeth to Battenburn and back again. "What is he saying precisely? What is this about, Elizabeth?"

She did not respond to her husband but looked pleadingly at Battenburn. "Do not do this thing," she said softly. "It is not necessary."

Battenburn shrugged, then adjusted his coat a second time. "Show him what you have, Elizabeth. Tell your husband who you are." When Elizabeth did not move, or change the set of her mouth, Battenburn began walking toward her. "You did not put it back, did you?"

She pretended not to understand. "What?" she asked weakly. "Put what back?"

"Whatever you took. It is still on your person, is it not?"

Elizabeth recoiled as Battenburn stretched an arm toward her. Almost without thinking, her own hand lifted protectively to her breast.

North took a single step forward. "Do not touch her, Battenburn. Do not lay a hand on my wife."

Battenburn's arm wavered, then dropped slowly to his side. "Show him, m'dear. Louise and I cannot protect you from him forever, not when you are so reckless."

"Elizabeth?" A crease appeared between North's dark brows. "I confess, I am losing patience with this. Explain yourself." When she did not move, he advanced on her. With no warning of his intentions, he caught her shoulder in one hand and curled his fingers in the lowest point of her scooped neckline, just at the point where her own hands sheltered her breast. "What do you have there?"

Tears rimmed her lower lashes. All of her trembled beneath his hold. "Please," she whispered. "I can explain."

Northam did not wait any longer. His fingers dipped inside her ivory gown. He felt Elizabeth suck in her breath and the hammering of her heart and then the very thing she seemed to be protecting. North slowly pulled the pearls from between Elizabeth's breasts. The choker folded smoothly in his palm. He said nothing, merely regarded the tightly strung pearls and the unbroken silver clasp.

Elizabeth stared at North's open palm, then watched his long fingers close slowly over the pearls. Her lips parted, but no sound came out.

North said, "Since you are still wearing your mother's diamonds, I can safely assume this choker is not yours." He cocked an eyebrow at her. "Well?"

Battenburn hitched a hip on the ambassador's desk and crossed his arms. "It should be plain enough, Northam. She stole it. She can't help herself. Tell him, Elizabeth."

North waited and Elizabeth's silence damned her. "He's speaking the truth? You stole this?"

Her nod was almost imperceptible.

Battenburn's clear blue eyes remained steady on Elizabeth, but it was to Northam that he spoke. "She's been about it for years. Her father couldn't manage her, and Louise and I have had so little success that we do not congratulate ourselves. She is the Gentleman Thief, Northam. She'll tell you herself when she recovers her wits."

"The Gentleman Thief?" North shook his head. "You most definitely jest, Battenburn. I have to help my wife negotiate the stairs on occasion because her hip troubles her. It is well known the Gentleman can enter a home from an attic window. Pray, tell me the purpose of this."

Battenburn's expression did not change. The heel of one satin pump beat a light tattoo against the desk leg. "No jest, I'm afraid. Think back, Northam. She stole Lord Southerton's snuffbox. Of course, Louise and I insisted that she replace it and devised the treasure hunt to make it possible. We felt she was so dangerously close to being caught that Louise created a story to remove suspicion from her."

Elizabeth shook her head. Her eyes implored North. "He is lying. Louise pretended her own necklace was stolen to remove suspicion from herself."

North's gaze narrowed fractionally. "But you knew it was a pretense," he said uncertainly.

"I—I knew she had—"

Battenburn interrupted with a long-suffering sigh. "Elizabeth could not permit Louise to have the last word. She stole my wife's necklace and placed it in your trunk."

"That's not true, North," Elizabeth said. "I swear it."

Northam dangled the choker between his thumb and forefinger. "Explain this, Elizabeth."

She looked to Battenburn for help. "Tell him why I do

it," she said sharply. "Tell him that you ordered me to take it."

Battenburn's features were pitying. "Elizabeth," he said gently, "you are overwrought. Replace the necklace and we will speak no more of it."

"Replace it? But you sent me—"

North took Elizabeth's wrist and forced her clenched fist open. He placed the choker in her palm. "Put it back. Now. Before someone comes."

Elizabeth drew back her hand as if to pitch the pearls at him. Before she could complete the throw, Battenburn's arm snaked out and stopped her. Elizabeth made a grave attempt at dignity when her instinct was to recoil. "Release me," she said quietly. This time it was her husband to whom she applied for aid. "They are lies, North. I cannot say it plainer than that. If I am a thief then it is what he has made me."

Lord Battenburn did not wait to be ordered to let Elizabeth go. He did so of his own volition, watching the effort North made to reveal so little of his thinking. The strain was there, though, in the tightness around his mouth and in the iron lock he had on his jaw. Battenburn stepped back, removing himself from the threads of tension between husband and wife. "I think, Elizabeth, that your husband is already well on his way to believing me. Is that not the way of it, Northam? I collect that you have had some suspicion about our Elizabeth."

Northam chose not to respond to Battenburn's observation. What he did instead was point Elizabeth to the adjoining room. His manner brooked no further argument.

Clutching the choker, Elizabeth spun on her heel and quickly disappeared into the ambassador's private library. North and Battenburn followed and watched her from the doorway. Battenburn imagined any lingering doubts Northam possessed were disappearing as Elizabeth managed her task with an economy of motion that spoke of skill and familiarity.

North stepped aside to let Elizabeth pass into the larger room and closed the panel of shelves behind her. It slid into place almost soundlessly. The fit into the wall was seamless. He regarded the rows of books for a moment before turning on Battenburn. "What is to be done?" he asked with a certain weariness.

Battenburn ignored Elizabeth's short gasp at what was essentially her husband's betrayal. With those few words Northam had chosen one of them over the other. The baron answered in the same tired vein, communicating clearly his own worn spirit. "It is a matter of protecting her from herself," he said. "And it is becoming increasingly difficult. She slips away at a moment's inattention. You must have seen that for yourself. Now that she is married and firmly set in society, Louise and I have despaired that anything can be changed. Rosemont has long ago given up and all but disowned her."

North remained stoic, his cobalt blue eyes flat and unrevealing. "May I call upon you tomorrow?" he asked. "You will allow there is a great deal to comprehend here."

Battenburn's assent was gracious. "Certainly. I hope you will understand that if there had been a less dramatic way to present you with these facts, Lady Battenburn and I would have done so. We could not know how willing you would be to hear us out. It seemed offering you the evidence was our best hope." He made a slight bow, his features set just shy of sympathetic. "I am sorry, Northam." Sparing no glance for Elizabeth, the baron took his leave.

Muted strains of music and distant laughter could briefly be heard when Battenburn opened the door to the hallway. When he closed it behind him, there was only silence.

Elizabeth looked at North. He returned her gaze. Neither of them spoke, afraid that even a whisper would give them away. Elizabeth's ivory satin gown rustled softly as she gave in to the need to sit down. North pressed four fingers to his brow and massaged it, the beginnings of a headache forming behind his eyes.

"We will bid our host good evening," North said finally.

Elizabeth nodded. She wanted to be away from this place

also. "Allow me a moment to compose myself." A small apologetic smile surfaced. "I am afraid I shall be sick."

Inside the carriage, Elizabeth removed her turban and shook out her hair. She idly fingered the jeweled brooch that held the ostrich plume in place. The tip of the feather tickled her chin as North stepped inside and the door was closed firmly in his wake. He sat beside her, his caped greatcoat brushing her shoulders.

The carriage rolled forward, setting them both back against the soft leather cushions. Tossing his hat onto the opposite seat, North turned a little toward Elizabeth. Her dark lashes created a pale shadow just below her eyes. She appeared to be studying the brooch under her fingers, but North doubted her thoughts had moved beyond the encounter with Battenburn.

He lifted the feathered turban from between her hands and let it fall beside his hat. Cupping the curve of Elizabeth's cheek as she raised her face, North lowered his head. His lips touched hers, lightly at first, then a second time that lingered with more heat. When he broke the kiss, he did not draw back. "You cannot know how much I wished you elsewhere this evening," he said. "If there had been any other way . . ."

"I know." Her lips brushed his. "I was never afraid of him. Only that you might come to believe him." She searched North's features for some sign that that was true. "I could almost believe him myself."

"He was very convincing." North touched his forehead to Elizabeth's. "But then, so were you." Seeing Elizabeth's confusion, he chuckled. "It's difficult to know whether to be flattered, isn't it? But I did mean it that way. You were splendid." He leaned back and took one of her gloved hands in his, lacing his fingers in hers. "You are splendid."

She flushed, averting her eyes from his own darkening ones. "We still do not know that it's worked."

North wondered how he would ever reconcile this vision

of a shy and reticent Elizabeth with the woman who had once stared at him so boldly and called herself a whore. He would plant an apple orchard at Hampton Cross, he thought, and practice contemplation under every one of those trees. If he was no closer to understanding her at the end of his life than he was now, it would still have been a worthy pursuit.

"North?" She glanced at him, frowning. "Did you not hear me? We still do not know if it worked."

He swallowed his smile. "We will know soon enough. I am assuming that you found no documents among the jewelry cases."

"None. You are certain they were placed there?"

"The colonel gave the task to West. He has never not done what was expected of him. The jewelry was there as he promised it would be."

She nodded. "How is it that West was able to engage the ambassador's assistance?"

"I believe it was the colonel who applied the pressure. The ambassador has his reasons for not wanting to appear uncooperative. West's part in it was to make certain there was no detail left unattended. Since you found nothing except the jewelry we can safely assume Battenburn had already lifted the documents before you arrived."

"He was not in the library when I got there, North, yet he was there when you came in. When could he have done it? And where did he come from? I heard no one enter until you did. East was in the gallery with Lady Sophia and would not have let the baron pass without a warning to me. If he came from the hallway as you did, why didn't I know it?"

"Because he didn't enter that way," North said. "At least not immediately before I did. I would say that he actually entered the room a little earlier in the evening, took the documents, and waited in the ambassador's very private library until you let him out."

"Let him out? But I—" She stopped because it suddenly became clear. "Oh. How clever of him. When I sprung the shelves from my side he slipped out after I went in. Do you know, I thought I heard something just as I was opening that door, but it did not occur to me to look inside for the source of the sound." She sighed. "How annoying. Then he was standing there in front of us with all those stolen documents on his person and neither one of us could be certain of the fact of it."

North shrugged. He had considered much the same thing. "It would have been a risk to confront him. He might have hidden them again. They might have been anywhere in the library. It is better to wait and see what he does with the information. I cannot imagine we shall have to wait long."

Elizabeth's relief was evident. "I am glad for that. I do not think I should be very good at waiting, North."

Now that the trap had been laid, North knew his own patience would be tested. "One of the things I learned in the army is that it helps to keep oneself occupied."

Elizabeth's eyes expressed her doubts, but she offered gamely, "I have started a new embroidery piece."

"Very industrious. I used to polish my buttons and my boots."

"You have Brill to do that for you now."

"I had Brill to do it for me then. There were times, though, when it was a thing better done myself." He rubbed his chin with his knuckles while he regarded her. "It seems that at present we should engage in something that will occupy us both."

"Cards?"

One of North's brows lifted. "You are carrying cards?"

"Now? Well, no. But when we arrive home we can play a few hands of whist. It is a certainty I shall not be able to sleep."

North looked for some sign that Elizabeth was not in earnest and could find none. "Perhaps I am not being clear. The activity should offer mutual pleasure."

"I thought you enjoyed whist."

"Elizabeth."

She blinked up at him, her smile perfectly innocent.

North shook his head. "You cannot be so obtuse."

"I assure you I can, though it pains me to say so."

He leaned toward her so that his lips brushed her ear. She had a more difficult time pretending she wasn't moved when his warm breath ruffled a silky tendril of hair. North whispered his intentions in no uncertain terms.

Elizabeth's eyes widened a fraction. "You can do that?"

"I am hoping you will help me."

Her expression was doubtful, though she had to work to keep it that way. "Are you certain you would not rather play cards?"

In response, North simply hauled her into his arms. "You delight in giving me the very devil of a time. No, I do not care to hear your opinion. Kiss me, Elizabeth."

She did. Her arms slipped around his neck and she laid her mouth across his, nudging his lips open with one sweet pass of her tongue. She swallowed the soft groan he could not quite hold back. Her fingers threaded in his sunshine hair. She tugged on the ends and felt him shiver in her embrace. "Was that a frisson?" she whispered against his mouth.

North drew back and let her see his smile.

Elizabeth's delicious shiver was not entirely feigned. "Aaah. All that from a mere smile. Can you teach me?"

"Not bloody likely. It must be used responsibly."

Laughing, she launched herself onto his lap and kissed him again. He unbuttoned her pelisse while she opened his greatcoat. Their mouths locked, their fingers remained busy working the buttons and fasteners and strings that frustrated their need for a more intimate joining. Elizabeth straddled North's lap, lifting herself up just enough to allow him to raise her gown. He ran his palm along her silk stocking from ankle to just above her knee. Higher than that he was met with her silky skin. Her gown rustled as it was bunched around her hips. Her breath fell softly on his jaw and neck. Behind his back she stripped off her gloves. She kissed him just below the ear and bit his lobe when he settled her back. His satin breeches were smooth and cool on her bare thighs.

Almost without conscious thought, she rubbed against him until cool became warm and warm became a flash point.

"I want to see your breasts," he said.

The centers of Elizabeth's eyes were already dark and wide. Something about North's tone made them go darker and wider. "If you think to find more pearls, my lord, you are sadly out of it there."

That she could manage to be so serious and saucy at once made North want to plunge himself into her. He settled for pulling her more tightly against him and frustrating her with the erection straining his breeches. "Your breasts," he said again, this time fairly growling the words.

Elizabeth's breasts actually swelled against the bodice of her gown. She moaned a little as his fingers tugged on the neckline. She had to help him, and in the end she was eager to do so. Her breasts ached to be touched.

"Pearls," he said, brushing her nipples with the pads of his thumbs. "So you are a thief, my lady."

"Fool."

"For you." He urged her upward until these pearls were presented to his mouth. He took one in, sucking, laving, drawing on it so hotly that she gasped and dug her nails into his shoulders. "Oh, North . . . Brendan." Her breath came quickly. The cool air inside the carriage swirled around her, but North's touch made it of no account. On either side of his legs her own thighs tried to squeeze together. She began to ride his solid frame.

North palmed her buttocks and felt her wriggle when he wanted to hold her still. She was fluid in his hands, lifting, rocking, sliding against him. He caught her other breast. He rolled the tender tip between his teeth and lips. She cried out this time, something between a laugh and a sob, incoherent, unintelligible, and primal. It communicated everything she felt and desired and needed in that moment. North understood perfectly.

They both fumbled with the front of his breeches, cursing the slippery satin and their own clumsy fingers. Her hand glided along his engorged penis, stroking the underside just before she rose up and guided him inside her. Their breath mingled, hot and humid. He kissed the corner of her mouth until she moved and took him fully, first with her lips slanting across his, then with her body sinking deeply onto him.

His fingers pressed against her bottom, lifting her, supporting her, helping her find just the right rhythm. She was tight around him, wet and slippery, her muscles contracting as she rose as if she did not quite want to release him. It was sweet torture. He would have told her how the colonel manipulated the French ambassador, how he managed to make the Prince Regent leave the ball early, and why the ambassador's daughter wore the emeralds instead of the pearls if she had but asked. She didn't, though, so these small secrets remained untold.

"You're smiling," she said, kissing the faint dimple at the corner of his mouth. "Why are you smiling?"

"Madam," North said dryly, "you have me to the hilt. Need you ask?"

She settled more firmly against him, wriggling just a bit to make him seize her bottom tightly. The carriage bounced and her eyes widened as he seemed to touch her womb. "*Now* I have you to the hilt," she said softly.

"Indeed. Shall you have your wicked way?" He was both agreeable and hopeful.

Elizabeth pressed her brow against his. "Do you know what sort of books the ambassador keeps in his private library?"

"Elizabeth," he said, "we shall be home soon."

"I have never seen the like before."

"Then it was not filled with Gothic novels."

Her small laugh was cut off abruptly as he moved under her. One of his hands left the curve of her bottom to trail slowly around her hip and dip between her thighs. Elizabeth's lashes fluttered closed and her lips parted. She was a moment collecting herself. "Not Gothic novels," she said in a rush.

"You must have been sorely disappointed." His index finger began to rub lightly against the fleshy hood of her

clitoris. A strangled sound came from the back of her throat.
"My lady?"

"Oh, please, Northam. We will be home soon. Have
pity."

He did, of course, as much for his own sake as hers.
North's mouth caught hers, his tongue sweeping deeply,
drawing on hers as he let her hips move again. When she
broke the kiss he feasted on her neck. Her tender breasts,
warm and achingly full, rubbed against the gold threads in
his waistcoat.

The well-sprung carriage was not proof against the rock
and sway of their bodies. The clatter of the wheels on the
icy cobblestones was lost to them. Elizabeth reared back,
thrusting her hips forward, and Northam set his heels hard
against the opposite bench. She came noisily, and a moment
later so did he.

Heart hammering, Elizabeth sagged against him. Her hand
lay gently against his open collar, just above the pulse in
his neck. It thrummed pleasantly against her fingers. She
breathed deeply of his scent, relishing the mixture of musk
and brandy and the lingering fragrance of his cologne.

North was no quicker to recover than she, but he was the
first to notice the carriage was slowing. He lifted the blind
on the window and peeked out. "Merrifeld Square, I'm
afraid." He dropped his feet to the floor. His heavy-lidded
gaze fell on her flushed breasts. "You will have to put those
away."

She looked down at herself, then at him. "You took them
out."

He gave a hoarse laugh. "Pray, do not invoke that nanny
tone. You will put me to a blush."

Elizabeth kissed him sweetly. "Too late." She lifted herself off his lap and began to right her clothes, smiling when
he brushed her hands away and raised the bodice of her
gown over her breasts himself. They narrowly managed to
present themselves in order as the door to the carriage was
opened by the footman. Northam alighted first and held out
his hand for Elizabeth. Her legs wobbled a bit and she

accepted his assistance gratefully. Out of the corner of her eye she saw their driver's son shifting his weight from one leg to the other, almost dancing in place, as he tried to get a glimpse inside their carriage. The young tiger's expression was equal parts worry and curiosity.

Elizabeth slipped her arm into North's but held him back while she addressed the boy. "What is it, Will? Is something wrong?"

"I'm looking for the cat, my lady." He ducked under the footman's arm that was still extended to hold the door open and peered inside the carriage. "She must have sneaked in when I was not looking."

Elizabeth's eyes flew to North's. His were filled with that unholy gleam. That look changed abruptly when he heard the tiger's next remark.

"But the dog, my lady, I don't know where he come from."

Elizabeth cleared her throat, prepared to tell young Will that the animals must have already made their escape, but North was moving quickly toward the house, pulling her in his wake.

Careful not to catch the other's eye, they comported themselves with dignity as they were relieved of their wraps at the door. North asked for a brandy to be brought to him in his room and tea for Elizabeth. In their bedchamber he dismissed Brill and Elizabeth's personal maid, and when they were alone he sank slowly into the large wing chair. Elizabeth did likewise on the edge of the bed. They both stared at their hands a moment before lifting their faces simultaneously and taking full measure of the other's expression.

Mortification warred with amusement, but the latter won out. They laughed until tears glistened at the corners of their eyes. Elizabeth used one corner of the coverlet to dab at hers while North used his handkerchief. On two different occasions they tried to talk, but each attempt sent them back into paroxysms of laughter.

The arrival of brandy and tea sobered them somewhat.

When the butler was gone, North loosened his cravat and removed his jacket. Standing near the fire, he warmed the brandy in the cup of his palms. "What sort of dog do you think I was?" he wondered aloud. "Not one of those yipping lap puppies my mother is so fond of, I hope. I shouldn't like to think I sound quite so shrill." He thought a moment. "Or annoying."

Elizabeth almost choked on a mouthful of tea. "Please, North, choose your moments with more care. But if you must know, you howl like a giant mastiff. Does that please you?"

He cocked one brow. "Truly?"

"Like a pack of mastiffs."

North chuckled. "You flatter me, my lady."

Elizabeth's smile was wry. "I certainly do."

He grinned. "Do you want to know the sort of feline you are?"

"Absolutely not." She held up one hand, palm out, to make certain North knew she was serious. "I shall never let you make love to me in that carriage again."

North sighed. "This is what comes of spending so much time in my grandfather's company. You have become a prude, my lady. It is not becoming."

"Hah! At what age do you think young William will know what we were about in there?"

"Unless I miss my guess, his father and the footman are explaining the way of it to him now."

"Oh, surely not."

"He's of an age. I had already seen Madame Fortuna's quim."

"You saw a peach."

"That is neither here nor there. I was prepared to know and see a great deal more."

Elizabeth's teacup hid the part of her smile that did not reach her eyes. "You will understand if I cannot look at him properly again."

"You will have to, else he'll think he's out of favor."

She had not thought of that. Her embarrassment would

have to be a secondary consideration. "This is your fault."
Elizabeth set her teacup aside and stood. She ran her fingers
through her hair and shook it out. Crossing the room, she
presented her back to Northam for assistance with her gown.
"I depend on your reserve. We both know I have none
where you are concerned. I never have."

North grasped Elizabeth by the waist and pulled her back-
wards onto his lap. "Is that true?"

The edge of gravity in his voice stayed Elizabeth's flippant
response. She turned slightly, settling herself in his arms
and regarding him solemnly. "Yes, it's true. Never doubt
it." She touched his cheek with her fingertips. "I wonder
sometimes about you and the women you've known." Elizabeth smiled faintly when she saw his surprise. "That never
occurred to you, did it?"

He shook his head, almost regretfully. "I'm sorry, but it
didn't."

"I suppose that is the way of things. Women must march
to one drummer and men to another." Elizabeth circled
North's wrist and lifted his hand and the brandy snifter
toward her lips. He tilted the glass so she could drink. It
was warm in her mouth, and warmer yet when it settled in
her stomach. "When I make love to you, it is different. I
cannot explain it better than that. It allows me to hope that
it is different for you also. I have never permitted myself
to believe I did not love Adam's father, for if I did not, then
everything that followed would somehow be tainted, and I
would be more foolish than I could admit even to myself."
She searched his face, willing him to understand. "But sometimes I wonder about that love now, because it is such a
pale thing compared to what I have in my heart for you.
When you touch me, Brendan, nothing is as it ever was."

He took her to bed then, loving her with gentle passion
this time, smiling wryly when she stretched languidly against
him, replete, sleepy, and actually purred in his arms.

Chapter Sixteen

Northam met with Lord Battenburn the following morning, but the interview provided no new information or any clue that the baron had truly taken the bait.

"He mentioned nothing about the documents?" asked Elizabeth when Northam returned. She placed the book she had been attempting to read aside. In truth, during North's absence, she had spent more time glancing at the clock and looking out the window than reading.

"I didn't expect him to say anything overt." Northam warmed his hands at the fireplace. Flakes of snow melted on his boots. "He would not give himself away in such a manner. Certainly not to me. But I thought there might be some hint that he would be meeting with one or two of the men who agreed to have their names included in the ambassador's papers. Battenburn does enjoy dropping a name from time to time. That is what I thought I might hear."

Elizabeth sighed. "It is really too bad of him." A lock of hair fell across her forehead and she blew it up and away. "Then we can't know with certainty that he has the papers."

"I stopped at West's briefly. He assured me that all the documents were put in the same hiding place as the jewelry. You could not have missed seeing them, he said." North dropped his hands and pivoted on his heel toward Elizabeth, his brows drawn slightly. "West did ask about the books, though. About whether or not you had mentioned them. I said you had not and he seemed rather relieved. It struck me as odd; then, as I was returning home, I remembered you had indeed said something about the ambassador's private library. As I recall, you began the discussion at a rather . . . well, I believe we were quite sufficiently occupied, and I certainly had no interest in whatever books the ambassador may have collected."

North noticed Elizabeth's eyes darting ever so slightly to a point past his shoulder. She also grew suddenly restless, drawing her feet onto the chair and arranging the plaid woolen rug across her lap. "Hmmm," he murmured.

Her head came up. "What does that mean? 'Hmmm'? What sort of notion does that signify?"

Amused, realizing he had struck a chord and knowing Elizabeth's talent for diversion, he kept his tone casual. "It is merely observational in nature. You do not seem to want to discuss the ambassador's books this morning."

"This is hardly the place."

North looked around. "Elizabeth. We are in the library."

"I have only recently had my breakfast."

"And that is relevant in what way?"

"It is not. It is merely a statement of fact."

North laughed. "I'm afraid you have intrigued me. Out with it—what sort of books were they? Pray, do not tell me now that you do not know, for we are well past the point where I might believe such a Banbury tale."

Elizabeth could not muster the right note of indignation to suggest offense so she surrendered to the inevitable. "Did you interrogate spies for the colonel?"

"No. Do you think I would have been good at it?"

"Very." She pushed back in the chair a little, bracing herself as she drew a deep breath. "I cannot speak to the ambassador's entire collection. Indeed, I only opened one book, and I only regarded two pages."

North waited for her to go on, but Elizabeth's tongue seemed to have cleaved to the roof of her mouth. "And . . . ?"

"And I saw a pair of illustrations."

"Yes?"

"They were . . . they were . . . ummm . . ."

North inclined his head. " 'Ummm'?"

"They were naked."

"The illustrations?"

"The man and the woman."

"Aaah."

Elizabeth arched one eyebrow. "You knew."

He shrugged. "I suspected. West said nothing. It was your manner that suggested it to me. Now I understand why you mentioned the books last night and want to say nothing of them in the light of day. I take it this is the first time you have seen illustrations of an erotic nature."

"Well, yes. I did not make a study of it in the classroom." She paused a fraction and regarded him. "Did you?"

"In the classroom? No. Eastlyn had some French cards, though."

"French," she said, as though it explained everything. "Libertines."

"Licentious."

"Loose."

North thought a moment, then raised his brows wickedly. *"L'amour."*

Laughing, Elizabeth came to her feet and started for the door. One come-hither look over her shoulder and North was immediately trailing after her.

Colonel Blackwood tapped the bowl of his pipe against a silver tray to loosen the blackened residue. He repacked it with his special blend, which Elizabeth had picked up for him at the tobacconist. He started to light it and paused, looking to Elizabeth for permission. "You do not mind, do you?"

Elizabeth shook her head. "I like the fragrance of a pipe."

North glanced at her, surprised. "You do?"

"Not on you," she said in no uncertain terms. "But on the colonel it evokes very pleasant memories."

Blackwood chuckled appreciatively at the helpless appeal in North's eyes. "You cannot expect me to interfere." He lit his pipe and puffed several times to draw the fire. His long exhalation was a most satisfied one. He looked from North to Elizabeth and back again. They were sitting on the sofa opposite him, neither entirely relaxed, but North making a better show of it than his wife. "I have heard from Whittington and Sutton. You will recall they lent their names to our enterprise. Lord Sutton received a post from the baron yesterday requesting his presence at Battenburn. The country residence, I mean. The correspondence is unexceptional. The baron has committed to nothing. He only promises to make Sutton's trip to Battenburn worth his while."

"And the Earl of Whittington?" asked North.

"Much the same, except the manner of approach. Battenburn cornered Whittington at their club. Whittington confided that if he had not known what was toward, he would have thought Battenburn was discussing some sort of lucrative trading scheme."

Elizabeth leaned a little toward her husband, brushing his shoulder with her own. His arm came around the back of the sofa and provided a shelter. Neither of them noticed the colonel's small, self-congratulatory smile through the wreath of his pipe smoke.

"What of the others?" Elizabeth asked. "Reston. Albermarle. Dunwithy."

"Nothing yet. It is of no matter. For our purposes, Battenburn need only to have contacted one. When he reveals that he has information that could have been gleaned in no other way except through the theft of the ambassador's private papers, we will have him."

"What of Louise? She is his supporter in all things."

Blackwood nodded. "I'm afraid her capture largely depends on her taking part in the baron's meeting with Whittington and Sutton. If she absents herself, it will be more difficult to prove her involvement.'' He noted Elizabeth's thoughtful expression and went on. ''North, you will go to Battenburn's country estate. The meeting is planned for the ninth.''

''You do not intend I should invite myself, do you?''

''Heavens no. It would do no good at all for him to know you were there. I wondered why Battenburn would choose to meet with these men in the country when there are so many private clubs and even his own town residence available. I think it may be that he is suspicious of a trap. Lord and Lady Battenburn feel safer in their own home. Would you agree, Elizabeth?''

''Yes. But I know every inch of the Battenburn estate.''

The colonel smiled and released a puff of smoke. ''Just so. And you will teach North what he did not learn during his summer sojourn.''

''I will not.'' Both men stared at her. ''Not unless it is agreed I can accompany my husband. Oh, do not look at me so. There is more danger to North alone than with me as his companion. He has explored little of Battenburn and could easily get lost in the passages without my help. It is not enough for me to teach him the way. Not with so little time. We have waited more than a week for Harrison and Louise to act on what they took from the ambassador's residence. That they have chosen to reveal their plans at Battenburn is to our advantage rather than the opposite. There are few rooms there that do not connect to another, either directly or through a little-used corridor. The baron and baroness are not even aware of the extent of them. They have never fully appreciated the novelty of the estate and its place in history. I was the one who explored the passages.''

Elizabeth regarded the colonel levelly. ''I imagine you mean to use the passages to permit North to eavesdrop on the baron's conversation with Sutton and Whittington.''

''Perhaps I need to rethink it,'' Blackwood said sardonically. ''It does not seem so remarkable a plan when I hear it from your lips.''

North's chuckle was cut short when Elizabeth dug her

elbow into his ribs. He grunted softly. "What was that in aid of?"

"You were taking his side." To the colonel, she said, "Have you both forgotten that I am the Gentleman Thief?" They both remained stoically silent, careful not to catch the other's eye. "I am much better suited to gaining entry to Battenburn than North, or any other member of the Compass Club for that matter. I am quicker and lighter and I know my way without hesitating. And if that were not enough, I know where Louise keeps what remains of the jewelry I have stolen for her over the years."

North could still not credit that he was not alone on his journey to Battenburn. Elizabeth rode beside him and had the good sense to say little, recognizing that his mood was almost as black as their riding clothes. It did not appease him in any way that she looked little enough like the woman he married. Her attire was thoroughly male, borrowed from the servants when Brill steadfastly refused to allow her to pilfer from his own wardrobe. His manservant was determined to sleep in the dressing room if it meant saving North's chitterlings and frock coats from Elizabeth's hands.

In truth, the borrowed togs were a better fit for her than anything she could have found among his things. Everything had been laundered and pressed so that no odor of the stable or kitchen clung to the material. It was little comfort to him. His wife was wearing trousers and riding astride, and when he mentioned those things she called him a prig.

And she had not been teasing.

Elizabeth slowed Becket to a walk as a coach thundered on the road behind them. She raised her scarf to keep dust from flying in her face. The capes of her greatcoat fluttered as the coach passed and her gelding shied a little to the sloping side of the road.

North came parallel with her immediately. "Control your mount," he said tersely. "And do not let the coaches run you off the road."

Elizabeth's chin came up and cleared the folds of the woolen scarf. "I do not know if you could be more determinedly unpleasant."

"I assure you, I can."

"Then, pray, do not restrain yourself on my account."

North's mouth snapped shut. Seeing her dressed in such a fashion reminded him of her escape from London . . . and him. He did not need to hear it from her lips to know that she had changed into such clothes on her way to Stonewickam. The most likely place had been at the inn where she seemed to have simply vanished. The thought of her traveling across the countryside—then and now—chilled his blood.

"I have already apologized for calling you a prig. Twice." She spared him a glance and sighed loudly when she saw that his jaw was still tightly set. She had many reasons for wishing there was less moon this night, not the least of which was that its glow made North's countenance all too visible to her. "Would you have me wear a gown for this work? It is deuced difficult crawling around those corridors in a dress. I know, North, because I have torn more hems and bodices than you can imagine doing it. And what manner of man sets out this time of night with his wife on horseback?"

He gave her a sharp look.

Elizabeth went on quickly. "I mean a wife who appears to be just that. The innkeeper would have been shocked. Dressed in this manner he thought nothing of you riding out with one of the grooms and assumes your lady is safely in your bed."

"Had I come alone," North was compelled to point out, "my lady would be safely in my London bed, and I would have ridden to Battenburn in a single day. No such ruse would have been necessary."

"You would have been surpassingly tired. The trip is tedious and overlong to make in a single day. You will thank me for insisting on stopping when you are cramped inside one of the passages for hours on end."

North's jaw clamped shut again. This time a muscle jumped in his cheek. He jammed his hat lower over his brow and thwarted the chill wind that pressed against his face.

"You would not have objections if I were South or West or East," said Elizabeth.

"Bloody hell, Elizabeth, I wish you *were* south, west, or east of here."

"That is not what I meant and you know it."

"You are my *wife*."

"I suppose you mean that as an explanation of this obdurate position you have taken, but frankly, North, I think it speaks most eloquently to your prejudices."

"My prejudices?"

"Yes," she said tartly. "Precisely so. It is because I am a woman that you find my assistance so difficult to accept."

"Dammit, Elizabeth! It is because I *love* you." Out of the corner of his eye he saw her flinch in the saddle. Even Becket faltered a little at the thunder in his voice. "I love you," North repeated more softly this time. "I would not have you hurt."

"And I share that sentiment in the same way about you," she said. "I could not have stayed behind and waited for your return. Do not misunderstand, Northam. I know there will be times when I have to do exactly that. I do not believe for a single moment that our marriage will make a difference to the colonel when he is choosing a man for his peculiar assignments. I *will* wait then. I will hate it, but I will do it because I can offer nothing but my support. This is different. We are safer together than we would be alone."

North wasn't certain he believed that, but it was clear to him that Elizabeth did. "When we reach Battenburn you will do as I say."

"Of course. The colonel said I must."

He gave her a sideways look. "I say you must."

She saluted him smartly.

"Other hand, Elizabeth. You salute with your right."

"Oh." She dropped her chin below her scarf to hide her quivering smile.

* * *

They arrived at Battenburn before dawn would have made their approach impossible. The horses were tethered in the wood. North hid their caped greatcoats and hats and carried only a pouch slung over one shoulder. They traveled across the frozen ground on foot. North had to admit that finding a way in would have been difficult without Elizabeth's help, though he did not share this aloud. All the doors to the main hall were bolted, and the underground entrance from the stable to the kitchen was where they were most likely to run afoul of a servant.

North had known of country estates with underground passages, but he had not realized Battenburn had such a corridor. They existed largely to give the illusion that the bucolic palaces were managed as if by magic, with servants coming and going from town without ever being seen by the lord and lady of the manor. Elizabeth was correct: The entrance was of little use to them.

She suggested instead that they climb to a window. North stood back and looked up, wondering how they would narrow the choices to one that was likely to be open. "The gallery," she told him. "There is a window there that does not latch properly. It will require only that you give me a leg up. I can easily let you in another way."

It was accomplished with alacrity. The house remained silent, the occupants unaware of the intruders. Lord and Lady Battenburn slept undisturbed and the servants who were beginning to rise were still making their way down from the attic. Whittington and Sutton were not expected to arrive until the noon hour, which meant North and Elizabeth had a long wait before them.

Elizabeth led North upstairs through a passage that paralleled the servants' staircase. She kept her hand cupped around a stub of a candle so the light would not slip through cracks in the wall. The corridor was narrow and steep and their jackets had attracted a thin layer of dust and cobwebs by the time they reached the top. He helped her push their way through to an empty bedchamber by moving aside a large armoire.

He recognized the room at once. "This is where South slept." He brushed off one of his shoulders.

"Careful," Elizabeth admonished him. "You will leave a trail that will make one of the chambermaids suspicious. Here, let me wipe your boots." Before he could stop her, Elizabeth was kneeling in front of him, giving his boots a buffing with the sleeve of her jacket. She rather clumsily did the same to her own.

North hauled her to her feet. "Enough. The fact that we are standing in the middle of a room with no excuse for our presence at the ready is more my concern than cobwebby boots."

He was right, of course. Elizabeth carefully opened the door to the hallway and listened.

Behind her, North asked, "Did you get into South's room through the passage?"

"No. I slipped in this way. It wasn't difficult. He sleeps like the dead." Elizabeth gave North a quelling look when he chuckled. "You are too noisy."

North dutifully reined himself in. "Where are we going next?"

Elizabeth closed the door all but a crack before she answered him. "There is a drawing room in this wing that connects to a passage that in turn connects to many other rooms. It is our best hope to wait there. We can move somewhat freely, and perhaps learn which room the baron will use to meet with his guests."

"Lead on."

Elizabeth slipped into the hallway with North on her heels. Entry to the drawing room required that they remain in the open for just more than half a minute. Once, when Elizabeth thought she heard a servant on the backstairs, they ducked into a bedchamber and waited for what seemed forever. When they finally reached their destination, North rounded on her, kissing her soundly.

"What was that in aid of?" she whispered when he drew back.

"In aid of an apology," he said. "You were right. I could not have managed finding these rooms on my own."

"Oh, that's all right, then." She slipped out from under North's arms, which were braced on either side of her shoulders. "This way."

The drawing room's passage opened through a panel beside the fireplace. It required North and Elizabeth to crawl for a distance of some twenty feet before there was enough headroom to stand. The passage then dipped downward with a set of steep spiral stairs. Elizabeth led him to a halfway point before she halted. "We wait here," she said softly. She sat down on one of the narrow steps and leaned back against the wall.

North took a seat a few steps above her. His shoulders almost filled the space between the walls. He raised the stub of the candle briefly, looked around him, then blew it out. There was a complete absence of light in the corridor, and the darkness was not something one could adjust to. It was impenetrable. "Where are we?" he whispered.

"In the innermost part of the house. This passage winds its way to at least a dozen other rooms that I know of. The walls are not uniformly thick, though. When everyone begins to stir we will have to be even more cautious. Keep in mind that when we can hear others, we can also be heard."

"Are we close to the gallery?"

"This will take us there. It is below and to the left."

"And what about the baron's library and the private room you both mentioned? The one that is similar to what the ambassador has."

"It is also connected by this passage. There are many ways out, North, but only one way in. Once we make our decision to enter any room we cannot return by that same route. These panels operate on springs that cannot be found from the other side. The design is very clever and made it difficult for the king's men to find those in hiding."

"Then it makes sense for one of us to remain behind in the passage."

"Just so. Another good reason to have me along." To her credit, Elizabeth did not gloat. She had tried to tell North some of these things prior to accompanying him to Battenburn. While the colonel had listened intently to what she was saying, she now believed North had heard as little as one word in three. She unerringly found his knee and laid her hand lightly upon it. "You will not regret having me beside you," she said softly. "Really, North. I promise I will do as you say."

He said nothing for a long time. Had Elizabeth not been touching him she would have questioned whether he had abandoned her. Finally his hand closed over hers. He squeezed her fingers gently, reassuringly. "*Precisely* as I say," he told her. He felt her slight movement. "Are you nodding, Elizabeth?"

"Yes."

"Good."

Louise put down her cup of hot chocolate and examined her face in the mirror above her vanity, lifting her chin and turning first one cheek, then the other, in a careful inspection for wrinkles, blemishes, and the odd stray hair.

From his perch on the window seat, Harrison watched her with mild amusement. "You are perfect as always, my dear. Dazzling, in fact."

Louise's eyes lifted to the emerald and diamond brooch she had fastened to the green silk band in her hair. "You do not think it is too much?" she asked. "Our guests arrive early in the day. I should not like to be thought garish."

"No one would ever think that," he said gallantly. "Sutton and Whittington will be favorably impressed." Battenburn smoothed the line of his gray frock coat and made a slight adjustment to his cravat. "I expect them shortly, so have finished with your preening."

Her head swiveled sideways and she gave him an arch look. "Pot calling the kettle black."

Coming to his feet, Battenburn smiled thinly. "You are right as ever." He paused at her side on his way to the door and dropped a light kiss on her cheek. "I will await you in the library."

She caught his hand as he straightened. "After today there will be nothing of a political nature that is not influenced by us. It is everything we have worked for. Our place in society is set. We have more ability to persuade others and fashion the outcome of events than if you had been named to the king's inner circle of advisors."

"As I most surely should have been."

"Of course," she said sincerely. "And as you will be soon. You are invested in schemes certain to bring about greater wealth than we enjoy now. That we will want for nothing is assured for our lifetime. I should be surprised if you are not to be granted a title more deserving of your stature. Marquess, for example."

"Duke."

"Or duke."

"Your point, Louise." He removed his hand from hers. "I hope you do not intend to refine upon my playing at cards. A man must have some pursuits outside of politics and society."

"I understand," she said quietly. "It is Elizabeth I wish to speak of."

"What of her?"

"I think she may still be of some use to us."

"Did you not just say that we have achieved what we wanted?"

"Well, yes, but that is not—"

"I have made my decision, Louise. And you agreed. As I recall, you were the one who first suggested that our association with Elizabeth had exceeded its usefulness. I was never as taken with the idea that she should marry Northam as you were. The man does not impress me as someone who can be easily controlled."

"That is why Elizabeth is valuable. He can be guided by us through her. You said yourself that he pledged silence in regard to Elizabeth's thefts."

"That is what he said."

"You don't believe him?"

"I don't trust him."

"He has the ear of Colonel Blackwood," said Louise. "We were never able to make Elizabeth's connection to him work to our advantage. This is a second opportunity."

Harrison sighed. "You are changing your mind, are you not?"

She smiled a trifle guiltily. "I confess I am. Please say you will indulge me, Harrison."

He regarded her shrewdly. "What is it you really want, my dear? And, pray, do not say it is only the colonel's ear. I know you too well to be gulled in that manner."

Louise's laughter trilled. "Your perception does you credit, my lord. I have been admiring Lady Everly's ruby bracelet for some time. With Elizabeth's help, it should not be so very difficult to acquire."

"You are incorrigible, Louise."

"Then you agree? The Gentleman Thief will venture out one more time?"

"One more time," he said. "Then it must end, Louise. Our association with Elizabeth must be finished."

"Of course. I will see to it myself." She smiled. "Don't I always?"

Elizabeth was more puzzled than frightened. She relighted the candle and carefully led North through the passage to the library. There was more space for them to stretch in the wider corridor that adjoined Battenburn's private reading room. "I think she means to kill me, Northam. I am to steal Lady Everly's bracelet for her and then she means to kill me. Do you not think that is her intention?"

North regarded Elizabeth's bemused features in the candlelight. His own were not so soft or bewildered, and there was nothing tentative about his response. "I think it is exactly her intention." He took the candle from her when her hand began to tremble. "Do not be afraid, Elizabeth. I shall—"

"Afraid? Not bloody likely. I am angry, North. Furious, really." Her eyes dropped to the pouch Northam had slung over his shoulder. "Do you have a pistol in there? I am certain I could use it."

He was not at all sure how serious she was. "No pistol," he told her. "I take it you are persuaded how intent the baroness is on making her acquisitions, whether it is jewelry or influence, and how little regard she has for anyone who has assisted her."

"Little regard? Clearly that is an understatement." Elizabeth's grave expression turned a little sad. "It has only been about more, hasn't it?"

"Pardon?"

"More," she said. "More wealth. More lands. More influence. A more prestigious title. More power." Elizabeth raised her hands helplessly, shrugging. "More."

His voice was gentle. "What did you imagine?"

She was quiet a moment, turning her face away from the candlelight. "I suppose I thought they had some grand plan, something they thought would change things for others, not simply for themselves. Even when they were doing their worst I wanted to believe their intent was noble."

"Noble?"

"Well, good, then."

"Elizabeth."

"Very well. I did not want to believe they were complete villains."

North found that he still had it in him to smile. "You are neither so cynical nor so worldly as you would have me believe."

"I suppose not." She was more than a little disappointed in herself. "You must allow that I have tried."

He put his arm around her shoulder and blew out the candle. "You certainly have."

* * *

Lord Whittington was finding it difficult to sit. His long frame did not fit easily into the overstuffed chair by the fireplace, and the spindly-legged, claw-footed appointments had never been to his liking. He got to his feet for the third time in three minutes. "It is beyond my comprehension that Battenburn would keep us waiting," he said to his companion. "Why the deuce we should have had to come so far is also beyond my ken."

Sutton sighed. His stocky frame was better comforted by the wing chair than Whittington's. "You are jumping about like grease on a griddle. Calm yourself, Whittington. I am sure Battenburn has planned every detail of this meeting. If we are to wait, then it has some purpose for him. You would do well to take it in stride. Apoplexy can be the only outcome otherwise."

The Earl of Whittington was not subdued in the least. "I want it over," he said, pacing. "Even the countess has remarked to me that I have been out of sorts, and my mood has never been of any importance to her."

"All the more reason for you to mind yourself."

The heavy doors to the library parted and Battenburn stepped inside. "I hope you have not been discommoded by your wait," he said genially. "There was a small matter requiring my attention that delayed me. I see you have refreshment." The doors were closed soundlessly behind him. "How was your journey? Did you travel together?"

Sutton raised one fiery red brow. "Not possible, Battenburn, and you know it. I was unaware Whittington was to come here until my carriage met his on the road. You did not intend us to know about the other before today."

"True, but one never can be certain. My caution to speak to no one aside, it would have been understandable if your association with the ambassador had prompted you to seek each other out."

Whittington pivoted toward Sutton. "That is why you are here also?" he asked. "The French ambassador?"

"It appears we both are," Sutton said mildly. "Is that correct, Battenburn?"

"I am delighted to say that is precisely the way of it." He carefully reached inside his frock coat and extracted two neatly folded sheets of vellum. He held one up in each hand. "Do not attempt to thwart me by destroying these. They are copies, written in my own hand. The originals are elsewhere. Quite safe. You will be able to attest to the veracity of the contents. I copied them exactly. Even the misspellings." He gave each man his own correspondence to prove the truth of his words; then he had them trade the letters and poured himself a glass of Madeira while they read.

Whittington was silent as he reviewed Sutton's missive. Lord Sutton only spoke once, and that was to remark on Whittington's lamentable spelling.

Battenburn tossed both letters in the fireplace when they were returned to him. They sparked immediately and were consumed in a flash of flame. "So there you have it," he said calmly. "Perhaps you did not realize how much you have in common with the other, but now I have brought it to your attention. Your correspondence with the ambassador can hardly be construed as diplomacy. It is more likely to be viewed as treasonous. Your interests are not those of the Crown and, in fact, fly in the face of the prime minister's ambitions. One can only wonder what you hoped to gain by putting such ideas to paper."

Agitated, Whittington began pacing again. His long stride quickly took him from one side of the library to the other. "How did you come by these letters? Sutton, do you know? He said nothing to me."

"Nor me." Lord Sutton looked to the baron for understanding.

"It is of no importance," Battenburn said. "What you should concern yourselves with is my intention to use them if we cannot arrive at some agreement."

"Agreement on what?" asked Sutton.

"My proper place among the king's advisors."

Whittington stopped pacing abruptly and stared hard at Battenburn, surprised and somewhat relieved. "Is that all?"

Sutton was equally comforted. "Why did you not say so? It is easily enough arranged."

Battenburn was not appeased by their willingness to oblige him. In fact, the mere effortlessness with which they could give him what he coveted so dearly enraged him. He drank deeply from his wineglass to calm himself. "There may be certain monetary requirements from time to time," he said. Until this moment he had not considered asking them for a single farthing. It was really beneath him. It was also an insult to them, since he clearly did not require their money. "Only from time to time, my lords."

"Now see here, Battenburn," Whittington blustered. "I will not—"

Sutton held up one hand, interrupting the earl. "You will, Whit. We both will. We know it and Battenburn knows it. I read your correspondence and you read mine. Perhaps we were too trusting of the ambassador. It may be that he betrayed us."

"I cannot believe that." He looked to the baron for some hint that this might be so. Battenburn's cool blue eyes were without expression. "I will want the original letter. The one in my handwriting."

"Of course," said Battenburn. "I will return it . . . eventually."

The Earl of Whittington remained insistent. "I will see it now."

"I shall have to do the same," Sutton said. "You understand we must know with certainty that it is in your possession. There would be no point in acceding to your wishes otherwise."

Battenburn was regretting his last demand. Clearly he had pushed both men into taking this stand. "Very well," he said easily. "My wife will bring them. Louise? You heard our guests. They want to see the documents."

Sutton and Whittington regarded their host in some confusion. His speech, it seemed, was made to the air. Their attention shifted simultaneously when a panel of book-shelves suddenly separated itself from the wall and swung open into the room. Their alarm was not entirely feigned when they saw who came through the opening.

Northam stepped into the library, his hands held level with his shoulders. Behind him was Louise. She held two vellum sheets in one hand. The other held a primed pistol.

"You will not credit who I discovered in your reading room, my lord," Louise said. She nudged Northam forward with the pistol. "He has heard every bit that I have, I'm afraid. And he did not seem to be overly surprised. I fear we have uncovered a problem we did not foresee. I am convinced they are all in league, Harrison."

"What?" Battenburn's eyes darted between his guests and his wife's prisoner. "In league? How do you mean?"

Louise tossed the documents to the table at her side. "These are fakes," she said. "Certainly they were written by our guests, but I am now persuaded that they were engaged to do so. Is that not correct, Lord Sutton?"

"If you say so, my lady," he said easily. "It does clear me of any wrongdoing. I am in favor of that."

The baron regarded Whittington. "Is this true?"

"I am also in favor of redemption," he said. "If you prefer to think of my letter as a fake, then it pleases me."

"They are making light of us," said Louise. "Northam's presence is telling. Elizabeth has betrayed us to him. He could not have found the passage without her aid and he would not be here, not at this time and place, if these two had not informed him of this meeting. We are found out, Harrison. They meant to trap us."

Battenburn put his drink down and picked up the letters. He was certain Louise was right. It was only a question of how to manage an outcome that was to their advantage. He jerked his chin toward Northam but addressed his wife. "Was there any sign that Elizabeth accompanied him?"

"Do not be foolish, Harrison. He would not permit that."

Northam smiled thinly as Battenburn flushed. "I certainly would not."

Harrison said nothing. He opened the middle drawer of his secretary and removed a small pistol. Out of the corner of his eye he saw Sutton and Whittington exchange glances. "You must revise your plan to overpower me, my lords, for I assure you, I will not hesitate to shoot." He exchanged pistols with Louise because the one he had was better suited to her small hand. "What is to be done, my dear?"

"We must be rid of the evidence and the witnesses, of course."

"My thoughts also." He walked to the fireplace and tossed both original letters into the flames. "I will get the others. I assume they are also fakes." Battenburn did not have to leave the library to retrieve them. He walked briskly to the bookshelves and chose Schlegel's *Lectures on Dramatic Art and Literature*. Opening it, he removed the pages that were not bound and tossed them onto the fire also. "That is the evidence," he said, with no concern that anything had been lost. "These three present a slightly different problem."

Northam raised a single brow. "Not so easily thrown in the fire, are we?"

It was Louise who answered. "No, not into the fire, my lord. I have something else in mind. You will proceed." She jabbed him in the small of his back with her pistol. "Through the doors, please."

Northam realized she did not mean for him to go back the way they came, but to head toward the hallway. Battenburn indicated Sutton and Whittington should follow. Louise closed the shelves that led to the reading room and then caught up quickly to her husband.

"Up the steps," she said, pointing to the main staircase.

Northam continued to take the lead. He suspected their direction was the parapet, but he paused dutifully at each crossroads in the hall, waiting for instructions from Louise or Harrison. Could Elizabeth hear them? he wondered.

It was something of a miracle that Louise had not stumbled on her in the passage. North had already moved into the baron's private library, leaving Elizabeth behind in the corridor with orders to stay there, when Louise had come into the small reading room using the same entrance he had. Her approach had been silent, but then he had also been listening to Sutton and Whittington discuss their arrival before the baron met with them. He was impressed that they had gamely accepted the roles the colonel assigned to them. The usually unflappable Earl of Whittington was suitably agitated by the impending interview. Lord Sutton was more at his ease but equally prepared to allow Battenburn the upper hand until they had the documents.

Northam had expected Louise to appear, but not in the way she had. Elizabeth, wherever she had gone, had not been able to warn him of the baroness's approach. Now she could be anywhere in the house and equally uncertain of his whereabouts. She was in possession of his pouch, however. It could offer her some protection if she but looked inside it. What he would do remained a mystery to him. Saving himself would be difficult enough, but he had Sutton and Whittington to think about as well.

A rush of frigid air met them as North pushed open the door to the roof. He stepped out, his chest tightening upon drawing his first deep breath. Behind him, Sutton coughed. Whittington began stamping his feet in an attempt to warm himself. When North glanced back it seemed to him that neither Lord nor Lady Battenburn were affected by the cold. It came from having ice water in their veins, he supposed.

Louise waved her pistol to the left and ahead of the small party, indicating the perimeter of the crenelated wall. "There," she said. "At the battlement."

Northam was of no mind to hurry the journey. "You do not really believe you can succeed in this, Battenburn." His voice was carried on the back of the wind. "More than the three of us know of the letters you took from the ambassador's library."

"I took?" asked Battenburn. "You have mistaken me for your wife. She is the thief, Northam. Not I."

"The documents were already gone when she arrived."

The baron chuckled. "Is that what she told you? It's not so. She put them under her turban and carried them out. A bit of misdirection, I'm afraid." He was watching North closely and saw the slight pause in his step and the stiffening of his shoulders. "What else didn't she tell you?"

Aware he was being goaded, North did not reply. Sutton and Whittington were similarly silent, both of them looking for an opportunity to seize the moment.

"She will have told you about her child, of course," Battenburn went on. "Some explanation for her less than virginal state would have been in order on your wedding night."

It pained Northam that Sutton and Whittington were privy to the baron's discourse. Since he fully intended they should escape unscathed, it meant that Elizabeth's secret would hardly be that any longer. He believed he could rely on their discretion, yet he hurt for Elizabeth.

Louise gave her husband a quelling look. She did not approve of this talk in the least. It was a measure of Battenburn's anger that her silent entreaty went unheeded.

"Turn around," the baron said as Northam reached the crenelation. "All of you." Northam's body filled the space between the stone merlons, making him vulnerable to a frontal charge. Battenburn could envision himself heaving North through the embrasure and then leaning over to watch his body hurtle toward the ground. He would take some pleasure in it, in fact. "But did she tell you everything?" he asked as if there had never been a pause in his thoughts. "Did she tell you about her child's father?"

North's mouth tightened imperceptibly. On either side of him Sutton and Whittington were pressed against the stone battlement. Icy fingers of air tugged on the back of his frock coat. The sensation of pulling and pressure was so real that North almost turned to look behind him. A frisson took hold of his spine and he clamped his teeth together, steadying himself solidly to block the opening in the wall.

"She did tell you," the baron almost crowed. He glanced at his wife. "Did I not say that she would? She told you that pathetic story that Louise helped her concoct. It soothed Elizabeth, I think. She wanted to believe it was true."

"Harrison," Louise remonstrated with him mildly. "This serves no purpose."

"I want him to know." Battenburn's thick hair whipped in the wind, but his jaw remained stubbornly set. "It is a small thing, Louise. Let me have this one small thing." His eyes shifted back to Northam. "I was her lover," he said. "The father of her child. I had her first, Northam. Think about that as you—"

Elizabeth's cry was positively feral as she vaulted through the embrasure and over Northam's shoulders, hurling herself at Battenburn. North pushed Sutton and Whittington broadly to the side, ducking and throwing himself forward as the baron reflexively fired off his pistol. He caught Battenburn just below the knees as Elizabeth's body collided with the baron's chest. They brought him down together. Louise's cry could not quite smother the sound of her husband's skull cracking on the cold stone floor. Northam rolled off Battenburn and made a grab for Louise's ankle as she recovered her wits and began to run for the door. He missed her boot, scrambled to his feet, and gave chase. One thought propelled him forward. If Louise managed to flee to the secret maze of corridors in Battenburn, even Elizabeth might not be able to find her again.

Elizabeth shook off Lord Sutton when he would have helped her to her feet. Her eyes followed the trail of blood from Battenburn's supine body to where Northam was prepared to throw himself at Louise's retreating back.

Her warning shout came a moment too late. Louise turned suddenly, brandishing her weapon. She waved it wildly, not at her pursuer, but in Elizabeth's direction. Northam's vision was clouded by a red haze, part terrible anger, part mind-numbing fear, and part something he did not quite understand, a sense that all was not just as it should be. Not entirely of his own volition, he pitched forward, his outstretched arms grasping the baroness's gown. Caught off balance, Louise stumbled through the open doorway and into the stairwell. A heartbeat later, Northam's momentum propelled him through the same opening.

Elizabeth, Sutton, and Whittington were all running to
the door as the pistol fired. The report echoed hollowly in
the stone stairwell. Louise's body tumbled down the spiral
steps, twisting limply in a flurry of petticoats until it lay
still some twenty feet below. Elizabeth caught North by one
leg before he snaked and rolled along the same route as
Lady Battenburn. Sutton leaped over Northam's body to
lend aid to Louise, while Whittington helped Elizabeth get
her husband to his feet.

Northam staggered up, leaning heavily on both supports.
They were uneven bookends. Elizabeth's shoulders were
below his own, while Whittington was taller by several
inches. Still, he was grateful for their assistance. He was
finally able to identify the thing that was not quite as it
should be.

"You are shot, North," Elizabeth said. "Come, rest here.
I will stay with you while Lord Whittington finds a—"

From the stairwell they all heard Sutton's robust voice
reverberate against the stones. "Her neck is broken. Lady
Battenburn is dead!"

Elizabeth had no feelings to spare. She steadied North.
"Come. Sit here. You must—" She stopped this time
because her husband was paying not the least attention to
her.

"Where is he?" he demanded.

Elizabeth followed the direction of his gaze to where the
baron had been lying. A smear of blood marked the spot
where his head had hit the floor. The drops beyond it, though,
were from North's wound and led directly to where they
stood. There were no such markings to identify the path of
the baron's escape.

A feeling that was akin to dread, though not nearly so
powerful or compelling, made Elizabeth's eyes lift to the
same opening in the battlement that she had climbed through.
She glanced at Northam and saw that he was of a like mind.
Knowing she could not hold him back, she chose to assist
him instead. Whittington helped her get him to the wall. By
the time they reached it, Lord Sutton had joined them.

Like knights of old they lined up between the stone merlons. Instead of tipping cauldrons of boiling tar over the lip, they leaned forward through the low intervals and stared down.

Below them, ignominiously sprawled on the frozen ground, lay Harrison Edmunds, the last Baron of Battenburn.

Epilogue

So many well-wishers trooped through the residence at Merrifeld Square that Northam remarked he was as popular an attraction as a two-headed calf at the Hambrick fair.

"Oh, I wouldn't say you were as fashionable as that," South said. "We stood in line for above an hour to see the calf." He looked to Eastlyn for confirmation. "We did not have to wait so long as that here."

Eastlyn leaned back in his chair and propped his heels on a footstool. He accepted the glass of port that West placed in his hand. "No waiting in the least," he said. "Shown right in."

"The two-headed calf was a fraud," West pointed out. "And North's injury is quite genuine." He paused in the act of pouring a glass of wine for Southerton as though struck by the possibility they were all being gulled. "It is genuine, isn't it?"

"Must be," South said practically. "North's already married. It's not as if he requires a ruse to garner the sympathies of the muslin set."

"Would you like to see?" North asked dryly.

The patient was ignored and South went on. "He has Lady North to take care of him, and she appears to be doing the thing right. Fretting. Coddling. Nurturing. Scolding."

He sighed and held out his hand to West, who promptly placed a glass of dark ruby wine in it. "One is quite envious."

Elizabeth's lips twitched. "Why, thank you, my lord. I think." Sitting at the foot of the same chaise where North reclined, Elizabeth could easily reassure herself of his presence and his fitness. "Do I scold, North?"

"Only with the most loving intent," he said dutifully.

His friends hooted and Elizabeth smiled serenely. When West looked to her for permission before he handed North a glass of wine, she nodded, which only made them laugh harder.

North pretended to be unamused. He accepted the wine West offered him with a long-suffering sigh. This earned him several sympathetic pats on his blanketed legs from Elizabeth and more laughter from the Compass Club. "I would gladly keep you entertained, but I fear I may be delaying your departure."

East, South, and West all exchanged glances. "I have no plans," Southerton said.

Eastlyn raised his glass. "None here."

Westphal dropped onto the sofa beside South. "I am also without another engagement. Came to hear the story of what happened at Battenburn. The colonel gave us an account, but it's not the same as hearing it from you."

"Perhaps he isn't up to it," East said. He did not look to North for a response, but Elizabeth. "Will it tire him overmuch?"

Elizabeth smiled sweetly and assured him, "He is well enough to land you a facer if you keep having him on."

Now it was North who laughed. "Nicely done, my lady." He regarded his best friends with a sheepish grin. "She is my champion."

West raised his glass in a gesture of salute. "So we are given to understand. To the fair Elizabeth."

"Here. Here," Eastlyn chimed in. "To Lady North."

Southerton leaned forward and touched his glass to theirs. "Lady North."

North lifted his own glass and added huskily, "Elizabeth."

Touched, Elizabeth's beautifully expressive eyes grew luminous as they toasted her. With a smile that was somehow both modest and radiant, she waited until they were finished before she held up her own glass. She looked at each of them in turn. "Gentlemen, I give you the Compass Club."

The members grinned at one another. With no word passing between them, they shared in unison the secret toast from their Hambrick Hall days.

> *"North. South. East. West.*
> *Friends for life, we have confessed.*
> *All other truths, we'll deny.*
> *For we are soldier, sailor, tinker, spy."*

Delighted, Elizabeth made them repeat it before they drained their glasses. She showed more prudence and sipped from hers, reflecting on how suited they had become to the pledge of their youth. She sat back, quiet and perfectly content to listen, as North related the particulars of the events at Battenburn Hall. His audience was attentive throughout, interrupting only occasionally for clarification or an admiring aside. They showed restraint in not heaping praises upon her for her timely rescue of Sutton, Whittington, and their own dear friend, correctly surmising that North would not thank them for encouraging such activities as climbing out windows and scaling battlements in the future. Neither did they express any overt interest in North's description of her manly attire, but the looks they cast in her direction were rather more appreciative than disapproving.

They were curious about North's account of the recovery of a certain cache of jewelry, all of it purported to have been stolen by the Gentleman Thief. The strongbox was hidden in Lady Battenburn's bedchamber, but North explained away the find as a happenstance discovery without ever revealing Elizabeth's other identity. By now the rest of the Compass Club had worked this out on their own, but they showed admirable restraint in keeping it to themselves.

They were considerably more vocal in their judgment as to whether Lord Battenburn had met his end trying to escape or because it was his intention. North and West thought it was the former, East and South, the latter. Elizabeth refused to weigh in with her opinion and effectively ended the discussion with her telling silence.

Somewhat sheepishly, Southerton flung his arm around the curved back of the sofa, settling back as North's tale drew to a close. "I've been wondering how Elizabeth knew where the baron and baroness had taken you and the others."

North smiled and gestured to Elizabeth. "You must ask her."

"Elizabeth?"

"I followed in the passage. Northam kept talking, you see, and I could hear him. He made certain that Lady Battenburn gave him directions. When I realized their destination must be the roof, it was not so difficult to find a way out to the outer wall. It was the window in the room where you stayed that provided the most efficient exit."

Southerton could only shake his head, remembering all too well the difficulty North had had negotiating the stone wall outside that window. "But the parapet at Battenburn is enormous. You couldn't have anticipated where along the crenelation they would take North."

"It was not entirely good luck that sent me in that direction. I knew which way the door to the roof opened. I considered it likely that they would march North and the others straight ahead to the wall. It was the shortest path."

Eastlyn rubbed his chin. "How did Lady Battenburn not find you in the passageway before she came upon North?"

Elizabeth set her wineglass aside. "I heard her approaching. There was no time to give North warning, but I was able to escape farther down the corridor. When she disappeared into the hidden room off the library, I went back and waited. North had given me his pouch to hold, but it did not occur to me to search the contents. I thought it contained candles and some foodstuffs." She gave her husband a mildly reproving look. "I did not believe that he would lie about having a pistol in his possession."

Northam immediately looked to his friends for support. "Would you have told her about the pistol?"

"Not the point at all," East said. "You didn't, and now you're in Dutch. Don't want to be in Dutch with you. No one does."

Elizabeth covered her mouth with her hand, hiding her smile. She cleared her throat, bringing their attention around to her. Her hand fell back in her lap. "I have never fired a pistol before," she admitted. "My lord's decision was perhaps the wisest one."

Eastlyn snapped his fingers. "There. You see, North, just like that you are out of Dutch. Very forgiving sort, your lady. I wish Sophie were of a like mind." He glanced at Elizabeth. "Do you think you could speak—"

"East!" The three other members of the Compass Club said his name in unison.

"Oh, very well," he said. "I shall keep my own counsel." While his friends enjoyed a chuckle at his expense, East took solace from the fact that Elizabeth offered him a surreptitious wink.

"Go on," North encouraged her.

"I was only going to say that had I found the pistol and attempted to use it, I might have been a worse shot than Battenburn."

"Or a better one," North said, looking down at his shoulder. Beneath his white linen shirt, the bandages were visible. After a week the wound was still tender but already showing signs of healing nicely. He had been the one to insist on leaving the Battenburn estate after only four days' recovery. Elizabeth had warned him there would be a parade of visitors to Merrifield Square once it was known he was returned to London, but he had been insistent. "I think if I had but ducked another inch it would have missed me entirely."

Elizabeth closed her eyes briefly. She did not like to think of the consequences had North not ducked at all. "It is behind us now and I am glad for it.'' She moved from the end of the chaise toward the middle when North extended his hand. His fingers threaded through hers.

Westphal stood suddenly and motioned South and East to do the same. They rose together, acknowledging, as West had, that Northam and Elizabeth were both tiring. For all their good humor and willingness to speak of what had happened at Battenburn, the retelling was not completed without exacting a toll on them.

Elizabeth escorted them to the front door. ''It was kind of you to come today. I know North was hopeful that you would.''

South bent and kissed Elizabeth's cheek. ''You have our thanks.''

''Your thanks?''

''For watching his back,'' East said.

''For saving his life,'' West added.

Elizabeth's smile was gentle. ''You have it quite wrong,'' she said softly. ''He saved mine.''

Turning carefully on his side, North propped himself on his uninjured arm and caught a glimpse of his wife's bare white shoulders before they were lowered under the water. The fragrance of lavender was lifted in ribbons of steam above Elizabeth's bath. Her elegant neck was exposed in a smooth, glistening arch as she leaned her head back against the lip of the copper tub.

North sighed. ''You might have tarried until I was situated. It cannot be safe to dive into such a shallow pool.''

''I did not dive.''

''Well, then, you were very quick about it.''

''I am a modest woman,'' she said coolly, soaping her washcloth. ''And you have a lamentable tendency to ogle.''

North did not take issue with Elizabeth's description of herself as modest, but the stirring of blood in his groin was evidence that he was prepared to do much more than ogle.

"It remains a fact that you will eventually have to get out and I shall be lying in wait."

She turned her head sideways and regarded him through half-lowered lashes. "Please say you do not mean to pounce. I do not think you are well enough to be pouncing."

"I shall lie quietly," he promised.

Elizabeth smiled and tilted her head back. Her eyes closed as she ran the soapy cloth across one raised arm. The water was deliciously hot, just a degree or two below her tolerance. It suffused her skin with heat and color and made every movement richly languorous. The smooth surface of the water was broken as she lifted one foot and rested the heel on the edge of the tub. Water droplets ran over her calf and fell back in the tub, shifting the rising pillars of steam.

"A post arrived from my father after the Compass Club left," she said.

"Oh? You have left it until a late hour to tell me."

"You were resting when it came." But that did not explain why she hadn't said anything when he awakened or later, over dinner. "He is asking permission to visit us here." She glanced at North to see if he was as surprised by this notion as she had been. Her answer was there in the lift of both his dark brows. "I did not know what to make of it. My father has never applied to me for permission for anything. I needed to think about it before I told you. I hope you will understand."

He did. In Elizabeth's place he would have done the same. "Rosemont will have heard that Lord and Lady Battenburn are dead. While he cannot know of your involvement, he must entertain a great many suspicions."

She nodded. Few people knew that Elizabeth had been at Battenburn, and it was her intention to let it remain so. Colonel Blackwood, the Compass Club, Sutton, and Whittington were those privy to the truth. Even North's own mother thought Elizabeth had merely ridden there when news of the shooting was delivered to her. "Perhaps he wants to make amends," she said, unaware of the wistfulness

in her voice. "I still do not know what I want to tell him.
He will not approve of me accompanying you."

North gave a short laugh. "I had not realized he and I
would find agreement on any matter so soon."

"Do not be smug. He will blame you for permitting it."
She saw that sobered North's grin, and her own expression
became earnest. "We have not talked about it, North. I
confess, I have been afraid to broach the subject, and today,
when you were telling the others what happened on the roof,
you never mentioned it."

"Elizabeth," he broke in gently. "It will remain between
us."

"Lord Sutton . . . the earl . . . they both heard what Battenburn said."

"And they will never repeat it. You must harbor no fear
on that score. They are in your debt."

Elizabeth pushed herself upright. A cascade of water fell
over her shoulders. Her movement caused a small tide to
lap at the curves of her breasts and against the side of the
tub. "But you, North? I do not want your silence because
of some imagined debt. I want us to speak of it now and
never again because you know that Battenburn lied."

North heaved himself to a sitting position. Pain made him
wince, but it was all the attention he gave it. He threw his
legs over the side of the bed and closed the distance to
Elizabeth in a few strides. His nightshirt billowed around
him as he hunkered beside the tub. Ignoring both her startled
look and the way she pressed herself against the copper
tub's curved back, North cupped her chin and held her
steady.

"If ever I believed Battenburn's accusations—and I did
not—the notion would have been immediately dismissed by
your own response. I do not know if he could have said
anything that would have unleashed so much fury or so
much strength. When I felt you clawing at my back, seeking
purchase to haul yourself up to the embrasure, I was not
certain you could do it. In order to help you I would have
had to reveal your presence. It was Battenburn who made

that unnecessary. He put forth a lie so abominable to you that it had the power to catapult you over that wall.''

Elizabeth searched North's face. He met her gaze frankly, willing her to believe him and put this demon doubt to rest. ''Why did he do it? Why should he want you to think he was my—'' She broke off, unable to even say the word.

''How can we ever be certain? Battenburn did not know you were there, so what he said was meant for me. I suppose he intended that I should go to my death mistrusting you. He expected to see you again, Elizabeth, and I have to believe he would have taken some satisfaction in relating what his final words to me were.''

''He would have tortured me with it,'' she said softly.

''And he *has* done exactly that. You have never understood that it doesn't matter to me if he was lying or telling the truth. I have always accepted there was someone before me. Not only did you make no secret of it, you painted yourself with a very black brush. Was there ever a time I wished it were different? Yes. Do I wish it now? No.''

Elizabeth's brows knit. ''You don't?''

North found her hand. ''No, I don't.''

''It seems odd to hear you say so. Don't men want a . . . I mean, isn't a . . .''

''Virgin?'' he asked.

''Yes.''

He chuckled. ''I cannot speak for other men, but I want the woman who stumbles over a word like *virgin* and can say *whore* without raising a blush.'' His smile faded and he spoke soberly. ''Your soldier . . . your first love . . . and every circumstance that followed in some way brought you to me, and while I can wish that you had never had your heart hurt, that you had never suffered even a moment of doubt, of pain, of sadness . . . of betrayal, I also know that you would in some way be changed. It would have made your life different. Mine also.'' North gave her hand a light squeeze. ''Whether we are shaped by the circumstances of our lives, or by our perceptions of them, I still find I very much admire the shape you have become.''

A hint of a smile lifted one corner of her mouth. "Is that so?"

North blinked, suddenly aware of his double entendre. "I didn't mean . . . that is, I was being . . ."

"Prig," she whispered affectionately. "The tips of your ears are—"

Releasing her hand, North stood and drew off his night-shirt, whipping it over his head in a fluid motion and letting it fly backward to the bed. Elizabeth was laughing and pro-testing and warning and all the while trying to make room for him in the tub. A tidal wave washed over the sides and spilled across the floor as North lowered himself into the water. He drew Elizabeth forward onto his lap. Her slippery thighs opened on either side of his. Her arms lifted to his shoulders and her breasts brushed his chest. She raised her face and touched his lips with hers.

"I suppose we do fit," she said.

"Mmmm." He kissed her with a thoroughness that left her flushed to the tips of her ears. Now that they were a matched pair, he leaned back and rested his arms along the sides of the tub. Hers slid down his chest and disappeared under the water. After a bit of fumbling she gave him a wicked look. "Soap," he said succinctly.

"Oh." Elizabeth dropped the bar and found him. She repeated her wicked look and this time wrested a small groan from North. "I collect this is better?"

"Infinitely." The word came out brokenly but perfectly intelligible.

Elizabeth smiled. "Yes, it is." She rose to her knees and tipped her hips forward, guiding him into her.

He watched her intently, his eyes darkening as she settled back on his lap. He listened to her breathing change; heard the water lap against the tub. He smelled . . . lavender. North tipped back his head and groaned softly.

Elizabeth stilled. "What is it? Your shoulder?" She began to rise, but he grasped her hips and held her securely just where she was.

"The bath salts," he said deeply. "I am going to smell like a veritable garden."

Her laughter was husky. She kissed him lightly on the mouth. "I like it. You'll be wearing my fragrance."

"I'd rather be wearing you."

She wrapped her arms around his neck again and tipped her pelvis ever so slightly. "You are."

"Mmmm. So I am." He found the soap and began lathering her back. She sighed, leaning into him and burying her face in the crook of his neck. "Don't fall asleep," he murmured.

"Not bloody likely." Elizabeth bit him gently on the neck, then kissed him in the same place when he affected a grunt of pain. A moment later she kissed him on his bandaged shoulder and then raised her face and touched her lips to the corner of his mouth. "I have plans," she whispered.

North turned, catching her mouth with his. The soap fell and he let it go, running his hands down either side of her spine and cupping her bottom. She rose, breaking the kiss, something like a sob caught in her throat. Her tight nipples grazed his chest, and the shiver that started in her ended in him. He lifted her higher and accepted her offering, taking the tip of one breast into his mouth. She did cry out then. Her fingers threaded into his hair and she held him close, guiding him in time to her other breast, wanting nothing so much as the sensation of his teeth and tongue and lips tugging on her skin, drawing out the pleasure that was still wound tightly inside her.

More water splashed onto the floor. Neither of them noticed. Their shared passion was like the moon's pull on the tides. Water lifted, crested, and cascaded over the side. Elizabeth's damp hair clung to her temples and neck. The tips curved darkly around her shoulders and spilled into the water each time she rose and fell against North's body.

He kept her close. Every heartbeat was like one of his own. Her passion enveloped him. Her slender frame surrounded him. She carried him with her to pleasure's end, drawing him out so completely that he might have gratefully sunk below the surface if she had not also been his lifeline.

There were slippery, slithering moments on the wet path to the bed. Laughing, grappling, they managed to finally fall on the mattress, the groan of the giant four-poster not so different in pitch and timbre from the one North gave up. Elizabeth was immediately solicitous of his wound, but he would have cut off his right arm at the shoulder rather than admit to any discomfort.

"Martyr," she said.

He supposed it was an improvement over *prig*. His head fell back against the pillow while Elizabeth scrambled over him to retrieve the towels. She dried him off with linens warmed near the fireplace and drew the blankets up to his neck before she wriggled under them herself. He reached for the candles at their bedside and snuffed them.

For a long while neither of them spoke. The silence was meant to be appreciated, comfortable. North's arm fell lightly around Elizabeth's waist. She rubbed his foot with her own.

"I suppose," she said rather absently, "that we shall have to find a way to explain how my limp has disappeared. No one commented this evening, but I thought West was looking at me rather oddly."

North pressed his smile to her damp hair.

"What?" she asked. "What is it?" Elizabeth strained to turn her head around and see his shadowed features, but he pressed her back. "What are they up to? A wager?"

"I'm afraid so." He added hastily, "But nothing to do with your limp, or lack thereof."

Elizabeth remained suspicious. "Well?"

"West is trying to determine if you are *enceinte.*"

Her eyes widened. "He has ventured a wager on . . . on . . ."

"On whether I have got you with child, madam." North heard a strangled sound coming from Elizabeth's throat but could not divine what it meant. "But he is not alone. I warned you. South is in for three shillings. Eastlyn, of course.

My mother is bound to raise the stakes, and do not think for a moment that my grandfather will not take part. It may be that he is the one who started it.''

When Elizabeth made to turn over this time, he let her. ''And you, my lord? Do you have an opinion in the matter?''

North's palm slipped along the curve of her naked hip until it came to rest on the flat plain of her belly. ''My opinion is that if you are not, you soon will be.''

Elizabeth arched one brow. ''Really? You seem very certain of yourself.''

He shrugged modestly. ''I have it on good authority.''

That gave her pause. ''On good authority? I do not even know myself, North. What exactly are you saying?''

''Madame Fortuna,'' he said. ''When I went to her weeks ago looking for you, she told me—''

''North!''

''I did not seek the information,'' he said quickly. ''She offered it.''

Elizabeth considered this, drawing his hand back to her belly when he started to pull away. She held it there, wanting to believe what he was telling her, almost afraid to do so. ''She said we would have a child?'' she whispered finally, her voice husky.

Emotion closed North's throat. He merely nodded and held Elizabeth tightly when she launched herself into his arms. He stroked her hair, her back, and kissed away her tears. In time she slept, and he cradled her with his body, mutual comfort in the curve of arm and hip and thigh.

Someday he might tell her, he thought, that Madame Fortuna had not precisely spoken of a child. Perhaps, he decided, when they were celebrating fifty years together and surrounded by three generations of loved ones, he would find the right moment to tell her that Madame Fortuna had spoken only of a certain ripening peach.

Apparently he and Elizabeth were to bear fruit.

Please turn the page for
an exciting sneak peek of
Jo Goodman's
next historical romance
EVERYTHING I EVER WANTED
coming in March 2003!

Chapter One

September 1818

Laughter erupted from the private theatre box. Hearty. Rolling. Sustained. It came at her like a succession of wavelets and played hell with her timing. She waited for it to recede so she could speak her next line. Even before she finished there was another ripple of laughter from the same box. Wavelets be damned. What was coming toward the stage now threatened to pitch her under and press her down.

She paused mid-phrase and pointedly stared past the candle footlights in the direction of the disruption. The four actors sharing the small Drury Lane stage with her did the same. The audience, largely male, fell silent. They turned in their seats if such was required for a clear view of the box that had stopped the players cold. It was not that the audience was as ignorant of the private box's occupants as the leading lady. Quite the opposite was true. It would have been difficult to find someone in the packed house this evening who did *not* know the Marquess of Eastlyn and his boon companions were in attendance.

From the wings came a loud aside: "Line! *You cannot expect that I will always save you, Hortense!*"

"I know the line," she said without rancor. "What I cannot know is if I will be permitted to speak it."

This had the effect of raising sympathetic chuckles among the general audience and finally wresting quiet from the private box as those occupants realized they had become center stage.

"Now you've done it, East. I believe she is speaking to us." The Earl of Northam indicated the stage where Miss India Parr was standing with her fists resting on the wide panniers of her gown and her elbows cocked sharply outward. Her painted lips were pursed in a perfect bow and her darkly drawn eyebrows were arched so high they fairly disappeared into the fringed curls of her powdered wig. This exaggerated demonstration of impatience would have been more amusing if it had not been so clearly directed at them.

The Marquess of Eastlyn turned from his friends and once again gave his attention to the figure in the footlights. He made a good show of appearing much struck by this turn of events. "Why, so she is. Odd, that. Doesn't she have a line?" His deeply pleasant voice carried easily across the craned heads of the audience below his box.

It was Evan Marchman in the chair beside East who answered, *"You can't expect me to save you, Hortense."*

This prompt, offered as it was in dry, uninflected accents, lifted more chuckling from an appreciative audience. Looking toward the stage as almost no one else was doing now, South knew the lady was in danger of losing her support and her momentum. He shook his head as he came slowly and with some care to his feet. It remained for him to make amends. It was his ribald aside, after all, that had sent East into a paroxysm of laughter that turned out to be as contagious as it was ill-advised and ill-timed. South braced his hands on the box's balustrade, curving long fingers over the side. He leaned forward, grimacing only slightly when he realized that behind him North had made a fist in the superfine tails of his coat. Did Northam seriously think he was in danger of falling overboard? The notion was absurd. Half asleep, he could still climb a ship's frosted rigging in a pitched North Sea storm. In clear, commanding tones, South announced, *"You cannot expect that I will always save you, Hortense."*

On stage the lady's eyes narrowed. She lifted one hand to block the candlelight and peered more intently in the direction of the scrupulously modulated voice. "Thank you, my lord," she said politely. "You have it exactly. Shall you go on or must we?"

South thought she looked perfectly at her ease now and even willing to seat herself comfortably on the stage and allow him to finish all the parts if he wished it. He certainly did not wish it. "I most humbly beg your pardon," he said, inclining his head in an apologetic gesture to her, then the audience. "For myself and my friends. Pray, continue."

The lady inclined her head in a like gesture, then she stepped back into the circle of light, lowered her hands and covered herself in the mantle of her character. This transformation, done so expertly as to seem both instantaneous and magical, was greeted by thunderous applause. From the back of the theatre where there was only standing room the men stomped their feet and cheered. In the Marquess of Eastlyn's box the response was equally appreciative, if more subdued.

The four friends did not leave the theatre immediately upon the play's final curtain. They remained in East's box as the audience filed out toward the street or, as was the case with many of the hopeful young Corinthians, toward the dressing room.

Marchman pointed to a small group that was headed for the stage doors. "They don't all think they can get a glimpse of her, do they? What a stiff-necked business that would be."

"Don't fancy yourself craning to view the lovely from a more agreeable distance?" asked East. He stretched long legs in front of him and made a steeple with his fingers at the level of his midriff. A lock of chestnut hair had fallen over his forehead and he made no effort to push it back. His eyes were heavily lidded, their focus vaguely sleepy.

Mr. Marchman shook his head as he considered East's question. It sounded like a ridiculous effort. "I don't fancy making myself a clear target for what would surely be physical retribution on the part of the lady."

Reviewing the possibilities raised East's smile. "Polite slap, do you think? Or a blow?"

The Earl of Northam saw immediately what direction this conversation was taking. As the only one of their group who was married, albeit recently, he believed he had an advantage in determining the outcome of a confrontation of this sort. "Three shillings that it's open-handed."

"Open-handed," Marchman agreed.

East shrugged. "I was going to say the same. No wager there unless South takes an opposing view. What say you, Southerton? Will she use an open hand or a fist?"

Southerton's cool gray eyes regarded each of his friends in turn. "I'd say it depends a great deal on which one of us invites her to do it."

North held up his hands palms out, eliminating himself from consideration. "I fear I cannot be the one. Elizabeth would hear of it before the night was over and I am not up to explanations involving actresses. It is not the kind of thing that is generally well accepted."

Marchman snorted. "You have only to say that you were with us. She knows that any manner of things can happen."

"My wife is with my mother," North said dryly. He raked back a thatch of hair the color of sunshine. "I can appease one, but not both. It is the very devil of a fix when they join forces. Like Wellington and Blücher at Waterloo."

The others nodded sympathetically. It was uncharacteristic of any of them to find empathy for the defeated Napoleon, but Northam's description was not off the mark.

Eastyn moved to extricate himself as well. "I'm afraid I must also refrain," he said. "I'm in a damnable coil as it is. No sense in tightening the spring."

Marchman grinned wickedly and a dimple appeared at the corner of his mouth. "You're referring, I take it, to your engagement."

"I am referring to my *non*-engagement, West."

The marquess's statement had no impact on Marchman's grin. It remained unwaveringly stamped on his fine features. "*Non*-sense." He easily caught the playbill East tossed at his head and used it to lazily fan himself. "The announcement in the Gazette was pointed out to me by . . . well, by someone among my acquaintances who attends to such things. The wags have the story. There is betting at White's. There must be an engagement. Your mistress says it is so."

"My mistress—my *former* mistress—started that particular rumor." East actually felt his jaw tightening and the beginnings of a headache behind his left eye. "The only thing Mrs. Sawyer could have done to make it worse was to have named herself my fiancée."

"Then you will not mind being leg-shackled to Lady Sophia."

"There is to be no leg-shackling to anyone," East said in mildly impatient tones. "You only have to look at North to see all the reasons why I choose to avoid wedlock."

North's scowl had no real menace. He couldn't pretend that he hadn't been distracted this evening. His marriage was too new, the circumstances of it too unusual, and the nature of the alliance too uneasy to give him much comfort or confidence when he was away from his countess. Instead of being at his country estate in Hampton Cross where he would have had a chance to court his bride, at her request they were in London, where he discovered the fiercest competition for her attention often came from his own mother and his best friends.

"Marriage hasn't precisely put a period to my freedom," he said, feeling compelled to make that point. "If you will but recall, I was the one who suggested we go out tonight."

Marchman shook his head. "No. It was South's idea when we found you alone at home. At sixes and sevens, you were."

"Well, I had been thinking about going out," North said somewhat defensively. He allowed his friends to enjoy a moment's laughter at his expense before he joined them. "I *am* pathetic.'' He started to rise. "Perhaps I should be the one to beard the lioness in her den.''

South laid a hand over Northam's forearm and exerted a bit of pressure to reverse the direction of North's movement. "Sit down. If you care nothing for remaining in your wife's good graces—or your mother's—there are those of us who do. East is right. He shouldn't go. Not with a mistress and a fiancée to consider. His plate is already full. We can't send West. Have you noticed no one ever hits him anymore?''

Marchman's grin deepened and he tipped his chair back on its hind legs, balancing it carefully while he considered South's observation. "It's true, isn't it? I'll have to think on that.''

Southerton used the toe of his boot to nudge West's chair back into place. "Don't exert yourself overmuch. The explanation does not strain credulity. For the Corinthian crowd it has something to do with your reputation and that blade you always carry in your boot. For the Cyprians, I believe, it has something to do with how well you wield your sword.''

Marchman gave a low shout of laughter. "You flatter me.''

"I do,'' South said dryly and without missing a beat. He stood. "Allow me a few minutes to reach her through the pandering gaggle at her door.'' He rubbed his jaw as if anticipating the blow. "You may as well give me your money now. No one ever pulls their punches with me.''

Though she pretended not to, she saw him as soon as he reached the periphery of men crowded in and around her dressing room. She realized he could not be sure that she would know him again. Her glimpse of him in the theatre had been hindered by the candlelight in her eyes and his distance from the stage. During their brief exchange she had only an impression of his dark hair, light eyes, and a mouth tipped at the corners in secret amusement. None of it may

have been accurate. She could not know with any degree
of certainty that it was he until she heard his voice.

But somehow she did know. There was no mistaking this
small flutter beating against her rib cage. It was not her
heart. That was steady, as was her breathing. She had no
name for this part of her body that shifted or tensed or, in
this case, fluttered, when she had a certain sense of things.
Just as she had no name for it, she also had no understanding
of its exact workings. She only knew that it did and that
she had come to trust it.

Inside her feeling had become fact.

This man standing quietly at the back, patiently waiting
his turn for admission, was someone she wanted to know.
And then know better.

The flutter became a steady thrum.

India Parr smiled politely in response to what was being
said to her now. It could have been praise or condemnation
and she would have accepted it with the same public face.
"You are very kind to say so," she whispered demurely.
Then she turned her attention to another and went through
the same motions, giving no hint that she wavered between
exhaustion and excitement, expressing nothing so much as
unflagging grace in the face of the onslaught of admirers.

While the crowd did not precisely part for the Viscount
Southerton in the same way the Red Sea parted for Moses,
there was some stirring and jockeying and ground was surrendered. The natural curiosity of those acquainted with him,
whether familiarly or by reputation, assisted his advance-
ment. His apology had already been made to Miss Parr and
accepted by her. It seemed to many that it was unwise to
raise the thing again.

South could not decide her age. Onstage she had seemed
older and playing at someone who was young. Standing a
few feet from her, trying to peel away the layers of powder
and paint that placed her character in another century, she
seemed much younger and playing at someone with considerably more years. He watched her eyes for any hint they
could give him. They were dark, so deeply brown that the

pupil and iris almost blended seamlessly to a shade that was very nearly black.

A shutter suddenly closed firmly across her eyes, making South blink. Had she been so aware of his scrutiny? Threatened by it? He had not meant to be obvious and he was not sure that he had been. He glanced around for another cause or to see if anyone else had noticed this faint distancing. India Parr was farther from all of them now than she had been when she was behind the footlights. She was protected better by this invisible shield she had thrown up than she was by the transparent fourth wall of the stage. Rather than being put off, South was intrigued.

One could be forgiven for supposing that was her game.

There was a slight commotion at the back of the room as India's dresser pushed her way in. With the brisk determination of one who wants to see her duty done, she began moving the admirers aside. Her spine was stiff, if slightly curved, and her shoulders sloped forward, hunched as though against her will, as if she had not yet surrendered to the realities of her age. She carried an armload of material with her but from beneath that mound the sound of her clapping hands could be heard as she started to shoo the crowd. "Out wi' ye now," she said firmly. "Miss Parr's a rare one, it's true, but she cannot lally here. Go on wi' ye."

Tipping her head back in the direction of the door, she exhorted the squeeze of men all around her to use it. Her lips pursed tightly so that vertical creases deepened around her mouth. A large brown mole sporting three frighteningly aggressive hairs actually twitched on the corner of her right cheek. Her nostrils flared and even the stalwarts among Miss Parr's legion of devotees shrank back in anticipation of flames roaring from those dark openings.

There was a rolling wave of bobbing heads at the door, then the hall, and very slowly the room began to thin. South stayed his ground though he would not have been surprised if his rumpled coattails were now singed. From somewhere behind him he heard the familiar voices of his friends trading easy barbs as they worked their way against the exiting tide.

He stepped into the breach when the dresser began another harangue and his closest competitor for Miss Parr's attention was carelessly diverted.

He inclined his head toward the actress much as he had from the marquess's box. "Viscount Southerton," he said by way of introduction.

"My lord."

Her eyes were most definitely brown, he decided. Like windows at night they had become dark mirrors, reflecting his own image back to him and hiding what was just beyond the glass.

"Your servant, Miss Parr."

She smiled slightly, and the coolness of it touched her eyes briefly. "My heckler, you mean."

He did not apologize again for it. "Aaah, so I am unmasked. It is not to be as I hoped, that I was safe from your scrutiny in the low lights."

"Safe enough," she said. "But your voice gives you away. It is unquestionably distinctive."

"Really?"

"To my ears."

South considered those ears in turn. They were small delicate pink shells perfectly symmetrical in their placement on either side of her head. A veritable chandelier of paste diamonds hung from each lobe and glittered brightly as she fractionally lifted her chin. "Truly wondrous, your ears."

Her lush mouth still creased with its slim smile, she casually unscrewed each earring and pressed them into her fist. "So they have been remarked upon." She regarded him patiently as he simply stared at her and when he didn't speak, she prompted, "If there is nothing else, my lord . . ."

"What? Oh, yes. The reason I have come. Pray, do not look, but just beyond my shoulder hovering in the hall are three wholly disreputable—" He sighed, his voice dropping huskily as her glance shifted in the exact direction he had asked her not to look. "Don't *look*," he said, drawing her attention back to him. "They are hardly worthy of your notice."

"I believe they are your friends, my lord. I recognize their laughter."

Indeed, they were chuckling again and working out the details of another wager. This time it was the dresser whose antics had their mirth and money engaged. The old woman was none too gently using physical persuasion to remove the hangers-on from her employer's dressing room. Safe as East, West, and North were in the hallway, they were no doubt waiting for the dresser to turn her attention in his direction.

"Pretend I have given you a grave insult," South said quickly. "And chuck me on the chin."

"I beg your pardon?"

"Go on. It's all right. I'd rather not insult you and I am not concerned a blow dealt by your hand will hurt overmuch."

India Parr said nothing for a moment. "You are a Bedlamite, aren't you?" It was the only plausible explanation for his behavior. She was more curious than alarmed. One cry from her lips and any number of the men Mrs. Garrety had herded out would simply stampede back in. She was likely to be hurt in the crush before she was harmed in any way by the oddly engaging viscount. "Is there nowhere you can go this evening? Perhaps Mrs. Garrety can arrange for a room here for one night."

He shook his head. "Just here," he said, tapping the side of his chin lightly. "There's nine shillings in it for me. I am quite willing to share my winnings."

This did nothing to clarify the situation for Miss Parr. Her dresser's voice had risen shrilly as another man was shooed from the room. "Oh, please, Mrs. Garrety," she said after a long exhale. "Put a shiv between their ribs if you must, but remove the last of them quietly. I cannot bear more caterwauling."

South's brows lifted in tandem. In the hallway the rest of the Compass Club fell silent. The last two admirers slipped out. And Mrs. Garrety's jaw clamped shut.

India Parr raised her glance to South. Her lips moved around words he could barely make out as she murmured to herself, reviewing their conversation as if she were reaching for her lines. "Now, where were we ... servant ... heckler ... voice ... ears ... grave insult ..." She caught herself and her expression became considering. "Yes, grave insult. Very well, though you may wish you had delivered one, you know."

Rearing back, she plowed South's jaw with her weighted fist.

The blow actually moved him off his feet. He shifted right, caught himself, and cupped the left side of his face in his palm. He felt a warm trickle of blood against his hand. His slow smile was a trifle disjointed as he worked the kinks out of his jaw. "I forgot about the earrings," he said,

India's expression was without remorse. "I thought you might have." She glanced over his shoulder toward the hall. His friends were gaping at her. Over the top of the armload of clothes she held tight to her bosom, Mrs. Garrety was also open-mouthed. "Will that be all, my lord? Or do you seek another boon?"

South's humor asserted itself. "One boon is all these bones can stand." He pulled out a handkerchief and touched it to the corner of his mouth. Even when she saw the evidence of his blood she remained unapologetic. "You know," he said, "about our laughter during your performance. I feel compelled to point out that the play *was* a comedy."

"It wasn't *that* amusing."

He allowed her own words to sink in, let her critique serve in place of one that he might have offered, then said rather drolly, "You cannot expect that I will always save you, Miss Parr."

On his way out he dropped five shillings—the better half of his winnings—on top of the dresser's stack of clothes.